Cloaked Press

pres

Shane Porteous
Andrew P. McGregor
Barend Nieuwstraten III
James Pyles
Betsie Flynn
Alex Minns
Toshiya Kamei
Ioanna Papadopoulou
N. R. Williams
J. F. Sebastian
Ceilidh Newbury
A.R. Turner
Vincent Morgan
Frank Sawielijew

Winter of Wonder

2021 Edition: Superhuman

A Cloaked Press Anthology

Published by:
Cloaked Press, LLC
PO Box 341
Suring, WI 54174
https://www.cloakedpress.com

Cover Design by:
Fantasy & Coffee Design
https://www.fantasyandcoffee.com/SPDesign/

Contents

Of Teeth and Termites

by Shane Porteous

Many had mistaken what it was, but Kaowu didn't blame anyone for believing it was a blade. It certainly was the size of a sword, a very large one. She had also wielded it as a weapon, a very effective one. It had incorrectly been called a rectangle, but its rounded ends made such a remark untrue. She stood holding it at her side, the way a shaman holds their sacred stick. It wasn't magical, but it was mandatory for the duty she needed to do. She had a weapon on her womanly waist, a curved cutter sitting in a simple sheave, something she never heard said wasn't a weapon. Her hair fell in waves, washing down from her scalp to her shoulders, some strands were black, others teal, the two colours touching but never tearing into each other. Amongst the strands were rings that could fit on her fingers, small circle shapes that no thief would ever be tempted to take, tied in amongst the teal and black.

The same colours shaded her clothing, which consisted of a top that covered her chest, but kept her shoulders and stomach,

1

trim and toned, bare. Her forearms were attired by lengths of leather, again the same twin shadings of teal and black. What she wore on her waist downwards was little more than a loincloth, half black, half teal. Being half naked certainly helped with the heat. She had sauntered shadow oil upon her skin, saving it from being burned by the bright sun overhead. Her boots, again one teal, one black, were terrific enough to tempt a thief, although none had ever tried. She seemed far more interested in her footwear than the sun over head.

A sight few could blame her for, considering the surrounding land consisted of sand and nothing more, not even shadows could be seen somewhere far off. This land so dead and dry it hadn't even made mountains in the distance. She could feel a frail wind on her face, too weak to narrow eyes, but just strong enough to slip through her hair and feel the rings that found themselves there. Kaowu kept her eyes, which were a green so dark they could be believed to be black, as well as large and worth looking at, towards her boots. She watched as the sands didn't move, so much as shadows, smaller than the grains that grew them, could be seen.

A second passed before the air was assaulted by the sound of said sand suffering.

She tossed herself upwards, turning her body like a tomahawk, spinning into and through the air with skill and swiftness. The thing she held, now before her, becoming like the blade. She had saved herself from the sudden ascent of something from the ground. A hill seemingly had hurled itself up out of the ground, one soaked in sand. What harm such a hill could've done to her if she hadn't heaved herself upwards, aided her adrenaline as she landed on both feet, both hands holding what she held before her, as if she indeed had turned herself into a tomahawk, one that was ready to be thrown again.

She watched with wide eyes as the sand on the hill began to billow downwards, slowly at first, then in droves, revealing that this hill wasn't made of mud or rock, nor was it a hill at all. Two eyes, black and as big as boulders beheld the sight of her as the sand continued to crumple down all around it. This revealed its lips, which were far longer than logs, belonging to a mouth that could swallow a comet, if the sky was stupid enough to send one. Its body was a behemoth no hound would ever dare hunt, hell even a dragon would wander elsewhere for its dinner seeing it. Compared to its massive bulge of a body, its legs were short, although they were taller than trees. It sat with its stomach still suffocating the soil underneath it, but there was no doubting what this fortress sized frog was staring at. Hence why Kaowu was holding the dark blue length like a weapon.

A second-long stare off ensued, focus far more than fear filled either set of eyes. As the frog opened its mouth it let out its tongue, as big as a bridge, advancing through the air with the fast force of an attacking army. As the tongue's tip struck the shape, she held Kaowu's boots became like blades, bringing her backwards across the terrain like she weighed no more than a walnut. The intensity of the impact infected every inch of her, her bones shook so much it was surprising they didn't break. But as the tongue threw itself back into the behemoth's mouth she was still standing.

What she held wasn't a shield, but it certainly worked as one. For a moment the mammoth frog seemed unable to fathom that such a small shape (at least for the frog) had stopped its slurp. But that moment didn't last long. The frog's tongue found its tip touching the shape again and again, as it unleashed attack after attack. Despite the earthquakes that emerged inside of her each time the tongue torpedoed forward, she found ways to keep what she held between her and it. With each torpedoing she turned what she held slightly, each time stopping the tongue from tasting her flesh. It was clear such an accomplishment was well earned, as every collision caused a cracking sound a whale sized whip couldn't conjure. They were loud enough to lay off the sounds of her grunts, which never reached the giant's ears, or whatever it was frogs heard things from.

After a dozen such assaults, the tongue came towards her like it had done before. But what she did in response wasn't what she had done before. The shape stopped the tongue, but it did far more than that, not only did it find itself on top of the tongue's tip, it drove it downwards, the dark blue length laying over it like a latch. Kaowu didn't smile, but her eyes were aimed by accomplishment as she looked into the giant's now gaping mouth.

The tongue depressor had done its job.

With it now under her feet she travelled up the stuck tongue, sliding over it like a leaf in a landslide. The dark blue shape kept the tongue depressed and therefore out of her way, leaving the frog's mouth wide open. The giant gazed upon this oncoming woman with both fear and fascination as she entered its mouth, showing no fear of the shaded green darkness that dwelt within. The sunlight at her back was bright enough so she could examine the monstrous mouth. But its throat remained dominated by darkness, a danger sunlight stayed clear of. Still Kaowu could see it, glistening with grievance, bright green and bigger than a bread loaf, it had grown out of the side of where the throat started. Which is why her hand went to her waist and claimed the cutter, smoothly and swiftly removing it from the sheave before removing the growth from the frog's flesh in a single slice.

The cut was clean, whatever blood may have washed out from the severing Kaowu didn't see, with the weapon back upon her waist and the glistening growth grasped under her arm she claimed the depressor back in hand as she turned herself into a tomahawk once more. The axe she had become accelerated out of the mouth away from the tongue, just before it was entirely back inside the frog's mouth. The cave sized opening was firmly closed before Kaowu's feet found the ground was once more. Despite the distance between the frog's lips and the land, the sand didn't stir under her feet when she landed, as if scared into stillness. The frog was still for a moment, its huge eyes harboured both insult and intrigue, which is why Kaowu kept the depressor before her as a shield.

The frog then swallowed, as if everything had happened so fast, its muscle memory believed it had captured its meal. It swallowed again, but this time was due to something different. Kaowu's stare stayed as a set of stones as she watched the giant gulp down half a dozen times. While its eyes stayed as dark as shadows, it appeared oddly satisfied as it sunk back beneath the sand. Still that didn't stop Kaowu from keeping the depressor raised until its descent was complete, the sand slowly shifting back over where it had sprouted. Even then she kept it raised for a moment more, standing like a statue, until she was satisfied she was safe. A well worth of wind seemed to leave her lungs as relief rounded through her. That had been close, if her task had taken a moment or two more than the tongue would've escaped the depressor entirely and she would have been eaten.

Of course, the fortress sized frog wasn't filled with hunger but hatred. Kaowu couldn't blame the behemoth for feeling so, an inflamed tonsil was a terrible thing. Just like she was thankful the frog fathomed the fact she had helped it. Hence why it had sunk under the sand instead of striking her again. She had trained for such a task her entire life, and this wasn't the first time she had found herself inside the mouth of a fortress sized frog. She was just grateful it wasn't the last time. These behemoths weren't normally baleful, while on occasions hunger had caused them to swallow a whole herd of sheep. Most of the time they stayed away from the shepherds that called home the same place she did. But when the sickness had made them sore, such giant frogs could fill graveyards.

Kaowu did what she always did after surviving such severing, she inspected the infected tonsil. It was heavier than a smith's hammer and within the sunlight it seemed more green than grey. They always did, these diseased designs. She kept it under her arm as Kaowu turned, despite the terrain being dominated by sand, she never got lost in this land of grains. Just like she never mistook her tent for a turnip. She had never known anyone that had made such a mistake themselves, but still it was surprising how she could always spot her own dwelling despite its identical design to all the tents made in town she called home. She wasn't at home, that would be half a day's march away.

The trek hadn't taken long, but she had come back to her simple camp, her only company being what she had brought with her, a depressor and an infected tonsil. But she hadn't come back to her camp for conversation anyway. Her task was not quite done, it would be before long. She just needed to take the infected tonsil and conceal it inside a chest, the same one that was sitting by her tent, the same one where a week's worth of such severances also sat.

The same one that had a huge hole in its side.

She only noticed it when she had knelt and seeing it her eyes seemed the size of the frog's. It shouldn't have been possible; the purple plating was supposed to be impenetrable. It *was* impenetrable, she was sure of it, just not as sure as she was that the hole haunting her vision wasn't a hallucination. Having dropped both depressor and taken tonsil she held the chest at its sides. Before she had begun to lift it, she knew it was too light. That didn't stop her from unlocking it with the only key (she kept it in her black boot) that could've unlocked it, throwing open the lid so tersely the chest nearly toppled backwards. Her eyes remained the size of the frogs, for the chest was empty. It shouldn't have been, but it was. This shocked her so much that she soon found herself standing over it, as if that would somehow change what she was seeing.

It didn't.

Kaowu's eyes crawled across every crook and corner, she saw nothing save her own shadow. She looked in every direction outside her camp but saw only sand. Someone or something had taken the infected tonsils. Thoughts tossed themselves through her mind like trouts that had trouble swimming. Kaowu didn't bend back down, even though both knees were wounded by weakness. Her eyes studied the sand all around her, but the dead soil seemed determined to keep its sameness, there was no slight sinking anywhere. It was the reason why she had chosen to camp here, there were no tracks anyone or anything could follow to find her in this place. That fact was proving itself a tooth that tore both ways. Meaning there was no sunk spot for her to study, no way of knowing which direction they had walked.

She looked back at the hole; the puncture was perfect for plucking out the tonsils. The problem was the hole told her no more than this. Hence why her eyes moved towards the only tonsil left in the camp, not knowing what it would tell her, but hoping it was something helpful. Kaowu wasn't sure how helpful it would be, but at least it was something. A bug, a kind she had never seen before, was traversing across the tonsil. This tiny bug, strange and square shaped with a touch of teal on its white back, was enough to make her bend her knees. The closer inspection didn't reveal what the critter was, again she had never seen something like it before. But seeing it move across the tonsil did make her think of an ant, one that had found a dead antelope and now needed to deliver the news to the rest of the colony. She watched as it slowly travelled off of the tonsil, moving up at the sands slowly away from her camp.

Kaowu was utterly bewildered by the bug, not just because her inspection hadn't revealed its identity, but she had never seen so much as a dung beetle in this desert. These dead lands were so dry, that flies couldn't even be found in them. Hence why the fortress frogs normally lived under the sand, staying away from the heat above. But wherever this critter was crawling to, it wasn't somewhere concealed.

The bug being her only lead, she chose to follow it, deciding to take her depressor with her, something wordless told her this was a wise decision. It seemed neither afraid nor even aware of the fact she was following it, the bug simply marched on through the desert. As she followed it, terrible thoughts tore through her mind like teeth. Something was able to cut through the chest, more importantly, the material it was made from. She didn't want to think about what that meant, anymore than a cripple wanted to walk with a limp. Being her only lead, Kaowu didn't look away from the bug, knowing it was so small that she could easily lose sight of it in the sand. Hence why her head remained lowered and her eyes wide as the critter continued crawling.

Both insect and its investigator had moved perhaps a mile out of the camp when Kaowu noticed a slight change, the sunlight, forever hot in such a hellish place, seemed to be homing in on both her and the bug. The specific sunlight was so severe that the strange bug seemed to cover itself in caliginous, becoming a speck of a shadow in her sight. She kept her eyes upon it, although the sun was gnawing enough that she had to narrow her vision.

That was until a sound seized the air, dark, dominant, dangerous. With wide eyes she looked up, seeing that she was now standing at the start of a slope and on its top was a shadowy sight. It was a strange shape, one that had concealed itself as much as the crawling bug had. But it made Kaowu conjure in her mind, a vision of a small pond rounded by rocks with a strange shaped plant growing out of it, alongside a small leafless tree. The shadowy sight, solid and sizeable seemed still for a second or so. Until she saw something stirring, on what her mind make-believed was a leafless tree. Things were travelling down from its tops, things that crawled, things looked similar to the speck of shadow she had followed from her camp.

She didn't know what this meant, or whether she even wanted to know. But she could feel her grasp tightening upon the depressor she had wisely taken with her. Whatever this was, clearly it was the destination the teal backed bug desired, but Kaowu couldn't determine why. The sound had stopped her steps, clearly the bug was braver than her. But she began to walk once more and a few footsteps closer caused her to stop again.

Like sheets shoved off a bed because of bad dreams the shadows slipped away revealing that it wasn't a pond with rocks rounding its edges, nor was there any strange plants. The closest thing her imagination had gotten correct was the leafless tree, it clearly was once a tree, where else did logs come from? It stood upright, with teal backed bugs crawling across its caliginous surface, it sat seized in a huge hand. One that belonged to the being that was sitting on top of the taken tonsils. He was so huge in height that if standing he could see over any hut. He had fists that seemed formidable enough to flatten fortresses. He was as muscular as a mountain was tall. He was shirtless, revealing the red rounded circle spots that sat spread out across his shoulders, back and upper arms. The shapes seemed a kind of camouflage, but what he would ever have to hide from Kaowu couldn't comprehend. His pants were as red as a bloodbath and just as brutal. His long flowing hair was as black as a crowd of crows, but far more murderous. His eyes, big and baleful, were brown instead of white and his pupils were tiny terrible shapes, at least ten in each eye, and they all seemed to float like dead flies in a drink. He certainly had a face that could frighten a corpse back to life, just so it could get away from him.

9

But it was the sight of his mouth, wide and wicked, that wounded Kaowu the most. His mouth seemed a hole to hell itself, a place so harmful not even darkness dwelt within. She couldn't look away from it, especially as the bugs came back into her view, crawling off of the long black log and up his arm, entering his mouth with an eagerness that didn't belong to bugs.

That's because they weren't insects, or even spiders for that matter, they scurried and then sat in his gums, placing themselves where teeth were supposed to sit. Terrible teeth with a touch of teal, but teeth all the same. Any doubt about what they were was driven from her mind, along with a slice of her sanity as the last tooth, the one that had traversed from the camp, right to this very place, crawled up his chin and completed his smile, a sight that could chase clouds out of the sky.

Kaowu didn't have to look upwards to know just how clear the heavens were. Nor could she blame the clouds for clearing out, it was quite clear what they were hiding from.

The shifting of his lips from smiling to puckering didn't make them any less petrifying as he lifted the log, moving it upon his mouth. He looked like he was taking a drink from the log, like there was a lake inside of it. But whatever he was devouring wasn't water and it sounded too dry to be a liquid. There was no wetness in the wicked whistle that warbled from his mouth as the top of the log still touched his lips. It had been difficult to tell what any of his twenty pupils had been aiming at.

The same couldn't be said for the deluge of blue that barreled out from the other end of the log.

Kaowu managed to move the depressor in the sandy stream's path before it could butcher her. She had no doubt over its destructive capability, it touched the depressor with the terror of a typhoon, one taken from a sideways sea. It wasn't water that wanted to wound her, but some sort of sand, small, sinister and sharp, the sound of the spraying spoke a wordless wickedness that wounded her ears. She could feel its wind weaving itself through her hair and wrecking havoc across the rings, like it was snacking on every strand like a spider. The blowing blue pushed her backwards, close to falling over.

She suffered seconds like they were harmful hours, but Kaowu survived the spitting sandstorm. Still when the blue began to fall like autumn leaves all around her, her stare didn't reach into the sky to see any rainbows. Her eyes stayed on him as he slowly moved the log from his lips, showing that he was smiling once more. The sound of the log's end touching the ground haunted the air, revealing just how heavy a thing it was, one wouldn't know that seeing how easily he handled it. Despite the power his spitting attack had been driven by, the depressor remained undamaged, something that didn't seem to sting him. …

"Rowlingel," she said with strained speech and not just because of the battering her body had taken stopping his sandstorm.

Her words only made his smile widen further and for the first time in her life she silently begged to be blind.

"Impressive," Rowlingel said, his voice was deep and dark like he spoke in shadows.

The compliment couldn't make Kaowu lower the depressor, keeping it before her as both a sword and a shield. Something told her she would need both before long.

"The fact you remember that night, where with a single breath I blew out every light in the city, you must've been one of the young children that watched me."

Kaowu was one of those young children and before that night, before he brought blackness to her city, she had never been scared of the dark. Before that baleful black had come, she had never been scared of a lot of things. How times change. She didn't speak, not just because she was still scared of that night and the

11

monstrous man who had brought the blackness. Her silence was a simple defiance of him, but a defiance nevertheless.

"Tell me," he said, because such a beastly man never asked for anything. "Were you also one of the many who screamed that night?" he said, his smile increasing to a sinister size.

"Yes," Kaowu couldn't stop the word from slipping out of her lips, his presence and the pain he had caused that night still poisoned her memory.

She noticed how wide his smile became, a nightmarish shape.

"I was also amongst the countless who clapped when you were driven out of the city and into this desert."

Even she was surprised by this sudden act of bravery, watching as his mouth stayed wide but he had stopped smiling. He seemed to stare into the distance for a moment, again it was hard to tell what his twenty pupils were peering at. He was a hard sight to keep staring at, watching him weighed down her eyes, causing them to descend and look at the baleful blue she had beaten back that now lay listlessly all around her. When her eyes reached his again, Rowlingel was smiling. Once again, she felt very wise in her decision to bring the depressor with her.

"Do you remember what they called the dust storm that battered the city for 17 days straight?"

"The Blue Butcher," she said, no longer sure how defiant her words were.

Such a comment caused his smile to increase, which only infected her with more horror.

"Ever wondered what had caused it?" Rowlingel asked, keeping his smile.

She had, hundreds of times, as did many in the city. Those terrible 17 days haunted her head more than a hundred thousand ghosts ever could. Kaowu didn't need his tapping of the blowpipe he held to tell her the truth. He had clearly extracted the evil earth, the baleful blue that should have stayed buried deep beneath the desert, using the sinister straw he held to suck it out and send it towards the city. Rowlingel had always possessed an inhuman inhale, it was said he could keep a cyclone in his chest. He could also blow it back out to decimate what he decided to see destroyed. The sound that then left his lips, deep dominate and dangerous, a cough that was a comment on what he kept inside his chest now. The same thing he had shot out at her only moments ago.

"The city survived, it stayed standing," she said more to herself than him.

"Yes," he said without a smile. "Although the same can't be said for the many shepherds that couldn't reach the city before the gates were locked." he paused. "They all screamed," he added *with* a smile.

Those three words tore through Kaowu, causing her to shudder like a blizzard had bitten her.

"Why so appalled?" he asked, appallingly. "Surely you are use to death, after all how many children died taking small doses of the blue dust? In order to build up an immunity to its infection?"

He didn't so much stay smiling, as he was showing off his teeth to her, specifically the teal upon them, the same colour that had claimed half her clothing and hair. They both knew this wasn't a coincidence.

"Too many," she replied simply, because it simply was the truth.

This indeed made him smile again.

Her eyes became heavy once more and they lowered, not to the baleful blue, but to the pile of green shapes he both sat on and was surrounded by. In a certain light such colouring could be called teal.

"Trophies," she said, making the monstrous mystic narrow his nightmarish eyes. "That's why you took the tonsils from my camp, you wanted something to show off the sickness you spread."

13

Unlike her people, the fortress frogs had no city to sealed themselves off from the baleful blue Rowlingel had brought back to the world. But unlike them, he was baleful long before the blue had been brought back. His horrid eyes suddenly became huge as he brought the blow pipe to his lips again sucking up one of the tonsils, like an ant eater upon a sizeable ant.

Before Kaowu could gasp at the ghastly sight the sucked-up tonsil was shot out directly at her. It barreled into the depressor just as the dust had. But unlike the dust it drove straight through it, the sound of the depressor shattering scorched the surrounding air like a scream. How Kaowu managed to jerk her head just enough to stop the tonsil from shattering her skull, she would never know. But she knew the tonsil had harmed the side of her scalp, it had move so fast she could actually hear the wind wailing through the rings that had been ripped out.

But this bashing didn't hurt her as much as seeing the destroyed depressor did. It was made from the same material as the chest, the one that shouldn't have been able to be punctured. The protective paint, that made the depressor dark blue instead of purple, should have further made it indestructible. Not magic, nor a million marching men could break the material, the same material her city had been built from.

Which is why her face was bruised by bafflement as she looked back towards Rowlingel, blood billowing from her brow. He lowered the blowpipe from his lips, revealing Rowlingel was both smiling and showing off his teeth.

"There was a time when I thought the only way to break through the city walls would be by chewing them up completely." He paused, just to lick his lips, the sound stained her more than any other memory. "But even my teeth can't pierce the protective painting," he stopped again just to tap his blowpipe, telling her the terrible truth. "Finally, I found something strong enough to do the impossible, to pierce the protective painting, to wound those walls, which will allow me to wound those inside. I suppose I should thank you," he paused, and the silence was a kind of soundlessness Kaowu had never suffered before.

"Because of you soon the screaming will start again in that city."

Repulsion ripped through her like ravens through red meat. She didn't know how he had found her camp, but she knew what would happen if the taken tonsils found her city. What remained of the desecrated depressor dropped from her hands before they went to the weapon at her waist as she ran forward. She couldn't move as fast as the tonsils, or the sands, but she was swift, he needed to die today, before he could reach her city, before the screams could be summoned once again.

But before she had taken two steps another tonsil had been sucked up and shot out. It was amazing that her ankles hadn't snapped, considering the contortion her body had to take to avoid it. She managed to keep moving, knowing staying in one spot was now a very dangerous decision. The tonsils were torpedoed so swiftly the sound of their shooting could barely keep up with it, the wicked whooshing of each, wounding her ears as she avoided one after another. She was forced to change direction, unable to move directly forward, at least if she wanted to keep living. Not only was Rowlingel fast, he was an excellent shot. Many that called her city home couldn't move the way she did, which only made it ever more important that today was the day he died.

Kaowu continued to move in a wide arc, it was the only way to gain ground while not being gutted by his shots. As she did so, for a second at least, he became draped in shadow once again. She couldn't tell if this was a trick of the sun or her subconscious showing her the horrors that would happen if she let him live. But the sight stained her all the same.

She raced onward, the sand that was struck up by his shooting sliced through the air like a razor blade just behind ever swift step she took. Apart of her was tempted to throw her sword, his chest was certainly a big enough target. And she was certain he had a heart, a dark hate filled lump, but one he couldn't live without if it was cut into. But if she missed than there would be no way for her to end his existence, it was a chance she couldn't take.

She was moving in such a wide arc that Rowlingel actually stood to keep her in his sights. Before long he even had to take a few steps towards her, all the while whooshing out the tonsils. She could see there was no chance of his footfall taking him too far away from the pile of taken tonsils. His breath was too big, too baleful. He simply turned his blowpipe behind him, sucking them up effortlessly before bringing it forward and exhaling them. She had managed to move a considerable distance, but Kaowu was no closer to him.

She hoped that would change in a few moments.

She hadn't moved in an arc just to avoid his attacks, although this was still a large part of it. Having twenty terrible pupils surely made his eyesight excellent, surely it also made his sight sensitive. Which is why Kaowu had woven her way around in such an arc, placing herself so the sun was now at her back. It was also why she chose now to leap up and let the sunlight completely consume the sight of her. She could feel the solar light like spears shooting over her shoulders, just like she could feel it across all of her anatomy. It was extremely hard to hit what one couldn't see, at least she hoped that was the case concerning her cruel attacker. She unleashed her sword, wanting to hold it in both hands, knowing she would only have a few seconds to reach Rowlingel before he could see her again. All she needed to do was have her blade bypass his blowpipe, it couldn't bend, the black cylinder simply wasn't made for that. Meaning once she passed it, the only thing for her sword to find was flesh, his flesh. He could survive storms and sand, but he wouldn't survive her sword. At least she hoped.

A moment came then, just as the shape of her had descended close enough to darken the sight below enough to see him. This was the moment, one her subconscious seemed to slow down for her to see. The blowpipe was lowered, no longer on his lips, this was a good thing. His glare seemed to be gutted by the sunlight still around her, this was also a good thing. It seemed he didn't want to waste a shot if he couldn't see his target, again this was a good thing. Suddenly just when it seemed the sword would reach him Rowlingel snapped his head back towards the blowpipe, bending his head down so his lips touched it as he began blowing.

This wasn't a good thing.

It was neither tonsils nor dust that drove out of the blowpipe but air. Appalling and all powerful, like a hurricane it seemed to hit the sand before him, sending it swirling in a circle, digging a hole deep enough for a horse to fall into. And clearly Kaowu was smaller than any stallion. The sheer force of the wind he sent out didn't just create a hole it heaved him up into the air, propelling him like his body was an arrow from a bow. What made it all the worse, wasn't that he was now well out of the way of her weapon, it was the fact Kaowu couldn't stop herself from falling into the hole. She landed in a way she didn't like.

Neither it seemed did the dead soil. The sand determined for sameness, shifting in an avalanche all around her, seizing Kaowu completely like a claw. Her head was now the only thing not underneath the sand. She tried to shift her body in any direction she could, but the sand wouldn't be deterred from its sinister stillness. The only thing she could move was her eyes, but she couldn't bring herself to look away from Rowlingel as he landed as gracefully as a green leaf in autumn.

Turning the ground itself into a trap, was something Kaowu would never have thought of. She found herself cursing the fact that the cruel were often so clever. She also found herself silently cursing his stare, there was no doubt what all twenty of his pupils were now peering at. Kaowu thought about screaming, shouting so loud that the sound would slice her lungs apart. But she knew no amount of passion and pleading would be powerful enough to let her cries be heard in the city, it was simply too far away for her lungs.

But not for his, a fact she couldn't flee from. Just like she couldn't flee from him. He was smiling, showing that some of his teeth were missing from his mouth, having already turned themselves into termites again, ready to traverse across the landscape and claim the tonsils once more. Rowlingel would reach her city before nightfall, she knew this, just like she knew there was nothing she could do to stop it.

"I have a gift for you," Rowlingel said, his missing teeth making his words even more monstrous. "For collecting the tonsils in that chest, let it never be said that I don't show gratitude."

The sucking sound he made as he brought the blowpipe back to his lips told Kaowu he wasn't going to spare her life, but end it swiftly, saving her from dying from dehydration. If that was gratitude, she just wished she could give it back to him. But she couldn't, she saw a tonsil being sucked up before she lowered her gaze from him. Ensuring he wasn't the last thing she ever saw. An act of defiance that wouldn't matter in a moment.

Her eyes lowered in time to look at the sand that surrounded her, more specifically towards the shadows that spawned next to each speck. Before she could look up her body was burst out of the sand shooting her into the air as something as huge as a hill had suddenly spurt out of the dead soil behind Rowlingel. She saw those eyes, black and as big as boulders, before he did. The action was so sudden it seemed Rowlingel had almost swallowed the tonsil into his throat, his neck bulged as he turned his head to see it for himself. He saw blackness, just not in its eyes, but there was much darkness in its mouth as it devoured him whole. If he had screamed the sound had been swallowed up with the rest of him.

Kaowu had landed on her back before the frog's lips had closed completely. She saw that not even the sand dared to try and shift back into sameness around the behemoth. Just like she had seen there were no ghastly growths tormenting the side of its throat, when its mouth had been opened. Both behemoth and now breathless woman stared at each other with satisfaction that Rowlingel had been slain. As her wide eyes watched the giant slowly sink back into the soil, she couldn't help but think about how fascinating fortress frogs were.

They had amazing hearing, so much so they could actually hear the near silent sound of the wind whirling through rings, no matter how small they had been made, hence why Kaowu kept such rings in her hair, how else would she get the frogs to come above ground and let her lacerate the infected tonsils out of their mouth? She didn't know. What she did know, and was far more fascinated by, was the fact this fortress frog hadn't forgotten how she had helped it. Clearly Kaowu was far more thankful for the giant's gratitude than she ever was for Rowlingel's.

Shane Porteous is a mastery of the legendary 77 donut devouring technique. He lives in a place of strange dreams and even stranger reality. A lifelong writer, he has an immense passion for the fantastical and prides himself on being alternative and if possible original with his storytelling. He has been published both traditionally and independently. The single guarantee he gives with his novels is not whether you will like or hate them, but he guarantees you will remember them.

Assassin's Bucket

by Andrew P. McGregor

Debbie adjusted the scope on her rifle and wondered, not for the last time, why she hadn't taken up assassination earlier. She clamped her mouth shut lest the recoil knocked her false teeth out again and turned off her hearing aid. She took a deep breath to calm her shaking hands as she sighted the visiting Prime Minister.

Damn, I love this part, she thought.

Debbie smiled and pulled the trigger.

Though it wasn't the most powerful gun she'd ever handled, the recoil kicked harder than she expected, and she yelped, letting go of the rifle. The rifle clattered to the wooden floor of the fifth story hotel room and she eased herself down underneath the open window. She shook her head and turned her hearing aid back on. "That'll bruise," she said to herself while rubbing her shoulder. She levered herself up against the wall next to the rifle and tried to slow her breathing. Despite being over a kilometer away, she could already hear shouts and screams from the streets below.

"S***," she said, then giggled. This was exciting.

She grabbed her walking stick and pushed herself up onto her slipper-covered feet, grimacing as pain shot through her hips. She loosened her gown, ready to distract anyone barring her way, and caressed her stick's trigger.

Debbie tossed her black, oversized gloves into the hotel room's sink and left the unmarked rifle against the room's window. Her employers would hate her leaving the rifle, but they had more than enough hush money to make it disappear from whatever evidence room it ended up in. If not, then she would start her next adventure.

Debbie started off towards the Spartan hotel room's door, her walking stick tapping to the rhythm of her favourite song. She started humming 'Can't get no satisfaction' by the Rolling Stones, but paused when she reached the bedroom door. More screams.

"A gun, I think I heard a gun," a man on the other side of the door said, his voice shaking.

"Do you think we should check it?" a woman asked.

Debbie rolled her eyes and whispered, "Idiots."

"What was that?" the man asked, hearing Debbie's whispered words.

"Help," she shouted at the hotel employees. "Help, the gunman's in here."

Something heavy fell to the floor on the other side of the door, followed by echoes of running feet receding down the hallway towards the hotel's stairs.

Debbie snorted at the employees, opened the door and walked towards the gold-rimmed elevator on the opposite side of the wide hallway. The hotel employees must've been in quite a hurry. A cleaner's trolley had been tipped over just outside her door. At 11am, the hallway was deserted, most of the guests having vacated or out touring the city.

The elevator doors, coated in polished limestone, slid open and the smiles of a young family of three, dressed as if they were going to a funeral, greeted her on the other side.

"Going down?" the father asked. He was tall, handsome, with a clean-shaven face and square glasses on his large nose.

Debbie grinned and nodded at him. Perfume wafted from the mother, smothering the scent of crappy coffee on Debbie's breath.

"Hello, my name is Beatrice," the family's little girl, barely old enough for kindergarten, greeted her. The girl's mother frowned at Debbie's choice of clothing and whipped out a mobile phone. The mother started tapping on her phone while the doors closed.

"I'm Debbie."

"What's that for?" the little girl asked, pointing at the walking stick.

"Don't be rude, Betty."

"But why, dad?" the girl pleaded.

"It's okay," Debbie assured the father. "It's for jabbing people if they try to hurt you."

"Oh… cool. Can I try it?"

Debbie shook her head and frowned, pretending to be annoyed. "No, you can't. It's much too dangerous. Most people would fall to sleep if they were jabbed, but if it hit a girl like you? You might not wake up. If you ever see someone else with one of these, you better stay out of their way."

"But you wouldn't hurt anyone, would you Debbie?" the father asked, his brow creasing.

Debbie winked at Beatrice. "Of course not, *daddy*." They felt the bump of the elevator as it stopped. The doors opened a moment later and the young family exited without hesitation.

"Strange woman," the father said to his wife.

"I don't think she's wearing any clothes," the wife replied.

"Can I have a stick like hers?" their daughter asked while jumping in front of them, full of excitement.

Debbie shrugged and stepped into the foyer; the young family already forgotten. The tanned, curly-haired concierge at the front desk had a worried look on his face while he spoke into a UHF radio. Two hotel staff, a man and a woman in white cleaning clothes, ran down the hotel's main staircase. They must be the people who belonged to the voices she'd heard earlier.

"Gun," the woman announced as she reached the bottom of the.

The concierge held up a hand to shush the cleaners, but to no avail.

"*Gun,*" the male cleaner, old bald and overweight but with legs made of wings, bellowed at the concierge. "A gunman's here."

The hotel's alarm started ringing.

This could've gone better. Debbie picked up the pace, heading for the hotel's entrance. The cleaners and several other hotel guests started running for the entrance as well. *My hips are going to feel this tomorrow.*

"Here, I'll help you," the concierge gently grabbed Debbie's arm. She almost swore at him to let go but allowed the man to escort her out of the foyer and onto the hotel's front steps. "The police will be here soon."

"What's happening?" she asked. Her voice quivered from adrenalin but sounded like fear.

"Didn't you hear?"

"I hear little these days," she said and pointed to her hearing aid.

"It's a gunman. Someone shot some science director, the guy that was making the next big bomb, I heard."

"My goodness, why would anyone want to do that?"

The concierge shook his head and flagged down a taxi for her. "Here, get in, please. I've got to go."

"Here," Debbie sat in the taxi's back seat and handed the concierge a ten-dollar note before he could shut the door on her. "You're such a good man for helping me."

"Yeah, okay, I have to go." The concierge snatched the tip from her hands and ran towards the hotel's underground parking bays.

"Dickhead."

"What was that, Miss?" her taxi's driver, a frowning, middle-aged woman with ears reminiscent of an elephant's, asked.

"The train station, please."

"Sure."

Debbie rested her head on the taxi's back seat and allowed herself a slim smile. Job well done. Not long after the taxi got going, police cars pushed traffic aside using their sirens and seemed to rocket past, heading for the hotel. "Could you turn the radio on, please dear?" she asked the driver. The Minister had been about to give a speech about military ties at a live event, so it should already be all over the news.

The driver glanced at Debbie in the rear-view mirror and grunted her approval before reaching out with a meaty hand to depress the radio's on switch. "—Shot in the neck," an announcer bleated from the radio's speakers.

A little low, Debbie thought, and frowned.

"Uh… It is believed the Science Minister will not survive his wounds…"

"Oh, good."

"Ma'am?" the driver asked.

"Good gracious, that's awful news."

The driver grunted again.

A piercing sound erupted from Debbie's hearing aid, followed by static. Debbie moved a hand to cover her ear but stopped the action halfway through when she realized what was happening. Her grandson had installed a miniaturized radio transmitter in her hearing aid so he could call her. Debbie had thought it cute. Now? With her ears still ringing, she felt like killing the pipsqueak.

25

"Gee Gee?" her grandson called. Debbie pretended not to hear him, staring at an increasing number of flashing lights headed in the opposite direction. "Gee Gee? Oh, sorry, you can't reply. Uh, you better come back to the shack."

A sigh escaped her lips.

"Somethin' wrong darlin'?" the driver asked over the radio and the boyish voice in her ears.

Debbie affected a smile at the visage in the rearview mirror. "I'm fine, thank you dear, but could you take me to my grandson's place?"

"Sure, where's that?"

#

The door to her grandson's dilapidated house, what could only be termed as a shack held together with duct tape and metal straps, opened to admit her. She tapped her way in, leading with her walking stick on the broken tiles of the shack's small hallway. Her grandson, a mid-twenties something lay-about in baggy jeans, bushy hair and a white singlet, led the way.

"Could this have waited, Johnny?"

"Uh… sorry Gee Gee but I thought you might want to hear the offer."

Debbie rolled her eyes. "Tell Mr Green I'm heading to see your aunt in Johannesburg."

"Um, you can tell him," Johnny pushed open the door to his bedroom and the picture of a half-naked woman adorning its white crusty paint rustled in the air where a bottom corner had come loose. Two men, both twice as tall as Debbie, sat on Johnny's bed. The first was her white, tattooed employer, and the other was a Chinese or Korean body builder by the look of him. The bed suffered under their combined weight.

Johnny closed the door behind her.

"Ah, there you are," one man said. Wearing a black, tailored business suit, Mr Green seemed out of place in the confines of Johnny's messy bedroom. He stood to his full height and reached a hand toward her. Debbie took a hold of it and they shook.

"What are you doing in my grandson's bedroom, Mr Green?"

He grinned with yellow teeth. They'd been brown last she saw him.

"I apologise, Gee Gee. I hear you completed the contract; payment will be forthcoming."

"You couldn't have told me that over the phone?"

"Yes, but then we couldn't have discussed other matters so openly. There is the matter of the rifle…"

"Dock it from my pay, just like last time."

Mr Green raised an eyebrow at her, the folds of skin on his bald head increasing as he did so. "Leaving it like you do is becoming a nasty habit. There are ways we could recover it more efficiently if you can't carry it yourself."

Debbie shook her head. "As I've said before, you want someone gone. Let me do it without distractions."

Mr Green huffed. "Fine, but you don't make this easy."

"It is fun, though. Now, who's this gentleman?" Debbie waved her walking stick at the larger man still sitting on her grandson's bed.

"Whoa." Mr Green skipped out of the way of the walking stick. "Watch where you point that thing."

The large man on the bed started chuckling. "Scared of a little old sheila, eh, mate?"

"Oh, you're Australian?" Debbie asked the larger man. The man, who she'd assumed was Chinese or Korean, had the broadest Australian accent she'd ever heard before.

He shrugged. "Does it matter?"

Mr Green cleared his throat. "This is Caleb. Caleb, this is our, err, liquidator."

"Her?" Caleb's eyes reduced to slits as he studied the diminutive assassin. Still seated on the bed, Caleb was as tall as Debbie's white curly hair.

Debbie smiled at him, flashing her false teeth at him. "Were you expecting someone else, young man?"

Caleb stood up from the bed and frowned down his nose at her. "Green, mate, you better explain."

"She just completed a contract."

"What contract? Escaping the nursing home?"

"Caleb, shut up. She's my best asset and, in fact, the contract was the Science Minister, the guy developing that new bomb and testing it on innocents without the President's knowledge, that guy."

Caleb's eyes widened to their full extent. "That was *you*?" He took a step back and gave her a better look. "*How*?"

"I nagged him to death. How the hell do you think?"

Caleb stared for several seconds before he could stand up straight again, absorbing the odd revelation. "You know they're going to catch you, though, don't you?"

"Maybe one day, but what are they going to do to me if they ever find out it was me? That's all part of the excitement." Debbie giggled at the thought of the SWAT tackling her. She'd probably be sent straight to hospital if they tried. "Why are you here, *mate*?"

Caleb rolled his eyes to the ceiling for a moment, probably trying to decide if this was all an elaborate joke, then he reached into his suit pants and fished out a piece of folded paper. "Your next target." He handed her the piece of paper and Debbie shifted her weight from the walking stick to grab it. It was well past nap time and her hands were shaking.

"Here," Mr Green said. He held one of her arms to help her steady herself and she leaned the walking stick against the bedroom door. The crisp white paper unfolded to reveal a picture of a woman on one side and printed text on the other.

"Height, weight, age, name… what's so special about her? Good gracious, the contract is worth ten?"

"Yes, ten million," Caleb replied.

"Dear me, why?" Debbie looked up at Caleb. "She's a nobody."

"Gee Gee… it is Gee Gee, isn't it?" Caleb looked over at Mr Green, who nodded. "This woman single-handedly murdered a dozen of my best army mates. I don't know how it'll be done, but the government, well, my government, wants her dead."

"Then have your Prime Minister speak to the President and have her dealt with. Have the FBI round her up."

Caleb's hands balled into fists and his eyes closed. "They tried. The officers are now missing, their records have been scrubbed, their families fled." He opened his eyes again. "We sent three other liquidators to take her down. I haven't heard from any of them, and someone cleaned out all of their bank accounts. No one that encounters her seems to remember who they are, as if their minds were scrambled. All we know is that, wherever this woman goes, secrets are stolen, and good people, good families, are wiped out. We do not know what she's up to, but with NATO's leaders meeting in the city in three days and the people she's after had grievances against the Science Minister."

"Oh, this sounds interesting." She'd forgotten her tiredness. "She's helping the Science Minister's experiments, is that it?"

The men both shrugged. "That's our best guess. We have a theory about why she's so dangerous, and what she wants," Mr Green said. He reached into his jacket pocket and produced a large, flat phone.

Debbie rolled her eyes. "Another film?"

"Yes… it won't take long this time. Here, please take a seat." Mr Green helped her sit down on the bed while Caleb folded his arms across his chest, visibly unimpressed by Mr Green's 'asset.'

Mr Green sat down next to her and they watched the small screen together.

The video had been taken from a black and white infrared camera in some sort of warehouse. The camera was high, pointing straight down at the many rows of low-lying of boxes. A glimmer of movement caught Debbie's attention on the left side. It was a person, searching through a box.

"Is that her?"

Mr Green paused the video. "Yes, this is the target. In a few seconds, a group of exactly twelve FBI agents are going to come in from the right side. What's important is that the woman kills *all* of them." He pressed play, and the video continued. Sure enough, the FBI agents burst through two separate doors on the right side of the screen. There was no sound, but Debbie could imagine all the shouting and general racket they were producing as they ran in and out of rows of boxes.

The woman stood up, then stepped into a side row and took out a pistol from her jeans. The motion was so smooth and relaxed it was as if she had been expecting the agents all along.

She pointed the gun at a box and fired. Two rows over, one of the FBI agents fell to the hard floor, clutching at his neck. The action seemed to intensify, with some agents moving to their fallen colleague and others searching frantically for the shooter.

The woman fired two more shots and two more officers went down.

"How did she see them through the boxes?"

Mr Green held a finger to his lips and indicated that she should keep watching.

The woman stepped into a different row at just the right moment to avoid an officer. She waited at the edge of a row for officers to run past, then stepped into the row those officers came from, moved a few steps along, and fired through the cardboard boxes to the other side, killing all three agents.

An agent finally returned fire at the woman. The woman was no longer there, she'd dived into the next row. Two more officers fell down. Debbie hadn't even seen the woman fire.

Two of the remaining officers started retreating while the last two tried to catch the woman in a pincer movement, flanking her from opposite sides of the warehouse. It didn't work. The woman knew exactly when they would arrive at each end, pointed the gun and fired.

The retreating officers soon suffered the same fate, and the woman looked at her left arm. She'd been hit.

"And you want little old me to kill that? What is she, a robot?"

"Psychic," Caleb called from the door.

"A psychic? Have you lost your marbles?" Debbie asked. "I would've believed alien, but psychic? That's just paranormal fantasy bulldust."

"It's ten million, remember? Why not add a psychic to your bucket list?"

Debbie coughed, gave both men a stare, and closed her eyes. Caleb cleared his throat, prompting her to reopen her eyes. "When do we leave?"

"Tomorrow, 0600 hours. We're going to the beach."

Debbie smiled. "Hope you have my casket ready."

#

Debbie licked her lips and slipped her right index finger over the rifle's trigger. She shifted her elbow on the car's beige-coloured dashboard and peered over the scope into the marketplace. They'd parked the car on a bridge overlooking the markets on the beach, giving her a bird's-eye view of the scene. Hundreds of other stationary cars, busses and trucks lay strewn around them, while a one-way mesh covered most of the window that Debbie's short rifle pointed through, making it hard for any observers to see inside the nondescript-looking white ford sedan.

Dozens of smelly fish stands lined the semi-solid footpath that ran parallel to the yellow sand and the curling waves further down. Garish banners advertised motley collections of new and second-hand junk, while steam rose from several stalls, blanketing prospective customers with alluring aromas.

Debbie's mouth salivated when she caught a whiff of the stinking aromas, her stomach churning at the thought of greasy pizza pieces sliding down her waiting throat. *Should've picked up a sandwich on the way*, she thought and sighed. She un-looped her fingers from the rifle's trigger guard and relaxed against the car's dirty woolen car seat.

"Problem?" Caleb, sitting at attention in the driver's seat, said. He'd been on alert since they'd arrived several hours earlier, in time to watch the sun rise over the peddlers, merchants and overeager hobbyists while they set up their stalls.

"Relax, big guy. I'm just hungry. Hell's bells, Caleb, why'd we get here so early if the target wasn't due for several hours? We may as well pack this puppy away in the safe house." She patted the brown and black rifle as if it were a pet.

Caleb peered at her through expensive sunglasses and opened his mouth as if to speak, but then took them off to rub his eyes. "You're serious, aren't you?"

Debbie re-focussed the rifle's scope and spied through its end, glimpsing a young family, the children dashing with mischievous intent between several stalls. "This is the longest waiting game I've ever had the displeasure of playing, and if you hadn't noticed, I don't have a great deal of waiting left in me. Why at the markets, full of innocent people?"

"Look, lady, my intel said the target would be here between—"

"Shut up."

"What?"

"Shut up, big guy, your girl's down there." Debbie sighted the scope on the target and tracked her for several seconds. She looked exactly like the woman in the pictures, even wore the same dark clothing she'd worn in the warehouse's video. "Prettier than the pictures," she muttered while turning off her hearing aid. Without waiting for confirmation from Caleb, she flicked off the rifle's safety and found the trigger before taking a steadying breath. The woman wandered among the merchants and customers, children and fitness fanatics, her slight frame slipping from concealing banner to banner, forcing Debbie to readjust her aim. Remembering the death and destruction the woman could unleash, Debbie wasted no time earning her ten million.

Just before Debbie pulled the trigger, the woman stopped. She looked up to the bridge, and cool eyes seemed to meet Debbie's through the other end of the scope, sending a shiver through her spine. The woman's eyes opened wide, and then she shifted her body as if she were a coiled snake, diving forwards into the crowds.

The rifle kicked as a pointed piece of lead-wrapped-death leapt from the barrel's black end. In a fraction of a second the bullet slashed through the warm summer air, passed the heads of innocents, punctured a brightly painted sign and went through a wide-brimmed hat before finding its mark. At least, Debbie thought the bullet found its mark. The psychic kept running through the crowd, her wide, brown eyes continually glancing up at the bridge as if she were a wolf that racing towards its prey.

The people in the crowds were looking around, confused, curious, and worried all at once.

"Drive," Debbie croaked at Caleb, turning her hearing aid back on.

"You missed. Green said you never miss."

"Just drive!" she screeched while lining up another shot. She flicked off her hearing aid and fired. She swore the bullet found the woman's neck, but the psychic didn't flinch. Several people ran and screamed, as if the second crack of the rifle confirmed their worst fears. "She's coming this way, you stupid fool, drive!"

With the hearing aid turned off, she didn't hear Caleb's reply, but the car lurched forward, and she dropped the rifle while rolling around in her seat. She steadied herself against Caleb's wild maneuvers and then snatched the rifle from the floor, flicking the safety switch back on.

She looked up at the windscreen, just as a bullet hole appeared in the middle of it. In the corner of her left eye, she saw Caleb gesticulating wildly at the back of the car. It hurt to turn around, so she flipped the rearview mirror in her direction to see what he was panicking about. It was the psychic, already on the bridge with a black pistol pointing at the back of the car.

The muzzle of the pistol flashed brightly several times and two more bullet holes appeared in the windscreen. Blood burst forward from Caleb's shoulder and the car swerved wildly. Debbie screamed when the car looked as though it was about to hit a parked bus, and she briefly wondered who was going to take care of her grandson. Caleb pulled the steering wheel in time to avoid a crash.

She turned her hearing aid back on and gazed at the bullet holes and blood that covered Caleb's arm, his seat, and the old music player that now sported an extra slot.

"Is she gone?" Caleb yelled at her while flipping the rearview mirror back to his side.

"She didn't follow," Debbie quavered. "Your arm…"

"It's fine," he said while wincing, "but we've gotta get the fuck out of here." He pressed harder on the accelerator and entered the highway, away from the beach. They moved in the opposite direction to her grandson's shack, passed the city's residential outskirts, and kept going, out of the city.

Several police cars flew by on the other side of the highway, but none had their lights on, or stopped to pull them over. Either Caleb had a lot of pull with the local authorities, or the cops completely missed seeing the blood and bullet holes in the windscreen. Caleb winced with every turn of the wheel, but the bleeding in his shoulder slowed.

When they'd left the city limits, Debbie decided she wasn't hungry anymore. They left the freeway and pulled over next to a field of sunflowers. The fresh air flowed through the bullet holes and into the car. Still shaking, Debbie took a breath of the fresh air and exhaled, calming her torn nerves. She forced a smile onto her face and looked at Caleb. "Well, that was fun. I guess I didn't really need the money, anyway."

Sweating profusely from his armpits, face, and back, the stains showing through his shirt, Caleb's eyes turned to slits, and he looked at her as if she'd just spanked his puppy. "You missed."

"No, Caleb, I didn't miss. That woman back there? That thing can't be human."

"Or she is, and she made you think you hit her." He loosened his grip on the wheel and planted his forehead on the top of it. "We're dead."

Debbie made a show of looking at her body and checking her arms and legs. "My back hurts, Caleb, but I seem fine."

"Lady, get out."

"What?"

"We have to split up, disappear. I need to get away from here. You better grab a taxi, lady, and go."

"Go where?"

Caleb leaned back into his seat, and his eyes fixed on the mountainous horizon. "Anywhere. Mexico, Spain, Cameroon, I don't know. Just don't go home."

"Why?" she asked, amused. She wasn't afraid of death this late in the game.

"She's psychic, remember?"

"Wait," Debbie said while frowning. "You're not kidding, are you?"

Caleb's mouth sat ajar, and he studied her face, amazed at the comment. "You," he shook his head, "you saw what she did, didn't you? I sure as hell saw it."

Debbie recalled the moments before her first shot, when the psychic seemed to know exactly where she was. She looked into Caleb's deep-set eyes and gasped. "Johnny."

"He's already dead," Caleb said. "Now get out so I can get the fuck away from here."

"Okay," she replied after several heartbeats. She absent-mindedly dragged herself, her walking stick, and the rifle out of the car. The door hadn't closed before Caleb sped away. Debbie watched the car turn a corner, lost to the fields of sunflowers.

She wandered over to the farm's fence line and dropped the rifle over it, hoping the sunflowers would hide it long enough for Mr Green's cleanup crew to get to it before anyone else found it. She noticed blood on her left arm, Caleb's blood, so she wrapped her shawl around her to hide it from any passing cars.

"Johnny," she whispered before setting off towards the nearest house she could see, several hundred metres down the road. When she got there, a concerned young man with bloodshot eyes let her in, cleared the beer bottles from his lounge room and gave her a phone to call for a taxi.

"Can you pay for a taxi?" he asked, alcohol on his breath, presumably from a party the night before.

"That's kind of you to ask, but yes, I can pay, thank you."

Feeling sick for her grandson's safety, Debbie waited on the house's front verandah, and the young man waited with her, giving her a large cup of water while drinking two for himself. "You look worse than I feel," he commented.

"I'm 83 years old and tired, kid."

"Uh, yeah, sorry."

She waved away his apology and looked visibly relieved when the taxi arrived. "You should probably move to a different house for a while," she said while standing up to go to the taxi.

The young man tilted his head to the side and frowned. "Why?"

Debbie pulled her cheek muscles down and gritted her teeth so that he could see. "Because I just dumped a rifle in the fields over there, and if you're still here when night falls, they're going to come knocking."

"Who's they?"

"You don't want to know." She turned her left arm so that he could see Caleb's blood on it.

"No kidding," the young man said, taking in the sight of her arm, and then looked at the distant sunflower fields in wonder.

#

Caleb was right. She shouldn't have come back. Her grandson's shack was on fire, with police, firefighters, and paramedics swarming around it. She covered her face and muffled a scream. Her grandson, her Johnny, was dead. Instead of getting out of the taxi, she directed the stunned taxi driver, the elephant-eared lady from the day before, to a nearby mall. She got out to go to the bathroom but asked the driver to wait.

Once inside the busy mall, Debbie cleaned up the blood on her arm, found the first clothes store with clothes that would fit her, and then bought a burner phone. She plugged the phone's charger into a wall socket in the mall's main plaza and set it up.

Fortunately, the phone company was having a good day, and it took less than half an hour to get it ready.

The phone dialed for several seconds before Mr. Green answered. "I can't help you," he said by way of greeting.

"Hello to you too, Mr Green."

"I don't know where you're calling from, Debbie, but you better get moving. Caleb told me what happened, and now your grandson's house is burning down. You need to get out of the city if you haven't already, and you need to never contact me again."

"But—"

"Sorry, Debbie. I need to cut you off. I dunno how, but she's tracking you."

"But what do I do now?" she asked, tears falling on gaunt cheeks. "Will you—"

Click. Mr Green was gone.

She sat alone, crying into her hands, until a middle-aged couple came to comfort her. She pushed them and stood to walk away. When they insisted on trying to help her, she waved the walking stick at them, her thumb on the injection trigger. The couple backed off, and she walked outside, handing the burner phone to a group of young girls with bemused looks.

The taxi came over to her, and she got in the front with the driver. "You know you're still on the clock, right?" the driver said while pointing at the meter, which had accumulated at an alarming rate.

"I don't care. Here," she said while opening her handbag and fishing out several large bills. "That should cover you for the week."

"The week? Lady, I'm not going with you anywhere for a week."

"Just keep the money."

"Then where do you want to go?"

Anger surged to the top of Debbie's mind, and she thought of the nice young kid with the hangover near the sunflower fields. "I want to get drunk."

The big-eared driver lost the colour in her face, and she forced herself to produce an uncertain smile. "Uh, to a hotel, then?"

"No, back where you picked me up." She wondered just how much alcohol it would take for her to forget. "But first, I need to make a stop at another house to pick up some things and leave a message."

The driver looked at her with a raised eyebrow, probably wondering what Debbie was playing at. She eventually rolled her eyes, flicked her ponytail out of the way, and drove towards one of Mr Green's safe houses.

#

The hungover kid was still at the house, but when he saw the taxi pull up with Debbie in it, as well as several wooden boxes on the back seats, he dashed inside, grabbed some shoes, and without a word started running up the road away from the house.

"Not very helpful, is he?" the taxi driver grunted while shifting one of the wooden boxes. "Grandson of yours?"

The kid kept running, almost sprinting to get away from them, and didn't bother looking back, fear driving his legs onward.

Debbie nodded and looked up the road to where she'd dumped the rifle. Mr Green hadn't asked for the details of the rifle's location, so it should still be where she'd left it. "Nice kid, but a bit of a slacker," she said. "Could you please unload the boxes onto the verandah? I'm going for a walk to get my gun."

The driver laughed. "Not going to shoot the kid, are you?"

"No, just going to shoot the psychic that put me in this situation."

The driver laughed nervously. "There's a lot in these boxes. By the time you're done with it all, I reckon you'd shoot at anything, or try to, anyway." Debbie ignored her and headed towards the sunflower fields, stabbing her stick at the road with every step, determined to get revenge.

The driver unpacked the boxes as fast as she could and waved at Debbie as she sped away.

Debbie retrieved the rifle and, fortunately, no vehicles came by to see her struggle with it back to the house. Once at the house, she opened the boxes and got to work, before popping the lid on the first bottle of whiskey.

#

The house phone rang again and again, forcing Debbie to pick herself up from the floor of the green kitchen with her walking stick and head to the hallway, where the phone was.

The world spun, and she wasn't sure whose house she was in. She pressed onwards through the confusion and pain and held her pounding head. She found the phone and ripped it off the wall. "What?" she barked into it.

"Hello, Debbie," a young woman's voice returned.

"Who's this?"

"The psychic. The murderer of grandsons."

Debbie almost dropped the phone but tightened her grip on it. "You found me."

"I got your message back in that safe house of yours. The note said, 'Come fight me, bitch,' with this address. Sound familiar?"

"Safe house?" she asked, genuinely confused. Did she go to one of the safe houses?

"Yes, one of ten, all burnt to the ground."

"But—"

"How did I know where they were? How did I know where to find your grandson? Oh, Debbie, you already know how. I'm psychic, to a certain distance. For example, I know you're confused and afraid. Want to know how close I had to get to find that out?"

"You're outside the house," Debbie said while trying to remember where she'd placed the rifle.

"Yes, around, say… two hundred metres away, in fact, right where you dumped your rifle, or where you thought you dumped it. Ah, you remember where it is now, don't you? It's in the house."

"Yes," Debbie whispered. She dropped the phone and moved as fast as her shaky hands and throbbing hungover head would allow, tap-tap-tapping rapidly with her cane in her haste. She found the rifle placed next to the front door, the cartridge already loaded and the safety off, as if she knew she would need it after drinking. She placed the walking stick at the front door and picked up the rifle before walking outside and raising the scope to her eyes it to search the road near the sunflower fields.

There she was, walking towards the house in the middle of the road. When she could steady the rifle on the verandah's small rusting fence well enough to place the crosshairs over the psychic's head, the psychic smiled at her.

Debbie turned off her hearing aid and fired.

The smile grew. The rifle roared again. The psychic dodged and then ran. Debbie fired four more times, apparently missing every time. Her hands shook as she tried to reload, something she rarely had to do. "How did I miss? How?" She locked a new cartridge into the rifle, sighted it up the road again, and caught a flicker of movement in the corner of her right eye, across the road from the house in front of more sunflowers. She spun to the right and fired on instinct, almost losing her right hand from return fire.

A bullet slammed through the rifle's midsection, the muzzle flash from the psychic's gun coming from across the street where Debbie had caught the flicker of movement, rather than a hundred metres up the road. She dropped the rifle on the verandah's wooden floorboard and backed away from the rusting fence, cradling her right hand.

"What? But you were up the road." She looked at where the psychic had been running, to where the muzzle flash came from. Her mouth went dry, and she fell onto one of the two chairs placed on either side of the house's front door. The psychic was talking, so Debbie turned the hearing aid back on and then held her aching stomach and head. When she recovered enough to focus, she noticed the psychic was bleeding from her left arm.

"You fascinate me, Debbie. I trick you into thinking I'm somewhere else, but you *still* hit me."

"I never miss," Debbie said, still shocked the psychic had hit her rifle.

"You almost did it, bringing my father's whole operation down. Do you know how we came to get to this point? To assemble the parts I need to bring the world's governments to their knees, and then you had to kill my father… wait, you're hiding something." She looked around the house and up both ends of the road. "I can't read you. What did you do to wipe your memory?"

Debbie leaned backwards, wondering the same thing. "Got blackout drunk, I guess."

"That's your grand plan to defeat me? Get drunk and wait to die by my hand?" She shook her head and walked across the road, mounting the steps with ease, ignoring the bullet wound in her left arm. "Odd plan."

"No, I don't think that was it," Debbie retorted while noticing the sun's rays dancing on a piece of string.

The psychic must've read her mind. She looked down at the string, carefully placed across the top step, right as her foot tripped through it. Her assessment of Debbie's drinking session changed in an instant. "Good plan—"

The explosion of shaped charges destroyed the steps, the psychic's bottom half, and Debbie's hearing aid.

#

The officers at the side of Debbie's bed unlocked her handcuffs and stood aside for the old man in a black, expensive-looking suit to enter the room. She didn't recognise him straight away, but he looked familiar. He started talking but soon realised she couldn't hear him; the hospital staff had ordered new hearing aids to replace the one she'd lost to the explosion, but they hadn't arrived yet. The man found a pen and started writing on a piece of paper.

"Well done," the note said. "You saved my life. I'm the President. Want a job?"

Debbie nodded and laughed. "That's item fifty-nine on my bucket list," she told him, feeling the words rather than hearing them. It wouldn't bring back her grandson, but it was *something*. She mentally checked off two items on her list. "I always wanted to work for the President."

Andrew P. McGregor lives in the rural town of Inverell near the East coast of Australia. He writes science fiction and dark fantasy short stories, most of which are collected in *Tales of Starships & Apocalypse*.

Pyrofang

by Barend Nieuwstraten III

O mesh sat upon his red cushion, focused on his breathing. Deep and slow, he fueled his meditative state as he sat with one leg folded over the other and the back of each hand resting upon his knees. A skinny boy of fifteen, his brown skin was covered only in a large red sash wrapped into a thick red loincloth about his hips and through his legs, with a smaller one wrapped about his brow. His red and yellow priest robes were folded behind him atop his unravelled sandals. Charged with sitting by the sacred fire, it was the only duty or task that allowed a priest to sit so underdressed within the temple, too hot to do so otherwise.

A sculpted cave, the temple of Pyrosian, sat high within the southern cliff wall of the Ravine of Purimah. A subterranean harbour city that could take no ships from the sea, only small boats if those aboard were willing to row for many days under low rocks, mostly in the dark. The preferred method was to dock on the south coast of Dor Vuldar and travel by land to the city's western entrance. A third of the way down a descending cliff road to the lowlands.

Omesh sighed as he heard visitors approaching. While dutifully honouring visitors to the sacred flame, he still preferred the tranquillity of days without them. But never begrudging those wishing to see the legendary sword within. All who viewed it dreamt of claiming it, but a mere moment of standing within a yard of the scared flame's heat deterred that ambition with its heat. A prison of rock with a thick cage-wall of dancing red flames that climbed from long overlapping fissures in the rocky floor while the sword itself sat upon a stand, crudely carved atop a narrow rocky pillar.

Omesh looked to the bottom of the stairs leading up to the chamber where he sat. Hearing voices as a monk brought them to the gates, he wondered whether they were merely sightseers or would-be heroes about to have some foolishly imagined dream of destiny shattered like every child who reached out when alone in their room, hoping to discover some natural affinity for magic.

He was surprised to see a man in imperial Kestrian armour. A centurion's, bearing the imperial griffin on an iron chest piece, with pauldrons, plated vambraces and shin plated boots, with a skirt of splintered strips of layered leather and studded metal tips. But the way this man wore a hood instead of a helmet, with a cloak obscuring the armour's proud design, it was clear he belonged to no legion. Carrying a gladius on either side of his hips was another unusual sight. An elven woman accompanied him in typical green leather armour of her kind's making. A third, behind them, wore the leather armour of the imperial soldiers who occupied the southern shores of Heruud. The elf had an olive complexion, while the other two had pale, pinkish white skin.

"Priest," the monk said. "There are visitors here who wish to see the sword."

Omesh gave the older monk a nod, who bowed in return as the visitors climbed the stairs until they were between the two side recesses; one for a statue of the man who made the sword centuries ago, and the place where Omesh sat. "Welcome," he said, pointing his left palm to the firewall atop the stairs.

The false centurion politely nodded as he raised a palm in greeting. Smiling, his head was drawn towards the statue from which Omesh sat across every day. He pointed his hand to it, the figure of a man with small horns upon his brow who had sat there almost as long as the sword lay behind the fire. "May I ask, who this is?" he asked. "For it looks like neither Pyrosian nor his son Burzuhl," he said, of the fire gods.

"His name was Gyraksin," Omesh informed the visitor, as he had done for so many before. "He was neither young god nor demigod. But a pyromancer who forged the sword that lays beyond the sacred flame, where he retired it, centuries ago."

"Pyrofang," the visitor said, with a knowledgeable nod. "I came here as soon as I heard legend of it."

"It draws the attention of many who wish to wield such a blade," Omesh said.

"All of whom leave empty handed of course," he said, turning back to the elf accompanying him and smiled at her. "What do you know of this Gyraksin," the visitor asked Omesh, again pointing to the statue.

"He came from another land when he was young and retired his sword here when he was quite old," Omesh recalled the tale. "He protected the northern passage of the borderlands, preventing the newly occupying Kestrians of the time from ever coming this far north. Forcing them to remain on the coast or venture into the lowlands where they'd have to contend with the wild roving kingdoms."

"How long ago was this?" the visitor asked.

"Just over four-hundred years ago," the young priest said.

The hooded man smiled. "So, he left it here to be collected."

Omesh tilted his head, wondering how the disclosed amount of time seemed to lead the visitor to that conclusion. "He left instruction that anyone able to pass through the flames unharmed was worthy to wield it."

"And presumably anyone who could survive being horrifically burned twice," the elf woman discouraged her companion.

"Have many tried?" the hooded visitor asked.

"In my short watch, I've only seen people step towards the flames and been deterred by the heat," the boy priest said, gesturing at his own lack of garments. "But I have heard tales from older priests, here, of warriors, warlocks, and sorcerers who believed they possessed some quality the fire would acknowledge or respect. All harmed themselves terribly. Some even died."

"There is no spell to completely protect oneself from fire," the visitor said, as he began unfastening a vambrace. "Only spells to repel magic or shield oneself from it. But this fire is not the product of magic. It burns from some mineral and alchemic reaction. There is no protective spell against that." He took a few steps closer, to where few could stand to stay more than a moment. "And none can jump through, because they'd fall down into the source of the fire. They must stand in the fire to retrieve the sword," he observed, taking a few steps back to hand his companion, behind the elf, his vambrace before undoing the next.

"Do you believe the fire will be more forgiving if you leave your armour behind?" Omesh said, guiltily excited that the man was appearing to make the attempt. "I should warn you that it won't."

"My only fear is that my armour and clothing will be harmed," he said, stripping his other arm. "That's a fueled fire, not just flames. Whatever steps through them, isn't just passing through fire, but that which sustains it."

"What is your name?" Omesh asked the rapidly disrobing man.

"My name is Elgaryk," he said. "My elven friend is Lelenya, and my squire: Sierele."

As the elf woman, Lelenya, stepped aside, Omesh finally got a clear look at this squire in imperial leather armour. She gave the young priest a polite nod as she accepted her charge's chest piece and pauldrons. Omesh was almost struck dumb upon seeing her face. His age, if not a year or two older, and her brief smile seemed to burn into his mind. He felt compelled to stand, suddenly aware of his lack of garments, while the man she came with was quickly piling his own in her arms. "Oh," he said, awkwardly running his arms over his bare skinny chest, wishing he'd grabbed his robes on the way up. "Nice to meet you."

"Nice to meet you too," Elgaryk replied, instead of the girl.

The girl smiled again; aware the pleasantry was meant for her. Her pale face was long and flat but with striking eyes, peering out from under her leather helmet, that just caught his attention like no other had before. Though the urgency of someone about to enter the sacred fire did wrestle her presence for his attention.

"Are you certain you want to do this?" Omesh asked Elgaryk, as the visitor slipped out of his boots.

"Strip naked before a boy priest?" Elgaryk asked. "No, but your own lack of attire makes me feel less awkward about it. So, thanks for that."

"It gets very hot in here very quickly in my full robes," Omesh explained, again reminded that he was almost naked. He settled his hands on his hips to remedy the awkward fidgeting of his arms and puffed his chest for good measure, hoping to appear better built in front of the girl.

Eventually the visitor pulled his hooded tunic over his muscly but slender and sinewy body and placed it on the pile of armour in his squire's arms. When he turned back to face the fire, he looked to Omesh and gave him a nod. His eyes and hair a reddish brown, on his square jawed long face. There were two small horns upon his head, pushing out from his brow, bending and pointing upwards. Omesh's eyes barely had to shift to see the statue beyond the man, where the image of Gyraksin, the sword's creator, sat with the same horns.

"Where have you come from?" Omesh asked.

Elgaryk pointed to the statue, before he continued up the stairs "The same place as him, and given the time he placed it here, I'm confident he left it specifically for one of his own kind to claim." The naked man stepped fearlessly into the flames at a calm pace. The flames licked at his skin but did nothing. The man wasn't even sweating as he reached over and claimed the sword, lifting it out of the small rocky spires carved to hold it in place.

Omesh stood in shock as he watched the naked man emerge from the fire with Pyrofang. Its blade was reddened with a faint swirling pattern in its metal. The hilt, two red dragon heads facing each other. Their racial colour only discernible beyond the metallic grey in which they were set, by the manner of the horns curling forward and upward. Below their meeting snarling snouts, a ruby was set in either side of the hilt, glowing by some magic. It's hilt, deep etched iron, void of leather gripping, as if its creator knew it was meant to pass through fire.

"Beautiful," Elgaryk said, as flames that still stuck to him were still slowly dying. "I don't suppose there's a scabbard for it."

"It's not kept in this part of the temple," Omesh said, strapping up his sandals. "But you don't want it. After decades by Gyraksin's side, it was in no great condition when he left it, four centuries ago. It's better in its display case than by your side, trust me."

"A shame," Elgaryk said, handing the sword to his elven companion so that he could redress. "I shall have to have one made. Know you of a fast tanner in Purimah?"

"The city boasts some leatherworkers, down here," the young priest said, slipping back into his robes. "But you won't find a tanner as such. I believe that requires access to the sun."

"Going somewhere?" Lelenya asked, looking up from the sword to see Omesh dressed and ready.

"I pledged to watch over the sword," Omesh said. "So, I suppose I must go where it goes."

Omesh's eyes glanced from her to the squire and back in what he considered to be the flap of a locust wing in speed, but the elven woman's eyes caught it and looked back to the young woman beside her and smiled at the priest.

"So, you wish to join us?" Elgaryk asked, as his squire helped fasten his armour. "And yet, you know nothing about us."

"I know that you were able to fetch the sword I was devoted to watching," Omesh said. "If it is the sword's fate to go with you, then it is also mine. I also believe we have many questions for each other. I know more about that sword than anyone. Anyone willing to travel at least."

Elgaryk looked to his elven companion with a raised brow as he continued redressing.

"It's good luck to have a priest in your party isn't it?" Lelenya asked, as more of a suggestion than a genuine question. She looked to his squire who shrugged.

"Very well," Elgaryk said, strapping his vambrace. "And I suppose if I should fall before, I can return the sword, you could always bring it back to this temple for me."

"Though it'll take a remarkable toss for me to get it back in its stand," Omesh suggested, pointing to the sacred fire.

Elgaryk looked back at the fire and laughed. "Indeed, it would."

\#

Omesh had not ventured far out of the temple in a long time. Priests and monks gathered to see the sword up close as Elgaryk proudly made his way back through the temple with it. The high priest approved of Omesh's commitment to follow the sword and gifted him supplies and coin to aid in his journey.

When Omesh had made his farewells, the group of four left the temple, taking the high southern cliff road. Looking down they could see fishermen far below them on wooden docks by the water, underlit by submerged sunstones. Yellow lights turned green by the subterranean seawater, made by the pyromancers and priests of the fire temple to attract fish and illuminate the low parts of Purimah. Through the water, the light reflected as a dancing luminous webbing upon the dark cliff walls above.

They passed through the upside-down gardens. Flowering vines that hung from the natural rocky archway of the city's main thoroughfare, reaching down towards the light of larger sunstones, suspended by ancient rope, overgrown by vines and roots. Elgaryk walked with his head turned upward, enamoured by the beauty of it.

"Even a second time, I can barely believe the sight of this," he said, studying the variety of plants that grew from the rocks above.

A native of Purimah, Omesh was proud to have his city impress a man who could walk through fire unharmed. "The Upside-Down Garden of Purimah is one of the great wonders of the world," he said.

"I can see why," Pyrofang's new wielder said. "Though, can a secret city boast a world wonder?"

"It's a hidden city, not a secret city," Omesh reminded him. "And not hidden, as a challenge. Merely from plain sight, to those walking the land above."

"So, we should feel no pride having found it," Lelenya added, as she patted her enamoured companion on the shoulder to guide him away from walking into others using the great passageway. "Even if you struggle to see it's people."

Omesh shared an amused smile with Sierele.

#

"So, how did you end up in Kestrian armour?" Omesh asked, as they sat at a table in the Undermoss Inn. "You do not strike me as imperial soldiers."

Tearing apart oiled flatbread, Elgaryk pinched a paste of spiced lentils in it and filled his mouth, ushering a hand towards his squire.

"We are not," Sierele said, as her master ate. "But we clashed with some, when our own garments and gear were in need of... supplementation."

"You... robbed them?" Omesh asked. "Not that I disapprove. They've no business occupying shores beyond Kestria."

"They cannot hold the kingdoms of Edenya, they name Kestria, and successfully conquer more lands without losing that hold," Lelenya said, taking a sip of vine water. "A lesson, I'm sure, they will eventually learn."

"We defended ourselves when an altercation became unavoidable," Sierele clarified. "So, more looted than robbed."

"I don't mean to continue wearing this Kestrian armour," Elgaryk said, looking down at the leather strips across his lap. "When we've coin for something else, I'll definitely switch to something that doesn't feel like a dress."

#

Elgaryk earned decent coin in the city's wrestling pits for a fortnight. His strength was remarkable, almost unnatural, defeating much larger strongmen who made their living there. The pit masters encouraged him to stay but despite his skill, it was not the path to fortune he desired. He thirsted for adventure and found the opportunity with a sorcerer, Tor Vishnad, who commissioned Elgaryk's party to procure a sanddrake egg.

They set out immediately, descending into the lowlands. After scavenging the sparse wood of the lowlands to build a campfire, Omesh used his fire magic to grow the first flame almost instantly into a full roaring fire.

"Shame I don't have any heatstones, though," he said, as Elgaryk and Lelenya laid down to sleep. "Stones that glow and heat in place of a campfire, though not as pleasant. Also, you can't really cook with them. But they're good in an emergency."

"Good in a rocky lowland wasteland where trees and bushes are far and few between, I imagine," Sierele said, sitting up with him as they took the first watch. "Are they what light the ravine of Purimah?"

"Oh, no, those are sunstones," Omesh explained. "They are made almost purely for light and can afford to be submerged in seawater."

"Heatstones can't?"

Omesh shook his head. "Heatstones resist water. They even work in the rain. But for some reason they do not survive seawater long. Though they are not completely destroyed by it, instead becoming aquastones. They expand from the size of a walnut shell to a large melon," he said, expanding his hands to demonstrate. "They capture and petrify the water into a large crystalised orb. As small fish tend to be drawn to the warmth and light, they often get caught in it, preserved forever within, with whatever plant life happens to be in the small surrounds. People who find them take them to jewel crafters who can polish them smooth for display. A frozen capture of sea life with a dull shimmer from within, they're the second most beautiful thing I think I've ever seen."

Sierele smiled a closed tight smile and squinted cynically as she looked at him. After an awkward pause, Omesh finally cracked at the silence.

"You don't want to know what the first is?" he asked.

"The problem is, I suspect I do," she said. "I have noticed the way you look at me, you know. But you cannot answer that."

"Why not?" Omesh asked, with trepidation.

"If you tell me it's me, I'll be embarrassed for you," she said, slowly shaking her head. "You would lose the respect you have earned so far and seem foolish to me."

Omesh swallowed, regretting his approach. "And if I said something else?" he offered, with an innocent shrug.

"Oh, then I'd be devastated," she smiled, as Omesh felt one creep across his own face.

"A tough situation," he said, leaning towards her. "Best say nothing."

She leaned towards him, and they kissed.

"If you're doing that," Lelenya's voice startled them apart, as she spoke without opening her eyes. "Who's standing watch?"

The pair looked at each, coughing embarrassed, as they straightened up. Sierele's hand found Omesh's and they sat in awkward but joyful silence for the rest of their watch.

#

They continued through the dry rocky lowlands of North-Eastern Dor Vuldar. With Pyrofang by Elgaryk's side, he donated one of his commandeered Kestrian gladii to Omesh. The other three taught him the basics of swordplay whenever they stopped to camp, though he proved a slow study. Omesh spent the last of his arcane energy each night, before sleep, pouring it into the sword so that it may one day take on an enchantment of his design.

"What do you mean to do with it?" Lelenya asked, as they walked.

"Most of the magic I know wouldn't really transfer to an object," Omesh admitted. "Priests of Pyrosian are a different breed of pyromancer. We manipulate existing flame for the most part. But I'll figure out something. Closer to when it's ready."

"Manipulate fire how?" Elgaryk asked.

"I can make it last longer, grow larger, and even borrow some of the flame."

"*Borrow* some of the flame?" Elgaryk raised an eyebrow. "What does that even mean."

"I can capture a small bundle of flame and carry it several inches above in my hand. A fire lotus, we call it. It can be used to light other objects, torches, braziers, candles. I could carry it around instead of a torch, but it gets far too hot to hold for long, and I know better spells for providing light."

"Perhaps, you could imbue your gladius with a light spell then," Sierele suggested, with a playful elbow in the priest's side. "It would be of more use as a magic torch than a sword, in *your* hand."

"I'm sure you were less gifted at swordplay once to," Lelenya said, to the young squire.

"If I was, it was before I remember," Sierele boasted, "buried with memories of my first steps and words."

"That sounds like a sad childhood," the elf said, with pity. "But Omesh is hardly going to improve if you discourage him by teasing him."

"Maybe he *should* be discouraged," the squire said, winking to Omesh. "With the skill of blade, the three of us possess, he's no reason to put himself needlessly in danger. Better he be preserved for talents, only he can provide."

"Oh, I see," Lelenya said, with a playfully scandalous tone of innuendo.

Sierele's face turned red, to the elf's delight. While Elgaryk did not look back, Omesh could tell with the forward tilt of his head and wiggle of his ears that was concealing his entertainment by walking ahead.

#

"The Valley of Spires," Elgaryk said, looking up from the crude map he'd purchased. Ahead the terrain sank into a long rocky valley before them, filled with tall naturally formed towers of light brown rock. Narrow mountains that reached up from the lowland, providing small platforms high above. "What a unique landscape to behold," the man who had walked through fire said, filled with wonder.

"Not as unique as you'd think, actually," Omesh hesitantly corrected.

Elgaryk turned back to the young priest. "You're saying there's other places like *this*?"

"More than a few," Omesh said, shrugging. "It's quite a common type of terrain in the Heruusian lowlands. There's the Canyon of Spears, Rockwood Ravine, the Gorge of Needles, Lamprey Gulch, Redrock Jungle, the Cleft of Teeth, the Hellfingers, and those are just the ones I remember the names of."

Eglaryk smiled. "Well, it's my first one so I'm still impressed. I can see why sanddrakes and other flying things would choose to nest atop those spires. It's going to be a challenge getting to them."

"Just a matter of climbing a spire that has a sanddrake atop it," Omesh said, with a sarcastic casualness.

"The real trick is knowing your dragonkin eggs," Sierele said. "You can't just grab the first egg you see. It's far too much effort to leave things to chance."

"What are you talking about?" Omesh asked, as they made their descent.

"The hatching cycle," Sierele explained. "Dragons who mate, produce dragon eggs. Dragons who don't, produce drake eggs. As do drakes who mate. But drakes who don't, produce wyvern eggs."

"And wyverns who don't mate?"

"Some will say they produce snakes," Lelenya said. "But don't feel too uninformed. I could not tell you which eggs are which by sight."

"Tor Vishnad wants a sanddrake egg," Elgaryk needlessly reminded them. "An egg full of wyverns won't do, and a dragon would be out of the question."

"Wouldn't he pay more for a dragon egg?" Omesh asked.

"Gods no," Elgaryk scoffed. "He most likely means to tame the beast he requested. A dragon is no mere beast to serve such purpose. Born with an abundance of wit, wherewithal, and wrath, they hatch far too clever to tolerate any pretender to the throne of motherhood."

Omesh couldn't imagine a sanddrake, even tamed, being allowed to dwell within Purimah. He suspected some strange ritual or experiment was instead at the heart of the sorcerer's request. "I don't see any nest from up here," he realised. "It's going to be even harder to see them from down there." He pointed into the valley below.

Elgaryk smiled. "What happens when you eat?" he asked the boy priest.

"I… stop being hungry?"

"And later?"

"I get hungry again?"

Elgaryk shook his head, amused. "No, it comes out the other end."

"Ah," Omesh said, realising the foreigner's point. "So, we just wander through the valley until we find the base of a spire piled in… oh," he grimaced at the prospect, "the first few steps of the climb are going to be unpleasant."

"Probably," Elgaryk said, lightly slapping the priest on the shoulder. "But hopefully they park their arses over the one side every time."

"And if they don't?"

"Then you'll regret wearing sandals instead of boots."

#

They made their way through the forest of towering rocky trunks that provided much shelter from the hot Heruusian sun, but at night they encouraged wind traps that embittered the cold. With Elgaryk refusing to host campfires that would herald their presence in the dark, they huddled together for warmth as they slept. Omesh supplemented their shared bedding by imbuing rocks with a low heat through his pyromantic spellcraft.

One day, Elgaryk halted the party as they travelled upon seeing a network of stretched canopies of animal hide, sewn together and suspended by rope over a small encampment. "I was told roving tribes don't come down this far," he said, of the Western Lowlands.

"The four greater tribes occupy the northern parts of the Heruusian lowlands, while the lesser are scattered across the middle, from east to west" Omesh said. "Low tribes travel where they may, but this far south is where the broken tribes dwell. Remnants of scattered and dwindled ones."

"Does being broken make them any friendlier?" Lelenya asked, pointing ahead to where a handful of tribespeople stood holding spears by their sides.

"Mostly the tribal people of the lowlands fight other tribes, even in their smaller numbers," Omesh said. "From what I've heard, they shouldn't have any real interest in us."

Standing in the shade of their suspended canopy, the lowland dwellers who defended the settlement watched the four approach while others moved about behind them. They seemed to spread to the edges of their shelter, watching in all directions.

"I think they think we're part of a larger group attempting to surround them," Lelenya said.

"Nobody draw weapons, then," Elgaryk suggested, raising his palms to the people before them. "What's the politest way to address these people," he asked Omesh.

The young fire priest shrugged. "These are the first tribal people I've ever met."

"Have you come to claim us?" one of the people called out, stepping into the sun. Like the rest of his people, he wore little over his dark brown skin. Layered wrappings of dark crude cloth covered him from knee to chest as his long copper spearhead sat upon a bowed shaft. "We will be no one's slaves."

"Slaves?" Elgaryk asked, confused.

Omesh pulled his head back in realisation and tapped on the imperial griffin on Elgaryk's chest armour.

Elgaryk shook his head at the tribesman. "We slew the men this armour belonged to. We're not with the invaders."

"Then why have you come here, to this place?" the tribesman asked. "And where have you come from? You speak our tongue far better than any I have seen with such pale skin."

Elgaryk smiled. "An exchange of stories for a night in your shelter, by your fire?"

The tribe welcomed them, and tales were shared. Omesh learned more of his companions and the elders spoke of past triumphs and glory. Lelenya spoke of her people, the Duscari, who were born on the borderlands of the two contiguous continents. A race mixed between the dark humans of Heruudand and the fair elves of Dantos, creating olive skinned half elves such as her.

Elgaryk and Sierele spoke of great trials fought, endured, and chased through the dragon lands to the east. There they fought for the rare honour to visit upon the rest of the lands about the Middle Sea to chase whatever destiny awaited them. Elgaryk impressed them with his mastery of the Heruusian tongue, both the high that Omesh spoke and the low that the tribespeople did. He explained that it was a gift of birth, for he spoke all languages while poor Sierrele had to learn, though by similar heritage she learned them easier than most, filtered through her rigid accent. Omesh had few stories to tell being both young and stationary until now. Though he had the stories of those who attempted to claim Pyrofang, inevitably leading to the tale of Elgaryk's claiming it, which lead to the foreigner showing off the blade that issued trailing streaks of rippling flame in its wake when swung swiftly through the air.

"So, you come from the dragon lands, bear horns like that of a red dragon or firedrake, though far smaller, and can endure fire as they do," Omesh observed.

Elgaryk nodded. "Like my Duscari friend here," he said, gesturing to Lelenya, "my blood Is not pure human, though more so than hers. But enough about me. Perhaps you'll finally show us this 'borrowed fire' of yours, now that you have a gathering."

Omesh nodded in agreement, pointing his palm at the fire. At first it seems as if he was doing nothing more than warming his hand, but when he pulled his arm back, an orb of flames sprouted from the fire, following his palm as he turned it upward. The orb hovered above it, with its flames licking upward like a flower of lashing pointed pedals of red and orange. Sierele was enamoured, as were the tribespeople.

"We call it the fireplume," the boy priest explained.

"And what else can you do with it?" Elgaryk asked.

"I can make it grow," Omesh said, leaning back and outstretching his arm. The flame grew tall for a few moments, spreading its light and warmth before he restored it. "I can't safely demonstrate much more under a canopy of hide."

Elgaryk scratched his chin in contemplation. "Can you take it from any fire?"

"I can manipulate any flame."

"Even a short lived one?"

Omesh nodded. "And the fire I extend keeps the properties of its original fire. For it has been tried with the sacred fire, and that of a warlock."

Elgaryk and Sierele exchanged an excited look before he asked, "Even dragon fire?"

"Not something I would want to stand in the path of just to try, but yes," the young fire priest confirmed. "Under the right conditions, and if I was not engulfed in flame."

"We could make Hellforged weapons and armour," Elgaryk said to his squire.

"Hellforged?" Omesh asked.

"Hellforge is a city in my homeland," Elgaryk explained. "A place where smithed iron is smelted in the fiery breath of red dragons." He drew a dagger from his belt and handed it to his new companion to examine. It had swirling patterns in the blade that seemed to change in the light of the fire as he turned it. "It makes swords that can cut through iron the way iron cuts through copper. It makes impenetrable armour that will halt even enchanted blades. A metal that endures fire, even dragon fire, where lesser metals would not. With your help, and a gifted smith, we could adorn ourselves in the armour and weapons that rarely exist beyond the shores of our homeland."

"But you still need a red dragon or firedrake."

Amused and knowing, Elgaryk and his squire exchanged another look. "Don't worry about that," he said with a sly smile. "I can get you a little dragon fire to play with."

Omesh furrowed his brow, confused at the notion.

#

When they left the next morning, the tribespeople sent two of their younger warriors, Mahrd and Esheh, to help them on their quest, knowing where the sanddrakes favoured nesting. They were skinny men, but agile with black wavy hair that twisted thick and wildly in every direction from their scalps and beards.

It was Esheh who pointed out from some distance that plants were growing around the base of one of the rocky spires. It was like a small oasis, but with a towering rocky protrusion instead of a pool of water. There were other plants and small trees that grew in sparse patches of fertile earth, but this was a small garden of green leaves and an abundance of red.

"Chilis," Omesh realised.

Esheh looked back and smiled. "Those of yellow scale love chilis. When the younger drakes and wyvern eat them, the plants grow below where they dwell."

"This is where we get ours," Mahrd said.

Omesh looked to Sierele who cocked an eyebrow back at him. She had suffered eating the spicy food shared by the remnant tribe. Elgaryk's resistance to heat seem to extend to his tongue, while both Omesh and Lelenya, having Heruusian blood, were raised on hot spice, leaving the poor young squire to suffer as most pale skinned visitors seemed to in these lands.

"Why would anyone living in such an arid climate choose to eat food that made them even thirstier?" she mumbled. "Then to quench that thirst with boiling water and dried leaves."

"You don't like tea?" Omesh asked.

Sierele shrugged. "Perhaps in winter and when my mouth wasn't already on fire," she suggested. "Even then, I'd prefer to drink glühwein."

"The boiled wine you told me of?" Omesh asked. "Didn't you say that was also spiced."

"With tasty spices, not... corrosive ones," she said, to his amusement.

Elgaryk examined the rocky tower before them. "A lot of natural grips in these spires. This shouldn't be too hard to climb." He looked to the two tribesmen accompanying them. "I cannot ask you to assist us here. This is our task and you have been most hospitable and helpful." He turned to Omesh, looking him up and down in his robes. "Perhaps you should stay here as well."

"Every child in Purimah climbs the walls of the ravine, just to jump back into the underground harbour where they were swimming." Omesh said, defensively.

"There's no harbour to break your fall here," Elgaryk said. "But if you wish to follow, lag behind, just to be safe. I need your help for far greater pursuits and would hate to have your journey end here."

"Agreed," Sierele said, gently patting him on the back. "Perhaps I should lag a little behind as well."

Elgaryk nodded and the climbing soon commenced. Eglaryk and Lelenya started up one side, and after a head start of several feet, while Omesh abandoned his robes and sandals, he and Sierele and began to scale the other side.

"You prefer to climb barefoot?" she asked him, as they began to pull themselves up from each protruding grip and deep recess.

"It's what I'm used to, and the flat sole of sandals and boots stop you from using your toes properly."

Sierele looked down at one of her boots as she purchased another foothold. "The Kestrians claimed a continent and continue to spread without using their toes properly," she mumbled.

Omesh smiled. "So, what am I looking for?" he asked. "How do I tell one egg from the other?"

"Scales, size, and colour," she said, lowering her voice as they slowly ascended. "Dragon eggs are quite large, heavily scaled, and coloured. Eggs containing wyverns are smooth and dark brown with only a speckling of colour. Eggs containing Drakes are somewhere in between; less pronounced scaling, stronger colour in the tips of each scale that fade to brown in the roots. With yellow scaled wyrmkind, we've not so hard a task. Black dragons and acid drakes are the hardest to tell."

A whooshing sound whipped past Omesh. He tightened his grip and hugged the rocky spire. He saw something fall, but it barely breached his line of sight, falling down the other side of the spire.

"What the hells was that?" Omesh asked, looking down. He could see what looked like a small, yellow, severed wing on the ground, a few dozen feet down.

Sierele climbed across to see what he saw. "Wyvern," she said, gesturing upward with her head.

With the sun at its highest, Omesh squinted upward to see movement in the air. Winged snakes hovering about the upper parts of the spire, slowly circling it. Their wings worked hard to keep their long bodies afloat, at least making it harder for them to suddenly lunge as snakes of the ground do. It gave his companions a fighting chance against them while holding onto the rocks. Elgaryk or Lelenya had sent one to the ground by crippling it.

"Stay back," Sierele said, climbing higher.

Omesh shifted around to his right for a better view of what was happening above. Elgaryk was swinging Pyrofang, slicing through yellow wyverns with a trail of fire and sending them to the ground. Some fell quickly, losing a wing or head, others flew away after losing the lower half their body, leaking blood as they fought the inevitable.

As Omesh watched in wonder, his right hand found a deep crevice in the rockface. Curious, he climbed around to get a better look. In the deep hole there was the thinnest shaft of sunlight making it all the way down to where Omesh was. There was no safe angle from which to get a proper view of the narrow, vertical tunnel. But the light told him all he really needed to know.

There was something strange about curvature of the base of this rocky shaft when he looked directly in. Though distracted by the sound of fighting above, and the odd spray of wyvern blood, he was drawn by what he saw. A round base to this shaft that opened to the rockface where he clung. He felt compelled to dust the dirt and smaller rocks that had fallen over time, until he saw a glimmer of yellow streak in the thin beam of sunlight. It took a few attempts but twisting and lifting with one hand while the other held him in place, he managed to dislodge it. A large egg, upside-down, with scaly ridges that yellowed towards their tips. He furrowed his brow, realising the egg must have slipped down the rock shaft and wedged itself there at some point.

"Come back down," he called. "I think I've got one."

Omesh laboured to free it, jostling it with his fingers to push It towards an opening that wouldn't accommodate his fingers around the egg. He negotiated upwards with small pinching movements, coercing it out with frustratingly subtle brushes as he maintained his grip on the spire with his other hand. After grazing his knuckles in the pursuit, he managed to shuffle it out, rolling over his arm catching it against his chest. After a sigh of relief, he showed it to Sierele who looked down in disbelief before calling to the others to return.

Omesh cautiously descended the rock only able to use one arm, cradling the sorcerer's prize in the other. More pieces of wyvern fell past him as he neared the ground where Mahrd and Esheh reached out to assist him. The remaining wyverns proved unwilling to pursue his companions below a certain point, hissing angrily at them as they started to pull away defeated.

"We should leave this place before the wyvern return to the peak," Esheh warned. "Before they return with something bigger."

Upon hearing screeching from above they took refuge in a cave within one of the wider rocky formations. Large shadows swept swiftly across the canyon floor and over the spire trunks as the sanddrake that birthed the wyvern looked for the slayer of her unfertilized offspring, accompanied by her sanddrake children. All but Omesh stood with weapons drawn, ready for a fight they all knew was better to avoid. For the mobile lightning storm that was the sanddrakes knew this territory better and might herd them into some trap, cooking their flesh in a single arc of their lightning breath. Even the cave was a gamble, but the winged beasts were loath to fight upon the ground on terrain that would obscure their mobility and sight while providing their pray tactical cover.

"An uncompromising stalemate," Elgaryk described it, when the sanddrakes eventually withdrew. "Each side refusing to provide the other their natural advantage."

"To have seen Pyrofang in action against a sanddrake would have been something," Omesh said.

"Had it been a single beast in a chance encounter," Elgaryk agreed. "Even then, I speak the tongue it understands and obeys. But the maternal rage of a nesting sanddrake is another matter. Especially with all the iron and copper about our bodies. One must choose their battles wisely."

#

As darkness fell, the moons and stars provided little light in a valley of shadows, casting most of their nocturnal illumination on peaks and higher ground. They relied entirely upon the two tribal guides accompanying them to lead them back to their encampment. Though Elgaryk saw remarkably well in the dark, he did not know the way.

"If you'll have us another night, we'll make for Purimah in the morning," Elgaryk propositioned his guides. "Assuming Sierele can survive another dinner," he added, to the group's amusement.

His squire shook her head before she halted the others. "Look," she whispered, pointing to orange light reflecting off the rocky rises some distance ahead. "Torchlight."

A group was moving through the rocky valley. One who did not know the way well enough to make it through the dark. Lelenya moved ahead, slipping into the dark forest of rocky pillars as the others stayed close to the rockface of the spires and waited. She returned, sometime later, moving with urgency. "A Kestrian patrol turned slaving party," she reported, before looking to their tribal companions. "Their prisoners looked familiar."

Mahrd and Esheh looked to each other and tensed, realising she was referring to their tribe. They made to move towards the patrol but Elgaryk stopped them. "Wait," he said. "There may be injured survivors at your encampment. Perhaps children who hid?"

"We cannot abandon our people who've been captured, "Mahrd said.

"We will reclaim your tribe," Elgaryk promised, removing his cloak. Without it, he looked like a Kestrian Centurion, missing only his helmet. "You took us in and helped us. Let us do this for you."

The pair reluctantly agreed, returning alone to their encampment as the other four pursued the Kestrian patrol.

"We should catch them," Lelenya said, leading the others quickly through the dark. "Taking tethered and bound captives slow you down."

After some time, trusting in the half-elven eyes of their Duscari companion and Elgaryk's mostly human eyes, the glow of torchlight shone upon rising rock formations ahead. Elgaryk and Sierele took the lead in their claimed Kestrian armour as Lelenya and Omesh slipped behind. Not only did they look to be part of the invaders' forces, in their uniform and pale skin, they both spoke the language.

They hastened their pace towards a rear scout, presumably back to spot any potential escapees. The pair approached him quietly and before he could react; he had a hand over his mouth and a dagger in his back. His torch passed to Sierele as if nothing had changed. She replaced his mobile position as the dying silenced man was dragged away effortlessly by Elgaryk and left behind the rocky trunk of a spire.

"Try to get me a torch as well, if you can," Omesh whispered to Elgaryk, who gave him an odd glance at first but soon nodded with realisation.

The next two soldiers were flanking the rear of the tethered captives. Neither terribly far behind other torchbearers. Omesh followed Elgaryk around the left while Lelenya took the right. Sierele maintained the position of the rear scout. Lelenya's curved sword impaled the guard in front of her as Elgaryk used his dagger on their counterpart, lifting him off his feet with his hand around his mouth. He laid the dying man down as Lelenya dragged her victim quietly away. Their stealth, however, was soon undermined by the captives, startled by the sudden violence.

The torchbearer on the right was the first to turn back, responding to the murmuring. What he saw first was Elgaryk rushing the torch-bearing soldier on the other side. A confusing sight in centurion's armour. Omesh followed behind him, ready to take the flaming stick, while Lelenya charged the turning man. The soldier managed half a cry for aid before the swiftness of her blade silenced him. She let him fall, clutching this throat and she caught his torch. There was no point concealing his body as further ahead, soldiers were already yelling back and forth in their foreign tongue.

The line of captives began to stretch as those at the rear ceased following their captors. Sierele was cutting them loose as another held her torch. Yelling came from the front as footsteps began to thunder on the ground ahead. Omesh shoved his way towards the front of the captives, yelling "Get down," as his companions engaged the soldiers in combat. As the captives crouched, he could see they were tethered to a cart where the elderly and children were held.

Soldiers approached with drawn swords, Omesh held his torch low in his left hand and presented his right palm to the flame. Muttering the necessary words, he expanded the small fire into a long burst of flames, briefly illuminating their surroundings as it unfurled forwards, making others flinch and duck as it reached and engulfed three Kestrians. As the burst retreated, he pulled from it a fireplume and sculpted it in the air into a large ball as Elgaryk attacked the men who evaded the stretched flame. The fire of Pyrofang rippled in the air, rumbling against the wind as it knocked enemy swords aside and sliced through arm and leg, leaving small flames on the leather armour and red cloth it touched.

With Lelenya standing alone against the soldiers who ran towards her, Omesh launched his ball of fire over the heads of the ducking captives into a pair of the attacking men, halting those behind them as the yellow ball exploded into those at the front of the charge. The distraction gave the Duscari woman the advantage she needed.

Soon Sierele joined the fight on the other side, fighting with a rare fierceness. Her skill and speed exceeding her enemy's. Their main strength was their formations, for which they were famed, but could not adequately form in this terrain nor in the fiery chaos supplementing the attack that had taken them unaware.

The Kestrians ahead halted as a single voice yelled orders. In the lull, Elgaryk turned his face half back so Omesh would hear him. "They are spreading out," he translated. He looked to the burning men who managed to put out their flames but as they rose again, Elgaryk slew them with Pyrofang in one hand and a Kestrian gladius in the other. "You're going to need a better fire."

"This is all I have," Omesh said holding up his torch.

"And you can do all that you have done with a plume of dragonfire?" he confirmed, confusing the fire priest.

"For as long as I could hold such a fire," he said. "But there are no-"

"Stay close to me," Elgaryk said, burying the gladius in the chest of an approaching soldier and snatching Omesh's torch and tossing it to the ground. He grabbed him, keeping him close. "Be ready, you'll only have one chance."

"For what?" Omesh asked.

"Dragonfire," Elgaryk said, as soldiers came around the far side of the rocky spire before them. "Ready? Now," he yelled, before taking a deep breath, a swallow, and convulsion. He opened his mouth and spreading his arms as an expulsion of fierce red fire burst from his face.

Shocked, Omesh still managed to quickly raise his hand and steal a plume of the fire with his devotional magic, before looking to three soldiers who caught the unexpected fire. They scattered and stumbled, not just ignited as the others had been by Omesh's magical extension of the torch flame, but instantly burned as if standing in a furnace. The very blast seemed to peal their skin and tear their flesh. Now Omesh held that very fury in a hovering ball of fire above his hand.

He was quick to take it around the spire as Elgaryk led him onward. From the plume, he expanded a cone of dragonfire into more soldiers while Elgaryk cut down any fast enough to doge it. It burnt as it had when the horned man had expelled it. Devastating and destructive it thwarted the incoming soldiers and deterred the few remaining. Many retreated with haste as an officer in charge of them yelled angrily in their tongue.

Elgaryk pointed to the fleeing men and soon the night air was filled with the sound of swarming insects that flew over them and into the dark towards the escaping soldiers. There were panicked cries of pain as whatever pursued them accosted them.

Their lieutenant stood his ground, too proud to run despite what he had seen. Omesh began to sweat, holding the hovering flower of dragonfire as far from himself as he could and clenched his wrist with his free hand as the heat was becoming intense.

"Release it," Elgaryk said, seeing it start to harm him. "I at least know you can hold it long enough for what I need."

As Elgaryk approached, the Kestrian lieutenant's eyes widened at the sight of Elgaryk's horns and he dropped to one knee, laying his sword in the dirt. Words went back and forth in the Kestrian tongue as the women finished off their own opponents and steadied the camel pulling the cart as they freed the captives. In the end the lieutenant bowed his head and left.

"What happened there?" Omesh asked.

"He knew where I was from," Elgaryk said. "He told me their first emperor had small horns upon his brow, also. He said he was honoured to meet one of my kind and asked if I would join their legion. But I told him to tell his superiors to avoid these parts in future." He looked to Sierele. "Gather all the iron."

#

After spending the remainder of the night within the tribe's encampment, Elgaryk and his companions left for Purimah with the camel drawn cart piled with the Kestrian swords, daggers, and armour of those they'd slain.

"You've been putting magic into that sword I gave you," Elgaryk said, as they walked the lowlands. "Each night before you sleep, for an eventual enchantment."

"When I can," Omesh said. "Whatever I have left. Not that I had much left last night. Why?"

"I understand that once a sword has magic in it, it becomes very hard to destroy."

"Once there's enough to seal an enchantment," Omesh said. "Why?"

"I want you to give that one to Sierele."

Omesh sighed, disappointed.

"I know you've been pouring what you have into it for weeks," Elgaryk said. "And I'm also going to need all of your magic for months to come as I make Hellforged swords and armour with your aid. But not without reward."

"What are you proposing?"

"You told me there are two types of pyromancer, yes?"

"Yes. There are priests like me, who worship Pyrosian, the god of fire, bending fire to our will. Any kind of fire that we may find," Omesh said. "Then there's the devotees of the demigod Burzuhl, Pyrosian's son. Students of the arcane who evoke magic fire. Creators of flame who send it on its way but have no further control of it once summoned and cast."

"I have seen what you can do with fire, and it impresses me greatly."

"That means a great deal coming from a man who can walk through flames and breathe dragonfire," Omesh said, recalling the events of the previous night, "and whatever that was with the insects."

Elgaryk smiled. "I have my talents, of course. Gifts of my forebears that cannot be relied up more than daily. I am no student of magic, favouring the sword. But it seems to me precarious that your talents rely on the availability of already burning natural fire."

"What are you suggesting?"

"That after we sell this egg to the sorcerer, you mean to stay with us, travel where we do, fight who we fight?" Elgaryk asked, earning a nod from the young priest. The man with small horns upon his brow smiled and unfastened his sheath. He presented Pyrofang. "Then perhaps it would make more sense if you carried this. Not just a sword, but a torch of magic flame when swung. Swung whenever you need to procure your deadly plume of fire."

Omesh was shocked, taking the sheathed blade in both hands. "I am merely the watcher of this sacred blade."

"Now you are its wielder," Elgaryk said. "It is of more use to me in your hands than mine. Especially after we forge a new one with my dragonfire, extended by your spells."

"When I first left to follow you, I had no idea this honour would befall me," Omesh said, overcome.

"I couldn't understand the making of that sword until I saw what you could truly do," Elgaryk admitted, as they continued the walk back to Purimah. "I believe Gyraksin's intention was to aid precisely the kind of magic you have. That's why he left it with a temple of Pyrosian. He left it for one like me to retrieve but intended it for a pyromancer to wield. Either he was such a pyromancer or perhaps, like me," he patted Omesh on the shoulder, "he knew a good priest."

Barend Nieuwstraten III grew up and lives in Sydney, Australia, where he was born to Dutch and Indian immigrants. He has worked in film, short film, television, music, and online comics. He is now primarily working on a collection of stories set within a high fantasy world, a science fiction alternate future, as well as a steampunk storyverse, often dipping his toes in horror in the process. With over twenty short stories published, he continues to work on short stories, stand-alone novels, and an epic series.

That Which Burns

by James Pyles

"She was beautiful, but she was beautiful in the way a forest fire was beautiful: something to be admired from a distance, not up close." -Terry Pratchett

Tyler Melody Ross sat masked in her padded cell in a sanatorium in upstate New York. In the common room, the first game of the 1954 World Series pitting the New York Giants against the Cleveland Indians was playing on the radio, but Tyler was never taken to the common room. She was kept continually sedated, not unconscious, but groggy enough so she could be handled. In that way, she could be fed, her toilet needs taken care of, and she could be walked around her cell for twenty minutes each day to get a bit of exercise. Other than that, she was alone and isolated, and the staff all felt safer because of it.

The mask was heavily laced with asbestos, as was the padding of her cell. There was no window, but a barred panel in her door where the glass could be slid open provided air. Her hands were encased in mittens, not that she really needed them, but if she were to have a lucid moment or two, she would be unable to remove the mask. Everyone believed that at all costs, the mask must remain on her face for the rest of her life.

No treatment had worked, not drug treatments, not electroshock, not repeated dunking in ice water, they all failed to cure or even marginally improve Tyler's condition. A lobotomy was still under consideration, but the hospital director kept putting off the decision. So, she remained drugged, provided brief company only out of legal and medical necessity, and otherwise was left to ponder whatever dreams she entertained inside her difficult and diseased mind.

Tyler's parents lived a mere forty miles away, but they never visited, not on weekends, not for holidays, not on Tyler's birthday, which was November 13th. Their daughter would turn twenty years old this year. Carl and Jean Ross told everyone their daughter had died after a long illness. Everybody in the town knew it was a lie, but they pretended to believe, knowing the hell the Ross's had gone through. There was even a grave with a headstone in the local cemetery:

"Here lies Tyler Melody Ross
b. Nov. 13 1934 - d. Dec. 25, 1953
Beloved daughter and child of God."

Last February, someone had painted over the word "God" with "Satan," but the town council quickly had Max Fischer from the Sanitation Department remove the paint and restore the headstone. The incident was never repeated. It was probably just a few bored kids from Fort Drum or Evans Mills up to no good.

The town rebuilt after what the locals called "The Christmas Incident," and like most rural communities, swept the ashes of the past under their floorboards and returned to the slow and regulated patterns of small-town life. The Ross's only child was dead to them, though it would have been better if Tyler's body was actually interned in her grave.

Melvin Gardner had been assigned as Tyler's primary physician and psychiatrist two months ago. He had been a student of J.B. Rhine's at Duke University as an undergrad but was later forced to publicly distance himself from Rhine's work for the sake of his medical career.

Secretly however, he continued to correspond with Rhine and kept up with his latest research, which hardly covered the phenomenon of Tyler Ross. Gardner studied such obscure cases as those of A.W. Underwood and Daniel Dunglas Home, but in all likelihood, their alleged abilities were the result of fraud. However, the details contained in Miss Ross's confidential medical charts, and in the few remaining copies of her hometown's small newspaper, those dated December 26th through 29th, 1953, could not be explained as such. Those copies were part of her private medical records and kept only for research purposes. All the others had been burned.

Dr. Gardner exchanged letters about Tyler with Rhine in strictest confidence, both because the consultation was conducted without the patient's or her legal guardian's (in this case the State of New York) consent, and because of the highly bizarre and inflammatory nature of his inquiries. Yet his former teacher and mentor was unable to provide any illumination or direction regarding research into Miss Ross's condition, other than to employ the time-honored axiom, "let sleeping dogs lie."

On the one hand, it was impossible to study such a manifestation without direct empirical evidence, which meant the ability to observe said manifestation. On the other hand, to do so would represent a significant risk to the patient, her doctor, the sanatorium staff, and the general vicinity of the sanatorium.

Gardner usually allowed the head nurse (the normal duty nurses being hesitant to even approach Tyler) to administer her medication, but on occasion he took the task onto himself under the guise of relieving the nurse of having to endure the patient's presence. His true reason was somewhat more obscure, even to himself. If he could look into Tyler's eyes long enough, would they reveal some remaining spark that might light up his path to knowledge?

Her eyes were just about all that were visible through the mask. They were blue with just a hint of copper, a sort of dull bit of orange applied as flecks among a sea of azure.

"What do you see through those strange eyes, my dear Tyler?" He stroked her dull blond hair to which she responded not at all, at least as far as he could perceive.

Behind those eyes, her vision jumped and blurred, like the images on the television set she once saw in the display window at Macy's when Ma and Pa last took her to the city. It was for her eighteenth birthday. Already she was becoming more withdrawn, physically restive, but psychologically absent, and the Ross's hoped that an outing and change of scenery would do her some good.

There had been a fire. All three floors of an apartment building were being consumed in the blaze, the numerous firemen and their trucks and hoses helpless to extinguish the conflagration. Tyler's parents tried to hurry her along as they were late for their dinner reservations, but the teenager was captivated, enthralled, not by the activity or the emergency, but by the flames themselves.

It was the only time in recent memory they had seen her smile.

She could see the fire now. Tyler could see herself, an unfocused, distorted vision in grey. She could see the mask, but the inside of the mask was rendered in shifting colors of green, blue, orange, and violet.

Then there was the bucket of fish. Pa used to take her with him to the pond when she was little. Tyler loved to put the worms on the hook, and then watch them dance before they became food for the fishies. Summer before last, she stared and stared into the bucket of fish caught by Pa, until the water boiled while the fishies were still alive.

They started locking her in the back bedroom when she was "bad." Tyler could still see the burnt and ruined remains of Pa's old Olympia typewriter and Ma's Singer sewing machine. She had trouble controlling her temper.

Then she saw the sanatorium just the way it looked the day she was taken there, all wrapped up in her straitjacket.

They'd given her the mask because of her face. It was the old Pastor who suggested it. He said she had to have her whole horrible, beautiful face covered up to keep her "curse" from working. The Pastor, and later the doctors, lied and said it was because she was disfigured, burned, her face didn't even look like a person's anymore, more like melted candle wax. The truth was, they were afraid of her face and what happened when people saw it.

Tyler imagined the sanatorium all brown, like the color of leaves on the ground in December just before the first snow. It was the color paper turned as it was burning, from white, to brown, and then to black as the fire consumed it, devoured it like a cat devours a sparrow, like the flames consumed the apartment in the city. How many people had been burned to death, turned brown to black, screaming until they burned out and died?

Dr. Gardner had taken to examining his patient on a weekly basis in her cell. On those days, and sometimes the day before, only he administered Tyler's medication. There were whispers among the nurses and orderlies about exactly what the doctor was examining, but that was none of their business, and making the rumors about a doctor more public would probably get them all fired. They needed their jobs, such as they were.

However, the truth of the examinations was less tawdry and more hazardous than they could possibly guess. If they could guess, then the doctor be damned, and they'd all testify that he was a dangerous quack who ought to be locked up with his patients.

"Let's just see what's under the mask, now shall we, Tyler?"

Her mask had to be removed periodically. It would have been unsanitary not to, and after all, there were laws about the kind of care patients required. However, only one nurse was assigned to this task. She'd been on the ward for nearly thirty years, and while it would be unfair to say she feared nothing, she was made of sterner stuff than most, and could endure this duty once per month, as long as the lights were low, the patient heavily drugged, and she didn't look directly at the face of this latter-day Medusa.

Tyler's breathing became noticeably faster as she felt her doctor's fingers manipulate the clasps at the back of her head that held her mask in place. She could feel it loosening, and then the light became brighter as his hands gently lifted the covering away, revealing her visage.

"You are such a beautiful young girl, Tyler." He held the mask in his lap for a moment, and then he put it next to her on the bed. Beside him on a small table, was a basin of soapy water, a washcloth, and a towel. Like a nurturing mother, Melvin cleansed her skin, lightly scrubbing her forehead up to the hairline, down both temples, and around her lids. She blinked as some of the water got in her eyes.

"Oh, I'm sorry, my dear. Let me." He replaced the washcloth in the basin and took the dry towel, dabbing it around her eyelids.

Tyler smiled slightly. It felt good, not being washed and dried as such, but the attention, someone actually caring about her. It had been a long time since even Ma and Pa loved more than feared her.

The doctor finished washing and drying her. At the end of the exam, he would administer the medication that would once again return his patient to her usual apathetic state. However, for the moment, she began to awaken from her long hibernation, like

Persephone rising from the darkness of the underworld into the bright and blazing light of day. In fact, Dr. Gardner started thinking of her as his Persephone, a child of darkness and light. It was not lost on the psychiatrist that the symbol of the daughter of Zeus and Demeter was the torch.

"Thank you, Doctor." She spoke as someone just awakening from a dream, like a child opening her eyes after a nap, not quite perceiving the world around her.

"You remember me, Tyler. Yes, it's Dr. Gardner. How do you feel today?"

"Sleepy." She giggled as if this were a joke shared between them.

"That's understandable. The narcotic has lingering effects." He used his fingers to open the lids of one eye and then the other. Golden bits of flame floated like tiny icebergs reflecting the light of the sun on the surface of an endless ocean.

"Do you know why you're here, Tyler?"

She looked around the room as if seeing it for the first time. "Where am I?"

"The sanatorium. Do you remember why you are a patient here?"

"Patient? I thought I was a prisoner."

"Oh no, not at all. You're my patient. I'm your doctor. I want to understand you. I want to help you."

"Help me?"

"Yes, I want to cure you, if I can. But I need to understand your condition first. Do you know why you are here?"

She looked down at her lap, her hands still cozy in their mittens, warm and comfortable, but nonetheless trapped, just as she was, cocooned in canvas.

"I…I did something bad." Her tone didn't communicate guilt or remorse, and it was difficult for Melvin to determine if it was fear he heard in her voice, or anticipation.

"Do you know what that was?"

"I don't want to talk about it." She pressed her face into her mittens, providing her own mask in place of the one from which Dr. Gardner had just released her.

"Now, now, Tyler." He took her wrists and slowly pulled her hands away, once again revealing her beauty, a glory both radiant and menacing. "It's quite alright. I'm your doctor. You can tell me anything. It's a secret just between you and me."

He'd meant to communicate the nature of the doctor-patient relationship, though he was aware of the clandestine tone of these meetings. However, she had become accustomed to keeping dread secrets, and realized she had found, in her shadow world, a co-conspirator, an ally, or so she hoped, who might free the Phoenix from her ashes.

"Secret?"

"Yes, Tyler. Whatever you tell me is just between you and me." A little white lie, because if he could achieve the breakthrough he hoped for in Tyler's case, publishing the results would make him internationally famous, outshining Rhine, Jung, and even Freud.

"What did you do? When was the first time you did it, and how?"

From that day forward, each Wednesday afternoon, Dr. Gardner freed young Tyler from her mask and her slumber, and they shared her secrets, the kitten that went missing when she was six, the tool shed's back wall that caught on fire the fall she turned ten, the fishies, the building in the city, the town where she used to live.

He wrote it all down and kept his notes in a private file cabinet in his office apart from her official records. He was the only one who had a key. It was too soon to publish. He dared not even reveal his findings to Rhine for fear of a leak. Tyler was too unique, too precious to be risked in such a fashion. Certainly, premature knowledge of his studies of the patient could result in him being stripped of his medical license. And she, poor dear, would never again find a soul to comfort her, and be condemned to an endless night and anonymous oblivion.

At thirty-seven, Melvin Gardner had never married. He didn't think it likely he ever would. His wife and lover were his career. He could have been attending psychiatrist anywhere, New York, Boston, Chicago, San Francisco, and yet he deliberately chose this little provincial facility because of her, for Tyler afforded him the opportunity of a lifetime.

There had been women of course. He was considered handsome in a Humphrey Bogart sort of way, not a classically manly face, but one that revealed a life lived at the edge of something dangerous. He discovered women were drawn to the forbidden, particularly married women, and many of the wives of his colleagues, and occasionally his patients, displayed unusual vigor and passion when liberated from the dull routine of their husbands' lovemaking.

Dr. Gardner didn't think of himself as a fool. He knew he was taking a risk, and he believed every single word of what was written about Tyler in her official files, for those facts almost exactly mirrored what he had written in his private records, the records of his patient's startling revelations.

He knew what he felt for her was part of the transference process, as was her apparent infatuation with him, and though he might indulge in a dalliance with the wife of a patient, he would never violate his sacred trust and involve himself intimately between the open wings of his Lycaena Mariposa, his fiery butterfly.

But he knew that great discoveries were not achieved without breaking boundaries, so he continually tested Tyler's limits and his own. Each week, he reduced the amount of medication she received one day and then two days before each examination, studying her increased awareness, and looking for even the slightest sign of danger or misadventure. Yet week by week, none appeared. Tyler was shy and yet charming in an immature, adolescent sort of way. As she became more comfortable with her Doctor's visits, she even revealed herself to be coquettish.

She asked favors. Could he bring a small radio with him during the exams? It had been so long since she had heard music. He managed to find a new transistor model, battery-powered, that was a little larger than the palm of his hand. It would just fit in his medical bag, and being a doctor, no one asked to search his belongings when he entered her cell.

Occasionally, he brought magazines, copies of "Life," even some comic books. She particularly enjoyed "Archie." It was gratifying to watch her come alive for him, to see her smile, observe her eyes flit back and forth as she read. He did have to caution her not to dance, and to keep the music down low so it wouldn't be heard. She was disappointed, but the word "secret" made it all better.

The final favor carried the greatest risk. "I don't want you to give me my medicine before you leave. Wait until tomorrow. Please? I want to remember our visit for a little while longer."

The first three times she asked, he said it was too dangerous and refused. The first time, just for an instant, her eyes flashed that golden copper light she held in blue, as if it were fire restrained by water, but then the light faded, and she smiled. "I understand, Mel…Doctor." He secretly liked it when she called him "Melvin," but cautioned her not to do so, lest it become a habit.

Tyler knew she had to be patient. When the time was right, Melvin would listen to her. She just needed to become a little less the wife of Pluto, and more the daughter of Demeter. Spring would come soon enough, and she would witness the dawn.

Finally, he relented, but only to the point of giving her a half-dose rather than dispensing with it altogether. The trouble with narcotics, and as a doctor he should have been well-versed in this, is that eventually the patient becomes accustomed to a particular dose and its effectiveness wanes.

Christmas Eve, 1954. All but the absolutely necessary staff had been released to their homes for the holiday. There was no tree or lights in Dr. Gardner's small rented house. He saw no need for them, neither being a Christian nor a particularly festive person. For Tyler, there was no Christmas either, since she was restricted from the general population of patients and their tree was in the common area.

She did get to hear Christmas Carols on the radio. Melvin paid her a special visit, since neither one had any place to go, or anyone to share the evening with. He couldn't give her a present, of course, since where could she keep it that the orderlies or nurses wouldn't find it? But they could spend some quiet time together, the now twenty-year-old's eyes being bright and flickering like a candle.

"Thank you for visiting me, Doctor. I really appreciate it."

"Not at all, Tyler. In any event, the snow has built up a great deal on the roads, so I'm likely to be spending Christmas Eve on the sofa in my office."

"I'm sorry. I didn't mean to keep you."

"Not at all, my dear. It's always a pleasure to spend some time with you." Earlier, he had shared some unauthorized "Christmas cheer" with the small number of staff who had drawn holiday duty, and he was feeling warm, relaxed, and just a bit euphoric. Tyler had received no "cheer" at all for the past four days, and was as remarkably clearheaded and focused, just as she had been last Christmas. As she remembered, the vision of the fire brightened in her eyes.

"I wish I had a present for you, Doctor. I know you wouldn't accept it because I'm a patient, but you have always been so kind to me."

"I have no present for you either. Perhaps this evening is gift enough for both of us."

"Perhaps…Melvin." She had been looking down at her lap, but as she spoke his name, she looked up into his eyes.

As typical, she was sitting on the edge of her bed, and he faced her in a small, wooden chair painted white. The radio was sitting on the table next to her bed playing "Silent Night." She glanced at his watch. Just a few minutes until midnight.

The "incident" had begun a year ago today almost to the moment. That was when she finally had enough of the judgments, the gossip, the rejection, and being treated like some "cheap sideshow freak," as Billy Thomas had once called her. She had to stifle a giggle as she remembered the look of astonishment on his face the moment his clothes burst into flames.

The newspaper article enshrined in her official hospital record, reported that forty-nine people lost their lives early that Christmas morning in the fire that started at the church where she and her parents were attending Advent services, and then spread throughout most of their quaint and charming downtown. Forty-nine people, fourteen burned to death, twenty-seven perished due to smoke inhalation, five were crushed under fallen debris. Old Mr. Taylor had a heart attack, the Reverend Matthews died of a stroke, and little Danny Baker ran across the street in a panic and was struck by a Fire Engine responding to the alarms.

"You know you shouldn't call me by my first name, Tyler."

"Why not, Melvin. You call me by my first name all the time."

"That's different, my dear. I'm your doctor and you're my patient. It's not the same relationship as if we were friends or…"

"Lovers, Melvin?"

"That will be enough, Tyler." He began to regret having those drinks earlier. It was difficult to think clearly, and if she should become unreasonable, he would find it harder to manage her with his faculties impaired.

"You called me 'my dear' before. Am I your 'dear,' Melvin?"

"It's just an expression. One designed to put you at ease in my presence, and please call me 'Dr. Mel…uh, Dr. Gardner'."

"I'm very at ease in your presence, my dear Doctor Melvin. I have been for a long time. You should know that by now. After all, you are my doctor."

Their faces were very close to each other. Her eyes and her lips were so inviting, and yet her beauty was that of a serpent or a forest fire, something to be admired from a distance, but not up close. Over the past three months, Melvin had allowed that distance to gradually erode, so that now the barrier between them was as thin as smoke.

"I think I should leave."

"Not yet. Wait until the song has ended. It's 'Silent Night.' You know. Silent Night, Holy Night, all is calm, all is bright. Round yon virgin…"

Tyler leaned forward just an inch or so more and their lips touched. Melvin could feel the warmth of her breath and her flesh. For a moment he also felt the enjoyment, and the slight beginnings of passion. Then he pulled back and sat up in his chair.

"No, Tyler." He was gentle, but the rejection still stung her. "We can't. It's not right."

"You don't love me because I'm a freak. You only want to study me." She was pouting, legs drawn up against her chest, lower lip jutted out, but her eyes were brilliantly alive.

"I must leave, Tyler. I'll check on you in the morning." He looked down at his medical bag and then back at her. "I should medicate you and replace your mask and mittens."

"No, Melvin. Its Christmas morning. You know what that means, don't you?"

"I'm afraid don't." And then he did know. It was the anniversary of the fire. She did it. He was convinced of it, just as the Pastor, the Sheriff, the doctors, and Tyler's own parents were sure of it.

Tyler stood up. Sometimes, during visits, she paced, but she couldn't go near the door and take the chance someone passing by would see her without her mask. Now she was facing Melvin eye-to-eye, the skin on her cheeks radiant, her eyes glowing.

"Sleep in heavenly peace, sleep in heavenly peace." Then she laughed as Melvin's white doctor's coat, the symbol of his status and power, smoldered, and then ignited.

He screamed and frantically slapped at the flames with both arms. He kept his keys in the medical bag. Melvin and Tyler had few secrets from each other, and she knew just where they were. Taking them, she opened her cell door, and stepped outside of her asbestos prison.

Floor by floor, the sanatorium exploded in fire as Tyler descended down toward the ground level. By the time she reached the bottom of the first-floor stairwell, everyone above her was a living and dying torch, and the few nurses and orderlies in between her and the outside were screaming in burning agony. The doctor's keys included those to his car, and the heat of a burning forest would certainly melt whatever snow that might prevent her escape.

She didn't have much time, but as she passed the office with the small brass placard proudly announcing, "Melvin J. Gardner, M.D.", she paused. She unlocked the door and looked into the room, so tidy, so orderly. Suit jacket and winter coat hanging on the coat rack, ashtray emptied, pens, and pencils in their proper containers. And then there was the locked metal cabinet, and the files which told her whole story.

If she did nothing, the fire would still consume both these and her regular medical files, all of the information and evidence that had been used against her. Her lower lip trembled. If only he would have loved her. Then they could have gone away together. She loved Billy Thomas too, but he also thought she was a freak. No one would ever love her. They would only make fun of her or be afraid of her. She would always be alone.

"Fine!" She stared at the file cabinet until it glowed amber and then belched smoke, as the papers, folders, and envelopes within ignited like the books in that story by Ray Bradbury she read right before last Christmas.

The screaming had stopped, and it was getting hotter. The fire would burn even her. She had to leave. Tyler spun, ran out of the open office door, and directly into something falling. Hot. Pain. She was bleeding. From the floor, she looked up.

"No, my dear. Not this Christmas." Melvin Gardner had second degree burns across his chest, arms, and lower face, but in spite of the pain, he had followed her downstairs. Fire alarms had been pulled by some of the staff before they died, but with the snow outside continuing to fall, it could take hours for emergency crews to arrive. She had to be stopped here, tonight. He raised the scorched two-by-four above his head, preparing one last blow.

"Melvin, no." Tyler tried to sit up, but then her head exploded in agony. She was dizzy, nauseous, she couldn't concentrate. He was going to kill her. "Melvin, stop. I love you. Please." She had to buy time, just a few seconds for her head to clear. Why was it so hard to think?

"Good-bye, Tyler."

The last thing she saw was the makeshift club rushing at her face.

The sanatorium was a loss by the time the first Fire Engines arrived nearly two hours later. Hours past dawn, rescue teams poured through the ashes and rubble, but no survivors were found. The bodies were burned so badly that positive identification was almost impossible in most instances, so no one would ever know that Tyler Ross and Melvin Gardner embraced each other in death just outside of his office.

Carl and Jean Ross were presented with a small box of ashes. They weren't hers. The gesture was symbolic. The following spring, Carl Ross planted a new tree in the field behind his house, fertilized with the remains of someone they pretended was their sweet, little girl. Her grave would remain vacant, but now she finally was given the rest she had never found in life. The fire had gone out, and from the ashes, something new and green would grow with spring, and the length of days.

#

On Christmas Eve, 2019, she smiled as she watched Tondo burn from across the Pasig River. They all deserved it. Nobody really loved her. Mommy and Daddy just said they did. When she got lonely, they wouldn't let her have a friend. They said she was too dangerous, but that she was too young to understand. Now she understands. Now they all do, too.

Mahalia had just turned ten years old. She liked to watch the flicking of flames as they consumed paper, cardboard, and wood. She also liked to watch the bodies of people as they writhed. She rejoiced in their screams, and even more, in the following silence.

Like most children, she liked to watch fire burn. Unlike most children, she could make the flames spark to life, leap, and dance, just by staring at things with those beautiful ocean blue eyes, brilliantly decorated with flakes of copper orange.

James Pyles is a published SF/F writer and Information Technology author. Since 2019, over 30 of his short stories have been featured in anthologies. He won the 2021 Helicon Short Story Award for his SciFi tale "The Three Billion Year Love." His first novella, *Time's Abyss*, was published this past October.

A Life is a Terrible Thing to Trace

by Betsie Flynn

"Another." He waited a beat, but when his long-suffering dealer didn't oblige, he asked again. This time, he teamed the word with what he was almost confident was a look so stern that it couldn't be opposed. He'd been perfecting it for circuits, ever since his mother had first told him "With a chin as weak as that, love, you're going to need some steel in your eye if you want to get anywhere in this life." When she'd added "A beard wouldn't go amiss, either.", almost as an afterthought, Peredur York saw how crucial cultivating such an expression might prove to be. Well, what landed on his face might not have been steel exactly, but the increasingly flustered dealer did as she was asked, nevertheless. The card was 'Star-Cropper'. Good, that would drive the bounty up nicely, Perry thought, especially as 'The Entrenched Botanist' had already been drawn. It was hard enough to root out growers in this zone – fertile patches were well-guarded secrets – let alone ones with expertise in both starlight fertilisation and tunnel growth. "Another."

"Come on, you're never gonna find anyone who fits the cards you've got already – don't add more! You know we'll both be affected by the outcome of this." Before Perry could butt in, the dealer continued, speaking with surprising precision for how quickly she rattled out her words. "I signed a legally binding document; Perry I can't set up tracks that don't have any hope of being filled – it's a bureaucratic nightmare. And the fines, don't get me started on the fines!" She took a deep breath and steepled her hands at the bridge of her nose. "I know, I know you've always made good on your contracts with the cards before, but even you can't hope to trace this level of specificity." He laughed. "Oh really, you think this is funny? Don't make me deal with all those forms, please! Take pity on a poor woman who works hard to scrape a living in this cruel world."

"Katrin, you and you alone have been dealing my cards for seventeen circuits. When have I ever caused you to fill in any more paperwork than was strictly legally necessary? And as for the specificity – remember when I tracked Thitis Cither? She was the fulfilment of seven cards, wasn't she?" Thitis had been the fulfilment of eight, actually, and they both knew it. Eight, including a triangulation that hadn't been logged as successful in the last century, at least. They'd both received hefty bonuses for that one. In fact, a bonus or two per cycle was becoming very much the norm for them. Whatever special relationship had formed between Katrin, her heirloom Awen deck and board, and Perry was something they both had good fiscal reasons to maintain.

"Okay, fine. But let's move this along, shall we? I do have other appointments, you know."

"I value your time, Kat, I really do." Relying on the hope that his charisma was stronger than his chin, he continued, "Could you do me the honour of drawing another card for me? Please?" She rolled her eyes, remembering how he'd first walked through her door. It had been raining so heavily that half of her clients – a small enough number to begin with as she was just starting out in the business back then – hadn't arrived at their allotted times. If she'd been more established, rain couldn't have held them away, of course, the slight on a member of the Awen Alliance in good standing would have been too great. There were stories about those who fell foul of even the lowliest members of that organisation, and it seemed as if everybody knew someone personally who had lost a finger, a home, or something even more sinister after a run-in with the AA. Not that people talked about such things openly. After a few drinks, though, clandestine tongues had been known to wag.

Katrin pulled her mind back to the task – quite literally – at hand. The cards. Sighing, she drew and then placed the card as firmly as she dared on the tenth port on her board. She was understandably wary, it had never been filled before – not by her or any of her forebears, that she knew of. She certainly would know if it had been, the lore of each set of cards and board was as carefully archived as the bounties of destiny that the decks revealed. Modern boards tended to peak at seven card connection slots, but in the early days the board-techs had been more optimistic. They'd been called artisans back then, and it showed in the nuanced intricacies of Katrin's board's interfacing. To look at, it was a work of art with cascades of spirals undulating across its surface and coloured lights gently listing from one end of the spectrum to the other. The boards they put out today were work-horses built to network with speed and put up with a lot of hard use. Katrin thought they looked clunky, but whatever. Not everyone was lucky enough to have a family interest vested in the industry.

That was something that Perry understood, too. The ghost of family work might have been part of Katrin's business equipment, but Perry had gone a step further in having his father's implant transferred straight to his own right temple. Genetically, it made sense. Transferring an identifier from recently deceased father to very much alive son rather than picking one up from the loser in a street brawl, for example, lessened the chance of tissue rejection. When the tech had been new, there had been widespread uneasiness that a person's memories, kinks, and proclivities would be passed on along to the next generation. Some people even relied upon this concept as a way to keep their family close, to get to know someone better than they ever would have had the opportunity to otherwise. Others had it written into their AA contracts that their implants be destroyed upon their demise, ensuring as far as they could that their secrets disappeared along with their consciousness when the time came.

"Ten cards have got to be enough, Perry."

"Yeah, you may have a point there. Ten should be enough. What's the total looking like, Kat?"

"Well let me just see now. I assume you'll be wanting it in gambits, not Awenwells?"

"You know me so well."

"Guilty." Katrin flicked the outer edges of the board in what seemed to Perry to be no particular order at all. It's not like there were wheels and levers she had to access. And yet, there she was, looking for all the world as if she was single-handedly on the cusp of technological revolution. "Here we go," she looked from the board to Perry and whistled low. "If you manage to pull this off – and that's an immense 'if' even for you, Perry – then you're looking at a payout of around sixty-four thousand gambits."

"I can work with that."

"Can you? You're one press away from this being logged in the system. Do I need to remind you how difficult it is to dial back something like that once it has begun to be processed?"

"Oh yes, Katrin, please do. You know how I love it when you treat me as your intellectual inferior." He took a breath so deep it likely could have calmed even a taxation officer's conscience. "Can't you just accept that I know what I'm doing right now as much as I ever have?"

"Perry, that's precisely what I'm afraid of."

#

"Destiny is dangerous" had been the mantra of the AA for as long as Gwenddydd Pierce could remember. It was supposed to mean that there were certain people society would do well to watch out for because of the calamitous changes they could create in even the most everyday of situations. As far as Gwenni could make out, though, destiny was the most dangerous for the people whose lives were skewed to fit those blasted cards. Normal people shied away from drawing notice to themselves, stood on the sidelines even in the face of events they didn't agree with, just so that nobody could point to them and say "Ah, so that's the kind of person you're looking for? Well, make it worth my while and I can introduce you to just the man!". Or, in Gwenni's case, the girl.

When she was twelve, she'd made the mistake of beating the seventeen-year-old Bachlach at Awelklap – the knuckle-bruising game of strength at which that particular tower of human-shaped stench had found local fame. Finding opponents for Bachlach had, in fact, become so difficult in the months before their bout that even wanderers from beyond Hlun Gloi-oo had to be promised serious compensation just for taking part. Gwenni, though, just had to be promised a fair shot against him. He'd had spittle, a hard hand, and crass words for her every day of her life for as long as she could remember, and she'd had enough. Every day she'd wake up with the intention of their paths not crossing, but somehow the very thing she kept hoping to avoid always ended up happening. When Gwenni won, she logged her chit-set from the official and moved on out within the hour. Sure, she'd been on the business end of some raised eyebrows on the serenboose, but that was to be expected. Girls, as young as she had been, did travel alone, especially in and out of Hlun Gloi-oo, but they were normally fancier than her. Or cleaner, at least.

Still, that Awelklap bout had topped up her chit-set balance enough that she was due a zone transfer. Without family to quibble or restrict her, her choices were as wide as the laws surrounding zoning perimeters would allow. And if Gwenni's life had fallen into something of a pattern since then, where she worked as hard as she dared until she'd saved up enough to get out of a place, well that wasn't so bad. It kept things from falling into a rut. If seeing the same things every day of your life was the goal, then why bother to try to make it on the outside? Stay in the office, hooked up so your electrical impulses fueled the archives. Watch whatever the AA decided you needed to in your downtime. Well, the AA would never choose to have their employees see the things Gwenni had. As far the tenets of the AA read, unsettling life stories were to be avoided or, failing that, erased.

Gwenni rubbed the small scar on her right eyebrow before tapping the departures screen. The time to move on was near at hand. She'd been to the local Kisegr and, once again, she'd hit a dead end. Unlike the AA, the towering archive of Kisegr information had never been digitised, so each Kisegr continued to hold detailed records only for those in each zone who believed in the old ways. That is, folks who actively went out of their way to register births, deaths, and marriages in actual writing that was stored in the vast catacombs beneath each Kisegr. Gwenni had no idea what would happen to all of that carefully stowed information when they ran out of space. All she knew was that of the seventeen Kisegr archives she'd visited so far; none had yet been full. Her back itched from her latest Kisegr tattoo, another part of the indelible map of her search.

The departures changed. Even this early in the morning, the population was moving. She was scanning the names of the zones, looking for a route she hadn't travelled before, when the man bumped into her. He was shouting something about "circuits of Patronage" and "being as good for it now as ever", but Gwenni was more immediately concerned about the set of telltale bumps on his temple. This guy was a card-tracer! Shit. She rubbed her scar once more for good luck before taking the plunge. "You look like a man who's seen better mornings, if I might be so bold." If he was making any attempt to disguise the fact that he was looking her up and down, he failed. Well, that was nothing new. Both men and women had looked at her before, would've done more than looked if she'd let them. Gwenni was taller than a lot of women were in Munuth Kathig, for all that she'd been average height as a child in Hlun Gloi-oo, and she had a way of looking straight at whoever she was talking to that tended to make them take notice. She shifted her gaze quickly from his eyes – doing her absolute best to ignore the small bumps at his temple while he was paying attention – to his lips. She ran her teeth along her own full lower lip. That should do it, she thought.

"Well, this explains it!" he grinned, and she had to admit that the effect was on its way to being disarming. "This finally explains why I'm still single if you've got to get up this early to meet the most charming women!"

"Charming, is it? Well, I guess I'll take that. It sure beats some of the things I've been called, no matter the time of day." Gwenni raised an eyebrow, looking for all the world as if she was remembering a litany of imaginative names she'd been called over the circuits. What she was actually doing was trying to size this card-tracer up. From what little she'd overheard of his less-than-private conversation, he was low on funds. That meant one of two things – either he was terrible at his job or he had some kind of irritatingly expensive habit. Or both. It could very easily be both.

He seemed well kitted out, though, so he probably had seen money before and used it wisely enough. That should have urged Gwenni to back away, to blend into the milling crowds of people at the serenboose station, but Gwenni had left behind doing what she should do on the day she'd challenged Bachlach ten circuits ago.

"You planning a trip?" she asked.

"Am I that obvious?"

"Oh, I'm sorry – were you trying to be subtle?" She forced innocence over her features. He laughed.

"I like you, so I'll let you in on a little secret," he took the opportunity – one he'd carefully crafted – to sidle up closer than he generally did to intriguing women he'd just met. Or closer than he generally would if he often met women that he found this intriguing. "I've just picked up a new assignment for work and I'm trying to come up with the best way to complete it."

"And by 'best', I assume you mean 'easiest'?"

"Well, maybe 'least strenuous', but yes, you're not far off." He ran his fingertips over his well-groomed beard before asking, "Is the lack of joy I find in doing more than I have to for a worthy payout that easy to see?"

It was Gwenni's turn to laugh, and her chuckle was decidedly conspiratorial. "If you think you're the only one who likes to do things simply and be paid well, I'm sorry to tell you that you've been grossly misinformed somewhere along the line."

"Well, maybe it's time that someone was kind-hearted enough to give an old fool like me a lesson in what I've got uniquely going for me."

"I don't think that anybody would describe me as being particularly kind-hearted, but I'm Gwenni and if you're looking to take on an extra pair of hands – no questions asked about your line of business – then you could do a lot worse than me."

#

When he'd looked her up and down, Perry thought he'd taken this young woman's measure. This Gwenni, he should say. She stood like she was waiting to dodge a punch. But still, a woman that striking taking the initiative in talking to a man? Well, that brought more questions along with it than it didn't. And she was striking, with those large cool eyes that raked across his face like she owned it. Not dainty, like some of the women he'd had the opportunity to get to know over the circuits, but Gwenni had cheekbones that were hard to miss even across an increasingly crowded serenboose station. There was no denying that it was more than odd for a woman to drag a man she'd never met into conversation and all but demand a job from him within a few breaths, though. Of course, that only served to pique his interest more.

"Gwenni, is it? From Gwenddydd, no doubt?" She nodded, seemingly accepting the telltale lilt that proved he'd said it the right way – the old way – with both the 'dd's treated gently, as if they had nothing to do with 'd's at all. "Well, that's a name I've not heard for a circuit or six. People are forgetting the old ways, but I guess not your people." He ploughed on before she could describe whatever family had raised her to carry the name of one of the most famous board artisans of antiquity. If they knew board history like that, doubtless they'd brought her up to recognise implant ridges like his. Maybe her asking to join him on his job 'no questions asked' wasn't so surprising, after all. Maybe she was scouting for a route into tracing. "Well, you look like you can handle yourself, don't get me wrong, but I'm not in the habit of agreeing to travel with people I've just met."

"So, get to know me. Look, I'm getting out of here as soon as I make my mind up on a destination, but I like to be useful and having a job going into a zone instead of scrabbling to find one as quickly as I can once I get there would be a welcome treat."

"Alright, how about this — if you can grab us some supplies for the journey, you can come. For some reason, shopkeepers who've known me for nigh on eighteen circuits are thinking that they'll get better prospects than a return on my word once I pick up my pay."

"I'd say it's a deal, but I make a point of knowing the name of people I do business with."

"Is that the way it is? Well, I'm Peredur York, but you'd do well to call me Perry." With his left hand, Perry squeezed the bicep of Gwenni's right arm in the age-old sign of honest greeting. That she hadn't initially offered the same to him wasn't anything to worry about — she was young, for all that she carried an ancient name. Traditions were important, though, especially in his line of work. When people recognised the scarring of his implant, slight though it was, they might as well have typed their identifier into an honesty pledge protocol — interactions between him and other people were that binding under the stringent rules of the AA.

#

Gwenni hadn't even considered that he could be a York. There were certain names you learned to avoid when you were young enough that you didn't think to question such a thing, and York was one of them. "Never answer blithely what a York has cause to ask" had been one of the sayings that whistled through Gwenni's ears even in her own sheltered early childhood at the Kisegr. She never thought she'd actually meet one of them, much less be sauntering across the marknad in search of the supplies that would win her safety in plain sight. What the Doythinebb Sisters of the Kisegr in Hlun Gloi-oo had drilled into her memory, alongside more history than most people her age would ever be aware of, could be distilled in three words: never attract attention. Most people lived by this rule regardless of their background, but the Doythinebb Sisters had made it abundantly clear that Gwenni in particular would be courting disaster if she didn't take the warning to heart.

When Perry had grabbed her arm, it had taken Gwenni a moment to realise what was going on. Once she did, her confusion quickly coalesced into alarm. Gwenni's arms were not unusual for someone with the work history that she had – the unusual part was that she was a single woman with that work history. Her arms had never been the same since her stint digging tunnels between one particularly reclusive grower's family moss-rich cave system and their cave-top star-crops. She'd enjoyed that job a lot. Not only was it physically demanding enough that she slept better than at any other time she could remember but it gave her the kind of arms that meant people should really think twice before messing with her. She wasn't, as far as she knew, related to any growers, but she'd been accepted into the close-knit family group due to their daughter Elin's shattered wrist. That Gwenni had strapped Elin up safely and kept her calm until a methug arrived was certainly a deciding factor in her hiring on. "You've got that kind of cool head in a heated situation that's more than useful in a tight space," Elin's father had said to Gwenni, once the methug's payment had been secured. "You don't happen to be looking for work, do you?"

"Almost always," Gwenni had replied, and from there her jaunt into the secretive world of growing began.

After the arm grab, Gwenni had smiled brightly. She'd been hoping that if Perry had noticed the surprising strength of her upper arms, he'd think positively about their usefulness. It must've worked, because he'd entered into a bargain with her, hadn't he? All she had to do was kit them out for this journey successfully and she would be one step safer from ever falling into a deal of the cards. Tracers could never pull in other tracers to fulfil a hand; the AA forbade it. And if anybody knew what really happened to those who had already been taken as the fulfilment of hands, it had to be the tracers – right? Gwenni didn't like to think of herself as a gambler, but luck often seemed to run in her favour, even if she did pick up more than a few bruises along the way. This move felt right, and that was all she could think about at that moment. Well, that and trying to puzzle out who would be the best marknad traders to begin a line of credit with.

#

When he'd sent her off into the thrum of the marknad, Perry had worried that he wouldn't see Gwenni again. It had been small enough of a worry, to be sure, with neither Awenwells nor gambits having changed bits between them – but he had a feeling that her company would be something worth missing. His line of credit would always be good at Brenin Pusgod-oor, which was why – not for the first time in his life – he'd found himself sat at a dimly-lit corner booth trying to make sense of the cards. "Thank you kindly," he said to Bran, who brought his loaded sandwich over personally just to get an eyeful of the draw. "You know I like to live vicariously through you, Perry," Bran smiled and stroked his thigh, "If it weren't for my mishap, maybe I'd have been a tracer…"

"…and there'd be someone better looking to take hands from Katrin!" Perry finished. The familiar pattern of their conversation was like a warm shower with clean water – always welcome, but increasingly hard to come by these days. Maybe he was getting old, he'd certainly felt it when he'd met Gwenni's gaze earlier. "Not so old you didn't send her away in the hope she'd come back. Bearing gifts, no less."

"What did you say, Perry?"

"Nothing, Bran. Nothing worth repeating, anyway. If the smell of this sandwich is anything to go by, business seems to be treating you well since my last visit."

"Better and better, it seems. I certainly can't complain!" Bran paused for a few breaths, favouring his good side with his weight. "You're going to make me ask, aren't you?"

"Ask what, my good fellow?" Perry was trying to keep his face free of the grin that so wanted to break out.

"The cards, man!" Bran set the plate of food down with audible force. The sandwich, a feat of construction that would dwarf other meals bearing the same name, remained solid. "Who are you looking for this time?"

Perry pulled his deck out of his pocket with one hand and reached for his food with the other. Most of the cards had dog-eared corners and, judging by the embedded crumbs, were often accompanied by a sandwich. Perry took a large bite before setting his meal back on its plate. Bran watched, used to Perry's pageantry. These cards might bear the names and illustrations made familiar by Awen decks like Katrin's, but they weren't masterpieces of digital encoding for all of that. They were simply cards, the same as anybody might play an illicit game or two on but that tracers used to look for patterns to quicken the fulfilment of their draw. Perry lazily thumbed the cards, pulling out ten in total. Bran whistled low. "Ten?"

"Ten." Perry confirmed, jaw set.

"What have you got yourself caught up in this time? I presume you were never here today, as usual."

"Exactly so."

"Well, turn them over. Let's see what you're working with."

One by one, Perry turned over the cards so that their faded pictures somberly faced Bran. 'Arrow-Shot' first. Honestly, when Kat had begun with that one, he'd almost called for a re-draw, but the bounty needed to be high and cards like 'Arrow-Shot' were the way to push it up. It wasn't in the same league as 'The Twins', sure, but it was a grand sight more than something everyday like 'Gap-Toothed Girl' or even 'Turned and Burned'.

Well, 'Arrow-Shot' might have been a multiplier, but there were some others too that shot up the specificity ranking alarmingly. 'Satellite's Shadow' and 'Tunnels' were two of those, nobody could question that. 'The Entrenched Botanist' and 'Star-Cropper' could be an issue as a pair but find the right family and everything would be fine. It would have to be. But where to find a grower who fitted the rest of these? 'Mutilation' – an accident with a shovel wouldn't cut it there, 'Mutilation' had to cover something intentional. Something inflicted on one person to another by distinct choice.

When Perry turned over 'The Brawler' and 'The Pilgrim' in quick succession, Bran laughed. He quickly turned it into a cough that might have been convincing without the look on his face. "I know," Perry said, "this is going to take some doing. But what is life without a challenge?"

"There are more, of course," Bran resisted the urge to find out the final cards for himself. He and Perry might go way back, but he knew as well as anybody what were and were not appropriate interactions with a tracer's cards. "Why stop here when things could get so much more interesting?" 'Left Forward' and 'Ring of Gold' completed the draw of ten.

"Well, I'll be damned to fifty circuits in the offices of the AA if I know where you're going to find a grower with a life that's been that interesting, friend!"

"That's what I was afraid of – you thinking along the same lines as me. Now I know for sure that my brain isn't as sharp as it used to be."

"I'll ignore that slight, Perry, but only because of the alarmingly immense amount of gambits I've prised out of you over the years."

"Oh well, that's comforting. You'll forgive me for my consumerism but not our near lifelong friendship? My heart is broken."

"Eat your sandwich, old man. Try filling that mouth of yours with something useful, for once. Maybe that will fire up the old synapses – give that implant something to work with!" Bran crumpled Perry's hair deprecatingly before walking away, back to the bar and the books he'd been attempting to balance before Perry had filled his familiar booth. More credit extended, well that couldn't be helped. Bran knew his friend would be good for it in the end, he always had been. But those cards? He whistled again just thinking about the draw. That level of specificity was a once in a lifetime thing. Bran just hoped that it wouldn't be the one to end Perry's career.

#

It hadn't actually been as difficult as Gwenni had feared, this supplying malarkey. The traders had been good-natured almost to a fault as soon as she'd keyed in her identifier, showing them her work history. As long as she kept her head – and sometimes coerced her cheeks into blushing by remembering things the sisters at the Kisegr had taken a dim view of – she was golden. Or at least, she seemed trustworthy enough to extend credit to. For her, the very image of gold had brought mixed blessings. Though she found herself thumbing the scar that cut across her right eyebrow whenever she had a decision to make these days, she could bring to mind very easily the blinding pain that had accompanied the cut that began it. One of her earliest memories, that was. She'd been back-handed so hard that the golden ring of Sister Arianrhod had drawn a welt. All for favouring her left hand, when everybody knew that for a sign of being a twin.

As she walked back through the marknad with two rucksacks of supplies – one on her back, the other swinging from her left hand – she tried to work out the best way to present herself to Perry. Of course, he had to take her along with him now, nobody could argue that her chosen provisions weren't sensible. No, what she was worried about was how to show him that she really could be useful to him. Could she bring up her Awelklap ranking without seeming like she loved to fight more than listen? Should her patient visits to each zone's Kisegr be mentioned, lest she end up looking appallingly devout? He'd have no reason to look at her back and see the map of Kisegrs she'd already had tattooed. At least that wasn't something she'd necessarily have to endure explaining. Sure, take on a tracing aid whose parents left her for the sisters to raise when her twin brother had been taken to fulfil the cards – that seems likely.

She didn't even remember them, this family of hers who'd either taken their leave or been taken away. She'd learned her lesson with the sisters – keep to the safest route. Hide in plain sight. 'The Twins' was the rarest card to fulfil, whenever it was it made people talk from zone to zone. It should have been easy to find records of what had happened to her brother once his paperwork with the AA had been filed, even to discover where her parents had gone after they'd left her. Work records, Awelklap wins – there should have been something, if not a trail of somethings for her to follow. But no, time and time again she came up with nothing. So, she had decided to go straight to the source: if she ever found a tracer, she'd earn their trust – or at least their respect – enough that they'd tell her where to start looking for her brother. She just hadn't expected to cross paths with one so soon. And what a one – a York, no less!

Gwenni vaguely knew the bar that Perry had mentioned, she'd liked the sign when she'd walked past: three fishes bound together and bearing a crown. That was memorable. Which, to be fair, was probably all you could ask of a bar sign. She didn't tend to stay in one zone long enough to gain regular status anywhere, but as she pushed the door open, she could see at once why people would keep coming back to this place. The light hovered somewhere between garish and cosy, depending on where you wanted to sit. Gwenni smiled at the well-cut man behind the bar before scanning the darker corners of the room. She had a feeling that Perry was not a meet under the bright lights kind of a guy, if he could help it. She walked slowly, yet purposefully, towards the bar itself, her eyes tracing the shadowed places as she moved. "Hello," she grinned slowly, letting the smile light up her face from bottom to top. When it settled in her eyes, which she knew were pale enough to draw notice from most people, she continued, "I wonder if a friend of mine might be here already?"

"Any friend of yours is lucky indeed, but as you see it's early yet to have many customers to choose from," Bran replied. He nodded towards a pair of elderly gentlemen she'd passed on the way in, "I don't suppose that Kay or Owain would argue if you found yourself looking for friendship with either one of them. They've certainly seen a variety of ladies in their time, but they don't tend to bring them in here."

"I think we might be at crossed purposes here," Gwenni's blush, this time, was very real and very bright. "It's possible I've got the wrong place – is there another bar with a similar name that might be popular with," she lowered her voice "those who enjoy cards more than most?" She hefted the rucksack she was carrying up onto the bar and Bran's face drained of colour. Before he had a chance to attempt to regain his conversational footing, they both heard "Over here, Gwenni!" It sounded like Perry was chewing almost as loudly as he was calling out. Gwenni shrugged, dragged the rucksack off the bar, and deliberately tried not to hurtle towards the man who – as far as she knew – hadn't taken her for a pitaeen upon first glance.

#

So, she'd come back, that was good. And she seemed to be lugging a bag as well as carrying one on her back – better and better. Perry wiped his beard free of sandwich remnants and ran his tongue across his teeth. He'd meant to push back his hair, but she was coming towards him with so much purpose that she couldn't have failed to notice such a primping maneuver. Oh well, he thought, perhaps looking rugged would be best served by a lock or two of hair caressing my manly brow. Not that a girl as fresh-faced as Gwenni would look twice at him, of course. That went without saying. But still, blaming a man for taking some pride in his appearance as well as his line of business was pretty low. Not that she had, Perry realised ruefully. He spent so much time putting cards together and creating possible life profiles from them that sometimes it was difficult for him to remember that not everybody was a potential draw fulfilment.

Gwenni dropped the one bag at Perry's feet, it clunked satisfyingly as it connected with the floor. "Well, it sounds like you've done well!" When he reached down and tested the weight of the rucksack, the strain on his face showed, "Scratch that. Whatever this is full of, you've done very well indeed! Just carrying it in along with its twin on your back shows me how capable you are." Did she flinch as she sat down? It didn't matter – he meant what he'd said. "Sorry about Bran, his tongue is quicker than his brain."

"That's not something he's alone in." The laugh that escaped from Perry culminated with a snort. She raised a sardonic eyebrow.

"Well, that's as maybe. You certainly won't get any argument from me on that score. I do wonder, though, if you'd like to turn that lightning quick mind of yours to something more… profitable?" He gestured to the cards still littering the table before leaning back against his seat. Gwenni shucked the rucksack from her shoulders and placed it on the floor next to the other bag. She slid into her seat, pushed her hair behind her ears, then rested her chin on one hand. With the other hand she traced shapes above the cards. It was a little painful for Perry to watch, this level of deference from someone so obviously capable. "You can touch them, move them around if you want." She met his gaze with wide eyes. This was an honour and they both knew it. Slowly, she extended her fingers, grazing their tips against the corner of one card, then another. The silence lengthened.

Perry was good at silences, especially ones where the person he was watching was as completely occupied as Gwenni currently was. For him, silences could be used to assess, to mete out marks on his mental checklist. What could he add to his first impressions of this woman – striking, strong, versed in the old ways, quick-witted, and bold enough to expect work in their first conversation – now that she'd returned to him, laden with supplies just as she'd promised. Well, he could underline strong, that was for certain. Add in capable and oath-keeper. She favoured her left hand when she touched the cards and when she'd carried in the extra rucksack, which was always an interesting trait. It didn't always mark a twin, but it made for an unexpected advantage in Awelklap if nothing else. She might be a pilgrim of sorts, or an archivist looking for more physical work, with a name like hers. Meddling in the shadowy records of even one Kisegr, unregulated by digitisation and away from scrutiny by satellites... But she'd clearly seen hard labour – the muscle on her upper arm had shone light on that truth. A grower grown weary of tending crops, perhaps? Maybe she'd have some useful contacts for this draw. Why, if she had picked up an arrow wound somewhere on her travels, she might prove fulfilment herself! But that was foolishness, he was letting his imagination get the better of his logic again.

Perry swallowed. Gwenni had fulfilled her end of the bargain, they were bound as travelling partners now. Technically, though, he hadn't taken her on as an apprentice tracer. He was almost sure of it. There should be forms to fill in for that kind of a bargain. Technicalities had been known to fail when there were implications, though, especially in verbal contracts. As far as he could see, she didn't look like she'd suffered mutilation. She wore no golden rings either on her hands or in her ears, also, which lessened her fit for the draw. Not that there weren't other places gold rings could be found, of course, but he didn't expect to find himself in any position to assess those areas for their precious metal content. He steeled himself to break the silence. "Any ideas on where we might start? Bran thought a grower with an intriguing past, I am increasingly tending towards an ex-grower who has followed a very interesting path in the time since their fingertips last met plants." He kept his tone light, asking, "I don't suppose you have happened to have crossed paths with anyone with a background in growing during your own travels?"

\#

Well, this was getting awkward. Gwenni had found herself straining in an effort to not gulp audibly when she'd seen the way that Perry had grouped the cards. He'd triangulated 'The Entrenched Botanist' with 'Tunnels' and 'Star-Cropper', which made sense. Of course it did. That she could glance over easily. He'd joined up 'Satellite's Shadow' with 'The Pilgrim' which, again, was sensible enough. 'The Brawler' and 'Mutilation' might go together, as he'd laid out, because in her experience a glutton for punishment didn't always stop at one source. Perry had gone a step further, though, by adding 'Left Forward' to make a second triangulation. Well, that struck a little too close to home, if she was being honest. 'Ring of Gold' and 'Arrow-Shot' he'd set to the side, floating as if they didn't quite fit with the incredibly specific life these cards required. She was just about to break the silence with "Ten cards, huh?", when he asked her about her own potential meetings with growers. Even if it was in jest, Gwenni didn't want this well-worn tracer slotting this draw against her lifestyle.

There was only one exit that she could see, and that was in full view of the barman, not to mention those two old men whose pasts might also have been fairly interesting in themselves. Owain and Kay, if she'd heard right. Why, they had names as far-reaching as her own. The three of them together with a Peredur – did this Bran always keep such historic-sounding company in his bar? It didn't matter right now. She was being too quiet, and she knew that this kind of silence shifted her into potentially dangerous territory. She flew as close as she dared to honesty with, "I actually might have come across a grower or two in my travels, as you put it."

Perry didn't move quickly, but he did break away from the relaxed posture that he'd been enjoying. In fact, he mirrored her own – leaning towards the cards and resting his chin on one hand. Gwenni noticed, too, that his legs stretched out in such a way that she'd risk tripping if she ran. Especially with those blasted rucksacks set where she'd put them – they all but hemmed her in. She gritted her teeth as if she was preparing for a hard blow. It was a posture she was, unfortunately, rather familiar with.

"Let's just say I do know a few places we might start looking. That I have a few faces in mind who would definitely fulfil, say, six or seven of these cards. That they might themselves even have ideas on where to look for someone as specific as this." She tapped a slow beating tune with her fingertips as she spoke, as if she was trying to remember a half-forgotten story from a childhood further away than she could lay claim to. "Where would I be sending this person to, exactly?"

113

"You want to know what happens to the people I trace?" Perry furrowed his brows. "That's simple. I take them to Katrin, and she begins to process them. Loves filling in forms, that one. Can't get enough of the bureaucratic hustle and bustle."

Gwenni stopped tapping her fingers and rolled her eyes, as if the two motions were discordant somehow. "Yes, yes, that's all very well and good. But what happens to them after that?" He had to know, he just had to.

"If I knew that – and I'm not saying that I do – it strikes me that it would probably be one of those things you don't mention to someone you've met all but twice."

"Ah, but as you've recognised, we've got a wholly unusual relationship going on here. We're business associates, after all." She wasn't going to give him room to sidestep the binding nature of their arrangement.

"Associates, is it? There's forms to file for that, and I'd need more than Gwenddydd to go on to complete those."

"If you need to know it to legitimize things it's Pierce, okay? My last name is Pierce. Now where does this ten-card person go once we find them?"

"If we weren't in a business relationship, I have a feeling that it wouldn't take long for you to find out." Perry sighed and reached for Gwenni's hand. "Only as long as it would take to walk you out of here and over to meet my good friend Katrin."

Betsie Flynn lives in Wales with her husband, children, and cats. Her poetry appears in various places online and she has a re-imagined fairytale in Fractured Mirror's upcoming anthology. She tweets @betsieflynn

Teacher's Puppet

by Alex Minns

Footsteps echoed from further down the corridor but coming this way. Jeremiah leapt into action. His treasured copy of Wells' latest book was thrust back into its hiding place, wedged between the struts on the underside of his bed. If one of the masters caught him with a fiction book, there would be trouble.

There was a sharp rap on the door. "Wilson. To the Hall." The commanding voice didn't wait for a reply. Jeremiah listened as the footsteps continued on past his room and towards the next one. The late-night summonses for extra training and assessments had been more frequent since Master Brown had left. For the last week, it had been every evening. Jeremiah didn't bother with getting into his bedclothes until it was well past midnight these days.

As he headed out of his room, into the corridor, he noted only one other boy. Their numbers had been rapidly dwindling: some had been sent home, others sent to serve in other institutions across the country but with each newly vacant seat in the refectory, the gnawing doubts grew.

As he made his way down the hallway, he couldn't help but stare up at the lamps on the wall. In his own home, a place he had not seen for some time, they only had gas lamps. The yellow greasy haze that caused shadows to dance and flicker in every crevice was far inferior to the glow of the aether lamps that filled these halls. A luminescent blue held steady in every lamp, highlighting everything in exact detail. He couldn't comprehend having to put up with the dim glow of a gas lamp anymore. When he had first arrived at the Academy, it had been like walking into a dream. Jeremiah had only heard whispers of the new discovery of aether when he had been selected, but to see it in action was indescribable. His initial fears about leaving home and joining the Academy had burned away by the glorious blue glow. The Academy had been the first to harness the power of the aether although there were still differing ideas on its source, even amongst the masters. Was it energy that lay dormant or the will of a greater being? Some even posited that it came from another dimension, bleeding through to ours. The only thing they all agreed on, was that the Mayans had known about aether thousands of years ago. Images on tombs had shown people with lightning that they drew from the sky. Some thought it was pure fiction, that they just had a good imagination, but the Academy had managed to obtain artefacts that were definitely devices used in harnessing the aether. Master Yellow had often lamented the loss of progress that could have been made if the Mayan empire had not succumbed and with it their advances lost for centuries.

Rumours has been spreading that the Queen herself was wanting to visit the Academy to see aether in action. To have the monarch adopt the technology would open the gates for it to spread across the globe. Jeremiah couldn't help but smile, the Academy was at the forefront of innovation and was going to change the world, and here he was right in the middle of it. He himself had helped Master Green just yesterday with some tweaks to a communications device he was creating. Several of the masters were engineers and had taught the boys mechanics.

Jeremiah had proven quick to pick up the principles and was regularly scoring the top marks in engineering assessments. He wondered what this evening's assessment was going to be about.

This week alone he had been required to undergo a marksmanship test, run around the field ten times in under one hour, re-construct a basic steam engine but the oddest of the tasks was a written assessment which gave a series of oral dilemmas where you had to explain what you would do in each. Jeremiah did not enjoy that one; he felt torn between what he thought the masters would want him to say and what he actually would do. Master Brown had often talked to him about philosophy and politics in the library after classes. He had introduced Jeremiah to a range of thinkers and their ideas about society and a person's place in it. It hadn't taken Jeremiah long to notice that Master Brown would often change the subject just as another master came near. All the boys had known that Master Brown was different, he was kinder and treated the boys as children rather than machines. Some of the other masters showed no sympathy and could not understand when anyone struggled to comprehend or not keep up. It was a sad day when Master Brown left. No-one had been formally told he was leaving but the night before he left, Master Brown visited Jeremiah and gave him the copy of Wells' book that now lay wedged under his bunk.

Fiction was frowned upon at the Academy. Initially, it had been allowed but since Jeremiah had arrived, how long ago had that even been, things had changed. He was still not yet fourteen years but even he could sense the political changes that had happened amongst the masters. Everything had become stricter, tighter, discipline had been enforced more strongly. All signs of play and imagination had to have purpose, there was no reading of fairy tales. Games were allowed but to be used as instructive tools on how to strategize and out-think your opponent. Even lessons had become competitions and every boy was striving to out-perform the others.

Jeremiah's musings on his life at the Academy were cut short as he entered the hall. His step faltered. This was the one room where candles still graced the walls. Usually, they were just for ceremony but, this evening, they were all lit and were currently the only sources of light. Shadows flickered up the stone walls which climbed ever higher to the grand roof. A domed skylight graced the centre of the ceiling, metalwork tracing its way to the middle of the glass. Tonight, the moon was full in the sky and was framed perfectly above them. It was a new theory that aether was at its strongest during the full moon, people thought it had similar effects on aether as it did on the tide. All the usual tables and benches had been placed against the edge of the circular room to make way for the impressive construction in the centre.

Jeremiah drifted to an open spot as all the boys gathered in a ring. There were only five of them present. His was the most senior year in the Academy and they had been decimated by the number of leavers. Where was Hadley? He had been present in Latin that morning. Jeremiah's concern was cut short as Master Red stood beside the main focus of the room. Jeremiah's eyes ran around the stone arch that sat in front of him. Carved, grey rock stood, propped up by metal vices attaching it to the base where the conduit sat. Symbols had been painted onto the surface in a special conductive paint. He had used the paint himself when assisting Master Blue with a prototype of a communications he was designing, one that drew aether from the atmosphere and focused it into a single beam, connecting two devices. Jeremiah caught sight of Master Blue now at the edge of the room. The Master met his eye and gave a small nod. Perhaps it hadn't been a communications device after all.

"Gentlemen." Master Red addressed the whole room. All the boys, and some of the masters, all stood a little taller. Master Red was an imposing figure. As head of the Academy, he didn't teach lessons. You usually only encountered him when trouble was afoot. He towered over most, and his features were very angular. His face often reminded Jeremiah of a hawk, watching for its prey. "Tonight, we would like to show you where all our hard work leads to. Some of you have already heard whispers of an aether gate."

Shocked gasps rippled between the five boys as they all stole glances at each other. Jeremiah saw his own excitement reflected in the faces of the other boys. He could feel a buzzing in his chest as adrenaline started to pump through him. When he joined the Academy, the lessons on aether fascinated him from day one. He had devoured all the masters had to say and went and read all their prior research in the Academy's library. He had discussed aether at length with Master Brown before he had left. Aether was everywhere, a hidden energy that existed in the air unless you find a way to harness it and withdraw it. Until it is extracted, it drifts through the breeze, inert and harmless. It was an accidental explosion in a factory where a man called Edison was trying to use something called electricity to power a lamp that allowed aether to reveal itself. Since then, the masters had been at the forefront of aether research.

Master Brown had told him that there had been resistance at first. People did not trust what they didn't understand, and some of the ideas of some researchers had only served to alienate them further from the general populace. Some masters decided that the presence of aether was due to some higher intelligence, something that influenced the universe and created the natural order of things. The Church had not been happy with this and there had been attacks on scientific establishments, including the Academy, well before Jeremiah arrived. He knew that some of the masters still taught this idea and propagated the theory, although less so in public these days. In fact, the masters did not share their work with the public much at all of late.

"We have constructed this aether gate for the purpose of travel. It has not yet been activated but this evening, we have decided to let this honour fall to the best of our students." Austin, to Jeremiah's left, immediately puffed out his chest. He thought he was the top of the bunch and made sure everyone else was also aware of this. The other boys were similarly enthused by this show of confidence from the masters. Jeremiah, however, was less sure. After all their work, they would let five children start the machine? It was another test; he was certain of it. "There is a table for each of you with the equipment you need in order to start extracting the aether. The conduit is the central point at the base, that is where you must channel your efforts."

The other boys immediately went to their tables and started preparing. On each table there was an aether glove. Jeremiah always though gauntlet was a better classification. It was a base layer of fabric, but strips of metal ran down the fingers, giving a silvered skeleton. Hoops also helped keep the rigidity as the sleeve went up to the elbow, but it also added weight. Jeremiah braced his arm as he donned the glove, flexing his fingers to ensure it was fitting correctly. He concentrated, mumbling a few words of the incantations. He felt a familiar heat start to build in the glove as his focus and the words allowed him to draw the aether from the air. The metal strips acted as capacitors, storing it up away from his hand.

The other boys took up their positions around the room. Two wore goggles in case of stray sparks. Jeremiah had worn them to start with, but his control had increased greatly, and he rarely had to worry about the aether escaping his grasp. The chanting began. Jeremiah instinctively joined in as he saw aether begin to coalesce around his peers' gloves. It took several minutes to generate a sufficient amount, but Austin was the first to attempt to connect.

He pushed out his aether into a flowing stream towards the conduit. It faltered and dropped close to the ground a few times but eventually hit the right area. Jeremiah waited a few moments longer, to build up increased stability but he was next to connect to the conduit, closely followed by the other three class members.

The conduit channelled the aether up into the arch. The gate blazed a brilliant blue as the space in the centre seemed to shake. Sparks shot from one side of the arch to the other as the gap began to coalesce into something more solid. It looked exactly like an aether lamp but much more intense. Jeremiah could feel the air grow coarse with static, an unnatural wind seemed to be growing from nowhere, pulling at his hair and clothes. He held firm, as did the other boys. The chanting continued, calling on the High Intelligence although some of the Mayan words began to slip, Jeremiah could hear mispronunciations and errors in the speech of his compatriots.

The crackling in the air grew stronger. Jeremiah stole a glance over to the masters, who he noted, were safely distant from the whole proceedings. His hand started to sting in the gauntlet, the metal around his fingers growing so charged with aether he could feel it starting to course through him. His teeth started to hurt, nerve endings screaming with the stimulation. Just as he thought he could take no more, there was an almighty crash and the portal snapped into focus inside the gateway. The pull of the aether was so great, the glove was ripped from his hand. Just as soon as the gateway activated, the light was broken by something emerging from the other side.

Shrieks filled the air as a beast with the head of an alligator flew into the hall and started snapping at boys. Children scattered in all directions, heading for the nearest doorway only to find them closed. Jeremiah remained rooted on the spot. He felt detached from his body. There was no way this could be happening. He had to have fallen asleep in his room whilst reading his book. There were strange creatures in the story, ones in the future. His dreams must have been influenced by that. The creature soared high into the air and paused, looking down at the scene below. Boys were still hauling on the wooden doors, trying to get them to budge. Someone had trapped them inside. Jeremiah looked across at the masters. Only now did he see a feint shimmer, a wall of aether between them and the chaos unfolding before them. They stood watching with a dispassionate air of curiosity, unmoved by the boys screams of terror. Master Red stood in the centre, his hands clasped behind his back and his black teacher robes hanging round him like a cape. The thin line of red ribbon that wove around the edge of his clothing suddenly looked line a line of blood. Jeremiah shuddered at the thought, not being able to shake the chill he got from the emptiness in the master's eyes. Why had he not woken yet? Were you not supposed to wake up when you realised you were dreaming?

Movement to his left drew Jeremiah's attention back to the situation in front of him. Austin had lunged forward with a pike he had removed from the wall and was yelling like a barbarian as he wielded the weapon at the creature. At once, the creature focused on the attacker. Its skin was scaled and a putrid green colour. The head was just like that of an alligator, a long mouth full of vicious teeth and eyes on the sides of its head that tracked you. That's where most of the similarity ended, however. The creature's limbs were longer than that of the Earthly alligator and on each joint there appeared to be another mouth, gnashing away. At the end of each limb there was a hand too, not the normal clawed feet of the reptile. As Austin readied himself to attack again, the creature hovered for a second. Jeremiah could almost feel it build the pressure around itself before it launched through the air and barreled straight into Austin, batting the pike away with one of its limbs.

The screams were renewed from his classmates and now the sobs of children started to join the sound. When the creature rose up again, it was clear there was no point in trying to aid their fallen companion. Still, when Jeremiah glanced across, the masters stood unwavering. Master Red seemed to sneer with disgust, or was it disappointment? This was no dream; this was just the latest assessment. A cold feeling washed over Jeremiah as he realised for the first time that this assessment, they could all fail, and failure would mean their deaths. Master Red noticed Jeremiah looking at them and cocked his head, a raised eyebrow challenging him. Fine, Jeremiah thought bitterly. He would complete this hellish test.

In the air above them, the creature circled again, searching for its next target. No-one dared take up arms now. The banging on the doors seemed to be attracting its attention. It swiveled as if in water and angled itself at the largest door.

"Move," he screamed at the boys. The commanding tone in his voice seemed to break through to the terrified students and they scattered again as the creature launched forward. Thankfully all the boys had dived aside in time and the creature smashed into the wooden door but still it did not budge.

The creature rose up, all mouths gnashing angrily as it locked its gaze on Jeremiah. He took a deep breath. Its scales were like armour, a normal weapon would do no good. His hand still felt heavy and warm where he had worn the aether glove. He flexed his fingers, feeling static between them as an idea formed. He circled round, moving until he could see the opening of the archway. Still it glowed blue although the light was starting to dim. It was draining already. As he moved, the creature turned with him, tracking his every movement. That's it, he thought, follow me. Jeremiah started whispering under his breath, reciting the words that he knew so well. He didn't know how the chant helped them focus onto the signature of the aether, there was so much he didn't know, so much the masters didn't know, or at least did not share. Staring down the ungodly creature in front of him he suddenly felt out of his depth, as if he were messing with forces not of this world, not meant for a mere mortal. And yet if he wanted to live… His hand began to sting, the aether gathered around it as it was drawn from the air. He daren't look down at his own hand but the gasps around him confirmed his plan was working, for now at least. No-one as far as he knew had ever attempted this without the glove as a conduit. And as his arm began to cramp and spasm he understood why. He ground the words of the chant out, refusing to release the aether. Not yet.

The creature drew itself a little higher as it prepared to attack. Its snout opened wide, saliva dripping from its gaping maw. Jeremiah ground his teeth together, he just had to hold out a little longer. Timing was everything.

The creature pounced. Jeremiah held firm. Shrieks went up around him, one hand tried to drag him out of the way, but he refused he move. The creature closed in. Just as it lined up with his eyeline in the archway, he released the aether in a straight line. Blue energy leapt from his fingertips and caught the creature mid-flight sending it tumbling through the air towards the gateway. It hit the portal releasing a thunderous crash as it collided with the window of aether. Jeremiah held his breath. Was it only one way? Sparks reached out and caught hold of the monster, swallowing it up before it pulled him back through to wherever it came from.

"Someone disperse it!" A voice cried out.

"It might come back."

Voices bounced around the Hall around him, but Jeremiah sank to his knees cradling his arm. It looked normal but he could still feel the aether buzzing through it. He shook it but his hand screamed in protest, so he went back to gripping it to his chest, massaging it with his good hand. He was vaguely aware of action around him; boys went over to the arch and disconnected the wires and cables that hooked up to the conduit powering the portal. The energy quickly dispersed, and light faded from the portal until it was inert again. Jeremiah looked through the now harmless looking stone. Directly on the other side was Master Red, staring at him with what he thought had to have been a grin on his face. It truly was a more terrifying sight than the creature itself. The protective barrier that had separated the masters from the chaos was gone and their teachers had returned to the room, already ordering the boys around and directly them to tidy the area. And the boys did as they were told. Jeremiah looked between his classmates, searching for one other who looked at least a little bit angry, but none seemed to have registered. Perhaps they were all too shell-shocked.

He was aware his searching gaze kept missing one particular area. Someone had already laid a sheet over the prone body of Austin and people just moved around him, refusing to acknowledge he was there. No doubt the masters would send in the caretakers after they were gone to clean up the mess.

Darkness swept over Jeremiah as someone moved in front of him, blocking the light. "An impressive display." He didn't need to look up to recognise Master Red's voice.

"Get up Wilson, show some respect." A hand grabbed at his shoulder making him hiss in pain.

"Leave him, I think after that display he can be allowed some leeway."

Still, he kept his head down and focused on his arm.

"Let him recover a short while and then bring him to my study in one hour. It seems we have finally found our subject." He watched the master's feet turn and walk briskly away. Jeremiah had stopped rubbing his sore arm, he found himself distracted by Master Red's last words. Subject?

"Hear that Wilson? Lucky lad, now let's get you cleaned up shall we." Jeremiah slowly managed to push himself up off the floor. His legs still felt wobbly as he stood. Master Green was nodding at him. "Good good. Right, Master Yellow. Can I leave you to ensure this is all tidied and the necessary preparations for the Communing are seen to?"

"This evening?" Master Yellow was frowning.

"Master Red wishes to waste no more time." He turned away before there could be any further protests or questions and put his hand on Jeremiah's shoulder urging him forward. "We've waited long enough to find someone."

#

Exactly one hour later, Jeremiah was stood outside Master Red's study. His right arm now hung by his side, still sore but no longer buzzing with shooting pains. He had barely said a word as he was guided along by Master Green. He had instructed him to put on his best, full Academy uniform. Buttons had been an issue at first but after enough tsking from the master, Jeremiah forced himself to manage. He pulled at his blazer; it was not the most comfortable fit. Normally, it was saved for Christmas or when dignitaries visited. Apparently, whatever the Communing turned out to be, it made the list of important events.

Master Green knocked sharply on the study door and waited for the response before entering. Jeremiah was ushered in impatiently but before the door could be closed behind them, Master Red spoke. "Thank you Master, you may leave us."

Jeremiah sensed the hesitation behind him, clearly Master Green did not want to be left out. Jeremiah didn't know whether to feel smug or more worried about the idea of being left alone.

"I shall help the others with the preparations."

"Thank you. We shall be along shortly." Master Red had already moved his gaze to Jeremiah and paused until the other teacher had left. "Well, I imagine you have a lot of questions, so I'll do my best to fill in any details, but we do not have long." He didn't wait for Jeremiah to respond before carrying on. "As you know, when we summon aether, we call on the High Intelligence to assist us." Jeremiah gave the barest of nods. "We do not do it lightly; it is not simply some fictional concept we use to hang the chants on. I know we are men of science, and this may be difficult to accept, however, we have determined that there is a force that coaxes the universe along its path. Some call it mother nature, some fate, but it does exist. It is not a godlike figurehead but a consciousness that helps things exist, creates energy. Are you following me so far?"

Jeremiah fought to not let his jaw drop. For all their banishment of all fictional stories, here was Master Red telling a fairy tale. He did all he could do and nodded again.

"By calling on the High Intelligence, we gain access to the aether that sits around us at all times. We are able to manipulate it, use it to further our knowledge, our technology, our access. That creature you fought off this evening, it was from another plane. We are not the only line of existence. The High Intelligence oversees them all and in using the aether, it has granted us access to these other realms."

"Did you know that monster was going to come through?" Jeremiah bit his tongue as soon as the words left it. He dare question the master? For a moment, he feared what the man might do, his face frozen in its expressionlessness. But then his mouth seemed to twitch into a smirk.

"We knew you were tapping into a dangerous realm, but only in the face of true danger and adversity do we either crumble or rise to our full potential. And you Jeremiah are the first boy to rise to the occasion and show you have full mastery over the aether." Master Red reached out and put a hand on Jeremiah's shoulder. The gesture seemed to be trying to be fatherly but the awkwardness with which the teacher held himself just made the whole situation feel wrong. Jeremiah could not help but notice the subtext of his words. He had been the first to rise to the occasion. How many other times had they tried this? How many other Austins had died? His distress must have shown on his face. "The advance of science is only gained by those who dare to take risks, make sacrifices. Without the need to defeat that creature, you would have never attempted to do what you did tonight." He moved away and started pacing round the room. Jeremiah daren't speak in case it betray his horror. He found himself wondering if Master Red had actually made any sacrifices at any point. "But how far you are willing to go Jeremiah, in the pursuit of knowledge, to further the evolution of the human race?"

A word he had heard earlier came back in his head, along with a deep sense of foreboding. "What is the Communing?"

"Ah, you are an attentive lad. Yes, you are a good choice. Of course, I already suspected you were a candidate when looking at your reports. Always near the top of all classes, just quietly getting on. But I digress. The Communing. Well, on a few occasions, we have been able to make contact with the High Intelligence. We believe the Mayans did once, but the results of their work were lost, we could only follow the documents left behind of how they managed it. However, when we have made contact, it has refused to interact, it says we need a spokesman, a champion who will represent us, one who it will imbue with the full gifts aether can offer. The Communing is where you will become that champion, and under the guidance of the Academy, you will lead humanity into a new era." The master turned and fixed Jeremiah with an intense stare. His eyes were wide with excitement that he was trying unsuccessfully to contain. His defiance to retain the look of composure just served to make him look unhinged. Jeremiah had never been more terrified in his entire life.

Three sharp knocks on the door nearly made Jeremiah fall to the floor. He spun round; his hands half raised to protect himself as Master Yellow appeared in the doorway. He barely gave

Jeremiah the most cursory of glances before he turned his attention to Master Red. "We're ready for you."

"Excellent." Master Red swept past him, his gown flapping and attacking Jeremiah's legs. "Come along."

As he followed the master back to the hall, Jeremiah's thoughts were lost in a maze. When they arrived back at the door, he found he couldn't actually remember leaving Master Red's study. The door opened but his feet refused to move. Flashes of the creature exploded in his head; images of Austin laying covered on the floor. It could easily have been him, or any number of them.

"Jeremiah." Master Red was already over the threshold and staring back at him. His eyes had narrowed, studying Jeremiah. He found the thought of displeasing the master greater than his fear of what had happened before, and his feet finally began to move. The frown on the master's face eased.

Jeremiah couldn't help but notice the lack of children. None of the other boys were anywhere in sight. Only the Masters stood around the edge of the hall, taking the places their students had done only an hour before.

"Go and stand in the archway." Master Red nodded to the centre of the room, where the stone arch still stood, reconnected after the earlier battle.

"In the arch?"

An eyebrow rose. Jeremiah had seen that look before, just after someone had given a wrong answer and just before the cane came out. "The archway." Jeremiah repeated with more certainty before moving round the master. He felt the eyes of all of the teachers in the room upon him. His feet carried him forward, but his mind screamed at him to find a way out of this. Standing in the arch when it was charged with aether was surely madness! If the portal's activation did not kill him, whatever monstrosity that came through first would!

As he positioned himself underneath the stone arch, a spark leapt from it and shocked his arm. Residual aether from the last activation he presumed. He rubbed the spot on his arm. If that was what left over aether felt like, how much would it hurt when they turned the archway on with him inside it? Not one of the masters was looking at him. They all had aether gloves on, one on each hand. Jeremiah had never seen anyone manipulate aether two-handed before. Tears threatened to fall no matter how hard he tried to be brave. He thought of his family; it had been so long since he had seen them. His father and older brother tried hard to provide for them all, but he knew that things were tough. He had hoped coming to the Academy would help, that he would learn so much he could earn enough money to look after them all, or at the very least, him being here meant there was more food to go around. But now, all he wanted was to be back home. He wished he'd never volunteered to take the entrance tests. He found himself missing Master Brown too, he had been the only teacher here to show any kind of concern or care for them. Jeremiah clung to the idea that he would not have let this happen to him if he were here.

"It is time." Master Red called to the room. Jeremiah took one last look around for a way out. There was none. The chanting began, but they were not the usual words they used to extract the aether from the atmosphere. Jeremiah could pick out the odd word but that was it. Blue glows started to gather round the men's gloves as the aether was drawn to them and activated. The air began to buzz, singing with the energy being drawn out of nothing. The voices began to rise as crackling started to build. Master Green was straight ahead, but still, he didn't look at Jeremiah. His gown was pulled backwards, billowing out from him as he was buffeted by the winds that had erupted from nowhere. The blue glow kept growing around the gloves. Jeremiah could see they were nearly at maximum capacity and then all the masters reached out towards other men across the room from them. Lines of aether erupted from the gloves and joined up with those coming from other people. Jeremiah spun on the spot. He had been surrounded in a net of aether. The energy lines crisscrossed around him forming an eleven-pointed star. This must have been the ritual Master Red had said the Mayans had written about for he had never seen anything like this before. Never had the teachers shown them anything beyond the basic applications and processes using aether.

Jeremiah's ears began to hurt, the pressure around him was increasing rapidly. Thumping in his skull brought him to his knees as the static built around him. They weren't channelling the aether into the arch but somehow it was still activating. Jeremiah clamped his hands over his ears, but it was futile. The aether was passing through him and around him, it was as if the portal was forming in the same space that he occupied yet still they remained distinctly separate. Another plane, wasn't that what Master Red said? The pain he had felt in his arm when he wielded the aether was now coursing through his entire body. A cry of pain tore from his throat but still they chanted on.

And then, silence.

He stayed huddled on his knees for a moment, confused. Had he fainted? The pain had gone, completely, not even any lingering buzzing in his limbs. The pressure in his head had lifted too. He listened for chanting, but it was completely quiet. Perhaps he had died?

"Are you going to stay down there for long?"

The voice seemed to emanate from inside his head. He let go of his ears and looked up. He was in the hall, alone. All the masters had gone. Gingerly, he glanced around, still searching for the source of the voice but there was no-one there. He frowned. Something didn't seem right. The walls were cracked. And the tables that had been around the edges of the room were gone. It looked like the room he had been in, but he was most definitely not in the same place he had been in seconds ago.

"Correct. We thought it best to try and mimic your surroundings to put you at ease. It seems we missed a few details." The tables materialised out of thin air.

Jeremiah stood up, turning around on the spot.

"Where are you?" He squinted, the light was not very bright here and he couldn't see into all the corners.

"We are everywhere."

"The High Intelligence?"

"That is what your kind call us." The voice echoed in Jeremiah's head again. "Humans like to put names on things, to classify them. It seems, unnecessary to us."

"Oh. Yes, I suppose we do. But how else would you keep track of what you know and what you don't?"

There was silence. For a moment, Jeremiah feared the High Intelligence had left.

"You make a valid point. Your kind still has much to learn. We know all so these things matter to us less. But that is why they have sent you is it not?"

Jeremiah kept turning, it was disconcerting to talk to a disembodied voice.

"Does this help?" The voice seemed to have a focus, and an actual accent now. In fact, a rather familiar one. Jeremiah turned again to see Master Brown standing a few feet away. "You seem to trust this human. Does this put you at ease?"

"Yes, thank you." Jeremiah mumbled. It was strange to think the High Intelligence could root through his mind without him feeling a thing, but it was comforting to actually have someone to look at now. He made a mental note to make sure he kept his thoughts polite just in case.

The High Intelligence looked down at himself, examining his hand. "It is a strange form. But then all things corporeal feel odd to us. This man was your teacher, yes?"

"Yes. Master Brown."

"Tell me, do all your kind give themselves colours as monikers?"

"No, only the teachers at the Academy." He cocked his head. "I'm not sure why they do to be honest."

The High Intelligence blinked, watching Jeremiah. It suddenly dawned on him that it was expecting an answer. "It is strange for those who purport to teach to hide behind pseudonyms. It is also strange for teachers to themselves claim to need more knowledge. How can they teach if they think themselves lacking in the knowledge they are passing on?"

"Striving for more knowledge makes us advance as a species. If we did not look for answers we would not find new technologies." Jeremiah watched the High Intelligence start to pace around the room, a frown had crossed his brow.

"I see why they chose you as their spokesperson. You are wise, young and very adept at harnessing the aether. Do you understand what they have asked from you?" The High Intelligence stopped and looked up at him, waiting patiently. Jeremiah struggled to focus on him, the light was dim, dimmer than in the real hall and the High Intelligence was shrouded in shadow.

"No," Jeremiah admitted. "Not really. They just said you would only share knowledge with one person."

"It is not knowledge sharing exactly Jeremiah Wilson. I would not teach you as you understand it. It would mean unlocking parts of your brain no human uses. You would have all of our knowledge downloaded into your mind."

"Down-loaded?"

"Oh, this word is not in your language yet is it. Hmm, we would place it in there, you would have instant access to it. You would also be able to use aether at will in many more ways than you know."

"Like how?"

"The how is not the most important question." His lips pursed, just like Master Brown when he was trying to encourage Jeremiah to think deeper about a problem.

Jeremiah bit his lip and considered this for a moment. The High Intelligence was offering to make him a genius, to make him understand the universe, to take all the knowledge back to the masters. He paused. "Why?"

"And that is the most important question." The High Intelligence smiled at him. Jeremiah couldn't help but smile back, he looked just like Master Brown. But then the words finally lodged in his mind.

"Why do the asters want me to have this power? Why would Master Red not take it for himself?"

"Why be the puppet when you can be the puppet master?"

A memory flashed into his head. Master Brown had lent him a book by Charles Dickens, about an orphan who was forced to turn to crime. Master Brown would often call him back after class and ask him what he thought; they would spend a great deal of time discussing the ins and outs of the story and the ideas behind it. At first, Jeremiah thought they were all just thrilling adventures, but Master Brown had shown him that often these stories were written to make you think, to challenge society and so he had started to dig deeper, question. In this book, the main thing that had perturbed him had seemed rather simple. Why did the old man get the children to steal and not do anything himself? Master Brown had uttered those very words to him that day.

"But why Jeremiah, would he be the puppet when he could be the puppet master instead?"

"I don't understand Sir."

"Who takes the biggest risk in this situation?"

"The boys Sir, if they got caught…"

"Exactly! This old fellow is nowhere near the crime, yet he reaps the rewards does he not?"

"The boys give him all they steal."

"But why do the boys keep doing it then?"

Jeremiah had sighed and drummed his fingers on the top of the desk, something he often did subconsciously when thinking. "Because they have nowhere else to go. He offers them some security and the fear of losing that is what makes them take the risk."

"Good. So of course, he doesn't go out robbing himself, he would never get his hands dirty when he can get someone else to do it. There are always people in this world Jeremiah that will control others, get them to take the risk and take the blame all for some promise or other whether it is a promise of wealth, of standing, or simply a roof over their head. But the rewards rarely outweigh the gains, not for the puppet. The puppeteer always wins."

It hadn't been long after that that Master Brown had left. When he had spoken, he had had an intensity in his stare he had not seen before. Perhaps he had been trying to tell him something.

"You would have an enormous amount of power." The High Intelligence dragged him out of his memories.

"And in turn, so would the masters."

"Yes." The High Intelligence nodded and started pacing round the room again. "They would have all the knowledge they desire through you."

"You have talked to Master Red?"

The figure before him flickered. Master Brown's friendly countenance was replaced by the foreboding figure of Master Red. Jeremiah took a step back before The High Intelligence reverted to Master Brown. "We have. Many of your years ago."

"Many years?" Jeremiah's gaze drifted towards the spot on the floor where in his plane, Austin had died. He thought for a second he could even see the blood. "A boy died this evening trying to prove himself. I'm not sure they would have stepped in if I hadn't sent that creature back through the portal either. How many times have they done this? How many boys have died?"

The High Intelligence paused, looking over the glasses that were perched on the end of his nose. It had managed to replicate a perfect likeness from his memories. "Quite." He clasped his hands behind his back.

"Do you know why they want the knowledge?"

"Interesting question. Why do you ask?"

"I," he paused, his thoughts were so jumbled he wasn't even sure he knew what he meant.

"Let me ask a different question. Do you want to unlock the secrets of the universe?"

"Yes."

"Do you want to master aether and use it in ways that would transform your world?"

"Yes."

"So then why do you hesitate? I am offering you something beyond riches and gold, but it is a one-time only deal Jeremiah. You take the knowledge back to your masters or you do not. If you do not, no-one else may take your place. You were chosen."

Why was he hesitating? He would be the most powerful human on Earth. He could do anything. His mind ran wild with ideas. If he could already summon aether without the glove, could he learn to wield it more precisely? He could build engines that would power cities. He could revolutionise the world. People would not go hungry, not sleep in the freezing cold. But something still made him pause. What was it the High Intelligence had said? Take it back to your masters.

"You have an answer?"

He waited an age before giving the nod. "It is a very generous offer but no thank you."

The High Intelligence paused, his hands behind his back. "Your reason?"

"This may sound childish, for I am only thirteen, but I don't think the masters are very good men. I may want to change the world, but I fear they will hold it to ransom. I would become a weapon or a tool. Power should not be in the hands of such men."

The High Intelligence studied Jeremiah for a moment. "It seems they did choose wisely after all. Although they may not see it that way." He smiled.

"That's what you were hoping I'd say?" Jeremiah frowned.

A smile touched the corners of his mouth, making its moustache twitch. "Knowledge is better when learned rather than taken. You respect it. It should not be used as currency. Your kind is not ready for all of this yet. It would do you more harm than good."

A thought crossed his mind and he was already speaking before he knew it. "The Mayans spoke to you long ago, didn't they? And not long after their civilisation collapsed; no-one has figured out why."

"Is that so?" The High Intelligence sniffed avoiding Jeremiah's eye. "As we said, knowledge can be dangerous. Now, we should send you home Jeremiah."

"Oh." Fear gripped him. The High Intelligence cocked his head in question. "I'm not sure what the masters will do when I return without being their new scientific marvel."

"You feel the world would be better off without them?"

"Well, I wish them no harm but," he sighed.

"It is done."

"What? What it done?"

The High Intelligence smiled. "You will see Jeremiah Wilson. And we believe you will find your Master Brown in Oxford; in case you wish to ask him to return. He will agree."

Jeremiah felt the static build up around him again; the portal was opening up, but the High Intelligence had not said a word!

"Do not fear, you will still be able to experiment with aether. You will just learn at your own pace. Remember Jeremiah, a great man is not made great by the power he wields, but how he uses it." Jeremiah opened his mouth to speak but the world around him flashed bright blue. He screwed his eyes up and when he opened them, the light was ack to normal and the walls no longer cracked. The High Intelligence was gone. He was back and it hadn't hurt a bit, he had barely felt it! It took a few seconds for his excitement to calm and for him remember the masters. He spun round, still standing inside the arch. There was no-one else here! He stepped forward, worried his legs would not hold him but they held firm. Soon he found himself running over to the main door. It was bolted on the inside. The masters had locked the doors to the hall when they began the ceremony. Perhaps the door behind the arch, the one that led to the masters' quarters was open. He turned and ran across the open space his feet slapping against marble floor. That one was locked too. They had gone, without a trace.

Now he understood. The High Intelligence had said it, the world was better off without them. He had made them cease to exist, warped reality until they were no more. They had not been harmed or had pain inflicted on them at least but they were no more. The sheer preposterousness of the whole night's events suddenly hit Jeremiah with full force. He slumped to the floor and sat cross-legged.

Hours must have passed when the first sounds outside the doors began to build. Jeremiah was still staring into space, oblivious. Only when the fists started to pound was he shaken out of his reverie.

He opened the doors with a flourish and a gaggle of boys stood, wide eyed and silent. Fewer stood there now than when they had started the term. A wave a sadness washed over him, and anger too, the masters had thought of them as expendable.

"Where is Master Red? No-one came to wake us this morning." A smaller boy was the first to speak, fear written across his face.

"I'm afraid the masters left." A sea of blank faces stared back at him. "They have gone and won't come back." Confusion reigned, but no-one dared speak. Jeremiah could see the warring emotions on their faces, fear and trepidation mixed with hope. "Master Brown will be returning and then." Jeremiah grinned and held up his hand, summoning a trickle of aether to play between his fingertips. "We have much to learn."

Alex Minns is based in England and has worked in forensics, teaching, PR and been paid to wield custard flamethrowers. She writes sci-fi, fantasy and steampunk and can be currently found forcing her mother to listen as she tries to untangle the timelines of her time-travel steampunk novel. You can find her obsessively creating   blog   stories   and   micro-fiction   on https://lexikon.home.blog/ and on Twitter under @Lexikonical

Patrona

by Toshiya Kamei

"Hermana Carolina," Lupe mumbled under her breath as she stopped sweeping and crossed herself with a deep reverence typical of an elderly woman. Carolina suddenly remembered her nun's habit and blushed. A smoky saloon in a tiny backwater town was the last place one would expect to see a nun, albeit an allegedly lapsed one. Even though she was no longer with the order, wearing civilian clothes seemed inappropriate, even indecent. She couldn't leave her room in Old Lady Lopez's boarding house without the loose-fitting, drab habit that hid the curves of her body beneath folds of crude linen.

Carolina gave Lupe a slight nod as she passed. She gazed around and saw early birds at crooked wooden tables, constantly drunk and drinking, who arrived before the saloon filled with local ranch hands. In the corner, an unfamiliar young man with a laconic air sat alone, toying with his unlit cigarette. He was slim, slightly built, and despite his close-cropped hair hidden under a straw hat, seemed androgynous. A pencil-thin mustache grew above his haughty lip.

She glanced in his direction. He held her gaze for a few moments before looking away. The plywood floor squeaked under her boots. As she took a seat on a bar stool, a plump redhead with a rose tattoo on her neck behind the counter glanced up.

"Can I trouble you for a drink, Josefina?" Carolina nodded at her.

"Hermana Carolina. How nice to see you again. What brings you back so soon?" Josefina's beaming smile made Carolina wonder if she was flirting. She felt her heart racing as she tried to calm herself.

In return, Carolina tried to think of something clever to say, but everything that came into her head seemed trite or inappropriate. She almost blurted out, "I wanted to say hello." Instead, she avoided answering the question by smiling.

She told herself to proceed with caution. After all, love was too fraught with risk. If Carolina could be honest with herself, she had never stopped yearning for the Patrona. Their parting was still fresh and raw in her mind. The inevitability of it on a rainy April evening. How her heart shattered on the Patrona's icy marble floor.

"What can I get you?" Josefina asked, smiling back. Carolina couldn't help but notice how Josefina's breasts were lifted high by her corset.

"The usual."

Josefina set a shot in front of her. Carolina drained it in one gulp. The fiery liquor burned her throat, almost gagging her. She took off her veil and shook her hair loose. Her own musky scent wafted up her nose. Then she exhaled.

"What's on your mind?" Josefina asked.

"Have you seen this? It's pasted all over town." Carolina took out a crumpled ball of paper and smoothed it out on the counter. She breathed out again and read aloud: "Wanted: Sister Carolina Sandoval. Dead or alive. $500 Reward."

"What did you do this time?" Josefina asked with a teasing tone in her voice. "I would have thought you had learned your lesson—especially when you were accused of, or shall we say credited, with helping fugitive slaves escape north."

"Nothing." Carolina settled her gaze on the freckles dotting Josefina's chest. Catching her staring, Josefina blushed and cleared her throat with a cough. Ashamed, Carolina lowered her head.

"Nothing?"

"She will never forgive me for leaving her."

"The Patrona?"

Carolina nodded; her face contorted with sadness.

Months had passed since her breakup with the Patrona. Time had mercifully dulled the pain. Or so she had thought, until her former lover began to haunt her dreams, some of which were erotically tinged. Now the mere mention of the Patrona's name made her knees weak.

Her real name was Alejandra Quesada, and she was the daughter of Don Adelberto, a notorious cacique who had ruled the town with an iron fist for decades. A lot of blood had been shed to satisfy the whims of the elder Quesada. Naturally, the news of his untimely demise came to most townspeople as a relief.

"I see. It's both personal and business. It doesn't help that you're working to foil your ex's machinations." Josefina flashed a mischievous grin. "What on earth did you see in her?"

"I loved her in my own way, but it wasn't to her liking," Carolina said with a serious look on her face.

"What do you mean?"

"I told her love has nothing to do with sex. But she disagreed. She thought I was a prude."

"I don't think you're."

"She accused me of taking sex out of the equation. And I've come to hate myself for failing to meet her needs."

"I'm sorry to hear that."

143

"I joined the order partly because I didn't want to reckon with my own sexuality. But I was naive. Believe it or not, having outlived everyone else in the world somehow failed to give me special insight into matters of the heart. I thought prayers would keep my carnal thoughts at bay, but they didn't."

"Weren't you kicked out of the convent?"

"No. I left of my own accord. I can't stay in one place for long without raising suspicion, so I have to move every now and then. But I do admit that the mother superior caught me with my fellow novice."

"I don't envy your immortality. But what were you doing with another nun?" Josefina teased, causing Carolina's face to turn red.

"I relished life in the convent. Sisterhood and all that. Time passes slowly in the convent, but it doesn't bother me at all."

"Life is short. That's why it's precious," Josefina said. A sense of despair flooded Carolina, because she detected pity in Josefina's voice. "Sorry, I didn't mean to—"

"No, forget it." Carolina shook her head, sighed in half-feigned desperation, and placed her hand on Josefina's arm. She swallowed a mouthful of saliva and braced herself for rejection. Josefina didn't stir. Feeling a bit encouraged, Carolina pressed a little. The touch lingered and became a caress. The warm skin seemed to welcome her caress.

"I wanted the Patrona, but not in the way she wanted," Carolina added, shaking her head, as if to shoo away the thought. "She took it rather personally."

"That's too bad." Josefina flashed a sad smile.

"Besides, she wants the oil running under our feet. She figures I'm in her way."

"We already know that. What are you going to do about it?"

Carolina shrugged. When she leaned in closer, her cross swayed slightly. Josefina pulled away.

"Let me take a better look." Josefina grabbed the crude wanted flyer. "It certainly doesn't look like you."

"It doesn't matter. Everyone knows how I look."

"Right." Josefina put the flyer back on the counter. "Dead or alive?"

"Uh-huh."

"Doesn't the Patrona know you're an immortal? Thanks to your gift, horse thieves leave us alone now." Carolina closed her eyes. Her mind flashed back to the night the whole town confronted a pack of thieves. The head of the gang raised his shotgun and pulled the trigger to scare the townspeople. A stray bullet went into Carolina's chest, splashing blood on the deputy sheriff's face. The next thing she knew, she was lying in a pool of her own blood. The funny thing was that her wounds healed immediately and left no scars.

"I told her many times, but she wasn't convinced."

"I don't know what to tell you. You surely scared the bad guys away that night."

"I know."

"I'll tell you one thing, though. You're too reckless to my liking. You don't care whether you live or die, do you? Immortal or not, it doesn't give you license to disregard your own life. If you don't care about yourself, how can you expect others to care about you? My God, you infuriate me sometimes." Josefina pretended to grab Carolina's shoulders and shake her hard.

"Hit me with another one," Carolina said and sighed.

"I challenge you to a duel," a voice came from behind her. Carolina turned and saw the young man standing before her. She could see him tensing. His fists were clinched, and his shoulders heaved with each breath. She quirked a brow.

"Hey, stranger. That's not the way to introduce yourself. It's too bad your folks didn't teach you manners."

"Leave my family out of this." He glared at her. "I know who you are."

"I can hardly say the same thing about myself." Carolina wore a bemused smile. "What's your name?"

"Most people call me Kid. I'm a gunslinger."

"You don't say." Carolina looked him up and down and held her posture straight. When their eyes met, she saw the look of defiance on his face. "How come I've never heard of you? Never mind. Nice to meet you, Kid."

"Do you accept my challenge?" Kid raised voice almost to a falsetto.

"Do I have a choice? I suppose not."

"At the plaza, at high noon tomorrow. Do you accept?"

"Deal." Carolina reached out and shook his hand. As she did, she felt him shake a bit.

Kid pulled away and stepped back, his lips quivering. Then she watched Kid walk away.

Carolina finished her drink in one gulp.

"Okay, I'm leaving, too."

"Are you really?" Josefina frowned, apparently disappointed.

"Yes." Carolina said goodbye to Josefina as she put her hand on Josefina's arm and gave it a squeeze.

"Good luck tomorrow," Josefina said. "I don't know if I'll be there. I'm such a scaredy-cat. I wouldn't want to see anyone get hurt. But if you need anything, you know where to find me."

Carolina nodded. She handed Lupe a few coins and stepped outside.

In the distance, grey mountains with snow-patched summits spread across the cloudless sky and boxed in the town.

#

The following day dawned like any other. The sun eventually reached its zenith, indicating midday. Carolina lifted her hand to shield her eyes as the merciless sunlight scorched her black habit and made her head throb. It wasn't long before sweat ran down her spine and between her breasts.

When she arrived in the plaza, a small crowd had already gathered. She spotted the local priest, Padre Fernando, in his black robe. He, looking solemn as usual, wrung his hands together nervously and whispered to the town undertaker, who adjusted his tie and tugged on the brim of his hat. The aura of impending death permeated the air. There was no wind. Nothing stirred.

"I was beginning to think you weren't coming," Kid said, fidgeting impatiently with his revolver.

Carolina felt uncomfortable, and a wave of pity washed over her. She reached inside her black veil and wiped the sweat off her brow.

The earth shook with hoof beats and wagon wheels. Carolina spotted some familiar faces in the multitude. She brushed away a strand of dark hair that had fallen across her face.

"Where's your gun?" Kid asked, raising his voice.

"I don't use one." Carolina slowly raised her arms and opened her hands to show her palms.

"Stop kidding. I'm serious."

Kid held his revolver in his hands, cocked it, and aimed at Carolina.

"Stop it, Kid. You're not cut out to be a gunslinger."

"Shut up. Enough already," Kid spat out. He fought to steady his shaking hands and squeezed the trigger. White sparks flew from the muzzle.

Screams erupted among the bystanders. The burning sensation in her side told Carolina she had been shot. Pain ripped through her, and she rolled over. The smell of gunpowder stung her eyes, and tears welled up. She opened her mouth to roar, but no sound came out. She lay on the ground, her eyes closed. Everything went black, and the last thing she recalled was the Patrona's face.

A few minutes had passed. She opened her eyes and blinked a few times. None of the landscape looked familiar. Everything was upside down in her sight, and she discerned that she was lying under a hedge on a dusty road. Her vision slowly started to clear. She noticed a face looming close. She made outa rose. It was Josefina's.

"What are you doing here?" Carolina asked. "I thought you weren't coming. You should be getting your beauty sleep right now."

"I see that you're well enough to make fun of me." Josefina said, feigning anger. "That's a good sign, though," she added and squeezed Carolina's hand.

Carolina slowly stood. Her cross swayed and settled crooked on her chest. With a slight grimace, she dusted herself off. The crowd let out a slow, collective sigh of relief.

Carolina saw Kid approaching. He staggered and almost tripped over himself, barely managing to stay on his feet. Panic clouded his face. He brandished his revolver wildly and emptied its remaining shots. Screams erupted, followed by the stomp of rushing feet. In her periphery, she caught a glimpse of Josefina. Carolina dashed toward her and tackled her. Josefina let out a loud groan as she hit the ground harder than Carolina had intended. But at least she was out of harm's way.

A bullet grazed Carolina's shoulder, tearing fabric and ripping skin. The impact knocked her off her feet, but the pain prevented from crying out. Someone knelt beside her and placed an ear next to her chest. A warm hand grabbed her wrist and checked her pulse. Carolina thought of Alejandra.

A few minutes later, she woke to the sound of a barking dog. As she stood, she felt lightheaded. She steadied herself and took a step forward.

"It's no use," Carolina warned and stepped closer. "Bullets can't kill me."

Kid dropped his revolver and cowered.

"Don't worry, Kid. I have no intention of hurting you."

"Are you some kind of monster?" he asked in a trembling voice.

"No. I'm an immortal. Sorry, Kid. You can't kill me."

"What do you want?"

"Why did you want a duel?" Carolina asked, ignoring his question. "The reward?"

Kid nodded.

"Why?"

"I need money for my operation. I have my chest bound, but it's very painful. I'm sick of it."

"Sorry to hear that." Carolina pictured his chest wrapped in bandages, but then she felt guilty for being voyeuristic. "Take me to the Patrona. You can collect your reward."

"Excuse me?"

"You heard me."

"Much obliged, ma'am." Kid touched the brim of his hat and tipped it.

"Don't mention it." Carolina waved off his thanks. For a moment, a feeling akin to maternal affection stirred in her heart. She wondered if she was destined to be a mother someday. She immediately dismissed such a possibility.

Carolina heard someone cough. She turned around and saw Josefina standing with arms akimbo.

"I can't believe you're going back to her," Josefina said.

"It's not what you think."

"Then what is it?"

"I'm helping Kid."

"That sounds like an excuse to see her again. I thought you came courting me yesterday, but I was wrong."

"Josefina, listen." Carolina reached over and held Josefina's hand.

"No," Josefina said and pulled away. Her hand slipped from Carolina's grasp. Josefina turned and moved away. For a brief moment, Carolina thought of going after her, but there was something that pulled her back. It was the same thing that prevented her from starting anew. Josefina was right: Carolina was willing to do anything to see the Patrona again. She stood frozen, watching as Josefina turned a corner and disappeared.

"You're not hurt at all," Kid's said. Carolina turned and saw him staring at her, amazed.

"No, not really." She flashed a bitter smile.

"How come?"

"I was born this way."

"Oh, I didn't know that," he said. She smiled at how awkward he looked. "Do you mind if I smoke?"

"No. Go ahead."

Kid took out a cigarette, lit it, and took a deep puff. He flicked ash from his cigarette and stared at the tip. Another puff drifted upward. Carolina followed the spiral of blue smoke with her eyes. She remembered how the Patrona smoked her pipe in bed. Once, she offered it to Carolina. When Carolina took her first puff, she went into a violent coughing fit. The Patrona rubbed her back while tears clouded her vision.

"Sorry. Would you like one?" Kid's words broke her reverie.

"No thanks." She shook her head.

#

Carolina climbed into a carriage, followed by Kid. She whipped the horses, and they set off toward the Patrona's house on the outskirts of town. As the carriage sped along the dusty main road, the wind felt refreshing on her face, and its noise saved her from making any more awkward small talk.

Fifteen minutes later, a familiar structure came into view—a two-story white-columned estate dotted with green hedges and long-standing trees. A cream-colored gazebo stood on the edge of the property. A snaking dirt path led toward the mansion.

They dismounted from the carriage and walked toward the house. When they reached the tall, heavy door, Kid shot Carolina a glance tinged with apprehension. When he extended a hand and knocked softly, an ancient-looking butler answered the door. Carolina remembered he had been with the Patrona's family for a few generations. Taciturn as ever, he acted as if he didn't recognize her. The butler looked at Kid suspiciously for a moment or two.

"What do you want? The Patrona is a busy woman," the butler mumbled in a tone that belied annoyance.

"I've got something for her," Kid said, pointing his chin toward Carolina. "I'm sure she'll be pleased."

When they stepped inside, the scent of marigolds wafted over Carolina. She knew there were dozens of bouquets on the foyer table, and that each flower came from the back garden. They were the Patrona's favorite.

With light, elegant steps, the Patrona glided down the stairs, one hand sliding along the banister rail. A draft blew through the foyer, making the flowers on the table sway. She knew she was beautiful and flaunted it. Her red dress with a sparkling marigold pattern lit up the already sunny hall. Her form-fitting bodice accentuated her curves and swells and revealed her shoulders. Carolina suspected she had sold her soul to the devil in return for her beauty. Hers was a kind that could charm anyone and make them bend to her will.

The Patrona nodded to acknowledge Carolina's presence. As the distance between them shortened, Carolina's heart ached at the memories—the perfume of the Patrona's hair, the caress of her cheek against hers, and the way Carolina's heart raced when the Patrona walked into a room. Carolina struggled to keep her knees from buckling under her.

"Well done, young man," the Patrona said, bowing in a theatrical manner. "Mission accomplished. I'm impressed." She laughed and clapped her hands.

Carolina watched Kid's face light up with excitement.

"Tell me your name," the Patrona said. Her voice echoed in the foyer.

"Kid, ma'am." He blushed lightly and tipped his hat.

"Kid. Would you like to work here?"

"Yes, of course. I'm at your service, ma'am," Kid said, sounding like a giddy schoolboy. He seemed quite smitten by the Patrona. No one was safe from the reach of her enchantments.

"In the meantime, see my butler for your reward," the Patrona said and waved Kid off. He scurried away to collect his money.

"Let's talk in the gazebo," the Patrona suggested and stepped outside. Carolina followed close behind. The Patrona headed toward a bench in the center of the structure. She sat and gestured for Carolina to sit next to her.

"Just like old times," the Patrona mumbled and cast her gaze afar as if to recall the past.

Carolina felt a soft breeze caressing her cheeks. She fought off the urge to reach out to the Patrona and call her by her name.

"How have you been, Caro?"

"I've been well. Thank you for asking, Patrona." Carolina gave a slight nod and faint smile.

"I'm offended you call me that. It's like me calling you 'Hermana' or 'Sister.' No one calls me by my name." A look of hurt flashed in her eyes, and Carolina regretted her own sarcasm.

"After my parents died, you were the only one who called me by my name," the Patrona continued. "I miss that. I miss the sound of my own name on your lips."

Taken aback by her frankness, Carolina fell silent. She looked around to gather her composure. She realized the Patrona's mere presence made her heart pound faster. She resisted her own desire to surrender herself to the Patrona. Again, and forever.

Carolina inhaled, ready to say something. Before she could, the Patrona rang a small silver bell. A delicate chime sounded, causing her mind to travel back to her blissful days with the Patrona. Carolina imagined the Patrona's arms wrapped around her as warmness spread throughout her body.

The sound of soft, shuffling steps interrupted her daydreaming. A maid in a billowing grey skirt appeared, carrying a lacquered tray with two glasses and a jug full to the brim with an opaque yellow liquid. Carolina remembered the Patrona liked her lemonade with a good amount of vodka. Ice cubes clinked as the maid poured their drinks. The Patrona nodded her thanks, and the maid slipped back into the house. The glass felt cool in Carolina's hand. She held her drink in front of her, and the Patrona's face warped through the glass. A wave of nausea flushed through her body.

"Do you realize how lonely it is at the top?" the Patrona asked. "Everyone wants something from me. Yet everyone is afraid of me."

"That's too bad, but I can't honestly blame them. You frighten me." Carolina was the first to break her gaze, as if frightened. That was a bit of projection on her part. She was fully aware of her own monstrosity.

"Besides," Carolina continued, "you're not the only one feeling lonely. As they say, lonely people attract other lonely people. Look at us." She thought they were a pair of monsters.

Carolina felt the lump in her throat growing as she struggled to keep herself together. Somehow, she managed a smile and a shrug.

The Patrona remained silent.

"After you took over your family business, you changed. You became as ruthless as your father."

"I had to," the Patrona said, after a pause. "I had no choice. It's a dog-eat-dog world, after all. I thought you understood that."

"Sorry, no." Carolina clutched her cross to her chest.

"We could rule the town together. They say oil is the future."

"With all due respect, I disagree. Oil contaminates." Carolina pictured the oil gushing out of the ground. The viscous liquid lashed against everything around her as a gale carried the spray from the gusher, tainting her once-pristine veil. The phantom odor of oil made her gag.

"Oil killed your father," Carolina blurted out and immediately regretted it.

"It was an unfortunate accident. But I must carry out the promise I made to him on his deathbed."

Carolina fell silent and watched the bumblebees buzzing around. Songbirds chirped in the trees nearby.

"I'd rather have you as a friend than an enemy," the Patrona continued. "Why don't you join me?"

"You know I can't. The townspeople depend on my protection."

"We can't have two Patronas in the same town."

"I know that."

"I can't change your mind, can I?" The Patrona sighed and finished her drink. Without waiting for a reply, she stood up.

Carolina smiled weakly and shook her head.

"Let us part as friends today, Caro. We'll go back to being enemies tomorrow."

"All right then. Goodbye, Alejandra." Carolina nodded, feeling her heart sink. The Patrona turned and walked back toward her house. Carolina followed the retreating figure with her eyes, knowing Alejandra wouldn't turn back, but hoping against hope that she would. In her mind's eye, the two of them set off in opposite directions, drifting further apart from one another.

Toshiya Kamei is a fiction writer whose short stories have appeared in such places as *Bending Genres*, *New World Writing*, and *SmokeLong en Español*, as well as the anthologies *Daily Flights of Fantasy* and *Enchanted Entrapments*.

The Hibernating Wife

by Ioanna Papadopoulou

The winter mornings were always the most beautiful ones despite Anastasis's loneliness. He strolled through the estate garden, watching all the sleeping creatures, wishing he wasn't the only one awake, and his wife was there to appreciate the sky with him. He reached the gate and headed to the lake outside the Manor's grounds. He wanted to visit it before the snow rose so high and forbade the journey. He hiked down to the lake. He exhaled into his hands to warm them and then picked up one of the purple pebbles and flung it across the icy water. He continued walking until he arrived at the small bench, he had built years ago. He sat on it, crossing his legs, and took out of his pocket his mother's mirror. He rubbed his thumb against the metallic surface, finding her initials. He turned it towards the sun, until the light filled the reflective facet. It absorbed the sun's power and the mirror transformed into a screen, showing him Evangelle.

The man he loved was eating breakfast, dressed for his morning walk, and lazily scanned the paper. Ever since Evangelle had retired, it was easier to watch him. Before, when he was a teacher, he was consumed by his work during winter, when Anastasis had the least work due to his wife's hibernation. Evangelle twitched and looked around as if he knew that someone was watching him. His eyes lingered, staring right into Anastasis's, but failing to see anything.

A croak snapped Anastasis's attention. He saw a rabbit like creature ran across him. Its fur had changed into a silver white colour from the yellow orange one it was the rest of the year. It was the only magical species that didn't hibernate, the only one at the estate at least.

He put the mirror back into his pocket and stood up to stretch his legs, resume his walk and return to the estate. He went past all the sleeping creatures in the garden and entered the manor. Inside it, Anastasis hang his coat and then walked to the apartment he shared with his wife. He opened her bedroom door and entered the dark room.

His wife didn't simply sleep but lay still and un-breathing on her bed, completely covered by a white sheet. Each winter, when he saw her like that, he remembered his grandmother's funeral. Her coffin was placed in the middle of the living room, also covered with a white cloth that reached the floor. He had the irrational fear his wife would rise as a ghost under the sheet, like he had nightmares of his grandmother as a boy.

He approached the bed and watched her, trying to find any sign of life and wanting to pull the cloth away. Decades ago, he had dared to touch it and she had woken up with scars all over her body. Even then, she wasn't angry with him, only looked at him in kindness and understanding.

He checked there was nothing out of place in the room before leaving. Once inside his bedroom, he took his shoes and clothes off, throwing them on the floor. He sat in his armchair, watching the sun, the wide horizon and all the colours of magic that vibrated beyond the estate.

The next day, Anastasis visited his wife again, checking that there was nothing out of place and then he began his walk around the garden. He pondered whether he wanted to go to the lake and watch Evangelle when he heard snapping wood. It echoed all over the estate and he watched as all the sleeping creatures stirred, their bodies twitched but none woke.

"Help me," a low but high-pitched voice was heard. Anastasis walked in circles trying to locate it. "Here," he heard, "Help, please," he spotted, under a leafless tree, a tiny animal. He approached and saw a ferret-like creature.

"Who are you?" he asked and dared to touch it with his finger.

"So cold, please keep me warm. Keep me close," the Ferret creature begged and Anastasis picked it up in his hands.

The creature curled in his embrace and Anastasis held it under the tree. He knew little about the world he resided in, only the estate, even though he had lived there since he was twenty. He wasn't sure if the creature was dangerous but watching it rest in peace eased his winter loneliness. He looked up at the sky. More snow fell onto the estate.

It wasn't the same kind that fell in his home world. It shone like diamonds and was more silver than white, reminding him of one of his mother's dresses which she wore when she went dancing. Anastasis lowered his face and breathed out slowly. Hot air left his mouth and the creature sighed in pleasure.

"You are a kind man," the Ferret murmured. "I am glad you found me. Are you her husband?"

He nodded. "Anastasis," he introduced himself.

It was past midday when it awoke. It turned over, showing him its belly and opened its eyes. "Anastasis," it spoke his name and smiled. "You kept me safe and warm, thank you." It jumped off his embrace and turned to look at the manor. "You must help me, please. I need to see the Maiden."

"My wife is sleeping. It is winter. She is never awake during winter," he explained, and the Ferret let out an annoyed grunt.

"But I *must* see her. I came all this way to find her."

Anastasis studied the little creature and crossed his arms. "Why?"

"Because she stole something of mine," the Ferret said. "I want it back."

His eyebrows rose in confusion at the accusation. "I don't know much of her affairs," he admitted. "You can wait until the winter passes to speak to her though."

The Ferret hissed in response. It climbed on him until they were eye to eye. "I don't have that much time. You need to wake her. Or let me get inside the house and search for my missing treasure."

Anastasis stayed silent. He wasn't allowed any guests in the house. He wasn't sure if the creature was a danger or not. He stood up and the small animal jumped off him, landing on the ground. "I can't help you."

The Ferret let out a growl. "You are just like all the other husbands," it said. Its words surprised him, and he turned to face the animal.

"You met the previous husbands?"

The Ferret turned its head at him and nodded.

"Why don't you come when it isn't winter then? You must already know that she will be sleeping during the cold season."

The Ferret laughed. "I can only come here when she is asleep, and most of the time, she puts traps for me. But this time, I must succeed. I am running out of time. Be different than the others, Anastasis. Help me!"

He shook his head. "I can't betray her. She is my wife and asked me to care for her and the estate while she is asleep."

The Ferret started to cry, a high-pitched shrieking sound, that hurt his ears. He walked away, entered the manor, locking the door behind him. He walked into his wife's room, towards her bed and watched her sleep, under the white sheet. He itched to pull it off her. To shake her awake and ask why she hadn't told him of the Ferret. Surely, one of her previous husbands would have told her of its visits and yet, she never gave him any advice about it. "Can you hear me?" he asked.

He didn't dare to speak aloud but it wasn't fear that stopped him. It was habit and care. He cared for her, loved her even, but not like Evangelle. Instead he loved his sleeping wife more like one loves a child and a parent. It was perplexing to simultaneously feel and expect her to take all his troubles away but still consider her frail and fragile like a newborn.

"Who is the Ferret? Why is it here and what have you taken?" His wife continued her dead slumber, unmoving and unbreathing. This was a problem she wasn't going to help him with. He gave up and returned to his room. He approached the window and to his horror he saw the Ferret had climbed onto his balcony.

"Please, Anastasis. Let me in and I will find my treasure," it begged him.

He approached the glass and looked at the small creature. "I can't. She has specifically told me that no one but me is to enter or leave the manor during winter. It must all stay as it is."

"You don't always have to do as she wants. You can be braver than the rest. You are braver than them because you still visit your old love. They didn't dare to do that."

Anastasis wasn't sure how the creature knew of his visits to the lake and his secret with the mirror but after five decades in his wife's world, he had stopped worrying over what made sense to him. He wondered if it had been watching him, if finding it had been part of a ploy. He shook his head at it, suddenly terrified that it wasn't a simple animal but a winter monster. He grabbed the curtain and pulled it over the balcony door. He rushed to do the same with his windows, trapping himself in darkness. He sat in his armchair and brought his legs up towards his chest, as he did when he was a boy, hiding his face against his knees.

The Ferret scratched onto the glass, making a cringing sound which hurt his ears No matter how hard he pressed his hands against them, the scratching sound still reached them.

"Please, Anastasis! Please!" The Ferret begged and Anastasis momentarily considered it. But he remembered his mother always said that marriage was a special thing in the world. She didn't mean the marriage he and the Maiden had but Anastasis still upheld her values. "It will only be a moment. She probably wouldn't even know that I found it."

The Ferret kept whimpering and begging all night. The sound of scratching didn't stop. He tried to sleep, to hide under the pillow, but the terrible noise didn't let him. He dashed out his bed when it was nearly sunrise and went to his wife's room. The moment he shut her door, there was quiet. He closed his eyes in relief and sank to the floor. He didn't bare to stay with his wife for more than half an hour, deciding that the annoying sound was better than the death that reigned around her.

He was trapped inside the manor. He was trapped between the two rooms as he didn't like walking alone in the house, when everyone was asleep. It was a magical place as well, a wonderland within a wonder world and Anastasis had no understanding of it. Anastasis wanted to curse under his breath, as he did his last night in his home world. He wanted to pull his hair, whatever was left of it, and scream in frustration. He was trapped and it wasn't the first time. That feeling had brought him to the Maiden's estate, making him her husband. He wondered where else that restless feeling of being caged would lead him.

Refusing to be like a leaf that the world moves about, Anastasis exited his wife's room and returned to his own. The sound was still there. "You are back, Anastasis! I knew you were braver than the rest of her husbands!" it exclaimed. The mention of the previous husbands had interested him the first times, but it now irritated him. He went towards the balcony and drew the curtains open.

He let out a shriek. The Ferret had grown during the night. It was as big as a dog, reaching above his knee. "What are you? Who are you?" he asked it.

"Let me in, Anastasis!" the creature begged instead of answering him. It lifted its one paw, with large claw like nails coming out of it, and pressed it against the glass. The sound was terrible and Anastasis saw the glass repair itself, screaming itself back out the same sound as it undid the damage. He was reminded how unfit he was to reside in the estate. Its healing practices hurt him as much as its damage.

He shut his eyes and breathed in deeply. "Please don't do that again," he said as he heard the Ferret place its paw against the glass again. He inhaled and exhaled three times and then dared to look at it again. "What is your treasure?" he asked the Ferret. "I can't let you in, but maybe I can search for it."

The Ferret stayed still. "So much braver than all the rest. How did you end up here, Anastasis? This is not the place for men like you. Only the weak of heart and mind come here."

Anastasis shrugged. He had never learnt why he arrived in the estate. He simply had and was given his title as the Maiden's new husband. He had protested, tried to convince her to expel him but whenever he saw her understanding, his resolve weakened, until he felt that there was no reason to go. Especially, when he discovered that he could watch Evangelle. "What are you looking for?" he asked again.

The Ferret shook its head. "I cannot tell you. You need to let me in."

"I can't do that. I told you," Anastasis said.

The Ferret looked at him sadly and then lifted its paw and scratched the glass again. Anastasis watched the glass fix itself, spitting the sound back and the Ferret repeated the act. It stared into his eye. It looked remorseful but there was something in the corner of its gaze that made Anastasis hate it. It knew the pain it caused him. It had him trapped inside the manor, trapped against the terrible sound. He closed the curtain and covered his head again, trying to push the sound away. It never stopped. It was even worse, as the Ferret was bigger and scratched deeper and longer.

He wanted to bang against the glass himself. To make a sound equally terrible and scare the Ferret. He was afraid though. He had always been afraid because he understood so little of the world he had lived in most of his life.

"Stop this," he shouted. "I am leaving, you stupid beast. Your sound can't reach me in her bedroom," he said and stamped his way out.

"You will come back. None of you can ever be with her for long. None of you understand her. Not when she is like that," the Ferret mocked him.

He slammed the door behind him, completely uncaring if he woke his wife. The moment he entered her room, he was enveloped in deathly silence. Like the terrible sound, it made his entire body cringe. He approached her bed and sat on its edge.

She lay there, unbreathing and un-real. "What can I do?" he asked her advice. He didn't expect a response, but he was saddened and deeply disappointed that she didn't offer him anything. "Come on! Do something! Give me a sign, even if you can't wake up."

He leaned against the wood panel of the bed. The silence ate him, but he forced himself to stay, focusing his eyes anywhere but the dead-like creature on the bed. Whenever his eyes wondered to her, the image of his grandmother as a ghost from his childish dreams popped and his whole body tensed.

The silence that made him hear his own heartbeat, feel it pulse in all over his chest, or the noise that made him want to tear his ears off? It was unfair these were the only two options he was left with in the world. He hated the Ferret because it knew the pain it caused him. He had seen the understanding in its eyes. He hated his wife for not waking and hiding that there was such a danger during winter. The more he thought about it, the angrier he grew. He leaned further and his hand accidentally landed on top of his wife's leg. He turned to it scared and stayed still.

She took a breath, a deep breath. Anastasis's eyes widened and he slowly moved his hand away from her. As he lifted his hand, there was a black handprint on the white sheet. It was a stain that would betray he had disrupted her. He jumped away, tripping over his own feet and falling with a loud thump on the floor. It was bare of carpets and the collision with the cold wood sent a pang of pain through his hip. His eyes went again towards his wife, who, to his horror, breathed a second time.

"Oh my God," he gasped and was back on his feet. He held his own breath, trying not to make sound and dreading a third inhalation. He dimly remembered her telling him that magic worked in threes. If she took a third breath, she was going to keep breathing and wake up, or something else magical would happen.

He curled his toes in fearful anticipation and waited for what felt like hours, until he couldn't take it anymore and let the air out. He slowly relaxed as she remained still and breathless. He retreated towards the door. He opened it slowly, his eyes still focused on his wife, afraid that at the last minute she was going to breathe again.

Outside her room, the sound had grown even louder. Anastasis went back inside his room, determined to face the Ferret. He was the lord of the manor. He was the Maiden's husband and while she was hibernating, the estate was his.

He gathered his courage to pull the curtain, bang his hands against the glass and order the Ferret away. He didn't believe that it had met the previous husbands or that his wife kept it away from the estate while she was awake. The Maiden was cool and unemotional, but she wasn't cruel. Throughout his life with her, Anastasis had never seen her refuse refuge to any creature. She had never turned anyone away, nor forced them to stay when they wanted to go.

When he pulled the curtain, he faced a giant eye. During his visit to his wife's room, the Ferret had grown so large that its head was too big to even fit inside the Manor. It supported its body onto his balcony and still scratched the glass, completely wrecking it. "Stop it!" Anastasis yelled. He put his face against the glass and directly looked the Ferret's large eye.

"You need to wake her, Anastasis," the Ferret said. It moved away from the balcony but as it did, it broke off. The Ferret moved around and Anastasis saw that many of the other hibernating magical creatures were writhing and twitching in the garden and there was heavy and thick snow falling. It shone like the whole atmosphere was filled with diamonds. "There is no other choice for me or you now. She needs to wake up and face me. Give me back what she has stolen."

"No," Anastasis refused. He pulled the curtains closed again. "No. No. No," he repeated but he still found himself walking out his room and standing in front of the Maiden's closed door. The sound at the glass began again. It still hurt his ears but, despite the huge size of the Ferret, Anastasis felt that it had reached the limit of its terribleness. The Ferret could grow as big as a mountain, but it couldn't scratch the glass more. It was possible that the bigger it grew, the harder it would eventually be to claw it. "Go back," he told himself. "Even at this size, it must not be able to break in. If it could, it would already try to do that."

There was a sudden change to the sound. It changed beats, becoming not louder but multiple. "You fucker," he muttered and covered his ears again. He stood in between his bedroom and his wife's, unable to decide which of them was worse. His ears screamed in pain; his eardrum pushed inside his ear as if it wanted to tear itself out of him to escape.

He was afraid of the Maiden drawing a third breath, but he felt his entire body shake and shriek itself at the sound of the glass. He momentarily looked at the hall that led to the rest of the manor, a place he never felt comfortable to explore. He wondered if the sound would manage to reach further inside it. All he knew was the way from the room to the exit door and back. He was about to walk there and hope that he would be safe behind it, when he felt the entire building shake. He looked up and saw dust falling off the ceiling.

The sound of the glass stopped. There was another loud shake and more dust fell and the ceiling cracked. The Ferret was trying to tear the manor down. Without thinking much, Anastasis dashed into his wife's room, completely uncaring if he woke up. He rushed to her side, flung the sheet off her, and waited for something to happen.

"Come on," he said. He remembered that in his world, hibernating creatures woke if they sensed danger. "Danger! Danger!" he yelled at her. She remained lying with her eyes closed. Her white hair was sprawled over her pillow and her hands were firmly set at her sides. "Wake up! I can't do this on my own! I need you!" he called her.

He moved his hand to touch her face and then paused as he saw her skin changing to purple – black around her neck. Then her hair shed off.

There was another shake. Her bedroom wasn't affected but he saw through the opened door that large pieces of the ceiling drop in the hall. He went to the window and pulled the curtains open, letting light in. The Ferret was nowhere to be seen outside but the world was changing. The snow fell madly and Anastasis saw the other hibernating creatures were different. Instead of sleeping peacefully as they did the last time, he had been outside, he saw dark-purple chain over their necks. The shackles joined and climbed up to the Maiden's window, going magically through it without damage, and then reached his wife. He approached her again and in the clearer light, he saw what he had thought was her skin changing colour was actually a neckband around her neck. "What's happening?" Anastasis asked and instinctively ran his hand through his own neck and hands. He was the only one not bound. He put his arms under her body and tried to lift her but as he did that, bonds formed around her ankles and wrists trapping her to the bed.

The manor was falling apart. Everything he knew, as little and faintly as he did, was destroyed. He sat by her side, terrified to act. He started shaking her entire body. "Wake up! Wake up!" he screamed at her but to no avail. "You need to wake up and help me. I don't know what to do. The whole world is falling apart. Nothing makes sense. Wake up!" he begged her, but the Maiden remained still.

"Anastasis!" the Ferret's voice was heard. He pressed his hands to block the sound, but it was useless. It was as if the sound was able to push through the matter of his own flesh, like the window glass was pierced without breaking from the chain. The sound seemed to be coming above him. He would run out of the door and give a piece of his mind to the Ferret, telling him that he tried to wake his wife, but she wasn't having any of it.

He headed determined to the exit when he saw it was blocked by fallen pieces of ceiling. He turned to face the hall that lead deeper inside the manor, to all the places he didn't dare go to without a magical companion. He saw a different chain appear through the door, leading down the dark hall, deeper into the manor.

He was about to climb over the fallen pieces to reach the door, as that seemed the better plan, but he noticed, just barely, that the chain moved. It was tiny, just a small tug, but it means that Anastasis wasn't the only one awake. There was someone else. Someone that might help him evict the Ferret from their estate. He took a deep breath, calming his nerves, and followed the chain. He didn't manage to see anything as the entire space was enfolded into darkness, until he reached a door. When he opened it, he went into a circular stairwell, which was light by a moon.

"Is this another world?" he muttered. He took out of his pocket his mother's mirror and let the light fill it. A slow, faded picture appeared showing him Evangelle. He was wearing his pajamas and was safely tucked into bed. Anastasis wished for the first time in years to return to him, to be safe beside him. It changed to the Maiden, whose eyes had snapped open, but remained still and motionless. There was a new collar wrapped around her bold head.

The image was too discomforting. "Show me Evangelle again," he asked the mirror, but it kept showing him the Maiden. The chain, which lead him further down the stairwell, moved again and soft wind blew against him. The door closed from it and the moon started being covered as snow fell.

Anastasis put his mother's mirror back into his pocket. He walked down, holding onto the wall as the steps were icy from the snow. He was surprised he didn't slip. As he reached the last flight of stairs, he saw the world he arrived to, a graveyard with a round wooden building, like a mausoleum in the middle. The chain broke into many directions. One went inside the wooden structure while the others lead to each of the graves. He carefully walked down the rest of the steps and explored the odd graveyard world. Behind the first grave, he saw the form of a boy with an old man's face. The old man child lifted its head slightly and showed him a dead ferret in his hands.

Unable to keep looking at his face anymore, Anastasis departed. Behind every tombstone, he saw another child with an older person's face and a Ferret in their hands. The chain that led into the mausoleum moved and rushed to find the other awake creature but inside it there only was a large erected stone tomb. He approached it and saw the Maiden. She was bald and chained but her eyes were open and calm when she recognized his face.

"You woke up!" he said, relieved, and put his arms to free her. Her eyes widened in alarm and just before he touched the collar, he paused. "What do you want me to do?" he asked her. She moved her lips to speak but no sound came out. "I can't leave you here. You took me in. How can I leave you, trapped like that? The winter will pass, right?"

She shook her head and the chains moved because of it. Tears rolled down her face. Anastasis took his mother's glass, which always showed him what he needed. "I will be back," he promised her. He filled it with light and then, without looking at it, he went back inside. He pointed the surface at her and the captured moonlight fell on her. "It always shows me Evangelle. I have told you about him. When I need to, I can see him. What do you need? It will show it and then I can find it."

The Maiden's eyes moved to the mirror and more tears fell down. Anastasis didn't see what she did. He only saw her take a deep breath. Then she took a second and, finally, a third. The moment she managed to do that, the shackles broke, and she frantically pulled them off. "You are free!" he proclaimed. "There is a Ferret and it says you stole something."

She tried to speak but no sound came out. She stamped her foot annoyed and then, as if a thought occurred to her, grabbed Anastasis's hand and lead him up the staircase. All the old men children watched them leave and lifted the ferrets above their heads, saying something that he failed to understand. He followed her up. The manor was in ruins. It was the worst winter, Anastasis had ever experienced in the estate.

She ran to her bedroom and he followed, slower as his old body struggled with the constant exercise. When he entered the room, he saw the Maiden get up from the bed, taking off her chains again. He didn't understand who he had freed and who had been trapped in the bed, but the magical woman stood up and walked close to him. "Thank you, Anastasis," she said, and her voice was hers but also different. She left the room and headed for the exit. He did the same.

The harsh snowstorm outside had calmed. He studied the sky and realized that it hadn't simply calmed. The snow was frozen in space. It looked like diamonds stars all around them. "Finally, you woke up," the Ferret said. It had grown even larger and was curled on top of the manor's roof. Its face was on her and then its large eyes moved to look at Anastasis, who hid behind the Maiden. "How did you get here, Anastasis? This is no place for you. Tell me how you got here."

The Maiden turned to look at him. "I just woke up here," he answered. "I was sad and scared after Mother died. I had to hide who I was, and I wanted to sleep. Then I woke up here and I was her husband."

"With a coward? You chose to be the husband of a coward thief?" the Ferret growled. "Have you no shame to leave Evangelle behind like that? Was that how weak your love was?"

"She is awake! You won!" he yelled at the Ferret. "Will you stop torturing me?" Its eyes turned back to the Maiden.

"I want it back," the Ferret pleaded. "Please, I need it back. My treasure." The Ferret lowered its head as it spoke.

"You broke my house," the Maiden accused it. "It is in ruins."

"You took my treasure. And every time I came here, none of your husbands ever returned and I was trapped for years in a world where there was only snow. Each time I escaped I was weak and near dead. I had to travel all over the world until I found where your estate had moved to."

The Maiden lowered her head sadly. "I am very sorry, little Ferret. Our world is not fair. My other husbands are still inside. They are still waiting."

The Ferret in its anger kicked the manor. "I will not be fooled by you again. Give it back. I have been empty without it."

"You are so very angry, little Ferret, and so tired," his wife said and approached the Ferret. She lifted her hand and caressed its face. The creature moved away. "But I don't remember taking your treasure or even what it is."

"You don't remember me," the Ferret said and let out a tear. "You forgot me. So, you need to put everything back and free me."

"I don't understand. Have we met before? I was also trapped for so long, split in my own self and buried in a grave. All my other husbands were afraid to wake me and got trapped themselves. Only Anastasis woke me. So, tell me what your pain is, and I will try to help you."

The large creature let out a wail of sadness and despair. For the first time, Anastasis realized that he understood its pain. The treasure, the insistence to wake her up and the Ferret's slight animosity towards him, suddenly made sense.

"It is your heart," he said loudly, and both the Maiden and the Ferret turned to look at him. "You gave her your heart, out of love, and she forgot. You are one of the husbands, aren't you?" he asked. "You are the one that left, right? The one we are all brought here to replace."

The Maiden's face was lost in thought. She was trying to remember. Anastasis took out of his pocket his mother's mirror and let the light fill it again. Without looking at it, he offered it to his wife. "I think you forgot what you saw down there. Look again." She took the mirror from his hand but didn't look at it. "Don't be afraid," Anastasis said. "Our fears grow stronger, the more we avoid them. Look how weak you and I have become because of them. You ended up buried alive, cut in two. I ended up here settled only in watching Evangelle, instead of fighting to live with him."

His wife shook her head. "But what if I can't? What if it is too late?" She turned to look at the Ferret. "Are you really one of my husbands?"

"I am your only spouse," the Ferret answered. "Anastasis and the rest aren't your husbands, not in any real sense. You aren't their wife either, simply cohabiting isn't what makes a spouse." The Ferret turned to look at Anastasis and lowered its eyes. "Maybe he is. He freed you."

"I am not," Anastasis said. "Look, Maiden!"

She fought him, trapped in her fear and pain. Anastasis, feeling braver and surer than he ever did in his life, put his arms over her shoulders. "Look," he urged her. "Our mind always makes things worse than they truly are," he whispered and softly moved her head to look. He felt her tears and hugged her tightly. "Look," he said and didn't stop saying it. He knew how the word and pressure pained her. It was the same way the Ferret had pained him with the glass, but it was the only way. He wished someone had done that to him when he was still young and had the chance to try to properly love the man that made everything more real. He clasped her tight and he felt her wanting to fight him. "I will never stop until you look!" The Maiden fought him, elbowed him but despite the pain, Anastasis kept on holding her. "Look!" he demanded. "It will be the same thing that took your chains off the first time. Can't you see that until you face the truth, those chains over you will never go?" She snapped her eyes open, looking at her hands which again had the dark purple-black shackles. He took them in his, which were wrinkly and tired while hers were smooth and white, like china. Despite that, she was his eldest. She squeezed his hand and then turned to look in the mirror. To Anastasis, the mirror remained empty, but he knew that whatever the Maiden needed to face was there for her. She let out a cry and then her body gave way. Anastasis held her tightly until the Ferret moved its face towards them. It was only then that he left her go. Her body fell on the Ferret and it held her.

Its eyes filled with tears and its body quivered. Whatever the Ferret had been looking for was found. He felt a snowflake on his nose. It had started snowing again, the wind blew and the Ferret, as it wailed and wept, started getting smaller. It cried its way to its old size until it was as small as when Anastasis had first seen it. The Maiden took it in her arms and held it tightly. All the chains which burdened her broke off, fell and were lost under the snow.

The Ferret's eyes opened slightly, and it kept looking at Anastasis. "How can you still be here, Anastasis?" it whispered. "This is no place for someone like you."

The Maiden held the Ferret in her arms, cradling it as a babe and rocking it. The estate started repairing itself. The chains around the creatures vanished, although they didn't break. Whatever was holding them was something they still carried. By the time the Maiden was finished rocking the Ferret, his old balcony was restored in its place and it looked as if the entire affair with the giant Ferret never happened. The Maiden started walking inside the palace as the snow kept on falling, burring the estate under its white-silver glow.

Anastasis stood on his own and looked around the estate until he was too cold, and his joints hurt. He walked back inside the manor. Its interior was fixed as well. He walked to their apartment. He opened the door to her room and saw her lying in bed. The Ferret was nowhere to be seen. "I need to sleep," she said to him. "Will you cover me, one last time?" He picked up the fallen white sheet and slowly moved it over her body. His handprint was still there.

"Rest," he told her as he placed the sheet over her head. He walked around the room, examining that everything was as it ought to be, closed the curtains and then exited her room, closing the door behind him. He paused looking at his door and then at the dark hallway that he had trudged through earlier. He wondered if he could find those other husbands again and ask them what they were holding. He wanted to tell them that they could be saved as the Ferret was defeated. But he was so tired. He needed his safe place. He opened the door and entered his room. He nearly missed the small Ferret which was curled in his armchair. His mother's mirror was placed next to its face. "I will keep you company while she sleeps," the Ferret said.

Anastasis nodded. He took a pillow and placed it on the small table and the Ferret jumped on it. He picked up his mother's mirror, put it in his pocket and then sat in his chair. He and the Ferret rested in silence together, watching over the estate as it was enfolded into deep snow.

They spent the cold season going on walks together and watching over the estate. On the last day of winter, they visited the lake. "The winter mornings are the most beautiful. I always thought so."

The Ferret nodded. "They will all start waking up tomorrow," it said. "Are you ready for that?"

Anastasis pondered over the question and then he took the mirror out of his pocket and placed it into the Ferret's mouth. "I am going back," he announced. "The Maiden has you again and you are all she needs. You don't hibernate like the rest, so you can watch over the estate during winter."

The Ferret nodded. "I still don't understand how your ended up here, in this unreal place."

They had had that conversation many times. "It was a moment of weakness," Anastasis said to it. "And it lasted all my life. Or I got braver this winter than I was the previous seventy years of my life"

"Are you not afraid it might be too late?" the Ferret asked.

"What if it's not?" Anastasis walked to the bench and sat on it. The Ferret followed him and moved to sit on his lap. It held his mother's mirror in its mouth. "Isn't that what kept you trying? What if it was possible?" He sighed and looked again at the morning sky. "You keep the mirror. Someone else will need it more than me."

The Ferret placed its head on his lap. "You made it magical, Anastasis. I don't know if it will remain without you here."

He shrugged. "Whatever. I need to stop finding substitutes. I need to face the world as it really is. It is about time." He paused and then he turned to look at the Ferret which basked under the sun. He put his hand over its body and caressed it. "When she wakes up, leave this place. This isn't a home. It is a prison."

The Ferret shook its head. "She will never leave it. I did once, with that thought in mind and look what happened. I think she and I will need to free everyone. That is the only way for the estate to change."

"Yes," Anastasis said. "Perhaps you are right. I think I will sleep and see where I wake up again."

The Ferret hid under his hand as he closed his eyes and waited for sleep to take him, mentally whispering to himself that it didn't matter how long he had stayed with the Maiden. He caressed the Ferret until suddenly his hands went through air and he drifted to sleep, feeling for the first time ready to face the unknown, all his fear and all his anger settled in his heart, even though he knew they would never vanish.

Somewhere, far away, Anastasis heard the sound of chains breaking and he knew they were his own.

Ioanna Papadopoulou is a Greek author, currently residing in Glasgow. She studied Art History and Heritage Visualization and has worked in museums, libraries and community centres. She is currently on a Museum studies course and works in timetabling at higher education. She has been published at Hexagon Magazine, Idle Ink and Collective Realms, Nymphs, Piker Press and Far from the Farther Tree.

Twyla's Tapestry

by N. R. Williams

Assignment
Chapter 1

They called her gifted. That was why Master Ganelon had given her the tower of the old château. No one troubled her. The other indentured servants and laborers all occupied the lower rooms. Twyla hummed a tune as she threaded her bobbin and ran the instrument through the wrap thread of the tapestry, switching colors as she worked, tamping it down when she reached the end.

Tirelessly she labored. Her song spun into the tapestry. Her fingers nimbly wove the bobbins through the threads. The greens of the meadow in the picture took shape and thrived. Soon, the stone walls of her room vanished, and living trees stretched their limbs through the roof of her tower. Birds began to whistle the tune Twyla hummed as she spun them in the treetops. They flitted from limb to limb. A unicorn with its ivory horn stepped from the birchwood forest of Anora into the meadow. Flowers bloomed, and sweet scents filled Twyla with joy.

The tapestry reached the sky, where a full moon peeked from the edge of a cloud and stars twinkled. Twyla completed her work. She'd put the back on the tapestry tomorrow. She stood, still humming, no longer in her room but in the meadow. She twirled in the tall grass with abandon. The unicorn approached. Twyla plucked an apple from a tree and fed him, running long fingers along his neck, still humming.

"Do you know my father? He is an elf. His name is Arunne."

The unicorn gazed at her with deep blue eyes, and Twyla felt as if the depth of a lake swirled before her. "I know him," the unicorn's thought was as clear as if he spoke out loud.

"Does he reside here? In Anora of the Elves? Does he know of me?" Her heart thrummed in a staccato rhythm, waiting for an answer.

"Arunne is an elf, he lives in Anora, but your human mother kept you a secret from him."

A knock interrupted them. Twyla stopped humming, the birds stopped singing, and the unicorn shook his head. The knock intruded again.

"I must leave." Twyla turned.

"Come and play again," the unicorn said

"I will." Twyla lifted her hand and waved it before her as if erasing the meadow. The tall grass, trees, unicorn, and birds all vanished, now confined to the nearly finished tapestry she'd made.

She went to the door that led out of her tower room to the landing and staircase. She put her hand on the knob and paused. Then, leaning against the door, she listened. Her elfin hearing was sharp. Voices. A high-born lord, she guessed, though he had a lisp.

"There are rumor-th," he said. "That this half-elf ha-sth the power to put a cur...cur...sth on a man."

A chuckle. Twyla recognized Master Ganelon. "Half-elf she is, but a truer heart you'll never meet. A spell of charm she'll cast with her talent, not a curse."

"We have our swords should she try anything, Your Grace," said a third man. Twyla had heard this one before in the village. His gravely voice sent a chill through her as she recalled his threat. Lucien Asselin. Once, he had pressed his sword against her throat and demanded she sing and dance for him in the streets of Lanteglos.

She opened the door to find four men. Master Ganelon wore his usual brown pants and cotton shirt. His well-trimmed beard hid his double chin. She surmised that the other three were noblemen because of their fine silk shirts and woolen pants nestled snug into knee-high boots.

Twyla curtsied and stepped aside to admit the four men. The three noblemen sauntered in and stood near her worktable in the center of the room, looking around at her nine tapestry looms and the small round table where she ate next to the wood-burning stove.

"Twyla." Master Ganelon took her arm and led her to the worktable opposite the noblemen. "Let me introduce His Grace, the Duke of Cuvillier, Jean-François. Their Lordships Jacques Longchambon and Lucien Asselin. Your Grace, My Lords, this is Twyla."

"Thi..th must be the one you were working on," Cuvillier said. He walked to the unicorn tapestry and touched it. "The for-es-th filled the tower steps." He turned back toward her. "Twyla, are you tru-wy half-elf as men claim?"

"Oui, Your Grace." Twyla pulled her hair away and showed the men her pointed ears, then raised her bangs to reveal her eyebrows that lifted high on her forehead.

"You alter the countryside whenever you craft a tapestry," Lucien Asselin said.

A shiver passed through Twyla, warning, but of what?

"Many of our friends also boast one or more of your inspired works. They come alive when you look at them. Like that one." Jacques Longchambon pointed. The unicorn lifted his head as he ate, gazing out at them. "Amazing." His voice was deeper and carried the twang of the east coast of Gil-Lael. Ganelon's factory, an old château, was situated mid-way between the Capital City of Terrel and the harbors in the east.

"What can I do for you, Your Grace?" Twyla asked as the duke turned toward her. He had a prominent nose and a mustache that was curled on the end. His chocolate hair was streaked with gray.

"I would like to present one of your tapestries as a gift to the king."

"To the king?" Twyla felt a surge of delight tingle in her stomach. What an honor. "What do you wish this tapestry to look like?"

"I am sending the king ten thousand of my trained men as new soldiers for his army."

"Ten thousand soldiers." Her excitement fled as anxiety spread within her.

Jean-François smiled. "Oui, a fine gift, don't you agree? I would like the tapes-th-ry to show myself, my friend-th here, and our men outside Château de Talaith. I should be standing on the royal porch adder-th-ing the men."

"And the king, where will he be?"

"Oh, somewhere inside, I suppose." Jean-François moved to join his friends.

Twyla frowned and glanced at Ganelon. If she made such a tapestry, it would come true. Did the duke know this? "Forgive," she said. "But I don't see how this will honor the king."

Master Ganelon glared at her. "Mind your place."

182

Twyla held her cheek and looked away from Ganelon. Now, the sense of dread made her nauseated. She took out paper and a pencil from a drawer in her worktable. "I must capture your likeness and that of your friends if I am to add you to the tapestry."

She glanced at each of them in turn and drew. Once she had their likeness, she took more paper and sketched Château de Talaith, having seen a painting of it many times. Adding the grand entrance and its massive staircase that curved around from either side to a porch, the stairs continued from the platform to the tall carved front doors above. As she drew, the men wandered around her workroom. Again, she glanced at them as Ganelon explained the process of creating a tapestry and the choice of backing that would finish it off.

Twyla frowned as she added the figure of Jean-François Cuvillier standing on the porch, looking away from the château with his two friends behind him. Next, she created a simple outline of Cuvillier's men gazing at him. The famous tree fountain was placed toward the bottom of the picture, the king's orchard along the side, and flowerbeds before the stairs. The drawing took Twyla less than an hour.

When it was done, she held up her drawing for Cuvillier's inspection. Twyla said. "Do you wish the soldiers to be dressed in the official uniforms of Gil-Lael or something else?"

"Marvelou-th," He said. "The soldier-th should be dress-th in my color. I'll have a uniform brought over."

"How soon does Your Grace require the tapestry to be done?" Twyla's shoulders hurt as if someone were sitting on them. She didn't like this. Her instincts shouted at her, trap.

"Ten months, I leave for Château de Talaith soon afterward."

When the men left, Twyla moved to the large window and gazed down at the courtyard. How could Ganelon approve such a thing? Didn't he see the danger? When next he came to her room, she would ask him.

Twyla wasn't one to spend time in hesitant worry. From her window, she watched the noblemen depart. Then she packed a small bag with yarn and bobbins and tucked a small loom under her arm. The tower had a back door on the ground floor that led outside and a second door that led into the hall and the rest of the old building.

Twyla went down the stairs, out the back, past the stables where the horses nickered at her, and headed west toward a lake through the forest. She knew the estate of the Duke of Cuvillier was opposite the clear blue waters of the pond. Nearly two hours later, she halted and set up the loom, stretching both warp and weft threads. Next, she set to work, capturing Cuvillier's estate, windows, and doors without adding the foliage. She didn't need any extra trappings to do what she wanted, just the building. As she worked, she hummed and found herself transported, standing before the door to the estate.

"Invisible," she whispered and knew her magic made her so. She entered. At once, she heard voices, and following them, she ended up in an office. Longchambon stood at a credenza while Asselin sat at a desk in front of Cuvillier. Twyla moved through the room unseen.

"That fool Ganelon didn't ask any questions after you promised him five hundred silver falcons." Longchambon brought three crystal glasses over, filled with an amber-colored liquid. The men each took one. Longchambon sat.

"I knew he wouldn't-th." Cuvillier took a sip from his glass.

Asselin laughed. "Greedy as always. Do you have 500 silver falcons, Cuvillier?"

"No, but I will have it-th and much more when I am kin…king," Cuvillier said.

"I think Ganelon will expect payment before you can claim the tapestry and the throne." Longchambon swirled his liquor before taking a sip.

"That i-th why the two of you will keep him occupied while I and sev...several men enter the back door and climb up the tow...tower stair-sth, grab the tapestry and the girl, and leave." Cuvillier sat back in his chair.

"Ah, she won't be able to create a new tapestry to stop you while she sits in your dungeon," Longchambon said.

"Ex...act...actly."

"Here's to King Cuvillier and the downfall of House Calimar," Asselin said, raising his glass.

"To war with Telaneasse. Bring their bastard king to his knees," Longchambon said. "Your Majesté." He nodded to Cuvillier and took a swig from his glass.

Twyla raised her hands and waved them before her to leave the tapestry. At the lake once more, she packed her supplies and headed back toward the tower. Jean-François Cuvillier intended to overthrow the king. Twyla must find a way to stop him.

Plan
Chapter 2

I n her tower, Twyla threaded the large loom which would become Cuvillier's tapestry. How could she stop Cuvillier? Long ago, she had seen a painting of the throne room inside Château de Talaith. Shutting her eyes, she began to hum. With her song, the room's colors came to her, the chairs of the councilmen, the men themselves, the long carpet down the center aisle, men at tables, and the king along with his friend-brother. High King Healden had three sons; they should be in the room, too. She must take a gift with her, something to prove her skill to the king. But what?

She stood and walked around her tower. Her hands felt cold, her skill imprisoned by fear, her stomach hurt, and her mind buzzed with tension. What would please the king and show her talent? The king's love for his queen was legendary. She would make a tapestry of the queen.

Twyla waited. Hours slipped by as she worked on stretching the initial threads for Cuvillier's gift. The moon was only a sliver out of her tall window when she crept down the stairway, paper and pencil ready. She needed to be sure. She needed to view the paintings of the throne room, of Healden and of the queen to be sure. And of his sons and friend-brother. Otherwise, she could end up speaking with a king a hundred years past. She could travel distances through her tapestries, but she couldn't control time.

Within Ganelon's storeroom, she found the paintings. There were also tapestries stored within which she had crafted previously. Those tapestries sensed her presence, and the animals or people within them turned to watch her. She remained for hours, drawing, thinking, and planning. She must craft these particular works when everyone slept, or Ganelon would know her secret, and so would Cuvillier. The throne room would come alive within the old factory, the queen would walk the halls. No, the night would hide her secret. The night would be her friend.

Twyla returned to the tower in the early hours and hid the drawings in her bedchamber attached to the workroom. In the morning, Ganelon would expect her to begin Cuvillier's tapestry. As massive as it was, it would take her all ten months. When evening sent everyone to bed, she would start the queen's tapestry. That night, despite her fatigue, sleep eluded her with thoughts of doom that wouldn't rest.

Spy
Chapter 3

A few days later, Twyla locked her tower door and retreated to her bedchamber where she kept the tapestry of Cuvillier's estate. Her memory of the grounds allowed her to finish the tapestry at home. Now, as she gazed at the foliage, she selected a group of tall evergreen bushes and concentrated, humming. A moment later, she was in the middle of the bushes, being pricked by their sharp needles. The scent of pine filled her nostrils. Peering past the foliage, she spotted hundreds of men sparring with swords or shooting arrows at targets. Dust engulfed her as more of Cuvillier's soldiers galloped past.

The men on foot before her were not unusual, but those on horseback had the short stature and angular eyes of the people of Shea-Talon. Twyla had expected Cuvillier's army to be made of Gil-Laelian men. As she watched the soldiers spar, Longchambon and Asselin walked among the men. She needed to be closer to hear what was being said.

"Invisible." She waved her hands and stepped from the bushes. At once, she had to dodge a man who charged his opponent. Next, a horse sensed her, screamed, and reared, dislodging his rider. Twyla threaded her way between the men and beasts until she stood next to Longchambon. Another man had joined him and Asselin.

"Green, unseasoned, rascals. You promised soldiers, Captain Gardet, not boys." Longchambon spit on the ground.

"I promise, by the time we leave, these men will be soldiers. The finest in the land." Gardet shifted his weight from one foot to the other.

"How many have reported thus far?" Asselin turned to peer unseeing, right through Twyla at the men. The intensity of his gaze made her shiver.

"Around six thousand." Gardet blinked and turned his eyes from one man to the other.

"Around?" Asselin asked.

"About," Gardet said.

"What is it? Around or about? Six thousand or less?" Longchambon glared at the captain.

"We have 5,712 men to date. I've heard reports of more on the ships coming to us."

"Greed is a powerful motivator." Asselin grinned, and Twyla stepped back.

"'Tis not just greed, My Lord. Those of Shea-Talon have come to secure Cuvillier's promise to give their country its freedom. Not all the men you see here are common. The horsemen are titled, lords." Gardet waved toward the men on horseback. Twyla looked their way as well.

Longchambon rubbed the tip of his nose. "Get them trained. Ten months isn't long." He turned along with Asselin and headed toward the estate. Twyla hurried to catch up.

"We must report the Shea-Talon lords to Cuvillier," Longchambon said.

"Oui," Asselin's stride was long as they climbed the grassy hill.

"How do you think he'll take it? Noblemen are not part of his plan."

Asselin's laughter was nasal and cruel. "I think Cuvillier will set a watch over them."

"Oui, oui, I think you're correct."

The two men entered the manner house, and Twyla almost followed, but she mustn't be gone from her room long. Waving her hands, she whispered, "Return," and found herself in her bedchamber. Someone was banging on her door.

Quickly, she brushed the pine needles from her clothes, letting them fall to the floor of her bedroom. Then, she ran into her workroom, taking care to shut the bedroom door.

189

Bang. "Twyla," Ganelon yelled.

She reached the door, unlocked it, and flung it open. Ganelon marched past her and turned to face her. His face was mottled red from anger. "Explain yourself."

"My apologies. I needed to relieve myself and couldn't leave the chair until done."

Ganelon took a breath, glanced around, and let the matter drop. He strolled to the tapestry requested by Cuvillier. "You haven't done much."

Twyla joined him. "It is massive, taking up the entire length of this wall."

"True. You have given a large list of supplies. I'm not sure you will need everything. Where do you plan to use the turquoise thread?"

"I have other projects as well." Twyla studied his plump face.

"True enough." Ganelon turned and looked at the other looms against the opposite wall. Twyla had put one in front of the other to make room for the loom that held Culliver's tapestry.

"Don't you find Culliver's request odd?" Twyla asked, hoping Ganelon wouldn't take offense.

"Odd? How?"

"Well…he wishes for a tapestry depicting an army at Château de Talaith. Does that not worry you?"

"Twyla, Twyla, Twyla." Ganelon turned to her and smiled, yet his eyes remained cool. "It is not your place to think. Do as you are told and let the noblemen of Gil-Lael think and worry. It is their lot in life." He strolled to the door and paused before leaving. "Now, get to work."

In the morning, when Twyla awoke, she felt lethargic. For over a week, she'd stretched the warp threads, ordered the colors needed, refined her sketches, and visited Culliver's estate twice. Her elfin heritage gave her strong endurance. She was rarely sick. Yet, the constant worry had taken its toll. For some odd reason, she continued to think of Gardet's assurances that more men would arrive. But…what if they didn't? Was there anything Twyla could do to prevent the arrival of more men? Of course, she could decrease the number in the tapestry, but would that be good enough?

An idea began to form in her mind. There were more Shea-Talonian men aboard a ship. What if they faced a storm? Not just any storm, but fierce winds and high waves. Could Twyla make that happen? And by doing so, the men would never arrive. Could she? Oui, but once again, she must wait for nightfall. And she must find a picture of one of their ships.

The hours dragged as she added to Culliver's tapestry. When the factory workers had retired and the night sky filled Twyla's windows, she returned to the storeroom and found a picture of a Shea-Talonian vessel. Part of her gift was the ability to remember in detail any subject, and so she returned to her room and set to work on a small tapestry. She hummed and threaded ships being swallowed by huge waves. As she reached the sky, her threads wove in the wind that dipped down upon the sails of the carrack. Humming, Twyla felt herself buffeted by the gale. The cries of hundreds of men reached her. A wave rose over the ship, smashing into Twyla. She lost her footing. Rocks rose close to the shore, and Twyla clapped her hands together, returning to her bedchamber. Drenched and cold, she stepped back, leaving a trail of water from the tapestry, and brushed aside her wet hair. What had she done? Those men would all die.

The king's life was in danger. She had done what she needed to do.

Predawn light flooded her window. No sleep tonight. Twyla rubbed her eyes and left the bedroom to put water on to boil.

Opening the iron stove, she put a few logs in and said, "Fire." The wood ignited, and soon, the oven would be hot enough to boil water.

Special Delivery
Chapter 4

Three weeks later, Twyla tamped down her tapestry of the queen. Now to finish off the back.

The queen gazed at her likeness from beside Twyla. "Lovely," she said.

"Do you think the king will like it?" Twyla worked at attaching the silk material to the back. The candlelight strained her eyes, and she paused to rub a headache.

"He will love it," the queen said.

Twyla glanced at her. The turquoise gown she had imagined was form-fitting with lace overlay in a matching color. A train fell from the queen's shoulders to the floor and a few inches beyond made entirely of peacock feathers.

"I must have a gown like this made." Her Majesté twirled.

Twyla smiled. "No need, Majesté, the gown will be there in your closet when I arrive."

Twyla lifted her hand, with the work complete, and the queen slipped from the room into the tapestry. For weeks now, Twyla had endured on a little more than two hours of sleep at night. Even with her elfin stamina, the stress had left dark circles beneath her eyes. She hid the queen's tapestry in her wardrobe next to those of Cuvillier's estate and the unfinished throne room.

Twyla left her bedchamber and lit her small stove to boil water. Cuvillier's commissioned tapestry showed the completed fountain tree before the king's château and a single line close to a thousand of Cuvillier's soldier's legs. Nevertheless, another minor tapestry was due tomorrow, and she'd have to spend the day working on it.

Twyla poured the boiling water over tea and set it aside to steep. Exhaustion left her body numb. She'd just set her head down on her arms while the tea finished.

From a great distance, Twyla heard a noise. Was it someone chopping wood? No, not quite the right sound. A muffled voice reached her, calling her name. "Twyla..." bang, bang, bang. "Twyla!"

A spasm shook her, and Twyla sat up. The light that poured through her window was much brighter.

Bang, bang, bang. "Twyla," Ganelon called.

She stood and hurried to her door. Ganelon stormed into her room with a tray of food for her. "What excuse do you offer this time?"

"I fell asleep." Twyla returned to the table and removed the tea from the now cold water. She took a sip and wrinkled her nose at the bitter taste.

Ganelon tapped his foot. "I am not bringing you any new work until you are close to being finished. But you still must finish what I've already given you."

Twyla nodded and took another sip.

"What are you doing today?" Ganelon set the tray down on her table and folded his arms over his chest, which made his belly look even bigger.

Twyla put her cup down and walked to the small tapestry of a woodland scene with deer. "This one is due tomorrow, I think."

Ganelon walked toward it. "Oh oui, I remember now." He rubbed his chin and then turned toward Cuvillier's tapestry. "You will finish it in time, won't you?"

Agitated, she said, "I have promised to finish on time, and I will."

"Why are you so tired? I thought elves could remain awake for days on end."

"I am only half-elf, Master, as you know, and I am staying up late with so many projects to complete." Twyla stepped closer to the massive tapestry. "I must count the number of men accurately, and that takes extra time." She fingered the yarn. "Does it not bother you even a little?"

"Twyla, Twyla, Twyla…how many times must I reassure you? Cuvillier merely wishes to honor the king with a gift of trained men and a tapestry to commemorate the occasion."

In his own way, Ganelon had always been good to her and his other workers. Not like her stepfather. A part of Twyla wanted to save Ganelon from a disaster that seemed to loom closer with each thread she wove.

"I will see you tomorrow," Ganelon said. "Your breakfast." He pointed to the tray.

Cold porridge wasn't appetizing. "I'm not hungry."

Ganelon shrugged his shoulders and left.

Twyla shut her door and set to work on the woodland scene. As she worked, she thought about the soldiers being trained at Cuvillier's estate. The duke must have been forced to hire from other countries. High King Healden of Gil-Lael was well-loved by the people for his generosity, justice, and the freedom he offered his people to be educated and rise above their station. Therefore, few would willingly participate in an uprising against him.

Was Ganelon as greedy as Cuvillier had implied? 500 Silver falcons! That was a fortune, and she doubted whether many had such a sum.

That evening she began work on the throne room of Gil-Lael. By the time she retired for the night, the council chairs were nearly complete.

#

Four weeks later, she finished at just after three in the morning. Later in the day, she would enter the completed throne room tapestry. Now that the time had come, her nerves were so numb from the stress that her fears slipped away, and, at last, sleep came.

#

Twyla prepared herself. She had changed into a skirt and blouse and rolled the queen's tapestry, tying a string around it to keep it secure. She folded the tapestry in her arms and pressed it to her body. It was bigger than she was and heavy. The throne room was still stretched on the loom. The figures within it moved. Now that the time had come, her fears resurfaced. Men had often treated her with disdain. She had been pushed, shoved, and even kicked for no reason other than that she was half-elf. Twyla was about to meet the most powerful man on earth. How would he receive her? Trembling, the panic started in her extremities and curled into a tight ball in her stomach. Twyla's heart thumped.

She glanced around at her bedchamber. The finished tapestry of the throne room remained within its fabric and didn't spill out into the room. No one in the factory would know she'd entered it. Taking a deep breath that was filled with the familiar odors of rose and lavender, Twyla whispered, "Enter."

A great sucking sensation overtook her, and pop sounded in her ears when she arrived. For a moment, she was disorientated. She'd never experienced that before. Perhaps it was the distance through space that had caused it. Then, opening her eyes, she found herself at the back of the throne room. The pleasant scent of lemon and cloves filled the air. The wall sconces gave off flickering light. Gold chandeliers hung overhead.

Others waited their turn to see the king. Twyla was pressed in among them. A woman in a heavy cloak who held a staff was on her left. An old man chewing on sarambor leaves stood to her right. His perspiration reeked and replaced the other smells. Twyla wrinkled her nose. Many more pressed in around her. She didn't have time to wait until they saw the king. She must be called soon. "Next," she whispered.

A man approached, ignoring everyone except for her. "Your name?"

"Twyla."

He motioned for her to follow. Moving down the dark blue carpet, past the seated councilors; he indicated for her to stand on the emblem of the House of Calimar woven into the carpet's fabric. Before her was the throne. Standing beside her, the man set his staff down and called her name. "Twyla." Once done, he stepped away and left Twyla facing the king.

Healden had light brown hair cut to his collar; his nose was straight, and his face clean-shaven. Next to him was his oldest son, and in appearance almost identical, and then the twin princes who both had hawk noses. And on his left, Friend-Brother Erard. Twyla trembled. What if I faint? She took a breath and willed herself to be calm.

"Majesté, I have brought you a gift." She unrolled it and held it up for the king to see.

Healden stood, stepped off the dais, and approached. He took the tapestry from her and turned so Twyla could see. The queen's image moved from the side view to face the king and smile at him.

"How did you do this?" Healden walked to the scribes' table. The men removed their paper and ink to let him stretch the tapestry across the table.

Twyla followed. "I am half-elf, Majesté. I use magic in my tapestries."

He gazed a little longer at it before turning to her. "Thank you for this. How may I help you?"

Standing this close to the king made her lightheaded. His spicy cologne filled her nostrils to erase all other scents. "I come with a warning. The Duke of Cuvillier is planning to kill you and take the throne."

Healden's brow wrinkled, and his mouth became straight. "I know the duke. Such a charge must be substantiated." His tone was stern. The pleasure she'd seen on his face was replaced by caution.

"He commissioned a tapestry from me, showing himself on the front steps of Château de Talaith with his friends and ten thousand soldiers before him dressed in his colors."

The king turned fully to face her. His brows pulled together. "Why should I fear a tapestry?"

Twyla clasped her frozen hands together. "Because my tapestries come true. The dress I created for the queen in this one with my imagination hangs in her closet even now."

Healden studied her for a moment. Twyla watched as his amber eyes darkened. "Liam, have your mother find this dress and bring it here."

Without a word, Prince Liam left.

"Take a chair Twyla," Healden said. He remained by the tapestry, gazing down at it.

The room had become hot. The councilmen were whispering behind her. The king's twin sons joined him to admire the tapestry. One of the princes smiled at her. Impatience edged along her mind. How long? She shouldn't stay overlong or her absence from the tower may be discovered. Finally, the king's oldest son, Liam, came back with the queen. She carried the turquoise dress on a hangar.

"This is beautiful," the queen said. "Do I understand correctly that his young girl imagined it, and it appeared in my closet?"

Twyla stood and curtsied.

Healden held out the gown and inspected it. "It would seem so. Council is over," he said. "Twyla, we have much to discuss. Come." The king left, joined by the queen. The Princes Liam and Jonathan followed. The other twin came to her.

"I am Eamon. May I?" He offered his arm. Twyla took it, and they stepped up the dais stairs and went around the back curtain to the rear door. Several other men followed.

Soon, they entered the king's library. The scent of old leather permeated the room. Twyla didn't know what to say and so remained quiet. A scribe sat at a round table and prepared his ink and paper. The queen gave Healden a kiss on the cheek and left. Prince Liam folded his arms and leaned against one of the bookshelves that lined the room. All eyes rested on Twyla. She dropped her hand from Eamon's arm and swallowed.

"Tell us all." Healden watched her with no indication of his feelings.

"I am indentured to Master Ganelon at his factory near the village of Lanteglos. A few months ago, the Duke of Cuvillier commissioned a tapestry from me." Twyla continued to tell them about her work, how she had spied on Cuvillier, and learned firsthand what he intended. She detailed the ships that carried more men and how she had sent a storm to stop them, and what she saw and overheard when she secretly visited the training of men on Cuvillier's estate.

"And what does your master say of this?" Healden had begun to pace and paused long enough to gaze at her.

"I have kept all hidden from Ganelon. He would not be pleased to learn what I have done. Cuvillier has promised him 500 silver falcons."

"500?! That is a fortune." Eamon stepped away from the scribe's table.

"Indeed," Healden said. "Does he have that much?"

"No." Twyla brushed aside a stray hair. "He intends to have his friends distract Ganelon while he and his men steal the tapestry and put me in chains."

"What will you do, Majesté?" Prince Liam let his arms drop and moved away from the bookshelves.

"How much time do we have?" Healden paced again, running his left hand through his hair.

"He commissioned ten months ahead. There are five months remaining."

Healden came to a halt before her. "Finish the tapestry to within a few strands. Then, I will come and make camp close by with my army."

Several men gasped. The scribe sat back in his chair with his mouth open.

"Father," Liam said. "The danger."

Jonathan put his hands on his hips. "No…no."

Eamon frowned and grabbed his father's arm. "Father, you cannot."

The men who followed them from the throne room seemed to talk at once. "You are king…you must not go."

"Surely others can take your place."

"Madness…the danger."

Healden put his hand over Eamon's and turned to him. A moment of silence followed, and the young prince removed his hand.

The king turned to face them. "Some of us will hide in Twyla's room. I want to see Cuvillier's face when I arrest him. You will remain here, Liam, in case there is a mishap."

Twyla felt her stomach somersault. The king would come. How will I know when he arrives? For now, however… "I must return, or I will be missed."

"Your absence must be known by now," Healden said. "It must be at least a two-week journey."

Twyla smiled, peered at the floor before raising her eyes to the king again. "It is but a moment. I use elfin magic."

Healden studied her. She waited.

"Go, I will see you the second month of spring. Look for me by the quarter moon."

Twyla held up her hand and waved as if erasing the library from her vision. "Return." She was back in her room and wondered what the king and those with him had thought when she vanished.

Map
Chapter 5

Once a week, Twyla took a day for herself, and tomorrow was her day. She'd been working straight through the last three months, and she looked forward to doing nothing if nothing was what one would call it.

In the morning, she loaded her pack with the sketchbook and pencil. The cooler temperature demanded her brown woolen cloak, and she pulled it on over her green tunic.

Her footsteps slipped past orange and red fallen leaves. The trees were almost bare. She hummed as she walked, gazing about her at red berries on evergreen bushes and autumn flowers. The air was crisp, and the scent of earth and rain filled her with happiness. Several deer saw her and began to follow.

There was a plan to this outing, and after several leagues, she stood in the center of a large meadow. A stream cut through the wilted grass, and an ancient building stood off to the side. One tall pillar remained on a pedestal of two steps. Beside it was slabs of ancient stone.

Twyla pulled out her sketchbook and drew the scene. Along the side, she gave the measurements as to how far it was from the road and Ganelon's factory. And which direction each one was.

She kissed the deer goodbye, returned home, and made a duplicate sketch while humming her magic into the scene. Then she pulled out the tapestry of the throne room and once again entered. No one was there when she arrived.

Twyla opened the heavy doors and left, finding herself in a hallway of the château.

A guard saw her. "You there!" He turned toward her.

At the exact moment, one of the twin princes also saw her. "Hold," he said and stepped around the guard. He smiled. "I've been thinking about you."

"Highness," she curtsied. "I have made a map and have a duplicate in my room. When the king arrives, I will see him."

Eamon took the picture and marveled at the detail. Then, looking up, he said, "Do you have to hurry back this time, or can you stay for dinner?"

"I have today to myself. I'd be honored to remain for dinner. Are you sure the king will approve?" She wasn't welcome to eat in the common room at Ganelon's because she was a halfling.

"Of course." He held out his arm again. "My parents will be delighted to have you."

Arrival
Chapter 6

Healden sat his fine black stallion and peered at the campsite. He'd ordered their departure from Terrel more than six weeks prior. Their travels had been long with a contingent of twelve thousand men, along with his twin boys and necessary supplies. In order to hide where they were going, the king had advanced through the forest once they were past Terrel, rather than along the road.

Hundreds of men now worked to make camp. Healden dismounted and marched toward the massive tent that would serve the dual purpose of sleeping and planning their strategy. The last time he'd been in a military camp was twenty-three years ago, during the war with Renwyk, Lord of the Smyberveen. At that time, a traitor came to light that despised his father's policy to bring greater status to the common man. He was a nobleman wishing to return to the former ways of oppressing the people of Gil-Lael. Now, it would seem that Cuvillier had a different agenda. What could he have against Tripada Pathak, Emperor of Telaneasse? Healden didn't know.

"Erard." Healden's friend-brother stood near the royal tent. The wind sifted, and smoke from a nearby campfire came their way. Healden entered the tent. "What do we know of Cuvillier?"

"He has a small dukedom which he inherited. His family has held it for a little more than two hundred years." Erard moved toward a large table where a map of this region was displayed.

"None of the Cuvillier ancestors has served as councilmen." Healden lifted a small clay château and put it down to indicate Cuvillier's estate. A nearby lake and woodland separated Cuvillier from Ganelon's factory. Healden placed an elfin figurine to indicate where Twyla worked. The village of Lanteglos was north along the road that meandered before Ganelon's factory.

"If Twyla's report is true, and Cuvillier has nearly ten thousand men, then we outnumber them but not by much." Erard put his finger on the clay château.

Healden had thought of that already. "We won't make war unless absolutely necessary. If Cuvillier walks into our trap..." Healden glanced at Erard.

"Oui, if so, then it will be a simple thing to send his men packing. But-"

"This is why we will hide archers in the woodland surrounding Cuvillier's estate."

"Some in the trees?"

"Most." Healden turned his back on the map.

"How do we contact Twyla?" Erard asked.

"She brought this picture I showed you earlier." Healden pulled the drawing out from an inner pocket. "She said she would see us when we arrived. If her secret hasn't been discovered, we wait for her arrival."

Erard lifted his goblet of wine. "To Twyla."

Healden raised his wine, and they both drank.

#

Twyla lifted the lantern. She stood before the nearly completed tapestry that Cuvillier had commissioned. Four days ago, when the king still hadn't arrived, she'd told Ganelon that she had run out of yarn. Since he made the yarn on-site, this delay only lasted until the following morning. Next, she blamed the uncompleted tapestry on an illness. Ganelon told her to work through it. Last night, as the quarter moon turned into a half moon, she despaired, knowing that she couldn't delay any longer. All that was left for her to do was to finish off the back and then run into the woodland so that when Cuvillier arrived to take the tapestry and kidnap her, he wouldn't be able to find her.

As she contemplated all this, the half-moon filled her window. For months now, she'd carried an ever-increasing fear with her. As the candle from her lantern brightened the bedchamber, she pulled out the drawing of the meadow she'd made and took a breath. There, within, were multiple tents, horses, men, and the king.

"Thank you," she whispered. Instead of changing for bed, she grabbed her cloak from the wardrobe and put it on. Humming, she soon entered the meadow through the drawing.

An owl flew off, startled by her sudden appearance. Squirrels hid in their holes. The scent of spring flowers mingled with rich dirt and evergreen trees. A nightingale warbled his tune. And Twyla stepped between trees toward the campfires of High King Healden.

A soldier approached her. "Mistress, this camp is not for one such as you." The young man blocked her advance.

"I am Twyla. Come to meet with High King Healden."

The man's eyebrows lifted. He must know her name. "Very well, follow me." He led her toward an oversized tent and spoke with another soldier who stood before the entrance.

The second man disappeared inside for a moment and then returned. "Come."

Ushered into the king's tent, she found herself in the company of Healden, Friend-Brother Erard, Princes Jonathan and Eamon, and several others. Twyla curtsied.

"Welcome Twyla, I'm glad to see you well," Healden said and smiled. "Tell me your progress."

"Ganelon has sent word to Cuvillier that the tapestry is done. He will come tomorrow sometime. The back entrance into my tower isn't guarded. If you come before dawn, no one should see you. Climb the tower stairs, and you will find my room at the top."

"Look for me then," Healden said. "Friend-Brother Erard will accompany me along with several of my guard."

"Forgive my curiosity, Majesté, but how will you deal with so many men in Cuvillier's employ?"

Healden stepped to the map stretched out on the table. "You said he had ten thousand men. I've brought twelve thousand. My archers will leave camp hours before dawn and climb the trees around Cuvillier's estate here, here, and here." Healden pointed to the trees around the property.

"This is an old map." Twyla took in the details. "To make room for so many soldiers and create a training ground, Cuvillier has cut down the trees here and here. The only significant forested lands left are those between Ganelon's factory here and Cuvillier's estate there."

"Ah…" the king said. "Then we will blanket the woodland to all sides of Ganelon's factory and along the road."

Trap
Chapter 7

Twyla slept only a little that night. Her fear had returned as a raging river after the snowmelt. Would the king's plan work? Twyla didn't know.

Before the sunrise, Healden, Erard, Jonathan, Eamon, and half a dozen soldiers arrived. Twyla opened the door and let them in. While they waited, she brewed tea and gave the king a short tour of her work in progress. The minutes inched along like a snail crossing a path to the garden. The smells of human sweat, campfire, leather, and horsehair permeated the atmosphere. Would Cuvillier notice when he arrived? Sure that he would, Twyla added aromatic oils to a small bowl and put it on the stove. Soon, the aroma of honeysuckle replaced the others.

Twyla stood by her window. The king and his men were all crowded in her bedchamber now. Anxiety pressed her jumbled emotions. What would become of her when this was over? She'd never known any other life, having been indentured to Ganelon since a girl of four. In the past, she'd gone to spy on her mother through a tapestry. Her stepfather considered Twyla an abomination. There would be no welcome there. Perhaps Anora of the Elves. How would she be viewed there? She was half-human.

Movement on the stairs alerted the two men who stood at the door. They joined the others in Twyla's small bedroom. Shutting the bedchamber door, Twyla turned just as a man burst through her door wearing Cuvillier's uniform. The duke followed him into the room. She lost count of the number of men who entered when Cuvillier grabbed her arm and forced her to the tapestry.

"Ganelon said it would be fin…fin…fin-sth-th." Cuvillier pushed her against the wall. "Get to work!"

"All that is left to do is the back." Twyla rubbed her arm.

Her bedchamber door banged open. High King Healden stepped out along with his men. Cuvillier pulled his sword and yanked Twyla against him holding her tight.

"Majesté." Cuvillier didn't bow. "The little weaver has-th betrayed me."

Soldiers on both sides drew their weapons, swords rang against swords. Prince Jonathan and Eamon joined the fight. Friend-Brother Erard stepped in front of Healden. "Release her," he said.

Cuvillier backed away behind his men, dragging Twyla with him and knocking over small tapestry looms. The beating of her heart was painful. Blood splattered Twyla's dress as a man was killed next to her, and the copper scent invaded her nostrils. The tower room echoed with the shouts of the men. Healden advanced on Cuvillier with the great sword of Carmelidrium in his hand.

"Treason is punishable by death," Healden said.

"You mu…mu…sth capture me fir…sth." Cuvillier tightened his grip around Twyla and threw away his sword, pulling out a knife instead and pricking Twyla's neck with the blade. She felt her blood trickle down her throat. More than half of Cuvillier's men were dead, while only two of Healden's soldiers were injured. A few more steps, and Cuvillier would be out her tower room door. Would he throw her down the tower steps or slice her throat?

The fear she'd lived with for so long ignited within her. Clutching the duke's arm, Twyla spoke, "Fire!"

Instantly flames shot up from the floor and consumed every inch of Cuvillier. He screamed and let go of Twyla. Her dress was ablaze, too. The fire crept up toward her waist. She turned to peer at Cuvillier while he danced around the room, trying to beat out the flames. Those fighting stopped and moved to avoid him, staring.

"Water," Twyla said. The roof filled with water and let loose, drenching everyone. The duke collapsed to the floor, wet and smoldering, and began to cry.

#

Every tapestry in her room was either soaked with water or splattered with blood, and several were burned around the edges. Twyla cut the threads from Cuvillier's tapestry, ruining it, then changed into a clean dress before joining the king and his men in the courtyard. A caged wagon held Cuvillier and his two co-conspirators. Ganelon stood before the king, held prisoner by two men.

"You," Ganelon said to Twyla. "I have given you everything. How could you betray me?"

Twyla said. "I tried to warn you."

"You chose greed over loyalty and have become rich off her talent," Healden said.

"But, Sire, I merely commissioned a work. Any good businessman would do the same." Ganelon said.

"Save your excuses." Healden waved his hand. The soldiers forced a stumbling Ganelon toward the wagon and hoisted him into it. "Your reward is to lose your business and your freedom, Ganelon. Let this be a warning to others."

Healden turned to Twyla. "It seems you have lost your employment."

"I have been indentured to Ganelon since I was four," Twyla said.

"Indentured?" Eamon asked. He stood beside his father and how he didn't know Twyla could only guess.

"When my mother married, her husband refused to care for me, a half-elf. So, Ganelon paid them two coppers to take me off their hands."

The king turned away from her, gazing at the wagon as it pulled away. "You have your freedom then. What will you do? Return to your mother? Open your own shop? Your talent will serve you well."

"Perhaps later," Twyla said. Freedom, the word tasted sweet. "I would like to meet my father."

The king's gaze returned to her. "He is an elf, is he not?"

"Oui, I know only his name. Arunne."

"Arunne," Healden said. "Erard," he called.

Erard approached. He wasn't as tall as the king, but he seemed a giant to Twyla, who was small.

"Friend-Brother Erard's wife, though human, was raised by the elves. He has been to Anora many times. Twyla wants to meet her father, Arunne. Will you take her there?"

Erard turned to Twyla. "My pleasure." Erard gazed at Healden. "I think she should be known as the king's eyes."

Healden nodded. "So, it shall be known with all due honor. But I do hope I never make you angry, Twyla. I shouldn't like being set on fire."

Twyla had no response except to turn a shade redder.

211

Conclusion
Chapter 8

Three weeks later, Erard led the team of men along with Prince Eamon and Twyla down an embankment into a valley surrounded on three sides by a birchwood forest. Twyla knew this valley and the woods too, though she had never been here before. The place seemed a part of her subconscious mind. This was Anora of the Elves, located within Gil-Lael. The tall grasses of the valley waved in the breeze. Wildflowers dotted the landscape and mingled their scent with the earth. A lyre played somewhere in the forest. The music toyed with Twyla's emotions. What would happen now? A tremor tightened her heart, making her second guess her choice to seek out Arunne.

"Welcome, Erard." An elf appeared from within the forest and approached. His light brown hair was styled to enhance his pointed ears. His green eyes traveled over the men to rest on Twyla. "I see you have brought several others with you."

Erard dismounted, as did Prince Eamon, who walked to Twyla. "Allow me to help you down."

Twyla accepted his aid, and they turned toward the elf together.

"Nimalith, may I introduce Twyla."

"Twyla, welcome to Anora. May I ask, why have you come?"

More elves began to emerge from the forest. Twyla was struck by their grace and the way they wore their hair. The females lifted their front locks, so their ears were enhanced. Twyla had always hidden her elfin features.

"I have come to meet my father, Arunne," Twyla said, looking back to Nimalith.

"Your father?" Nimalith grinned. He turned toward the crowd and spoke in the elfin tongue. "Nindrol elrolith Arunne."

213

Twyla felt a breeze and saw the leaves rustle in the trees. Instinctively she sensed that time flowed differently in Anora. A moment later, an elf strolled away from a thicket and approached. As he walked, his eyes scrutinized her. His pointed brows pulled together.

"Arunne," Nimalith said. "This is Twyla. She claims to be your daughter."

Arunne looked from Nimalith to Twyla but didn't speak.

"My mother lived on a farm just south of Anora. Her name is Karine Naudé."

"Karine," Arunne said. "My sweet girl. You say she is your mother, and I am your…why didn't she tell me?"

"I don't know. She married when I was four and sold me to a fabric maker."

"She sold you?"

Eamon cleared his voice. "Twyla was indentured to a man who over time made a fortune from her talent as a tapestry weaver. She has risked her life to save the king, and now it is her wish that you would accept her."

Twyla felt her nerves stretch as if she were being threaded on a loom. Arunne studied her as the minutes seemed to expand. Would he accept her? Would he be the father she so desperately wanted? Would he love her?

"It would seem that we have much to learn of each other." Arunne stepped to her side. "Come, let me show you Anora," Arunne held out his hand, and Twyla smiled, taking it before glancing at Eamon.

"Come to Château de Talaith when you are done. There, I'll be waiting for you." The prince leaned in and kissed her cheek.

Twyla smiled, "I will." Then, turning toward her father once more, she walked with him into the forest of Anora.

N. R. Williams lives in New Mexico with her husband and has two grown daughters and two grandchildren. "I have found such a release in writing. I do hope that my stories will entertain you. All my best."

She posts stories on her blog too. Check out the pages: Her blog: http://nrwilliams.blogspot.com/

Confessions of a

Deviant Mind

by J.F. Sebastian

LGCopperFan12 – June 18, 2022

Ofthe6, am I the only one to think there's something weird going on with all those deviant Neos, suddenly becoming the good guys?

Hey all, somehow I have a hard time believing how deviant Neos are suddenly turning into model citizens. I mean, I'm all for redemption stories and all. And we need to keep our streets safe, but something kindda feels off about it. Too good to be true? Plus they all seem weird. I'm not sure why. Thoughts?

▲ **15** ▼   25 comments

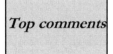

MikeyWay011 – June 18. 2022

I'd say def weird. Ok, it's cool that the govt and the ministry of Neos decided to help lesser known Neos get useful jobs and all, but do you see the way they speak in interviews? They talk like they're repeating something, or reading from a prompter. And their smiles? Nbody's that happy. They do look brainwashd to me. Creepy. We can't be the only ones to have noticed, right?

▲ **3** ▼   1 reply

LGCopperFan12 – June 18, 2022

Yeah, that smile… I def get creepy vibes. I mean, how can you do crime and stuff, and suddenly become all nice with people and almost, I don't know, religious? I usd to love Little Girl Copper and, suddenly she was different somwhow.

▲ *2* ▼

DarkMoonSinging – June 18. 2022

If you guys have been following the threads, there's been a lot of discussion in the community about that lately. There are rumors about Neos the government doesn't want you to know about. Ones with powers they want to keep secret for national security reasons. Others say they use certain deviants and their powers to do illegal things like remote assassination, destruction of property or propaganda.

▲ 3 ▼   2 replies

LGCopperFan12 – June 18, 2022

What about mind control? Like pushing certain thoughts in ppl's minds or, like, changing their personalities? Thoughts?
▲ *2* ▼

DarkMoonSinging – June 18. 2022

You mean a pusher? Who knows? We learn about new Neos and new powers every other day. I wouldn't be surprised if they did. It would be to their advantage. Imagine, if you could use Neos to change the minds of leaders of opposing parties?

ILikeBeards01 – June 18. 2022

Did you guys ever read the unedited version of Dr. Waste's "Confession of a Deviant Mind"? He's the Neo who got this whole "give deviants a chance" business started. I heard that it's a pretty interesting read. I think that's where the pusher theory came from. Dr. W was suspecting something had been done to him.

▲ 3 ▼   4 replies

LGCopperFan12 – June 18. 2022

Yeah, I remember hearing about it. How did the thing got published? FYI: I'm not a fan of Dr. Waste, tho, so wasn't too interested. I mean, his job is "faecal sludge management" (I checked). So gross!

DarkMoonSinging – June 18. 2022

It wasn't. An anonymous user posted the early draft of Dr. Waste's confession on our community board. It was quickly taken down, and the Ministry Of Neo Affairs apologized and said that anyone sharing that version would be prosecuted. A week later or so, an official updated version appeared on Dr. Waste's official page, but those who allegedly read the early draft said it was just bullshit. As it turns out, the guy was as toxic as his power… but still. It doesn't legitimize anything being done to him and others.

MikeyWay011 – June 18. 2022

Ddn't know about that. Is there a trace of that orignal post? Any idea how to get that frst version??

User108976 – June 19, 2022

You guys shouldn't talk about that online. They're monitoring everything we write and say. <u>Here</u> *is the original "confession". Download it before it's deleted again.*

TO-Neos-Official – June 20. 2022

If you guys want the whole Dr. W story, check out the updated website. It is approved by the Ministry of Neo Affairs and by Dr. Waste. himself. I've met him and he is the nicest guy, really! He told me about the day he met Lady Starshine. Don't believe that whole conspirationist business. Our city needs Neos, and we should all be thankful for them.
Here is the link:
http:///www.DrWasteKnowsBest.ca
I'm sorry, but I have to report your post, user 108976.

▲ 3 ▼   3 replies

221

DarkMoonSinging – June 20. 2022

Screw you, TO-Neos-Official. The Ofthe6 should be a place of freedom of speech. You should be ashamed of your obvious pro-Neo propaganda. There is enough of iton social media as it is.

LGCopperFan12 – June 20. 2022

Shucks. Looks like User 108976 was right. Link is dead. Can't download the doc.

ILikeBeards01 – June 20. 2022

This comment was removed due to terms violation.

User108993 – June 21, 2022

They won't be able to keep the lid on it for long, especially when changes come from within. Trust me, you guys are not the only ones to be suspicious.

Here it is again. Read it, share it and ask yourself: who is the real Lady Starshine and is she working alone?

▲ 3 ▼   50 replies

TO-Neos-Official – June 21. 2022

I have reported you!

DarkMoonSinging – June 21. 2022

Too late, A-hole! Got the doc. Sharing now!

ILikeBeards01 – June 21. 2022

This comment was removed due to terms violation.

Confession of a Deviant Mind

Let's start with something you might not know about *Neohumans* : it can really *suck* being one, especially if you were born with the "wrong" kind of power.

You don't believe me?

Think about Canadian superstars like Lady Starshine, Snow Gal Raven or their counterparts, Ghostblaze and Shadowstorm. What is it that *really* defines them, beyond their copyrighted names? What is it that *really* makes them celebrities?

The nature of their powers, of course.

Now let me ask you this: have you ever heard about I-Heat-Water-But-Below-Boiling-Point Man? Probably not, although he might have served your latte this morning. Did you know that there is a woman here, in Toronto, who can actually smell the future? A kid who can repair cracks in the pavement?

Of course not... So even though these people are all unique in their own ways, even though they can do things no one else can, nobody really cares about them because what they can do is not spectacular, nor marketable. Heck, they're not even use as comic relief!

Worse: some, like me, even end up categorized as "deviants" because they have developed a potentially dangerous ability. Why? Well, also because of their powers.

Take that gangly teenager I met who, once upon a time, realized that houseflies didn't follow him around because he stank (you know, being a teenager and all), but because he could unconsciously control them. I tried to encourage him to do something useful with what he called his "curse", but he had a hard time realizing his true potential, good or bad.

"Imagine what you can do with such a power!" I told him when we first met.

"Nothing... that's what..."

"Come on, think about it! You can go to any restaurant and get one of your flies to kamikaze itself in your plate for a free meal..."

"That's disgusting..."

I thought about telling him that a single fly can carry over 100 pathogens harmful to humans, and that he could basically control a biological weapon, but I realized that he would have been offended at what I was insinuating.

"Or... I don't know. You could go to one of those developing countries you see on TV and help sad-looking kids get rid of those flies stuck in their eyes." I suggested, testing him.

"That's offensive... Besides, I don't have enough money to travel."

"Listen, I'm just trying to help."

"Whatever," he said, moodier than ever.

"Look at the bright side. You could have no power at all…"

"Yeah, or worse, I could have *your* power…" he said.

I simply looked at him and managed to smile.

Cute. He's trying to hurt my feelings, I thought, resisting the urge to show him what I could really do.

That discussion, one of many I had with other "*lesser-Neos*" like him, slowly reinforced the realization that by putting forward certain types of powers, our mass-media society was neglecting those whose gifts were not as glamorous, forcing them to spend their lives in the shadows until… well, until they died or did something stupid and got arrested like me.

Well, let me tell you something: I'm not okay with that.

I believe that <u>no</u> Neo, whatever the nature of their power, should live in shame and guilt. I believe every one of us should be able to tell their stories like I am about to share mine

*

How could I define my "origin story"?

Well, first off, there was nothing glamorous about it. Unlike what you see in movies, my power didn't come to me because of trauma or destiny. It just happened on an ordinary, hot and hazy summer morning. I was having a coffee on my balcony, feeling already deflated at the sight of the ruddy haze of pollution enclosing the city (which would inevitably lead to a late-afternoon migraine), when I spotted a dark silhouette standing on top of another building, wearing what looked like a dark costume and a cape.

Squinting through my glasses, I thought I recognized a familiar shape, one I had seen on hundreds of pictures posted on social media, but never in real life. I felt my heart skip a beat.

Is that Lady Starshine? I thought.

As common as *Neos* are in the media, I had never actually seen one, except maybe as a blur in the sky or in the corner of my eye.

225

So, as blasé as I thought I was about the whole superhero business, I couldn't help feeling a mixture of awe and envy as I watched her standing on that building, proud, mysterious and, even from far away, powerful looking. Even though I had always thought that the concept of cape and costume looked stupid on most people, I had to admit that it did look pretty impressive on her, even from far away. So, torn between the desire to get my binoculars from my kitchen cupboard and the fear of missing her famous (and trademarked) take-off, I just stood there, barely sipping my coffee.

At first, she did nothing and I was about to turn towards my kitchen when she moved a little, her cape dancing in the lazy breeze and seemed to bend forward, as if she was looking at something below. This is when, even from where I was standing, I saw sunlight gather around her, forming a flickering gold and blue halo. She then crouched a little and, just like that, propelled herself upward, hero-style, before flying away in a blur, leaving her famous trail of glittering star-colored photons behind.

I had retreated to the cool darkness of blue shadows that was my apartment, feeling suddenly awkward and unimportant, when her signature sonic boom reached my building, rattling my apartment windows and making me spill my morning coffee all over the carpet.

*

Things didn't get any better when, a couple of hours later, I found myself in the sun-baked streets among the office crowds trying to get some lunch. It was a Wednesday, my self-appointed "burrito day". I was feeling already anxious at the prospect of preparing an undergraduate course on fungi and slime molds, when I found myself waiting in an unexpectedly long line at my usual fast-food joint. This is when a tall, muscular business-type guy with a thick reddish beard cut me off in line to join a colleague of his. Even today I remember his crisp, grey suit, and how loudly he talked and laughed, flaunting his masculine arrogance. I also remember how unimportant and weak he made me feel, especially when he took a step back and inadvertently elbowed me in the chest, triggering me.

"Why are you standing so close to me?" he said, lifting his hand as if he was about to slap me. "Oh, sorry, I thought you were a dude," he added, before winking, squeezing my shoulder, and turning to resume his conversation. I felt my ears burn and was immediately brought back to the savage wasteland of my high-school days. I looked at the back of the guy's neck, jaw grinding, and pictured myself grabbing a napkin dispenser and hitting him over the head until he fell to the ground. Finally, in a weirdly satisfying release of that anger, I imagined jumping feet first on his gut, emptying his bowels like a tube of toothpaste.

It was at this precise moment that I heard a growl-type grunt coming from the guy, as he suddenly bent forward and clutched his belly. Then came a wet sound, like blowing raspberries, and I wondered, for just a second, why a grown man like him would make such a sound in public.

It's only when the fetid smell of his diarrhea engulfed the line of gagging customers that I realized that the man had just emptied his bowels inside his crisp, grey suit.

*

The first time I *willingly* used my power was the following day. It happened at my community gym, and my first victim was a balding muscular guy in an orange Bugs Bunny tank top whose obvious OCD tendencies had, for some reason, deeply annoyed me. He arrived every morning at 8:45 sharp, always wearing the same orange Ninja Turtles t-shirt, and carrying a minuscule notebook and toothpick-sized pencil. Whenever one of his exercise machines was taken, he just walked up to it and, standing uncomfortably close to the person working out, pretended to scribble things in his notebook, looking up from under his bushy eyebrows every five seconds. Then, after a minute or two, he usually coughed a little and asked in a mumbled whisper how many sets the occupant (usually a decrepit old guy barely lifting any weights) had left to do. Once the occupant, who had not even done the proper movements anyway, had vacated the coveted machine, he took possession of it for at least forty minutes, spending half his time mumbling to himself and writing in his goddamned notebook.

Ok, I'll be honest here. I am pretty sure that, in other circumstances, I might have been (at least a little bit) touched by this guy's general innocent demeanour. He didn't look like a bad guy. Just an annoying one. I might also have been curious about his wedding ring and by the content of his little notebook… But having abnormal powers, even lousy ones, can make you feel… detached and, I have to admit, superior to the rest of humanity.

Yeah, I know.

I guess it all boils down to basic human nature: one doesn't have to be able to read minds or create and control fire to find a reason to feel superior to another human being. Any type of special privilege will do that to you.

Okay, I know this is an explanation and not an excuse… but this is why, in that moment, I saw this guy as a kind of nuisance on which I could test what I thought were newly found superpowers.

So this is how it happened: as soon as he took possession of his favourite machine (the chest press) I started concentrating on his lower digestive system and realized, without a hint of disgust, that I could actually "perceive" his bowels, and how they softly shifted inside his abdomen, even as he was sitting down. Concentrating a little more, I tried to conjure up feelings of liquefaction, sharp pain and contractions but without any success. Unaware of my failed attempt at making him shit his pants, he scribbled something in his notebook, and started to push.

Frustrated by my powerlessness, I looked at him and, for a second, saw him not as another human being but as some sort of a grotesque walrus grunting on his machine, unaware of my existence, and of what I could do to him.

He was in the middle of pushing his weights when I angrily tugged at his bowels.

Screw you and your fucking notebook, I thought. Hard.

Then, just like that, it happened: his brow suddenly furrowed and he just cried out, releasing the press with a loud clang. Then, red-faced and muttering something to himself, he just stood up, grabbed his ass to contain the disaster and hurried to the change room, leaving both his notebook and pencil behind.

It worked… I thought, feeling myself smile without a hint of shame, *holy shit, it worked!*

Then, the very next day, I made a speedo-wearing orangutan of a man release a dark beige cloud that engulfed a teenager swimming in his wake, causing the closure of my local pool for 48 hours.

The day after that, I made a cocky-looking guy shit himself in his Lamborghini. The day after that… Well, you get the picture: things kind of "escalated".

You might not realize it, but it's actually easy to drifts away from the path of normality and into the path of "deviance": you start using your powers discreetly, feeling slightly ashamed of what you can do, until you wake up one morning, feeling like you can't truly be yourself unless you use them.

To be clear: having powers *is* addictive.

As a result, I found myself in a conundrum: my ability, as far as I understood it, was to control people's bowel movements… But since soiling one's pants isn't something people typically enjoy, I had to accept that I affected others negatively. I was, therefore, a deviant, which meant that my choices were pretty limited.

To sum it up I could:
a) use my power and be a nuisance to society,
b) forget about it and be like everyone else.

Of course, I also considered using it as a force for good and imagined, for example, giving criminals cramps so painful they wouldn't be able to run away... but how many criminals have you ever encountered ? How many banks have you ever seen being robbed? Probably none.

So, fast forward a couple of weeks, here I was, administering my own personal brand of justice whenever I felt people needed it, which meant very often. That's how I found out, for example, that I needed to be in the presence of my victims to affect them (I couldn't make the Ontario Premier shit himself during a speech on TV, for example, although I tried).

A couple of weeks after that, it was simply a matter of having fun by ruining people's lives: I made old people and brooding teenagers shit themselves at family dinners, for example, or ruined lovers' dates in all the ways that you can imagine.

It never occurred to me that I might be hurting people. But what do you expect? Even though I could not fly and was perfectly destructible, I had a power that made me feel better about myself remaining anonymous. What more could I want?

*

Everything changed when I met a small group of *Neos* who, quite unwillingly, helped me change my mind about how and why I should use my powers.

It was I-Heat-Water-But-Below-Boiling-Point-Man who introduced me to the group after our chance encounter at the coffee shop where he worked. Lanky and with a face that looked like a bearded foot, I had disliked him as soon as I heard him use the Café's compulsory welcoming formula as he asked me for my order. I honestly think I would've flicked his gut even if he had written my name right on the cup. But, at this point in my life, I had started to make people sick without even thinking about it. So, it's only when I felt my coffee suddenly get ice cold in my hand that I realized he must've known I was responsible for his wet fart.

I got back into the coffee shop and found the guy staring at me, his curled-up moustache almost quivering with concentration.

I walked towards him, pointing to my coffee. "Are you doing this?" I whispered.

He looked around to make sure no one was paying attention and bent forward over the counter.

"Don't fuck with me…" He growled, turning the coffee hot again.

"Or what?" I said with a smile, triggering a series of wet farts in his pants.

He winced, obviously in pain, and grabbed the counter, almost knocking down the order he was preparing.

"Okay, stop…"

I released his bowels a little, enjoying my power over him. Another *Neo*.

"So that's your power? To cool down people's coffee?" I said.

At this point, I didn't even care if people overheard us. He looked around, panicked.

"Shh!" he said, before adding, under his breath "are you crazy?"

I twisted his bowels again but didn't want him to humiliate himself just yet. He grunted and closed his eyes. "Gnn, okay, okay…"

"So?" I said, maintaining a certain tension.

"T-take a seat. Let me finish my shift and we can talk, okay?" he managed to say, "I'll even get you a pastry while you wait."

"Sure, why not?" I said, feeling myself grin for the first time in days.

Just like that, I had won my first dual with another *Neo*.

*

"I can change the temperature of liquids… but I can't make them freeze or boil," the guy said, staring at the stale muffin he had offered me.

"That's pretty cool, actually. Why do you seem so embarrassed about it?" I said.

"Well, there's not much I can do with it. Why do you think I work here, of all places?" he said, gesturing at the coffee-shop counter.

"Seriously?"

"Yeah, the coffee we serve is always a bit too hot, so I always make it right…" He said with tired enthusiasm.

I started to feel sorry for the guy.

"Um, okay… That's not what I meant, though," I said.

"What *did* you mean?" He said.

"I meant that there are so many things you could do with that power! Why simply cool other people's coffee?"

"Oh yeah? Like what?"

"Well, for starters, you could change the blood temperature of any living thing…"

He looked at the other customers in alarm and leaned towards me.

"Are you fucking crazy?" He said between clenched teeth.

Feeling in control, I tried to sound innocent, hoping to shock him a little bit more.

"Why? What's wrong?" I said.

"It would kill them, that's what!" He tried to whisper.

"So? That makes you dangerous, and ill-fitted for this shitty job. Or, you know, you could also bring down fevers, if that's more your thing," I said.

He suddenly stood back in his chair, took a deep breath and looked in the distance, all animosity gone.

"I'm a deviant. I can't use my power to hurt people. But I can find the right place in society to use it," he recited.

I was so surprised by his tone, I actually turned around to see if he had said that to someone else.

"You sound... brainwashed. You shouldn't be ashamed of what you can do," I said, taking a bite out of the muffin.

He looked at me as if I had said something incredibly stupid.

"Dude, you simply can't use your powers if they harm people. There are *Neos* out there whose job it is to stop people like us, you know? You have no idea how powerful they are."

"How do you know that?"

His eyes darted from something behind me to his long, hairy hands.

"I just... know".

I gave a quick glance over my shoulder, feeling suddenly uncomfortable.

"How about, hum... helping victims of hypothermia? You could save lives," I said, just in case someone was listening.

He smiled and his hands creeped forward, making mine retreat under the table.

"Thanks, but I'm right where I should be. You should also find your place in this society... and accept it."

"What if I can't?" I said, sitting back, testing him.

"Well, have you ever heard of the LNSG? They could help you the way they helped me,"

"The what?"

This is when he proceeded to tell me about the *Lesser Neo Support Group*.

*

The LNSG was, officially, a support group for *Neos* with "less-than-super" powers. This is where I met a teenaged boy who could control flies, a woman who could smell the future, a girl who turned gold into copper, and several others with borderline ridiculous powers, like a guy who could control automatic sliding doors or an older woman who could help dust settle faster.

They met once a week, early in the evening, and had a hyper structured schedule organized around tearful confessions, teambuilding activities, and other "I can't find my place in society" moments. And, yes, they had stale pastries, coffee thermoses, and jugs of water with sad-looking lemon slices floating in them.

I initially thought the meetings would be about accepting our powers, and about being proud of who we were but, as it turned out, talking positively about powers or, worse, talking about *using* them was strictly forbidden. So, every meeting ended up with these "lesser Neos" complaining about indifferent partners, abusive bosses, divorce and/or about their kids hating them.

"We are deviants. We can't use our powers to hurt people. But we can all find the right place in society to use them," was their mantra, repeated in unison at key moments of every meeting.

If anything, spending several evenings with these people actually made me want to push my powers more, and I spent many of these meetings fantasizing about defying the so-called "Higher Neos" who, I felt, were pressuring us to be normal, even though we clearly weren't.

To their credit, the members of LNSG *did* try to make me see the path to righteousness… but it didn't take me long to come to a simple realization: helping Mrs. I-smell-the-future with an indigestion she hadn't been able to predict didn't make me feel half as good as making people shit themselves.

"But don't you feel good about the *unique* power you have?" I said to the group during my last session.

Copper Girl looked at me with wide eyes. I knew that talking about the intoxicating effects of our powers was not encouraged by the group, but I didn't care anymore. After that evening, I had no intention of ever attending another meeting.

"Really? Am I the only one to think that? You…" I said, pointing to Copper Girl, "you could go to the Tower of London, and turn the Crown Jewels into worthless junk. And you…" I said, pointing to Mr. I-Warm-Liquids, "you could warm a lake in Winter if you felt like going for a swim!"

"You're delusional... I can't heat a whole lake!" He exclaimed.

"How can you know if you don't try it?" I replied.

He crossed his arms and looked away, disgust spreading across his bony face.

"Oh my God. You're a deviant. Worse, you're a deviant with an ego!" he said.

I got up and looked around. I still couldn't understand how all these people wanted to forget what they truly were.

"You know what?" I said. "I really *do* think that our powers are gifts. That they make us unique."

"Even if it means we are deviants?" Mrs. I-Can-Smell-The-Future said.

"Yes, even if it means that society categorizes us as deviants... And let me ask you this: why are we deviants? Who decided where the line actually is between us and... *them?*" I said.

I saw a few of them roll their eyes but I continued. "Think about how unfair it is: out there, there are a few individuals endowed with awesome powers who make millions of dollars by 'making a difference'. And us? Here we are, drinking cold coffee while talking about our miserable lives."

"You're just *jealous*", said Mr. I-Warm-Liquids, his eyes now back on me.

"Of course I am. Nobody wants to be a normal human, or a half-baked *Neohuman*, for that matter. Everybody wants to be popular, loved, remembered... Don't you?"

I saw a few nods, so I continued: "so I can't help but cringe when I hear some of *them* claim, over and over again on social media that they wish they were 'normal'. But guess what? They are *not* normal. They will never be. And it's the same for us: we might be categorized as 'lesser' *Neos* or 'deviants', but we are still *Neos*. Society shouldn't deny us the right to use our powers freely."

"Ha! Like your shit powers?" Mr. I-Warm-Liquids sneered.

I resisted the urge to humiliate him and, instead, told them about an evening at the movie theater where I had made half the audience rush to the bathroom. It was a stupid move on my part, but I really wanted to impress them.

"You're disgusting..." Mr. I-Warm-Liquids said, looking at the door again.

"You know, I think I actually read about that..." Mr. Sliding-doors said, seemingly worried. Since I had joined the group, he had never said more than three words.

I was suddenly excited. "You did? Where?" I said.

"Online. On a couple of news threads. They said an unknown deviant might be to blame. That there was an investigation..."

I was about to brush it off when I noticed a lot of anxious side-glances. I felt my confidence suddenly evaporate.

"Hey, why the faces? I didn't even-" I started.

Then a member of the group stood up and came towards me. For some reason, I don't remember who it was. As much as I try to remember that moment, he/she/they are just a blur without a face and I suspect that, whoever it was, they have been partially erased from my memory.

"You are a potential suspect in a *deviant* investigation. You can't be here anymore... Please leave," they said.

"What? But-"

"I said leave!"

How dare they reject me? I thought, taking a step forward, ready to reach out to all of their intestines.

Then, just like that, something unexpected happened: my anger dissipated, and I realized that I had no wish to be with these people anymore, and that anywhere in the city would be better than being there, with them.

"And we have to report you to the authorities." Mrs. I-Can-Smell-The-Future blurted out, looking smug.

Humiliated and feeling powerless, I got up and headed for the door without a word. I was, as far as I knew, the strongest *Neo* present and yet there I was, compelled to leave peacefully.

"Are you going to make us poop ourselves?" Copper Girl said in her childish voice.

I turned around and tried to smile.

"Just ask Mrs. I-Can-Smell-The-Future…" I said as I closed the door behind me.

*

As I got home that night, the anger I thought I might feel towards the LNSG had melted away, replaced by a deep, dark kind of sadness. I wasn't even worried about the fact that they had probably reported me to the Ministry of Neo Affairs. Incredibly I was almost… hoping for it.

What is wrong with me? I thought as I entered my building.

Sitting in the comfort of my darkened apartment, the rest of the world just a whisper outside my window, I felt utterly alone. At one point, there was laughter outside my door, a couple of neighbours probably going out, and I actually sobbed.

Why the hell did I end up with powers if I can't use them? I thought. *I could make my upstairs neighbours, and probably the whole building shit themselves and here I am, feeling powerless. It's so fucking unfair.*

Then, slowly, the dark thoughts evaporated, revealing the tiny bud of an idea that had germinated over the last few meetings: people didn't care about *Lesser Neos* because they stayed in the shadows; because they were told to be ashamed of who they were and of what they could do.

My power could essentially be defined as bad… So what? I thought. *It's mine, it's unique, and it makes me who I am… Why should I be ashamed of that part of myself?*

I thought about all the movies I had seen about *Higher Neos* and remembered all the scenes where, after struggles and self-

237

doubt, they suddenly became who they were supposed to be by embracing their power.

Let's see if I can have my own moment. Let them arrest me, if they can, I thought.

Fists clenched, I closed my eyes and got up to stand in the middle of my living room, wearing nothing but an old pair of shorts. Just like I had done in the movie theater a couple of weeks before, I started by focusing on my own feelings of solitude and anger, before turning them first towards the neighbours around my unit, then towards all the people in the building. Unbeknownst to all, my power crept out of my apartment like sticky rhizomes, entering every tenants' body, ensnaring their guts. Then, once I felt ready and in control, I took a deep breath and inflicted a nicely calibrated surge of hot diarrhea to everyone.

Since life is not a movie, there was, unfortunately, no way for me to witness the end result. All I heard was a vague, muted series of cries coming from different apartments surrounding mine, a sudden rumble of chairs, tables and feet and the occasional clatter of dishes. Then, just like that, the moment was gone, life resumed its ordinary movement forward and, the temporary connection with my neighbors now over, I found myself isolated once more.

So, I guess that's that… I said to myself, as I walked towards my bedroom window.

I remained there for some minutes, until I heard the wails of a series of ambulances and police cars, all rushing towards my building in a carrousel of lights painting the streets in flashes of red and blue. I rushed to my balcony to look and noticed that people were leaving the building. I was so surprised that it took me a few minutes to realize that I was probably the one responsible for all the agitation and panic.

The world suddenly started to glow anew, and I felt a new rush of pride and confidence as I realized that I was, after all, quite powerful. This was also the moment I realized that I had no other choice but to become the *Neo* I was born to be: Shit-Man.

*

To be honest, I don't know why I felt compelled to pick a Deviant name. It just felt like the right thing to do when you decide to challenge a Super *Neo* like Lady Starshine.

I know what you're thinking: how could I even consider challenging a photon absorbing, indestructible, flying *Neo* when the only thing I could do was make people shit themselves?

Well, I never really thought that I could compete with her… I simply assumed that, since she had to eat and digest food like everyone else, I could at least try to humiliate her in public.

The first time I tried – and sort of succeeded – she was standing amongst the lighted stone guardians at the top of the Commerce Court building, in the downtown Toronto core. One of her more reliable online "Starshiner" had signaled her presence when she had landed there, and since I lived a few blocks away, I had rushed to the spot.

It was a cold and wet November night, but I couldn't help feeling a sudden rush of heat course through my body when I saw her walking amongst the huge, deco-style faces on the sides of the building. I was used to seeing her online yet there she was walking back and forth, casting an immense shadow behind her and looking quite photogenic.

She sure knows how to pick her spots… I thought, watching her from below.

I looked at the grinning people around me, holding their phones to film or take blurry pictures of the *Super Neo*, and I started to wonder how many of them were there because they had, like me, seen it online.

This is when it dawned on me that this moment might simply be a PR operation to upkeep Lady Starshine's presence in the media and to keep her relevant in a mostly safe city. After all, it had been a while since Toronto had been threatened by any sort of disaster.

Without their fans and followers, are Super Neos *still relevant?* I wondered.

I took out my phone, switched the camera on, and zoomed on Lady Starshine.

Maybe some of her "Starshiners" are supposed to post her location so that people can take pictures and post them on social media, maybe it's all about keeping her in the news… I thought.

I started to see a pattern: despite her popularity, there was the very real possibility that Lady Starshine was desperate for attention. It made so much sense to me that I found myself grinning. Throwing all caution away, I decided to allow my power to cross the space between her and me. Even though she was high up on that building, I was able to slip through her bulletproof costume and her skin to touch her insides, softly at first.

I waited a few more seconds before nastily yanking at her gut.

Unfortunately, it wasn't enough to make her shit herself, but she *did* stop in her tracks and I clearly saw her body stiffen. She then turned her gaze towards our group, and I felt, for maybe a second or two, that she knew that there was a deviant in the middle of crowd.

Yeah, I see you too… I thought.

I was about to tug at her insides again when she suddenly bolted upwards and disappeared into the mass of dark orange clouds that had gathered above the city. It took me a while to come out of my transfixion and to realize that, to the disappointment of the crowd and their social media feeds, Lady Starshine hadn't even displayed her trademark photon trail.

Emboldened by what I assumed had been my effect on one of the most powerful *Neos* active in the city, I suddenly decided I'd had enough of staying in the shadows to punish random people on the streets. As shallow as it might sound, I felt like I deserved to officially exist in the world and, for that to happen, I had to do something big enough for Lady Starshine herself to intervene and stop me. And what's bigger than a stadium full of people attending a popular music concert?

*

I felt confident as I entered the Rogers Center that day. I walked in with my hands in my pockets and smiled as I was searched at the security gates, for I knew that there was nothing that could detect the power I was hiding within.

As people started to enter the arena, I warmed my skill and passed the time by making distant, ant-sized fans rush to the nearest bathrooms. It still surprised me that I was able to control people's bowels without even touching them.

When the headliners entered the stage, the crowd suddenly went wild, lifting me like a tidal wave of sound and flesh as drums and bass started to beat a rhythm that put me in a trance-like state.

Subtly at first, I started to give rhythmic cramps to everyone around me but the band: two mild independent cramps, followed by a quick succession of three, gradually more painful ones.

Boom, boom, boom-boom-BOOM, boom, boom, boom-boom-BOOM...

The mood of the whole arena started to change as people started to fart and frown, the ones close to me looking anxious as they probably realized that they would have a hard time rushing to the nearest bathroom if they needed.

Unaware of what was happening, the bass player and drummer started to increase the rhythm of the beat, just as I increased the pain I caused, pulling even more strongly on the last beat of a new cycle.

Boom, boom, boom-BOOM-BOOM, boom, boom, boom-BOOM-BOOM...

I heard a few groans around me and saw some of my direct neighbours trying to get on their knees despite the crushing crowd. Others simply clutched their bellies as I increased their pain and continued to play with the rhythm.

BOOM, boom, boom-BOOM-BOOM
BOOM, boom, boom-BOOM-BOOM

The crowd started to get loud, the groans replaced by deep wailings and death-like rattles. I heard someone vomit right next to me, but I managed to keep my hold over every single person in the crowd, feeling more powerful than I ever had.

Excited by screams they understood as excitement from their fans, the band didn't immediately notice the situation as the lead singer started to address them:

"Good eeeevening Toroooooonto!" he said, lifting his fist in a perfect rock star cliché.

Since nobody replied, I tugged harder.

"WHAAAAAARRRGGGG!" Thousands of people screamed in unison, their mass suddenly turned into a wave-like entity trying to rush towards the exits and the bathrooms. The lead singer's face, visible on the big screen above the stage, suddenly frowned. He turned towards the band and to whomever was backstage as I struck their guts as well. The drummer dropped his sticks, followed by the guitarists and base players who dropped to their knees. The music then stopped as, above the stage, the projected image shook as the cameramen probably struggled to do their jobs.

The singer suddenly turned towards the crowd, eyebrows now raised, eyes wide with panic.

"W-what's happening?" he said, to no one in particular as rancid fumes rose to fill the hot, humid atmosphere.

The screen then turned black, and the man suddenly looked very small on that huge stage.

Most people in the concert hall had stopped moving to shit themselves or to vomit in their cupped hands, while others just stood there, with a look of pained disbelief on their faces.

Taking my time and keeping my hold, I stepped on dozens of people to avoid noxious pools of mixed excrements and slowly made my way towards the stage, under the increasingly worried eyes of the band leader.

"Who are you? What are you doing to these people?" He said, somehow unable to move away from the spotlights.

I felt hot, light-headed and curiously detached from my body as I climbed the steps to enter the spotlight. With thousands of desperate people now watching me, I realized that I had just passed the point of no return.

I walked towards the lead singer and pressed his guts. "On your knees" I said in a tone of voice I didn't quite recognize.

The guy fell silently forward with a muffled, wet fart noise and said something that sounded like "mumflub…"

Then, without really thinking, I grabbed the microphone and started to talk.

"Look at you all" I said, raising my hands towards the indistinct mass in front of me. "Where is Lady Starshine, when you need her? Well, let me tell you: she's probably standing on a building somewhere, having her picture taken!"

I pulled on their guts a little more, and heard low grunts, punctuated by high pitched cries. I shivered for a brief moment as I truly realized that I was not, after all, a *Lesser Neo*.

If only the losers at the LNSG could see me, I thought as I walked towards the front of the stage.

"Deviant!" Someone managed to shout from the mass of people crumpled on the ground.

I felt anger seeping through but managed to smile, taking reassurance from my total control over the crowd.

"Yes, I guess that's what I am…" I said, tugging at everyone's bowels again.

"D-deviant" said a few more voices.

"I heard you the first time!" I yelled.

243

I tried to tug harder, frustrated by their resistance, but felt my confidence evaporate as I saw several hunched figures stand up from the mass and point at me.

"Deviant!" they said, one after the other.

Coming out of nowhere, a water bottle covered with feces struck me in the face, making me lose my balance and my grip on everyone. I wiped my face and started to hear laughs as people started to chant "deviant, deviant, deviant" and throw more bottles at me.

Feeling another surge of pure, white anger, I raised my arms and, unaware of my clichéd theatrics, got ready to push my powers to the limit.

Well, screw you all… I thought.

There was a sudden flash and I ducked, thinking it was another bottle. Then the world exploded in a deafening shockwave of blue light, knocking the air out of my chest and launching me into the air a microsecond before the sound of the exploding stage reached my ears, knocking me unconscious.

*

I came back to my senses under a mass of wood panels, splinters and twisted bits of metal, my ears ringing and my vision a blur.

"Shit…" I mumbled.

I got on my hands and knees and looked up to see Lady Starshine standing in front of me, still surrounded by a shimmering blue glow. She was dressed in her typical nighttime suit, dark blue and green, her face half concealed by a hood. My first thought was that she was taller up-close than I had imagined, and more muscular.

Trying to keep my countenance, I managed a smile, and tried not to look too closely at the splinters that seemed to protrude from my arms and chest.

"Lady Starshine, I said, tasting blood, I've been… expecting you," was all I could come up with.

Her aura flickered out and she chuckled, looking at me with her arms crossed.

"Really? Do you think you're in a movie or something?", she said in an unexpectedly husky voice.

My body still filled with the echo of the blast; I had a hard time thinking coherently.

"Well, I… Err…" I started, before losing my train of thought.

"And what are you, exactly? Some kind of incel?" she then said.

I wanted to tell her that I wasn't a fan of people in general and that, if anything, I considered myself asexual but, somehow, words and sentences crumbled away, losing their meaning.

"I'm S-shit-Man," I managed to say.

She cocked her head and looked at me with an amused sort of grin.

"Excuse me?" she said.

"My name is Shit-Man…" I replied, feeling a sickening lurch in my stomach as I heard myself say it.

"Oh my God, you *are* serious… Well, Mr. Shit-Man. You're coming with me. Show's over," she said, as a blue halo started to flicker.

I took a step back as I started to feel pins and needles all over my hands and face. Behind Lady Starlight, I noticed two band members lying on the broken stage, dead or unconscious.

What the hell… I thought, wondering if she had killed them upon landing.

The feeling in my hands and face turned into a sunburn kind of pain and I instinctively reached for her guts but, to my surprise, didn't recognize them. Whoever was coming towards me was not the Lady Starshine whose bowels I had felt on that downtown building. I wasn't even sure what gender they were.

Suddenly afraid, I took a few steps back until I found myself against a mess of wood, twisted metallic beams and smoking projectors.

"Relax… it's all going to be okay," they said, coming closer.

It's when I tasted metal in my mouth that I really started to panic, for I realized that whoever was in front of me was not emitting a photon glow, but Cherenkov radiation.

"W-who a-are you?" I muttered, trying one more time to get at their guts.

"If you only knew…" they said with a grin.

Then came the punch and, right behind the hairy knuckles, sweet oblivion.

*

Yeah, I know: a radioactive, non-woman version of Lady Starshine? That sounds *crazy*. And maybe that's the point. But since I'm locked up somewhere like a goddamned villain cliché, and since I'm unable to use my powers, who cares? I'm back to where I started, alone and forgotten.

If I'm being honest, though, I kind of like being in solitary confinement. I never thought I'd say that, but it feels nice to be alone and cut off from the world. I almost feel… relieved.

There was a time I might have been angry, and I might have wanted to tell the world about what I have seen, but I don't really care about anything anymore.

Maybe it's because I know this bullshit confession will probably never leave my cell. Or maybe it's because I'm somehow being brainwashed, tamed into obedience by some mysterious *Neo* hiding behind this one-way mirror.

If that's the case, however, and if you're some kind of Neo Affairs employee who knows I'm being held illegally and against my will and doesn't do anything about it, I'll share these words of wisdom with you:

You don't have to make people shit themselves to be a shitty person...

Sincerely,

Shit-Man

LGCopperFan12 – June 23. 2022

OMG you guys were right. This is fudged up... Is that what happened to Little Copper Girl? She was so awesome... Even Dr. Waste/Shitman. Never liked him, but come on! I don't know what to think about Neos anymore. Thoughts?

▲ **0** ▼   0 replies

LGCopperFan12 – June 24. 2022

*Hello? Anyone out there? **Ilikebeards01**? **Darkmoonsinging**? We need to do something about this!!!!*

▲ **0** ▼   0 replies

DarkMoonSinging – June 24 2022

We're working on it… But we can't use the forum anymore. If you're really interested in joining us, we'll contact you. Keep an eye out. Good luck out there, LGCopperFan12.

▲ 0 ▼ 0 replies

Due to inactivity, this comment section has been closed.

J.F Sebastian, born and raised in the South of France, has been living and teaching in Toronto, Canada, for the last 17 years. Writing in English, and under a pen name, is a way for them to better express themselves beyond their social and professional "established self". Unfortunately, they don't own any quirky-named cats.

One Possible Future

by Ceilidh Newbury

I didn't realise this was Ana's ship. If I had, I never would
have tried to steal it.

Now, I'm perched on the bottom step in the main and
only room of said ship, with my hands cuffed to the railing and a
sense that maybe she both remembers me and is holding a grudge.

I haven't seen Ana since she was too short to ride on the hover
coasters at the fun fair. Back then she wore her coiled black hair
slicked tight in a ponytail. Now it's shorter, not tied up but flying
free in a cloud around her round face. Her dark skin is creased on
her forehead and around her eyes, and these wrinkles seem too
permanent for someone who's only just turned eighteen. And
maybe that has something to do with the biggest change about her
I can see: the screaming baby in her arms.

It's been screaming for the past twenty minutes and if my
hands weren't cuffed to the railing, I'd be covering my ears.

"Does it usually scream this much?" I ask, because apparently,
I have a death wish.

Ana shoots me a look I've seen before. But back then I would
never have been on the receiving end of it.

We were best friends, inseparable, and the only time she
looked at someone with this much hate was when they picked on

me for my gangly limbs or my glasses or the general weirdness that followed my family everywhere.

Ana keeps staring at me, but she's also bouncing on the balls of her feet, the baby's head rocking gently as she does. It's hard to look deadly with a baby in your arms, but somehow, she manages it.

The problem with turning my back on my family's abilities is that I can't predict things like this. I'm sure if I had been my brother, I would have seen this coming. And I would have turned around and found a different ship to steal. One occupied by someone I didn't know, who didn't know me, and who wasn't so goddamn scary.

Ana begins to pace the length of the bed. The bed, like Ana, like this whole ship, is a weird mix of old and new, hard and soft. It's covered in a faded quilt made of patches of all different colours, but its sides are a ramshackle of scrap metal that stick up to presumably stop the baby from rolling off it.

"Shh, baby," Ana says in an almost whisper. "Everything's okay."

The baby doesn't seem to believe her, because it screams louder.

She stops at the end of the bed and shifts the baby to her other hip, the one with her gun. The baby's socked feet just brush against the leather holster as it wriggles.

Ana's profile is lit up by the dim overheads in the tall space. She closes her eyes and presses her lips tight together, takes a deep breath, her nostrils flaring. Then her eyes flick open and she starts up the pacing-bouncing maneuver again.

It occurs to me that while all of this is going on, Ana has stopped looking at me. And the baby now blocks access to her gun.

Keeping my eyes fixed on her, I tug experimentally at the cuffs on my wrists. They are old-fashioned, just circles of metal chained together and locked manually, no electronics at all. That makes them harder to break out of if anything. As I tug on them, cold, tight on my wrists, they clank against the railing. Ana doesn't hear over the screaming and her own shushing.

I shift my gaze up the stairs. I could slide the cuffs up the railing. I'd be stuck at the top of the stairs, but that's also where the piloting console is.

Another reason I thought this ship was perfect: it's small, basically one room, and old. This means that first of all, no one (apart from its owner) will notice it missing because it doesn't have an AI, so it won't ping to the nearest police port when it's stolen. And secondly, it will be easy to fly. Older, smaller models like this aren't too different from flying on-planet transports. I've never flown anything bigger than a car, so I was hoping that by picking this ship I would... you know... not crash and die.

I stare at the console. At the place where the railing ends. I won't be able to get off the railing or use my hands to operate the console. But I don't know, maybe I can kick it, or threaten to kick it. It's pretty obvious from the state of the bed, the empty kitchen, the patchwork of different coloured panels all over the ship, that Ana can't really afford this thing to break. Leverage, however little, is better than just sitting here pulling against the cuffs.

I try to play the scenario out in my head. Creeping up the stairs, grabbing something heavy from the floor, threatening to destroy her only means of transport. But I'm rusty, and I can't tell if this scenario is really a possible future, or simply a plan I have and how I hope it will go.

"Who sent you?"

My attention snaps back to Ana. The baby isn't crying anymore and she's no longer holding it. She must have gotten it to sleep and put it to bed. And now she's focussed completely on me, no trace of the tiredness or tenderness she had with the baby.

251

She puts a threatening hand on her hip, fingers brushing the holster, and takes a step closer. "Who sent you?" she says again. Her voice is strong, but she's whispering. She doesn't want to wake the baby.

"Why? Should I be getting paid for this?" I ask. I don't know why I'm being so difficult with her, don't know why I'm not apologising and asking to be freed.

Her eyes narrow and her mouth turns down into a frown. "Do not play games with me, Elliot."

So, she does remember me.

"I've just spent the last three weeks hauling arse to get away with my baby and as soon as I get here *you* show up? Not a coincidence."

"No one sent me," I say, but I know how unbelievable that sounds. When I first saw her here, gun pointed at me in one hand, baby held in the other, I couldn't believe it either. I had even very briefly wondered if someone had sent her to bring *me* home.

"Try again," Ana says, her fingers slipping down closer to her gun.

My mouth is dry, my back is sweating. "Really," I say, hoping that maybe somewhere deep down the version of her that I used to know still trusts me.

She worries at her bottom lip like I'm right, but her fingers tickle the butt of her gun like she can't forget that I left her.

"Then why are you here?"

I could lie. Could try to think of something that would convince her to free me. But her fingers are a breath away from pulling the gun from her belt. Her hair is swaying gently as her breathing deepens. Her jaw is set in a way I saw so many times as a kid. And her baby is asleep behind her. Ana is more dangerous than I ever could have imagined she'd grow up to be and she will see through any lie I tell. She might not even believe the truth. But it's all I have; all I can offer as explanation for breaking into her home and trying to take it from her.

So, I take a breath and force myself to look at her eyes instead of her gun. "I'm trying to get to a funeral."

#

Ana doesn't ask whose funeral, so she's obviously heard about Reya's death. It may have even happened before she left, but she doesn't offer that information. Instead she just nods and turns away from me.

She's been looking at the comms screen on her wrist for about ten minutes before I start to think about maybe shimmying up the railing and trying my button mash plan. But just as I'm about to start, Ana whirls on me again.

"Why?" she asks desperately, coming closer than she has this whole time. Close enough that I catch a faint whiff of sweat and baby vomit coming off her.

"Why what?" I ask, trying to stop my nose from wrinkling at the smell.

"Why are you going?" she asks, and her eyes look kind of desperate, like she's begging me not to.

"I—" I'm not exactly sure why I decided to go. I haven't been back there in eight years. I fully intended to *never* go back. Until last week when my comms device pinged from an unknown number with the words: *Reya dead. Funeral 2/4/97 3pm.*

At first, I thought it must have been a wrong number. A different Reya. Because imagining my aunt's death was worse than thinking about my own. She's the one who got me out of Kalias, the one who heard my pleas for help and smuggled me away on a ship going as far away as it could. I owe everything I have here to Reya. And granted, it's not much, but it's more than I would have had if I'd stayed.

So, I went looking in the local news holos and found that yes, she had died. It didn't say how, but I could make a fairly accurate guess. Everyone in my family died of the same thing. Superstition is a dangerous thing on a conservative planet.

Reya would have seen it coming, and she would have let it. Because, unlike my mother and brother, Reya didn't like to change the futures she saw. She thought that her gift was in knowing who needed her and when. I think the only time she actually changed the fates was in smuggling me off Kalias.

So why? Why do I want to go all the way back there? When Reya is gone and all I would see would be the rest of my family, whose meddling had no doubt led to her death. Whose willingness to play with everyone's futures had made my family the target of every angry citizen in the capital.

My eyes start to tear up and I can't even wipe them away because my hands are cuffed. I close them instead and try to take a steadying breath.

"I need to—" My voice hitches and I swallow the rest of the sentence.

Ana's rough hand comes down on my shoulder. She rubs circles with her thumb and makes a shushing noise. It must be ingrained in her. That maternal instinct. That need to soothe someone who is crying. Or maybe, it isn't, and she remembers what we meant to each other.

I choke on a laugh and open my eyes, staring straight into hers. Big and brown and on the verge of tears herself.

"You make a good mother," I say and force a smile to change the subject.

Ana takes her hand back and her eyes harden.

"Is that why you left?" I ask.

She glances back at the bed. "Yes."

"It was a good decision," I say.

"Same one you made," she says, coldly.

Her eyes are back on me and she looks angry now.

"I don't know how much choice I had," I say, though I know it's not true. I just want an out, a way for this to not be my fault. "I was only ten."

"So was I," she says. "And I loved you more than anything. And then — *poof*," she makes the gesture with her hands and I flinch. "Gone. You didn't even tell me."

"I couldn't—" I try to protest, but she doesn't let me.

"You didn't say goodbye. You didn't leave a note. Do you have any idea what it's like to be ten years old and lose the only person you considered family?"

I try to form words, but there aren't any. Because I do. I lost her too. And Reya. But I hadn't been thinking of any of that when my aunt said she'd get me off Kalias. I was ten, and scared, and saw people angry and dying and all I could think was that I needed to get away. And then before I knew it Reya was pushing me onto that ship and someone was handing me a broom.

After a while, I convinced myself that Ana wouldn't even remember me. Convinced myself that she'd made more friends without me and my family's weirdness holding her back. She was doing just fine.

But the look on her face now says that she wasn't. She's been hurting this whole time.

"I'm sorry," I say.

She scoffs. "You're willing to go all the way back for Reya, dead, but you never thought to come back for me while I was living."

Something heavy lands on my chest as I realise the truth of it. I thought of Ana often, but I had never once considered going back for her. I couldn't fathom anything that would make me go back. Until now.

Ana frowns at my silence and turns back to the bed. She takes a few steps over to it and stares down at her baby.

It all flashes in front of me: Ana's face falling when some adult told her I wasn't coming back, the black fog of loneliness enveloping her like it had done to me on that ship with only the broom for company, her alone eating her lunch and doing her chores. For the first time, I'm seeing someone's past, not just thinking about their future like my family taught me to. I'm imagining her life up 'til now, not just looking at what she might do to me tomorrow. She grew older and tried to make new friends, there was laughter and love and heartbreak, good things and bad things and everything else dragged her through life, but she was always alone at the end of the day. Until she had a baby. And she looked out at the world that used to be my home and saw the anger and the dying, the suspicion and the injustice, everything I saw and wanted to escape, and she saw it all happening to her baby. So, she left. And she knew it would be hard, but she would never have to feel that fog again because she would always have this one person that is hers. And she's theirs.

"Do they have a name?" I ask, watching Ana watch her baby.

"Not yet," she says, so softly I barely hear her. "They aren't old enough to tell me yet. But I've been calling them my sunshine."

"They look like you," I say, which earns me a stern look.

"They don't look like anyone yet," she says. "They only look like a baby."

"Well," I say. "I think they will."

Ana turns so that she is facing me and crosses her arms over her chest. "Why do you want to go back? Really?"

She sees me. Sees past every defense I've ever put up against the world and everyone I've ever met on this planet. This has never been home, and I have never found a single person here to confide in. I've been alone as long as she has.

"I think," I say carefully, unable to break eye contact with her. "I think I'm lonely. And the last thing keeping me away was Reya's expectations of my life. My wonderful life away from Kalias." I shrug my shoulders in my raggedy clothes and lean towards Ana. "I'm nothing," I say. "No one. I tried to steal your ship because I have no way to afford the travel. I'm grateful to Reya for sending me away, to avoid winding up like my mother or dead like everyone else. But I also resent her for it. I have been alone and away from home for so long. And I'm tired."

Ana looks at me for a long time. "You aren't getting this ship," she finally says.

I laugh. "I figured that, yeah."

She nods. "But you don't have to be nothing."

I push down against the swell in my gut. I don't know what she's going to say. I don't want to hope that she could forgive me for leaving her.

"You could be someone," she says. "With us."

I can't help the warmth that surges through me and becomes tears. Ana steps closer to me and lets her arms fall to her sides.

"I'm still angry," she says.

I nod.

"But I've never been off Kalias before. And you've made it for eight years on your own."

"I won't leave again," I say, and my throat sounds ragged like I've been screaming. On the inside, I have been, for eight years.

"What about the funeral?" Ana asks. Her hands are clenched at her sides like she still thinks I'm going to try and rob her.

"I don't need it," I say.

"What about Reya?"

"Funerals are more for the living than the dead," I say. "And I've been to enough for a lifetime."

Ana hesitates, glances back at her sleeping baby. She reaches into her pocket and pulls out the small key for the handcuffs.

"If you hurt us," she says. "There will be no coming back from it."

I nod and hold her gaze.

She seems satisfied and reaches around to unlock the cuffs. When my hands are free, I suddenly don't know what to do with them. Apart from the grapple we had earlier when she cuffed me, I've hardly been in a position to touch anyone in a long time. But I want to show Ana I'm here.

I start to reach out and before I know it, I'm pulling her into a hug, grasping onto the back of her shirt like I'm afraid she'll disappear. She rubs circles on my back, shushing like the mother she is.

"Everything's okay," she says, and I don't even know if she realises she's doing it. But I don't care because it's the warmest I've felt in years knowing I have family again.

The baby stirs. Gentle cooing becoming worried fussing.

Ana pulls out of the claws of my hands and goes to her child. She picks them up and rocks them gently.

"Mama's here," she says. "And look." She bounces the baby over to me. "Elliot's here too."

I wave to the baby. Up close Ana's right, they really don't look like anything but a baby. But in their eyes, in the spark of the smile they give me, I think maybe they'll be like their mother. We can only hope.

And I suddenly see it. That twinkle in their eye will become the same fierceness their mother has. But they will be softer and trust more easily, because I see this baby growing up in a way that neither Ana nor I got the chance to. In a home small and poor but full of a family that loves them. I see their hair growing and twisting and mirroring Ana's when she was young and wild. This child will choose their name and pronouns and have friends and laugh and go to school. They will come home covered in mud from scraps with bullies. They will get lost and angry and fight us for no understandable reason. They will come back and ask forgiveness and so will we. They will learn to drive and even pilot and Ana will be a frustrating teacher. They will travel and make mistakes. They will eat every possible flavour and love so many people. They will bring partners home to meet Ana and I, who will be getting more wrinkly by the day, with worry lines that spell money problems and laughing crow's feet that show not everything is bad. Ana's child will become an adult and have their own child and we will be grandparents. And Ana will spoil this grandchild with too many sweets, but she will also teach them how, when they are older, to hold a gun.

It doesn't matter to me if this is the real future or not. If it is wishful thinking or a rusty remnant of a gift I left to stagnate and plan never to use again. I don't need to know, because any way it turns out, as long as I'm with Ana and her child, I know it's the future I want.

"Hiya sunshine," I say, leaning down towards Ana's baby who looks at me like they aren't quite sure what I am. They don't know who we are to each other yet.

"Gah-ga," the baby says.

"We're here little one," Ana says, and she looks at me with the intensity she had as a ten-year-old swearing that she was really tall enough to go on the ride, despite the fact that the attendant could see her height. "Always."

Ceilidh Newbury (she/they) is an Australian speculative fiction writer living on Peerapper land in Lutruwita (Tasmania). She is a fierce advocate for and creator of safe queer spaces, especially for young people. They enjoy big mugs of tea, singing to their cats and can be found screaming about books on Twitter @ceilidh_newbury.

Halka

by A. R. Turner

Pain flooded her eyes as they flicked open, and she was blinded by cold, white light. She hissed and threw her hands up to cover her face, shrinking from the sting of that brightness. She tried tentatively opening her eyes while her palms were pressed into them. Her vision was a bloom of red as the light penetrated her flesh and tried to blind her once more.

"Finally, she's awake," boomed a sonorous voice, loud enough to cause her eardrums to quiver. She groaned in response, whipping her hands to block her ears, but this only brought the bright pain back to her eyes. She hugged herself into the fetal position and sobbed. "Come on now, hurry up," it grumbled.

"Nearly there, dear. The pain will be over very soon. Hang on just a little longer," came another voice, croaked and genderless. Soft. Gentle. Calming. These words, in stark contrast to the previous speaker, settled on her like a soothing balm. The discomfort of the intense luminescence began to fade. The agony in her ears reduced to a dull throb, then vanished altogether.

Gritting her teeth, she opened her eyes by the smallest possible crack. Bleary smudges greeted her. Opening them wider still, the smudges sharpened into blobs, and opening her eyes fully caused the blobs to morph into people. And what people they were!

There were two standing a few paces in front of her. A huge man, rippling with muscles, a luxurious pair of bright blond mustaches framing a stern face. Those eyes! They glowed like a pair of suns, so bright it pained her to meet his gaze. She took in his expression of amusement before she had to rip her focus to the figure next to him.

The other was possessed of such regal bearing that, had she not been on the floor, she would have felt the need to kneel or bow. The figure wore her hair in an elaborate auburn braid that ran down the back of her ostentatiously jeweled dress. She looked... well, bored.

Who are these people?

A gentle tapping on her shoulder and she flinched, snapping her gaze to the hunched figure to her right. She hadn't spotted it at first. It looked old, terribly old, with bright white straggled hair and a threadbare tunic that dragged on the floor. It was not possible to tell if it was male or female. The figure's hands were shriveled and veiny, but its voice... it was the voice from before, the soothing one.

"That's it, my girl. Didn't I tell you that it would fade? Now, why don't we try standing up, hm? You can take my hand and lean on me, that's quite alright, I'm not so frail as I look. Here." A gnarled hand took hers and lifted her as if she were light as a baby. Her legs wobbled as she unfurled herself, but she did not stumble as her carer released her hand, letting her stand unaided. Only when she stood did she see where she was. There was no mistaking the golden slab floor, or the silver clouds, or the twinkling, shifting constellations above - visible, despite there being no sign of night's shroud. She recognised it from the temples. Which must mean...

Horrified, awestruck, she turned her gaze back to the two figures in front of her. She lowered first her gaze, then dropped to her knees in fervent, desperate prostration. The male figure with the sun-bright eyes sighed.

"Now, there's no need for that," said the King of the Gods in a voice much less painful to hear. "We do not expect such supplication from those of our ilk."

Ilk? What does he mean? I'm not-

Another gentle tap on her shoulder and she glanced up. A fourth figure, a beautiful young man with masses of black curls and a half-smirk, placed a hand under her elbow and guided her to her feet again. He produced a small looking glass seemingly from thin air and held it up, mirror side facing himself, then paused, waiting for some sign from the queenly woman. The matron considered something, then nodded, and the young man flipped the mirror so the newcomer could see her reflection. She glared at it.

And screamed.

#

"Your name is Halka," said Kona, braided Queen of the Gods and High Matron of Heaven. "You are the God of Winter, the Cold, Ice and Snow. All that… stuff." Kona's hand played idly with her dark plaits as she stood in silence.

Breathing slowly and deliberately, Halka tried to take this in. Roandi, the Caregiver, stroked her hand with an ancient palm, whispering soothing sounds. She was sitting on a hard-wooden chair in a simple stone room. There was nothing but a series of chairs in a circle, facing inwards. Halka herself occupied one, Roandi next to her, and Kona stood in the centre, addressing her. Halka cleared her throat and spoke, unsure of the protocol when addressing gods.

"But… mistress, why me? I am no great hero or worship-leader - beg pardon, I did offer my prayers and lit my votive candles, of course - but I don't understand why I should be, uhm, the word you used…"

"Deified?" said Kona with a slight sneer. She looked down her nose as she replied in an imperious tone. "Yes, well. It was not my decision. Your predecessor failed in his duty, and so we formed a council which selected you before he disappeared. I cannot reverse the decision, nor can we simply rid ourselves of you, so… We're stuck together."

"My… predecessor?"

"Yes, keep up for sky's sake. He ceased to be, and you are to follow his footsteps, continuing his important work. You are bound."

"His work?"

"This is precisely why I didn't want *you* as his replacement! You're obviously unable to grasp *basic* concepts!" Fury flashed across Kona's face, terrible in its intensity, but gone in an instant, replaced with a calm if irritated expression. "Yes, his work. You keep the heat of Solhiti at bay, just enough to allow life, but not so much to end it. You herald the season of winter. This you must continue."

Halka was scared to say anything else, so sudden was Kona's outburst, but the silence stretched on for long enough that she felt compelled. "But I… I don't know how…"

Kona rolled her eyes. "Vitneskja will teach you what you need to know. I'm done; you are dismissed." She stopped stroking her braid and waved a shooing hand at Halka. Halka rushed to her feet, fearing another of those terrible, furious glances, and rushed from the room. Stumbling into the light, she started walking in a random direction, following the golden slabs that covered the paths. Roandi appeared beside her and kept pace with no apparent effort, despite their elderly appearance.

How do they keep up?

"You'll get the hang of it, dear, trust me. The council wouldn't have picked you for no reason, you know."

"The council... I still don't understand why they chose me."

Halka had lived a quiet life, trying to stay out of trouble, obeying her parents, her teachers, the priests... The priests... obeying them, until...

Roandi shook their head, white hair bobbing. "I'm not surprised, dear. They keep to themselves. Only the most dedicated scholars among us could even begin to guess their motives, I say."

"You were not on the council, Roandi?"

"Oh no, they don't bother coming to me with such things, not these days."

They walked through impossibly intricate stone pillars adorned with infinitesimally detailed frescoes. Myriad beautiful flower arrangements snaked over every surface with brilliant colours. Any artist alive would have ripped his own arms off to get ten minutes to stare at these decorations.

"Did... I die?" asked Halka quietly.

"Of course not, you're here, aren't you?"

They turned a corner and the path started snaking through a forest. The trees bore enormous fruits, their branches bowing under the weight. Some of the trees turned towards them as they approached, lowering their branches to offer up their produce without the passing gods having to expend the effort to lift an arm. Halka ignored them. She felt no hunger, just a cold emptiness. An emptiness that she knew instinctively could not be filled with food. Around that emptiness, though... a searing heat, not *painful* as such, but terribly uncomfortable. A prickling, burning sensation surrounding that frozen void within.

"No, I mean... I can't remember... before. Not properly. Did I have a life? A family... Did I displease them? Or the gods?"

"Those are questions best left for Vitneskja, dear."

They walked in silence for some time. Birds of shapes and sizes completely alien to Halka flitted through the underbrush singing songs in perfect harmony in an orchestral range of perfect timbre and cadence. Despite the utopian warmth of the air and the picturesque beating down of the sun, a small wisp of mist accompanied every one of Halka's breaths.

The trees thinned out to reveal a clearing with a wooden cabin in the centre. A single stream of smoke rose from the chimney, smelling not of ash, but of wonderful earthy fragrances. Dotted around the house were benches and tables, tree stumps and bushes. As they approached, a figure opened the wooden door and walked to greet them.

He was a short, stocky man with enormous bushed eyebrows, a wide, flat nose and a bald pate that was surrounded by a ring of wild grey hair. He came to a stop a few steps away, Halka and Roandi doing the same, and he looked her up and down before grunting.

"You certainly look the part," he grunted, before breaking into an avuncular grin. "Roandi, my dear, you are looking radiant as ever."

"Oh, give over, you old billy goat." Roandi turned to Halka. "I'll leave you for now, dear. You're in safe hands." With that, the Caregiver shuffled off. Halka flicked her gaze from the old hunched figure to this new god, and back, but Roandi was gone.

Vitneskja tapped his steepled fingers together and took a step towards her. "Come, child. We have much to discuss." He swept an arm back and gestured at the shack. "Shall we?"

#

Inside, everything was carved wood and polished bone. Pouring two steaming mugs of something sweet smelling, Vitneskja bustled his way to the sitting room. He handed a cup to Halka, whistling a nonsense tune. His breath frosted in the air as he leaned in close, the whistle faltering a semiquaver. He shook himself and stepped back before landing heavily in a carved wooden armchair covered in furs. Taking a sip then clearing his throat, he began.

"You wanted to know a little more about your… origins. You did have a family, yes. Their fate, and yours, is not a happy one, child. Suffice it to say, a terrible incident befell your household, and you would have perished too, had Lunkinn not suggested you."

"Lunkinn?"

"Your predecessor. Moments before you were due to perish at the hands of, er- well, that is to say, he selected you as a candidate for his replacement. The council was formed and agreed on your…" He frowned. "Suitability. Thus."

Halka twisted the hem of the sleeve of her dark robe in her fingers. Fingers that were not the colour she was used to. Blue, dark enough to almost appear purple. Her veins stood out like silver rivers on a map through skin as thin as paper. Tiny crystals of ice formed on the cup where her touch fell. "Why can't I remember them? The events and my family? All I have are… flashes."

A warm set of eyes. Kind embrace. Being handed a piping hot bowl of something orange. A rumble in the distance. Enormous plumes of black-grey smoke, bursting from the mountaintop. Terror. Screaming. Flashes of recollection swirling and rolling like frozen blueberries around an empty bowl. Terrible loss. Grief. Hope.

The old teacher sighed. "I'm sorry, child. Some things are best forgotten. Lunkinn must have had the foresight to ensure you didn't remember. Cunning, that Lunkinn, but could be kind when the mood suited him. Of course, the mind raises its own barriers as well to protect itself under certain circumstances."

She felt herself reaching for that cold emptiness inside herself. Was that where her family would have been? Had they been ripped from her, cast aside, and left this freezing wound to fester? What was this intense… something? Something she couldn't focus on…

"Take a sip before it gets cold," he said. She did so, absent-mindedly. The drink was warm as she sipped, but Halka could feel the liquid rapidly cooling in her mouth. By the time she swallowed, it was chilled, like the breeze in autumn.

"Soothing, hm? My own recipe." Vitneskja's mug still steamed. Halka's did not. Glancing down, she could see a crystalline sheen forming on the surface, just next to where her hand held the cup. Realising he wasn't going to get a reply, the old man cleared his throat again and continued.

"You will find that your new position bequeaths certain… abilities. For, what is a god that cannot shape the cosmos to their will?"

As if to illustrate this, Vitneskja swirled his hand in a lazy ring above him. A galaxy of stars formed in the air, no wider than the circle he drew with his outstretched forefinger. Halka watched, transfixed by the sparkling spread of pinprick lights. He stopped, dropping his arm, and the stars vanished as abruptly as they'd appeared.

"You will learn to control your own divine will soon enough. Instinct will take over, probably without you knowing. I daresay it's already started."

Halka let the words wash over her, unsure of what to say. The old man frowned a serious frown, then changed the subject.

"Your duty, child, is of paramount importance. It is to keep the fires of Solhiti in check. His life-giving passion is bright, so very bright… His inner furnace heats the cold clay of flesh and stone, fueling life itself." A pause. "You will know this, of course."

It was true, or so the priests had drummed repeatedly into the young Halka. Solhiti breathed life, his warmth spreading through all that lived, nurturing the inner spark of his love into a roaring fire. And, upon death, the embers return to Solhiti so he may forge life anew. All creatures followed this same pattern. *Well, almost all.*

How strange that this lesson returned to Halka, now of all times. A disapproving priest lecturing her about how the fish, the lizard and some other creatures betrayed his light long ago, and so must find their heat elsewhere, their blood doomed to run cold. Such beliefs of Solhiti and his kindling humanity's flame formed the cornerstone of faith. Faith...

Another flash. A man gripping her wrist. Tightly. It hurt. Dragging her somewhere. Stone. Threats. Fury. A knife. Helplessness.

Halka frowned at her drink, her warped reflection frowning back at her. Vitneskja seemed to be waiting for her response. "Yes," she said quietly. He nodded and swilled his drink around his cup.

Do you know who I am, child? I am Solhiti's representative. I speak with his voice. Listen to me. There is but one way to calm the mountain's fury. One way.

"Solhiti's love for life is so great that he cannot contain himself. That, and humanity's draw on him is ever so much greater with every passing day. And so, he must urge his inner furnace to burn that much brighter. He must. But passion can boil and bubble, can melt and explode..."

He has spoken to me. You must offer yourself to me, his representative, to satiate Solhiti's passion. It is the only way. Do not fight it, simply- what are you doing? Come back here, insolent child!

Vitneskja stood up, placing his drink down. "Such heat threatens to burn man to cinders. Without a cooling influence on him, Solhiti will destroy all. He cannot help it. This is where you

269

come in. You are his opposite. You are cold where he is hot. Calm, where he is fiery."

You will regret this! You will live to regret this!

"Death, where he is life?" offered Halka with a hard grimace. Her hand shook. Vitneskja winced and bobbed his head from side to side, trying to figure out new words for the same concept.

"No, child, it is not as simple as that. Your predecessor performed this task without complaint for many-"

Cold fire washed through her blood as she felt the fury building. She forced her voice to remain calm. More flashes. Injustice. Panic. Regret. Justification.

"And what happened to my predecessor, pray tell? He retired to enjoy the rest of his infinite life on a beach, no doubt? I am snatched against my will, and what? So, I must eternally *mollify* another? I must *meekly react* to him, always looking over my shoulder to make sure he isn't getting carried away?"

"Those are not the words I would choose."

She is our only daughter! She's just a child. I can't...

If we don't, his vengeance will be terrible. I speak with his voice. You must understand. We have no choice. We will all perish.

No choice.

"No?"

"My dear, we-"

"Is this why I feel this prickling heat behind my eyes? In my core? Constant discomfort, as if fevered? My own body is fighting his relentless searing? My own lifeblood, forced against my will to balance this... buffoon's laziness?"

Vitneskja raised a hand in an attempt to stay her words. "That's the King of the Gods you're talking about! If he heard you-"

Halka sprang up and threw her cup at the wall. It shattered and covered the floor in a sprinkle of frozen crystal.

"He can play and *ignite his passions,* while I must pick up the pieces? I must keep him in check?"

"Child, I-"

"I am no child!" she screamed. The floor exploded in frost, covering everything in a carpet of white. Vitneskja cowered from her, hands shielding his face. "You have *chosen* me to fulfill a role? The role of winter? Of *babysitter?* Fine, I shall do as you require! But I shall do it my way, and I shall not do it calmly!"

A flash of light caught her eye and she turned, catching her reflection in a polished shield affixed against the wall. A terrible apparition stared back at her. Wild white hair flecked with blue. Dark blue skin veined with silver. Eyes whiter than winter. Snarled black fangs bared above white gums. A whisper of instinct, a flick of her finger and the shield, subjected to extreme cold, shattered into sparkling powder.

Halka turned and raised a hand. The door flew from the cabin, exploding outwards in a shower of icy splinters. Without looking back, she strode from the cabin and set off into the woods.

#

Vitneskja watched her leave. He hadn't told her why she was chosen. Truth be told, he wasn't sure if he would have ever told her. But watching her storm off, overflowing with such *sentiment,* proved that, once again, the Gods can, and do, misjudge situations *quite* terribly.

We need someone completely malleable; Kona had insisted. *Malleable, though robust. Someone who has experienced severe trauma but survived. Someone who can do so again without complaint.*

I have a candidate, Lunkinn had gasped while his skin peeled away. Light and heat were bleeding from his mouth and eyes. The heat within him was boiling him from the inside out. *I have just the*

271

candidate. His eyes had settled on Solhiti, burning with such intensity. *You might know her, in a way. She fulfills the requirements.*

How wrong they'd been.

Vitneskja was delighted.

#

"Keep him in check, was it? Hold back his passion, indeed?"

Striding through impossibly fine architecture, swirls of snowflakes swishing behind her, Halka growled a hail of outrages to herself. Figures stood aside to let her pass, whispering to their companions as they did so. Nothing as unexpected and exciting as a new god angrily stomping through the pathways and courtyards had happened up here in… well, time was hard to judge, but certainly a while. The denizens here knew better than to stand in a god's path, especially when sporting a face like an avalanche.

Angry thoughts formed a flurry within the blizzard of her mind. Thoughts of fear. Dreams of failure. Fury, injustice. Why her? Why should she be responsible? Chiseled from a life they didn't let her remember to play nursemaid to a god that couldn't be bothered to constrain his own power.

Well, why not let *him* keep *her* in check?

Looking up, Halka saw where her feet had taken her. She didn't recognise it, but something in her *knew* what it was. A squat stone tower, a perfect ring, with tall grey walls and no windows. The top of the tower was lost in an infinite taper that stretched forever upwards. A single wooden door was all that ornamented the structure. Walking through it, she saw what she knew would be waiting for her. A glass globe. She lifted it, staring at the faint etchings that marked the shorelines of the world.

Scowling, she let the cold spread from her heart to her arm, from her arm to her fingers, from her fingers to the globe. A globe that had given her nothing but misery.

Let him keep **me** *in check.*

#

"Why are the gods cruel?"

A small question from an innocent child. A question with no answer. "Where did you hear that question, Jetta?"

"Pa said it."

Brazen blasphemy, in my own household…

Tucking her granddaughter tighter into her enormous coat, Helti considered how to answer. "Well, sweetheart, the Gods have their own fears and tempers, and sometimes people cross them, so they react."

"Like grappo does when someone treads his flowers into the mud?"

"…Yes, just like grandfather did."

"Did?"

"Yes, it's what you say when someone, well, when someone isn't alive anymore."

"Oh."

Helti stood up. Jetta looked like a walking pillow, so layered as she was, but it was necessary in this particularly harsh cold. Helti looked up at the grey skies, clouds that threatened more snow.

Some in the village said that Solhiti had turned his gaze from us. Others blamed the moon, or the witch in the woods. That mad old hermit had been found frozen to death in his cave, his meagre belongings arranged in a symbol of supplication. Something was happening, that much was clear. But what could one grandmother do? Swaddle the young ones up and pray the cold away.

Oh, Kuppa, you stubborn old fool.

They'd found him by the roadside, barrel strapped to his back, the broth inside frozen solid. He'd told her he was going to drop it off to the blind teacher on the edge of the village, for if he didn't, who would? He wouldn't listen to reason, but his heart was so big. And now... his kindness had taken him away from her. That, and this blasted, god-forsaken, never-ending cold.

"Grappa, you're hurting me a bit."

Helti gasped as she realised how tightly she'd been squeezing Jetta's hand. It was the shock of herself having these shameful, blasphemous thoughts. "I'm sorry, darling one, I was just thinking."

"About grappo?"

"...yes, dear."

"Will they bury him?"

"If they can dig the earth, they will."

"What if they can't?"

"Then they will keep him safe and dry until they can."

Or they'll leave him somewhere.

She'd only known it too cold to dig once before, many years ago now. It must have been fifty winters past. An old memory of a sad time.

"Winter himself has come to visit," her own grandmother had said. "Keep a stove on and warm your feet, you'll get through it."

Helti smiled at the thought of her own grappa. She'd almost fainted when Helti said she thought of winter as a woman, not a man. Oh, she'd had to hide from her for a week until it was safe to emerge. Helti looked down at Jetta and squeezed her tight. *I must think of some mad witch-woman wisdom to pass onto this little one before...*

She stopped, releasing the tiny shivering Jetta and looking up at the black clouds. *Before it's too late.*

#

Time passed. On Earth, winter showed no sign of relinquishing its icy grip. Above, none had bothered to seek out the missing Goddess of Winter. None, save Vitneskja, who had found himself wandering the heavens, searching everywhere except the place he was worried she would be. Unable to put it off any longer, he headed to the clearing of Jardvoggur, the tower that housed the Earth-Cradle. As he approached, he felt it before he saw it.

An enormous, shimmering pillar of ice stood around the stone tower that Halka occupied. His stomach sank as his mind raced. He sighed and rubbed his balding pate. *I suppose I should probably tell them.*

Trotting back along the path, he couldn't help notice the sinister black clouds above the clearing. Clouds that had no place in Heaven.

#

Vitneskja arrived back in the clearing around the tower. Turning his head to look behind him he saw Kona walking down the path, trailed by a sullen Solhiti. The fiery King of the Gods scowled as the tower came into view, then flinched suddenly, shaking his head back as if stung by an insect. He held out a hand for a moment, palm up, then inspected it. Kona stared at him, her hands stroking her braid, doubtless ready to offer some snide comment, before she too recoiled, whipping her hand back. Looking down, she saw something that started her teeth to grinding. Snowflakes had settled on her plaited hair. It was snowing. It had never snowed in the land of the gods before. Ever.

"We… have a problem," said Vitneska.

\#

Kona was watching the light bounce and shimmer from the ice as Solhiti stared at it with his eyes two beams of brightness.

"I don't think she's listening to us," she said to her husband, with a touch of scorn. A growl was his only reply. Tiny rivulets of water wept from the ice where his gaze fell, but they froze as they trickled down the walls.

"Open up, blast you!" yelled Solhiti. The ice did not reply. "Open up willingly or we shall force you out!" He stomped from side to side, fists clenching and unclenching. He flicked his eyes from the ice to his wife, and behind her, Roandi, who had heard the commotion and come to observe. He snarled at them both. Roandi shivered, but Kona rolled her eyes.

"I wouldn't bother, husband," she said. "You know as well as I-"

"Of course, I'm not dense!" he yelled back. Her eyes darkened and the King of the Gods flinched at her gaze. He shook his head, mustaches flapping, and clapped his hands together. "Call them."

\#

Within the hallowed Hall of Garsalur, a council was formed calling for the wisest of all the gods to attend. Of course, every god considered herself the wisest, so every god attended the council - all except Lerra of The Thousand Smiles, who said the truly wise would know the fights that aren't worth fighting.

Habea, the law keeper, settled the participants with a gesture. His great white beard, tied in a wide knot, swung pendulously beneath his arched frame. He waited until each member of the council was silent and began to speak.

"A god cannot undo what another has put in place. This fundamental rule has governed the heavens since time began.

There can be no war amongst the gods if all are equal in strength. Any god can match another in a battle of wills, though can doubtless trick or outwit one another, or even overpower each other in a forceful battle of strength if allied in groups, but fundamentally it is all about the *spirit*. No god is superior in spirit to another, and this ensures that none can dominate another. To invite conflict ultimately wastes time for everyone. We will still have our spats and our feuds, of course, as the gods are perfectly capable of being petty and narrow-minded," he glanced sidelong at Kal of the Infinite Word, who rumour suggested had been saying most unkind things about Habea, whether they were true or not. Habea let his gaze and his pause linger just a fraction too long to be natural, then continued. "But infinity is a long time to hold a grudge. Knowing this, the gods may largely do as they please, answering to none but themselves and their own moral compass."

Some of the council held their heads in their hands and sighed. The God of Law had a habit of stating the obvious, the fundamental, the oh-so-bloody-boring... Either oblivious or simply uncaring, Habea plodded on.

"Yet, when the gods band together, fundamental laws of nature could be reinterpreted. Could be twisted. Could be *broken*. It is all a matter of effort, and determination. Thus, we must decide what course of action to be taken. I cede the floor to Solhiti, first among us, to suggest a course."

Solhiti waved a dismissive hand, signaling that the floor was open to all suggestions. A hundred voices all started at once. The King of the Gods rolled his eyes and selected one god at random. "You."

#

The council decreed that Halmar the Strong be charged with the tower's destruction; a challenge haughtily accepted by the patron deity of warriors, brutes, thugs and strength. Yet, the strongest of the gods, his mighty club in his hands, could not shatter the ice that encased Halka and Jardvoggur. A web of cracks bloomed from where he struck, but the ice reformed around them as quickly as he could damage it. Some had scoffed at the idea during the council, saying that a clever mind would be required, not simple brute force. Halmar snarled a challenge to any god that doubted him to test their strength against his, but none accepted.

Having wisely concealed his amusement at Halmar's failed and ever more furious attempts, the next to offer his skills was Tillitio the Sculptor. Assuming it was a mere matter of pressure points and craftsmanship, he nonetheless found no greater success in his attempts to split the frozen bastion apart.

His divine chisel, the formidable Ferrus, which once split the stone-giant Jyrkke's head in two with one stroke, carved from a meteorite, blessed icon of the craft, bent at the tip when Tillitio held it to the ice and struck it with his hammer. Furious, he threw it to the ground, where it fell to Earth to become the tallest peak in the Northern range, thereafter named Hook Mountain. Halmar made no attempts to conceal his own amusement.

"We must face facts," said Vitneskja, who had watched the proceedings with growing concern. "She's not coming out. Her cold shall spread, and keep spreading, until the whole world is frozen over."

A haughty sniff from Kona, who ran a hand down her braid. "I almost don't care," she sighed. "Let her have her tantrum then behold the consequences once she comes out. Which, of course, she must, in time."

"Don't care? But the people…" said Vitneskja, barely disguising his horror. Countless aeons he'd known Kona, yet she could still surprise him with her moral depravity. "They'll... well, they'll all..."

"Not my problem," came the reply. "I am the Queen of the *Gods*, not of the *mortals*. Why, I would sooner mourn a blade of grass than one of them. What really is the difference?" A final sneer flashed across her face, instantly replaced with a neutral bored expression. With that, she turned on her heel, strode out of the hall, and started humming to herself. The rest of the assembled gods followed her, including Solhiti, who had become more subdued of late. Dark circles formed under his eyes, which burned ever-so-slightly less brightly. He looked, in a word... tired.

Vitneskja turned his own worried eyes back to the window, from which he could see that impregnable wall of ice. What he didn't tell Kona was that this cold was spreading not just down among the mortals, but through the heavens as well. The trees whispered to him of bitter winds on the outer edges, of shriveled leaves and peeled bark. He noticed the smallest haze in front of his mouth and he exhaled.

Does her fury have an end? Or is it an end to everything?

#

Let them all freeze. Gods and mortals. Beginning and end. What does it matter? Who gives a fig for divine duty, for holy provenance, for natural law? Let them all freeze. May they feel as cold as the gaping tundra in her heart.

As she cradled that carved sphere of glass, she found her attention wandering across the plains and fields that mortals scratched a living on. As she did, the memories thawed within her, memories of her life *before*.

The Vilko mountain had been billowing smoke for six days, the ground rumbling in response. That terrible old prophet, that

Oracle of Solhiti's. He had gathered the villagers and told them what needed to be done.

"Trust me," he had said with his kind eyes. "I am Solhiti's representative. Stay in your homes. I will knock on your doors, and when I do, your first born must follow me without protest."

Murmurs, but agreement. What choice did they have?

She had seen through his plan the moment her door was knocked that evening. He'd had a wandering eye since she'd known him, and, despite his supposed holy inclinations, she'd long suspected he was not quite as ascetic as he purported to be. Meek Halka. Pliable Halka. He hadn't liked it when she'd shoved him down those stairs and fled his temple. *Where had that sudden, uncharacteristic flash of courage come from?* Her family had liked it even less when he'd sent word that Vilko would only be mollified with the pure life of a young woman. The mountain had belched ash and black cloud ceaselessly; They hadn't seen the sun in two weeks. They were desperate.

Being bound and gagged, dragged to the temple by her crying parents. A harsh grip of her wrist. A knife. A flash of cold. No more memories after that. She bared her teeth.

Let them all freeze.

A tiny voice, barely a whisper, stole Halka's focus. Turning her attention to it, she could make it out as clear as if the speaker were next to her. A female voice. Frail. Pleading.

Please... she doesn't deserve this...

Looking around, Halka was alone in her makeshift fortress. This voice came from... somewhere. Closing her eyes, she could see the speaker, kneeling down, hands clasping a... something? A bowl? She was in a wooden room, very small, very... cold.

Halka focused her will briefly and took a step forward, walking into the space behind the speaker. The room was smaller and meaner than it had appeared. Cold spilled in from cracks in the roof.

"Please, oh great winter goddess," said the old woman, her breath frosting in great plumes in front of her bowed head. "I beseech you, send me a sign that I might know your will."

Halka snorted an inelegant laugh. The old woman whipped around, and gasped.

"This enough of a sign for you, crone?" said Halka. She would never have used such language before, but... that was before. Who could stop her now? Who cared?

The old woman was lost for words. Her mouth worked but no sound came out.

"So, you beg me to hear you out, to send you a sign, yet when I manifest myself in your..." and she looked around at the room, as if searching for the word. "...your chapel, you decide I'm not worth your time?"

The woman clasped her hands in front of her chest and bowed. "I am not worthy, O great one," she intoned.

Halka dismissed this gesture with a lazy wave. "I'm not interested in your self-appointed worthiness, or lack thereof. What do you want from me, Helti Knapersson?" She didn't know why she knew this woman's name but know it she did. Getting used to the preternatural knowledge had taken some time, but now Halka couldn't imagine living without it.

Helti gathered herself and stood up straight. "I beseech you; please end this terrible winter. Our land will bear no harvest and our... animals have perished. We cannot last much longer, O great one."

"You don't want to freeze to death, is that it?" Halka asked.

"Uh, yes, your Divine Holiness."

A pause. Halka felt her rage writhing in her. When did she become so angry? Yet she couldn't stop it.

"Who is 'she'? She doesn't deserve this, you said?"

"My granddaughter Jetta. She is strong, and she's brave, oh so very brave, but she is struggling."

"With the cold? I thought children *loved* snow."

"Yes, great one, but too much of it... well, as I have said before, the impacts are far-reaching."

Halka hated herself for what she was doing to this world. When she thought of the human impact, it filled her with self-loathing. But, no one had ever shown her she was worth more than a hefty dose of self-loathing, so why should she treat herself any different? Ignore the lives, ignore the pain, become a villain, let the world outside match the world inside. Who could stop her, after all?

A terrible thought arrived unbidden in her mind. She thought of Kona as it manifested into a terrible idea. She lowered herself onto a rickety wooden chair, waving a hand in the air in a conciliatory gesture. "Mortal, you have convinced me with your eloquence. I will stop this cold and restore Solhiti's great warmth to your lands."

The old woman's face sagged with relief and she fell to her knees. "Oh, thank you, thank you-"

"On one condition."

A truly terrible idea.

"Anything, O great winter queen."

"Anything?"

"Yes, O blessed one, anything!"

Halka leaned back as if asking for the time. "It is a terrible thing to break an oath to a god, you understand."

The old woman pressed her hands together and straightened herself, still on her knees. "Yes, O great and merciful-"

"Sacrifice Jetta to me."

#

Vitneskja scowled into his steaming mug, then glanced around at the council. Something had just happened. Something...

unexpected. No one else had noticed yet. His eyes slid to the great frozen tower that was the focus of all this godly bluster. He swirled the liquid in his cup in a sloshing circle and thought of Halka. All he knew for certain about her is that she wasn't in that tower.

#

Helti blanched. "What?"

Halka pressed her fingertips together. "Today. You heard me. Offer your granddaughter Jetta in sacrifice." *What was she saying?* "Bring her here, kill her in my honour, dedicate the death to me, and I shall lift the curse of winter immediately." *Why was she doing this?*

Emotion warred on Helti's wrinkled face. She tried to speak several times, but nothing came out.

People are pathetic. Meek. Pliable. Any second now, she'll hop to it. Just like my parents did. This world deserves-

"No."

What did she just say?

Halka froze. She stared at this upstart, this *mortal*, this-

Helti's eyes returned her gaze, hard as tempered iron. "I won't do it. Goddess or no, I shan't harm a hair on that beautiful girl's head. No, no, three times I say to you: no."

Halka stood up. "You defy me?"

"Yes."

Halka took a step towards Helti. "You... dare?"

The old woman's face didn't flinch. "Do what you will to me, winter queen. I shall not betray her."

"Why?"

"She is everything to me. She is an innocent child, and no one, not even you, has the right to do harm to her. I will protect her with my life."

283

Halka's mind flashed back to her own brush with sacrifice. No one had leapt to her defense. She had pleaded with her parents, with her grandparents, with anyone within hearing. No one had heard. She fought the emotion of that terrible betrayal like a man might fight a dragon.

Something had softened Helti's face. Her kind eyes were full of concern as they sparkled in Halka's reflected light. "My dear, are you alright?" she asked.

The sheer impropriety of a mortal asking such a question of a god... Others would have struck her down where she stood, or transformed her into a branch, or a wisp of smoke. Halka stared at the old woman. Such genuine care in those eyes.

"You know, it's been a very long time since anyone asked me that," said Halka, and began to cry.

#

Vitneskja shivered and rubbed his hands together. It had been many, many years since he had felt cold. Proper cold. The others had left him to it, sitting here, watching the pillar.

"Let us know if anything happens," they'd sighed, already bored with the way this particular stream of excitement had slowed and dribbled to nothing. "I've a bet with Sylini that no one survives," he had heard Kona boasting as she'd walked off. Solhiti had scowled at him then turned to follow his wife.

Some feeling or other kept Vitneskja there, waiting. Halka was hurt, that much was true. There was pain, tremendous pain, yet there was something else to her. It was as if she was putting on a front, not quite believing all that she had caused to pass. He had seen it in her. A pearl of goodness buried deep within her, rolling around her like a dried pea in a bottle. It rattled if you knew how to hear it.

"Show an old fool that he's not wrong," he muttered. "Come on, girl."

#

Halka explained everything between wracking sobs. From her deification to the duties imposed on her, to her family and their decision to sacrifice her to Solhiti. Through it all, Helti patted her arm and stroked her hand, murmuring sweet reassurances.

For many hours they sat like that, mortal and god, god and mortal. Once there were no more words that Halka could think to say, Helti folded her in a motherly embrace, rocking her gently from side to side.

"It's okay," she said. "You are safe now." Halka clutched the woman's rags and let the sense of security envelop her. She could have stayed that way forever, absorbing the sense of familial care that she had craved her entire life. Eventually, she pulled herself away. She could not meet Helti's eyes.

"How can you ever forgive me? I've said such terrible things. Done such terrible things, and for what? My own warped sense of injustice." She looked at the largest crack in the ceiling, which still had snow drifting through it.

"You can make it right if you want to," Helti said. "But it is your choice. Let no one tell you otherwise." She lifted Halka's chin with her hand and gave her a warm smile. "You don't have to listen to anyone ever again."

Halka stared into those big, wrinkled eyes and a spark within her heart was lit.

"Helti," she said, pulling her face away and standing.

"Yes, my dear?"

"I was not blessed with a warm and loving family in life. I would ask you something. A request." She fiddled with her fingertips nervously, not making eye-contact with the old woman. "That is, well…"

Helti stood, taking Halka's hands in her own. "Halka, Goddess of Winter, I welcome you into my family. My hearth and home are yours." With a mischievous grin, she added quietly: "You may call me Grappa, if you like."

Halka squeezed Helti's hands, then released, and brushed her eye. "Grappa Helti…" Her dark blue face slowly drew itself up in a smile, not a frozen rictus grin, but a genuine, ear-to-ear face splitting smile. She laughed, and Helti laughed with her. They embraced, and Helti felt warmth from Halka, not the cold she was expecting. Drawing herself back and with a determined expression, Halka's voice became level and measured. "I must leave you now. I have many things to set right."

"Make sure you're back for the winter's end meal. I can't promise much in terms of fancy cuisine, but you are most welcome."

Halka nodded, smiled, then vanished in a swirl of white. The moment she did, snow stopped falling through the ceiling, and Helti closed her eyes, clasping her hands to her chest.

#

Vitneskja's breathing came ragged. His short legs were frozen stiff, the hairs on his arms were solid and crisped with rime. It took all of his effort to stay awake, to keep his eyes open, to let his inner furnace burn as low as possible without sputtering out.

He could hear the voices as they would be when he was discovered. "Old Vit's only gone and frozen himself," they'd say. "And for what? Waiting for some young upstart to thaw herself from her own aloofness. Serves him right, the old bastard."

Would they leave him here forever? If no one moved him, he supposed he'd never leave this place. This patch of grass. His tomb.

A sharp cracking sound pierced the air as a solid silver fracture appeared on the tower. The sound of ice rubbing together, that creaking, grinding cacophony, louder than the thunder, and the air filled with a heaving tension. Vit's eyes swiveled up; it was the only part of his body that he could still move.

With an echoing boom, the ice tower shattered into a billion splintering sprinkles of dazzling diamond dust. The light from above scattered into a rainbow with a million ends, discs and swirls of multicoloured coruscation. Vit stared, horrified, amazed, entranced, not wanting to look, unable to tear his eyes away.

As the cloud danced and spun, he caught glimpses of her. She was standing in the centre, where the tower used to be. Tall, proud, regally she stood, holding that globe, staring with intent towards the highest peak of heaven. Frozen as he was, Vit could not wave to her or call her name, but his heart was racing, pumping ice-cold blood through his unmoving body. He yearned to shout to her, to shake his fist in triumph, but he could not.

Then she was walking, striding, whipping up skirls of shimmering dust behind her as she did so. She hadn't noticed him! She couldn't leave him like this, could she? A statue, frozen? Halka walked past him, beyond his restricted sight. Vitneskja closed his eyes. Old Vit, his own worst enemy. Too trusting by half.

Halka laid a hand on his back, impossibly warm, and the ice sloughed away from him in thick chunks. He gasped, falling to the floor, coughing. Turning to look at her, he saw her face, not the dark blue face of a scowling blizzard, but the face of the hearth in the dead of the coldest night. The beauty of a world covered in a layer of silent white, of utter serenity. He saw this, and he understood.

She helped him to his feet and left without a word.

\#

The doorway to the throne room did not explode inwards as Solhiti had expected. Instead, the ornate doors swung open of their own accord in perfect timing with Halka's arrival. He had known she would be here soon, of course. It was not hard to piece the puzzle together. A loud crashing boom, a great cracking, a noticeable decrease in the air temperature… and some shift in his own inner furnace. He was used to his soul pressing outwards, straining against the desperate gossamer-thin wall that pushed him down again. Lunkinn had always dutifully maintained that icy protective veil around Solhiti, leaving him free to burn as brightly as he wanted, knowing he would be held in check. Well, until Lunkinn's own soul could withstand his onslaught no longer and had shriveled, blackened and flaked away to nothing. That of course had set this whole recent turn of events in motion. The gods selected the replacement for Lunkinn the way a woodsman would throw another log on the fire, paying no mind to the ash that gathered beneath it.

Amusing, then, that this upstart had proved far from the malleable puppet that Kona had insisted she would be. Instead of breaking under pressure like the icicles that she now ruled over, she had hardened, forming a soul tough and sparkling as the diamonds that icicles dream of.

Right now, she was standing in front of his curved metallic throne. Calm, collected, but with face that would brook no argument. Solhiti hadn't seen that sort of a face directed at him since he threw his own father out of heaven. The scolding his mother had given him… He grimaced.

"Yes?" he grunted.

Halka held up a finger. "You, and every other god, demigod or otherwise heavenly creature, will *immediately cease* your unwelcoming treatment of me or anyone else who you have 'raised up'. From this second on, I, and anyone else who visits this plane, shall be treated with the greatest of respect and welcome, something that was not shown to me," she said. "I hereby forbid any other course of action as my newfound self-imposed role as the Goddess of the Hearth, the Home and of Hospitality. Let it be known now that anyone that refuses to show such virtues shall know my disappointment." She raised a second finger. "What's more, Solhiti, Great King of the Gods, Sungazer, you *shall* learn to control your 'inner furnace' or whatever it is you call it. You will harness and fetter *yourself,* so I do not have to mollycoddle you. If you do not, I shall be forced to take *drastic* measures once again, and I will do so swiftly and without warning. Do I make myself clear?"

Solhiti's solar eyes blazed and he gripped the arm of his throne. Secretly, he was thrilled. Having someone brave enough to stand up to him, and what's more, in front of everyone, including his wife? He had not had this sense of excitement in… in…

Kona slammed her fist on her throne, her face a rictus snarl. "You dare presume?"

Halka's skin burned bright blue, her hair paling to white. "I do not think you understand. This is *not* a request." She stared Kona down, and as she did so, the temperature dropped, and kept dropping. Breaths steamed in the air, grumbles and shivers from the assembled witnesses. A pale glow emanated from her, getting wider and paler as time progressed.

"Enough." Solhiti raised a hand. He could barely keep himself from laughing, but for the benefit of those watching, he kept his expression stony. He had a reputation, after all. He turned his hand and opened a welcoming palm. "I'm sure we can come to an arrangement."

#

A knock at the door, and Helti lowered her tray of ginger biscuits. "It's her!" she said to herself. She fussed with her apron and straightened her hair. In the gentle chaos of her afternoon preparing the recently traditional winter feast a few irritating strands had come loose. "Oh, who cares." She wiped her forehead and examined her reflection in the steamed mirror, trying not to count wrinkles and trying to remember what she was in the middle of doing.

Another knock, no more insistent than before. *Of course! How could I forget!*

She shuffled to the door and pulled it open. A wash of warmth and homely contentment spilled both outwards into the world and inwards from the splendid outline of the guest at the threshold. Helti's face cracked into a well-worn smile.

"Come in, my dear, get out of that cold," she said, quite forgetting about her guest's particular resilience in that matter. "Come and meet everyone," her eyes sparkling with mischief. "I haven't told them who you are, oh they are going to spit teeth when they find out!"

"Actually… could you not tell them?" the guest asked. "I'd rather just be a… well…"

"Say no more. You're a friend of a cousin of my niece, and that's that." She swept the young woman into her living room and took her coat from her, before folding her into a motherly embrace. "And you're welcome for as long as you like."

"Oh, I hope you don't mind. I've brought a guest."

A guest? But who-

Halka stepped aside and he was standing there, as bright-eyed and cheekily grinned as that fateful day he'd left with the teacher's broth.

"Hiya, Helti," he said. "Room for one more?"

290

Alex Turner, born on the Isle of Wight in the south of England, now lives in South Wales with his wife and cat, where he divides his time between reading, writing and board games. Having always wanted to read a book about a lawyer in a fantasy world (but never successfully finding one), Alex finally realised that there was nothing else for it: he was going to have to write it himself. His other passion in life is a board game called Blood Bowl. He talks about it often in his podcast and one day hopes to compete in the Chaos Cup or other big global tournaments.

Check his podcast here:
https://anythingbuta1podcast.wordpress.com

The Cryo Kid

by Vincent Morgan

Distant Future - New Brazil - Medusa System.

Somewhere out there amid the dead apple trees and the tumbled mass of strangler-vines that killed them, something moved. It could be one of the refugees that looted and burned the Chang's place last week, or worse, a clatter bug. Either way, it meant trouble. Cameron racked his shotgun. "Show yourself, or I start blasting."

A dozen yards to his right, the strangler-vines rattled apart, and a thin-faced child with stringy, blonde hair stepped out. She wore a dirty, knee-length dress that hung sack-like from her bony shoulders. The only remarkable thing about her was her eyes. Large with irises a shade of blue so pale, they seemed almost white.

She thrust out a grubby hand. "Need food."

Since the fall of First Landing to the bugs, there were too many refugees for the outlying homesteaders to feed. Were she an adult, Cameron would have turned her away, but she looked half-starved. Muttering under his breath, he tramped over to his cabin and returned minutes later with a fistful of biscuits and his last can of apple juice. He watched in silence as the girl gulped down the juice and crammed the food into her mouth.

When she finished, he asked, "What's your name?"

The girl shook her head. "No name, just a cryo kid."

Cameron winced. A cryo kid! Oh crap. Some fool must've thrown open the cryogenic storage center. Then he shrugged. Probably doesn't matter a hell of a lot. The ship carrying the third consignment of cryos came out of jump too close to the Medusa. All those aboard got a lethal dose of radiation. After that, they were dead folk sleeping. Too bad for this Kid, of course, but whatcha gonna do?

Cameron gestured toward the strangler vines inching forward as they always did in the heat of mid-day. "Okay, Cryo Kid, you see any bugs on your way up here?

The girl bobbed her head. "Lots."

He ran a work-roughened hand across his unshaven chin. "Lots, huh? Well, it's time for me to up stakes, anyway. Think I'll try and make it over to Second Landing."

The girl glanced up. "I come Second Landing?"

Cameron shook his head and gestured toward the jungle-covered heights rising behind the cabin. "No, Second's way the other side of those hills, and it's real rugged 'tween here and there. Jungle's full of alien stuff so nasty, it makes strangler-vines look like house plants. No place for a man, let alone a kid."

The girl scowled and stuck out her chin. "I come."

"The hell you will. I'll have enough trouble looking after myself without you tagging along. I'll drop you off at Frankie's place. If anyone can hang on 'till the next ship arrives, it'll be her."

The Kid squinted up at the dust-laden, amber-tinted sky. "Another ship comes?"

Cameron shrugged. "Maybe, maybe not. An AI-controlled supply ship, the Vanguard, was supposed to be waiting in orbit for us when we arrived. Never found out what happened to it.

Anyway, Frankie's the best I can do for you. So, that's where you're going."

The girl made no response to this, other than to plump herself down in the shade of the cabin while giving him what he recognized from battles lost to his ex-wife as a this-ain't- over-look.

Cameron returned to the cabin, found the Kid a thick, long-sleeved shirt and a small backpack which he filled with apples. After loading a larger pack for himself and grabbing a machete, he shouldered his way into his faded spacer jacket with its astronavigator's silver bars and slung the shotgun across his back. Then swinging the machete as he went, set out along an overgrown trail that wound its way up into the hills. As he pushed deeper and deeper into the gloom of the alien jungle, he kept an eye on the girl as she scampered along behind him. She seemed to be doing okay.

Then she threw up.

Cameron winced. Aw, crap. Radiation sickness! Hope Frankie's still got some of her meds.

Two hours later, jacket soaked with sweat and hands crisscrossed with cuts and scratches, he came to an abrupt halt. Ahead of them, a clump of creeping, catch-you willows formed a thick, waving curtain across the trail. He swore under his breath. If I try going around those sticky horrors, I risk getting lost. Nothing for it but to keep the Kid close and try to hack my way through.

As he started forward, the girl grabbed his arm, pointed to the swaying curtain, and whispered, "Bug."

Cameron peered ahead. "Where? I don't see anything."

The girl grasped his hand and squeezed hard, "See like me."

The scene before him flashed to infrared. He jerked back, for there, not thirty yards distant, crouched a clatter bug. Its massive, crab-like, fighting claws and multiple legs ensnared by the catch-you willows. The creature's stalk-mounted eyes glared at him with murderous intent.

Heart pounding, he reached back for the shotgun. Before his fingers could touch the weapon, the girl whispered, "No, others hear."

He glanced around. Crap! She's right. There could be dozens of them out there.

The bug made the clattering sound, for which those tank-like creatures were named, and lunged forward in a desperate attempt to free itself from the smothering grasp of the catch-you willows. However, the bug's struggles served only to open a narrow tunnel running the length of its right side and the swarming catch-yous.

The Kid yelled, "Come, come," and shot past him, racing for the gap. Cameron followed, hacking off one of the bug's legs as it lashed down at her. They were almost through the hole when another leg slammed into the side of his head. The force of the blow drove him to his knees amid a swirl of stars.

The girl, now through the gap, jumped up and down, calling, "Quick, quick!"

Cameron clambered to his feet and staggered after her, trying to think amid the still swirling stars. *She can see in infrared! Okay, a mutation brought on by radiation, maybe? But how the hell'd she share her vision with me? Telepathy? Ye Gods!*

The bug continued to flail and clatter behind them, but the sounds became fainter and fainter as they struggled up the trail.

#

Cameron and the girl sat on the trunk of a fallen tree, sharing an apple. He studied her profile. *Hasn't thrown up again, but she's complained a couple of times of dizziness. Another sign of radiation sickness?*

She squinted up at the palisaded cluster of buildings looming above them and wrinkled her nose. "Bad place."

Cameron nodded. "You got that right, but beggars can't be choosers, so that's where you're going."

She shook her head. "Frankie bad?"

"Survivor more like. Led the parties that hunted down the boars for us."

The girl glanced up. "Boars?"

"Yeah, big, black, piggy things. Bite me in half. Swallow you whole. Like the strangler vines, the catch-you willows, and the clatter bugs, the boars came as a nasty surprise when we arrived."

"Frankie, still hunt boars?"

"No, even before the bugs overran First Landing, her people were raiding the outlying settlements."

"You not afraid of her?"

Cameron scoffed. "Frankie? No, worked for me on the way out. She was the queen of the cargo hold. Figure she'll cut me some slack."

He heaved himself up and extended a hand. "Come on. Let's go."

After another fifteen minutes of climbing, Cameron spotted a bush-filled depression running alongside the trail. Having first satisfied himself that the hollow was free of nasties, he whispered, "You stay here while I work things out with Frankie."

The Kid shook her head. "No, I come."

"No, you won't. I don't want you underfoot if things go sideways."

The girl scowled at this but settled into the hollow without further argument.

As he climbed the last hundred yards or so, Cameron studied the palisade. Looks solid enough. Frankie must've built it from the trunks of Sagan trees. Those GMO redwoods are doing fine out here. His sweat-streaked face twisted into a wry grin. Score one for the terraformers, who got pretty much everything else wrong.

At his approach, the palisade gate swung open, and a burly, young woman hefting a crossbow stepped out. "Hold it right there, Cameron. We got no food for you."

He made a calming gesture. "Get your mother, Thena. I'm just here to talk."

The sentinel called back to someone unseen, "Get Ma. Chet Cameron's here."

Minutes later, an even larger woman pushed past the first, squinted toward him, and grinned. "That really you, Chet Cameron, out of work astronavigator and failed orchardist?"

"Yeah, it's me, Frankie. Come to talk."

The cargo queen folded her formidable forearms across her equally formidable bosom and nodded. "Okay, Chet, but nothing's free anymore, not even talk. You got anything to trade?"

"Intel."

"Okay, intel's always worth something. Let's hear it."

"Some idiot's turned the cryos loose."

Thena snorted. "As far as intel goes, that's gotta be worth what, a jug of warm piss?"

Frankie gave her head an exasperated shake. "Get back to your post, Thena. Grownups talking here."

The sentinel shot her mother a resentful glance before stamping back inside the family fortress."

Frankie swung back to Cameron. "Girl's got a point, Chet. Why are we talking about cryos?"

"Because I got one with me. A young girl. Got radiated. Needs looking after."

"And you brought her here because you think I run a foundling home or something?"

Cameron took a deep breath. "No– I brought her here because you've got meds, and when you ran the cargo hold, you always came up with workarounds when things went all pear-shaped."

The cargo queen looked reflective for a moment, smiled, and nodded. "Yeah, I did, didn't I? And you were the only bridge bastard who came down to help trim the cargo after it shifted on the final jump." She peered down the slope. "Okay, call her up, and let's see what she looks like."

Cameron turned to summon the Kid and did a double take. She was standing close behind him. How the hell'd she get up here without Thena or Frankie spotting her? He grabbed the Kid, pulled her around to face Frankie, and tried for an ingratiating smile. "Here, she is. Calls herself the Cryo Kid."

Frankie glared at him through narrowed eyes, and, when next she spoke, her tone was icy. "So, help me, Chet, you pull another trick like that, and I'll have Thena put a bolt through your head."

Cameron made a calming gesture. "There's nothing to get bent out of shape over. Kid's got special talents, is all."

Thena, sounding rattled, called out from behind the gate, "This is bullshit, Ma. He could have dozens of those freaks out there. Just waiting to slip inside the wall and slit our throats."

Frankie yelled over her shoulder, "Zip it, Thena." Turned back to Cameron and said, "Talents?"

"Yeah. Kid can see in infrared. Some sorta mutation, I figure. Got me out of a bug ambush a few hours back. As for what just happened, I was as surprised as you. She must be able to bend light."

Frankie, her expression now speculative, cocked her head. "Okay, maybe I'm a bit interested, but if she's such a prize, why aren't you keeping her?"

Cameron shrugged. "With First Landing overrun and the orchard's gone, there's nothing to keep me here. I'm going to try and make it over to Second. Can't take a radiated kid along on a hike like that."

Frankie snorted. "You'd be a fool to try, Kid or no kid. I took a crack at it a year ago with a party of six and didn't get halfway. Lost two jungle-savvy hands trying it."

Cameron shrugged. "Still gotta try, Frankie. A few more months and there'll be nothing but strangler-vines and bugs down in the flatlands."

"Can't argue with that. Tell you what. I can use an extra hand around here, the Kid can't eat much, and we got no use for our radiation meds. Why don't you throw in with us for a while? See how it goes?"

From the other side of the palisade came the sound of voices raised in heated argument. Then Thena called out, "No way, either they go back where they came from, or we start shooting."

Frankie swung around to face the palisade gate and, fists clenched, snarled. "Since when do you give orders, girl?"

From inside the fortress came the sound of further argument followed by the thud of the gate's drawbar as someone rammed it home. Thena yelled, "Since now."

Frankie's face purpled. "I'll have your hide for this."

"Maybe, but you got Lui and Marcus killed on your stupid attempt to get to Second, and now you're willing to take in flatlanders and freaks. We're not putting up with any more of your crap. We'll throw you over a backpack with the meds he wants and some other stuff for the trail. After that– you're one of them."

#

Fifteen minutes later, a backpack came sailing over the palisade to land at Frankie's feet. The cargo queen glared up at the silent fortress and shook her fist. "This ain't over, Thena. Not by a long shot." She then scooped up the pack, slung it over her shoulder, and stalked off toward the jungle.

Cameron jogged alongside her. "Where we going, Frankie?"

300

"I'm looking for the trail we hacked out to Second last year. Have to find the supplies we cached when we turned back."

The Kid tugged at Cameron's arm. "We go Second now?"

"Yeah, looks like it. I hoped to get supplies from Frankie before starting out. Now, all we got is what's in our packs, and whatever's in that cache."

As soon as Frankie found the trail, she demanded Cameron's machete. Which he surrendered in return for Thena's meds.

Three sweaty-hours later, darkness fell with tropical swiftness, and a bone-numbing cold crept in from all sides. Cameron, Frankie, and the Kid huddled together for warmth while things unseen snuffled and slithered around them. The Kid was soon asleep. Cameron and Frankie dozed, but neither really slept.

At first light, they set off again and soon reached the hill's crest, up which they started climbing the day before. Ahead of them stretched rank after rank of distance-dimmed heights. Cameron peered ahead. "How much further to Second?"

Frankie shrugged. "We figured the other side of the furthest range you can see."

Cameron raised a scornful eyebrow. "You figured?"

Frankie glared back at him. "Yeah, Mr. Astronavigator. All our satellites got fried when Medusa flared, remember? That means no GPS, so, even if we had maps, which we didn't, the best we could do was head east 'til we found something."

Cameron made a placating gesture. "Okay, point taken. Any landmarks we should be on the lookout for?"

Frankie gestured toward the forest, stretching away below them. "We found the wreck of an aircar hung up in the trees somewhere down there. A bit beyond that, there's a river running real fast through a deep ravine. The only way across is a fallen tree."

Cameron nodded, said, "Okay," and took the lead, slip-sliding down the slope clutching at branches to slow his descent. The girl followed, leaping after him, never losing her footing or taking her eyes off the trail ahead. The cargo queen slid down behind them, cursing like a techie.

The Kid spotted the wreck first. The vehicle dangled high above them, caught in the topmost branches of a clump of Sagans. Cameron swung around to face Frankie. "That's not an aircar. It's an orbit to surface shuttle."

Frankie squinted upwards. "You sure? I was told we lost both ours to the Medusa flare."

"Yeah, I'm sure. I trained as a backup pilot. Flown 'em a dozen times. This one's gotta be from the Vanguard."

"The Vanguard? Holy crap!"

"Exactly. You recover anything from it?"

Frankie scoffed. "Course not. Didn't have anyone stupid enough to climb that high." She glanced over at the Kid. "Maybe it's time she started earning her keep?"

Cameron shook his head. "No way, even with the meds, she gets dizzy. 'Sides, she wouldn't know what to look for."

Frankie made a frustrated gesture. "Well, I'm sure as hell not going up there, so, either you go, or we head down to the river."

Cameron squinted up at the shuttle. "Maybe, if we had ropes, but–" He caught the stink of something worse than rotting flesh and gagged, slapping a hand across his nose and mouth.

The Kid mirrored his gesture and tugged at his arm. "Things come."

Frankie yelled, "Boars." Jumped for the nearest tree limb and hoisted herself up. Cameron grabbed the Kid, threw her up to the cargo queen's waiting arms, and spun around shotgun at the ready.

Two black boars, each larger than a Cape buffalo and both uglier than sin burst squealing from the jungle. Cameron scrambled for cover amid the Sagans. The boars skidded to a halt and peered about with small, angry eyes. Unable to spot their prey, they raised their snouts– sniffing the air. As soon as they caught Cameron's scent, they stalked forward.

The Kid leaned down from her branch, reaching for his shoulder. "Come, come."

Cameron batted her hand away. "Frankie, get her out of the way."

The boars, hearing their voices, closed in on Cameron's hiding place. Frankie's head and shoulders appeared amid thick foliage a lot higher than the Kid. "Pass up the gun. I've got a clear shot at the bastards."

A boar nosed around the base of the Sagan behind which Cameron crouched. The creature gave a triumphal grunt. But before it could lunge forward, the Kid swung her apple-filled backpack in a downward arc, smacking it on the head. Squealing in surprise and anger, the boar lurched up at her only to have Frankie's larger, heavier pack come crashing down on its now upturned snout. Cameron sprang forward, jammed the shotgun under its chin, and blew a fist-sized hole through the top of its head.

As the boar sagged to its knees, Frankie yelled, "Way to go, Chet. I still got eyes on the other one. Now throw me the damned gun and get your skinny ass up here."

Cameron, ears ringing from the gun's thunder, threw the weapon up to the Kid, who passed it on to Frankie. There was a moment's silence. Then the shotgun thundered twice more. Frankie gave a whoop of triumph. "Got the bastard right between the eyes!"

The Kid leapt down and threw her arms around Cameron, squeezing the breath out of him. It took him a moment to realize that he was shaking as much as she.

#

303

Frankie spat down the steep-sided ravine. "Yeah, I'm sure this is where the bloody tree was. You can still see some of the roots sticking outa that hole behind us."

Cameron peered at the river, boiling away below them. "So, what happened to it?"

Frankie gave her head an irritated shake. "I don't know, Chet. It was rotten as hell. Maybe the river got higher and washed it away. Maybe pixies took the damn thing. All I know for sure is we're screwed."

The Kid, silent until now, said, "Need rope."

Frankie swung around to face her. "Yeah, rope would be good, a prefab bridge would be even better, but we don't have either. So, what's your point?"

The girl ducked behind Cameron. "Boar tummies."

"What the hell's she on about, Chet?"

Cameron flashed back to the previous night. The dancing flames of their campfire and the skill with which the machete-wielding Frankie dismembered the boar carcasses. "I think she means the pig guts we left back at the Sagan grove."

Frankie paused, looked thoughtful, and nodded, "Yeah, yards, and yards of the stuff." She glanced at the Kid as if seeing her for the first time. "You know, she may be onto something."

Cameron shot her a skeptical glance. "Pig intestines? They be strong enough?"

"Should be. They're tough as old hell. If they aren't, we can plait them." She turned to the Kid. "Okay, we'll give it a try. You know the way back to the Sagans?"

"I know."

"Then, scoot."

The Kid gave an eager nod and scrambled up the slope down which they slid minutes before. As he turned to follow, Frankie clamped a restraining hand on Cameron's arm, waited until the girl was out of sight, and leaned close. "We need to talk about her."

Cameron frowned. "Why? By now, you know as much about her as I do."

"Maybe more."

"How's that?"

"You saw my pack hit the boar?"

"Yeah, nice shot. Thanks for that."

Frankie made an impatient gesture. "I didn't do a damn thing. One moment, I'm hanging onto a tree branch with both hands. The next, my backpack unclips, slides off my shoulders, and falls away, weaving its way down between the branches and picking up speed. Then whamo! Scores a direct hit on the porker's snout."

Cameron frowned and glanced up the slope. "And you think that was all the kid's doing?"

"Either that or Thena gimmie a magic backpack, which," she added sourly, "I very much doubt."

Cameron nodded. "Okay, in addition to her other powers, she has the gift of telekinesis, the ability to move objects just by—"

Frankie bristled. "I know what the hell telekinesis is, you smug bridge bastard."

Cameron made a calming gesture. "Okay, assuming she has the power to move objects just by thinking it, how's that a problem?"

"The problem isn't that or any of her other powers we know about. The problem's whether the Kid has other abilities. Abilities she isn't even aware of. Powers that could be a danger to us all."

Cameron shrugged. "Okay, but, even if she does, what can we do about it?"

Frankie stared up the hill, looking unhappy. "I don't know, but she's giving me the willies. Keep an eye on her, okay."

#

Next day it rained hard. Great, cold drops dripping their way through the jungle canopy above while the river frothed its way through the narrow canyon below. Cameron squatted near the edge of the ravine amid coils of plaited boar guts. Legs aching from climbing up and down the hill to the Sagans, he wanted nothing more than to curl up and sleep.

Frankie, with the Kid following, slid down the slope behind him. The Kid hopped up on a nearby stump and sat staring across the ravine. The cargo queen dumped two coils of plaited boar guts at his feet, saying, "Last batch, Chet. We've got more than enough to cross. You figured out a way to get a rope over to the other side, yet?"

Cameron heaved himself up and shook his head. "No. You?

Frankie gestured across the ravine. "Maybe. I figure we can use that big old tree over there to anchor our pig gut bridge."

Cameron squinted across the chasm. A giant purple colored plant looking like a much-swollen saguaro cactus stood close to the ravine's far edge. He straightened up. Don't remember seeing that before. She's right, though. It'll make a solid enough anchor if we can get a line around it. He swung back to face the cargo queen. "Okay, but I still can't see any way of getting a cable around it."

Frankie looking smug, smiled for the first time since they left the palisade, threw a comradely arm across his shoulders. "I'm thinking we use a scorpion."

Cameron shook his head. "A scorpion! What the hell's a scorpion?"

Frankie grinned. "A scorpion, Mr. Astronavigator, is an artillery piece invented by the Romans. Basically, it's a big old crossbow. We can make the stock and the bowstave from the trees growing around here, and we can make the bow cord from boar

306

sinews. Won't have to be anything fancy. It's only forty feet from here to the other side. We should be able to get our line across in one shot." She pointed over to the stump on which the Kid sat. "We can mount it on that."

"Okay, but how are we going to make an arrow for this, this—scorpion?"

Frankie picked up a wrist-thick tree branch lying near the ravine edge and held it high. "It's not called an arrow. It's called a bolt, and we make our bolt from a length of hardwood a bit thicker and straighter than this. I'll carve it into arrowhead at one end and fire-harden it. Then I'll fasten our pig-gut cable to a notch carved just behind the head. Once the bolt's buried in the tree, we'll tie the cable around the Kid's stump and cross hand over hand."

Cameron grinned, rose to his feet, clapped his hands in admiration. "Brilliant, Frankie. The best workaround, yet."

The girl frowned and shook her head. "Tree bad."

Frankie scowled and looked as if she was going to give the Kid a backhander, but, after a moment, she shrugged. "Maybe, but this's the best I can come up with. So, unless you have a better idea, it's what we're gonna do."

#

Building the scorpion proved harder than Frankie sketched out, a lot harder, but, after two days sweating and swearing, a contraption looking for all the world like a stump-mounted crossbow sat pointing at the purple-colored tree perched on the far side of the ravine.

Frankie turned to Cameron. "You care to do the honors, Chet?"

Cameron shook his head and backed away. "No way I'm touching that thing. It's all yours."

Frankie chuckled and, stepping around the lengths of pig-gut cable coiled beside the scorpion, crouched down behind her weapon, grasped the firing lever, and yanked it back.

There was a loud thwack. The war machine bucked and flung itself off the stump, but the bolt, trailing the cable behind it, shot across the ravine and slammed into its target. The tree screamed, a shrill ear-stabbing sound, twisted around on previously hidden stump-like legs and crashed away into the jungle, taking the cable with it. After a dozen yards or so, the pig guts, stretched to the breaking point, snapped. Cameron grabbed the Kid and threw them both flat as the cable came whipping back.

Everything went quiet save for the roar and tumble of the river. Frankie, now seated on her broad backside, dabbed at her bloody nose and glanced over at Cameron. "Okay, the Kid was right about the tree. But I never seen anything like that in all my time in the jungle."

Cameron got to his feet and peered down at her. "You sure there's no other way across?"

Frankie nodded. "Yeah, like I told you, we had to use the log here because we couldn't find anything else."

Cameron swore under his breath. "So, what do we do now?"

The cargo queen's shoulders sagged. "Beats the hell out of me." She picked up an empty boar-skin bag and a coil of pig gut rope and slouched over to the edge of the ravine to draw water.

The Kid, silent until now, jumped to her feet, pointed to the pig gut rope Frankie was tying to the water bag, and said, "Use to climb shuttle?"

Frankie shrugged. "Sure, why the hell not?"

#

Using the pig gut ropes to climb up to the shuttle sounded dangerous but doable when staring up from the ground. Only when they were high in the Sagans' wind-swept branches did Cameron fully appreciate what they were up against. They abandoned their backpacks after the first couple of hours, reworked some of their ropes as lassos, and continued their ascent.

They never stopped shivering now, and anything dropped, like the shotgun banging and bouncing its way down through the tree limbs, was gone for good.

Frankie threw a length of rope up to Cameron, which he looped around the branch he straddled and tied it off. They climbed roped together like mountaineers throughout the previous day and then slept tied to the Sagan's thick branches during the night. Cold, stiff, and tired, morning found them, in Frankie's words, "Within spitting distance of the shuttle."

Cameron squinted up at the craft's blackened undersurface. The shuttle, its delta shape, still, for the most part, hidden amid thick, green foliage rested on a crisscross of stout branches, including the one on which he sat. He fretted his lower lip. Looks like an older model, with no obvious signs of damage. And apart from that broken branch jutting up alongside it, nothing's blocking the airlock. He leaned over and called down to Frankie, "All looks good, so far. Toss me up a lasso. I'm going to rig a safety line before trying to get over."

Frankie threw up the requested rope yelling as she did so, "Careful of the branch you're on. Looks like the shuttle's weight's cracking it."

Cameron slung the lasso over his shoulder and began working his way along the tree limb. He managed to halve the distance to the shuttle before the branch gave an ominous crack and dropped what felt like half a foot. He took a deep breath and threw the lasso, hoping to snag the broken branch next to the airlock.

The line fell short.

The tree limb gave another louder crack and sagged yet again. Cameron pitched forward, grabbed hold of the branch with both arms, and dug his fingernails into the bark. Heart pounding, he lay there, for a moment cursing under his breath. Crap! No way forward. No point in going back.

Something landed behind him. He glanced over his shoulder to see the Kid standing there, hands outstretched. "Give rope."

Frankie called up, "Sorry, Chet. I don't know how the hell she got up there without me seeing. You okay?"

"Yeah, but I can't go further out on this branch without it breaking."

"There another branch?"

Cameron glanced around. "Nothing's closer to the airlock than this."

"Then let her try. We got nothing to lose."

Swearing under his breath, Cameron handed the rope back to the Kid then waited, heart in mouth, as she clambered over him, scampered along the creaking limb, and tossed the line. The lasso sailed over to the airlock, hovered for a moment, then drifted down to encircle the broken branch next to it. The Kid pulled the rope tight and tied it around the limb to which Cameron still clung.

He let go of a breath he didn't remember holding.

Frankie whooped. "Unbe-freaking-levable."

Cameron smiled and shook his head. "Great work, Cryo Kid, but I'll have to bind this branch with rope if it's going to hold my weight, let alone Frankie's."

Frankie made a rude noise before slinging up another coil of rope. Cameron bound the cracked tree limb together, then keeping a tight grip on the line rigged by the Kid, inched his way forward. A rising wind caused the branch to sway and creak as he worked his way over to the airlock.

Frankie called up, "Well, how's it look?"

Now within touching distance of the shuttle, Cameron yelled back, "Still no signs of damage. I'm going to try to open the lock." He pulled aside the plate protecting the access panel and pressed his palm against the cold metal.

The door grated open.

He clambered inside and sniffed. Air's stale as hell. Better stay near the outer door 'til we've got some circulation going. Readouts on the control panel set into the lock's sidewall went from forbidding reds to cautious yellows and, a short time later, welcoming greens. He palmed the access plate on the lock's inner door.

For a moment, nothing happened, then the door wheezed open a crack, and the shuttle's internal lighting snapped on. Cameron threw a fist up a triumphant fist. "Newton and Hawking, we got power!"

He pushed the inner door all the way open, stepped through, and glanced around. The cargo bay was a tumble of cracked and broken cargo pods. He grimaced. Frankie will have to sort this lot out. No sign of the crew, and no hint as to what caused the crash.

The Kid appeared beside him, looking sick and shaky in the harsh light of the cargo bay. "Where people?"

He shook his head. "Don't know yet. Let's get Frankie up here to check out those cargo pods while you and I climb up to the flight deck and have a look around."

#

Cameron studied the flight deck door. A stenciled notice read No Access AI Controlled. Chinese characters to the same effect appeared immediately below. He looked down at the Kid. "Well, what do you think?"

The Kid placed her palms against the door and closed her eyes, concentrating. "Door locked."

311

Cameron turned and called down to the cargo hold. "Frankie. We got a locked door here. Need a pry bar or something."

The cargo queen's voice boomed back, "Haven't seen anything like that yet, but we got mixed cargo here. Must be something we can use."

From behind him came a loud click. Cameron turned to see the girl sliding the door open. "Never mind, Frankie. The Kid's got it."

The layout of the flight deck was like those on which Cameron trained. Including a control stick and a monitor screen mounted alongside the power gauge. Tree boughs blocked the view through the windscreen and side ports.

Cameron settled into the pilot's seat while the Kid, looking tired, curled up in the copilot's chair. At his touch, the instrument panel lit up with a mixture of digital readouts and dust-dimmed red, green, and yellow indicator lights. As he watched, the greens came to dominate.

He called over his shoulder, "Frankie, finish up whatever you're doing and get up here. The freaking ship's alive and running a self-diagnostic." Beside him, the girl slumped forward. Cameron caught her, adding, "Bring up the Kid's meds and the water bag. She's fading on us."

Moments later, the cargo queen crowded in behind them, holding up the water bag for the Kid to gulp down the last of its contents. "This sucker really flyable?"

Cameron gestured toward the control panel. "I still see a hell of a lot of yellow-maybes, but, yeah, it's looking good."

Frankie gave him a close-to-lethal slap on the back. "So, we can fly this bird and her cargo to Second Landing? Hot damn, we'll own the place!"

Cameron threw up a restraining hand. "Whoa, we'd be lucky to get her across the river."

Frankie snarled an expletive. "How come?"

"Solar panels aren't picking up enough light, so our power reserves," he jabbed a finger at the flickering power gauge, "aren't building up."

Frankie glared at the offending indicator for a moment, turned, and began clambering down the ladder to the cargo hold.

Cameron called after her, "Where're you going?"

"To fix your power problem."

Cameron shrugged and swung back to face the control panel muttering as he did so, "What's she gonna try now? Not another scorpion, I hope."

The answer came minutes later when part of the foliage blocking the windscreen fell away to reveal Frankie macheting away other branches covering the starboard solar panels. Moments later, the flickering yellow power gauge changed to a still flickering, but more promising, green. Cameron waved for Frankie's attention and gave her an enthusiastic thumbs-up. The cargo queen grinned, waved back, and returned to her work.

The Kid wrapped up in blankets from the cargo hold was drifting in and out of consciousness now. But there was nothing more Cameron could do for her. He was getting up from his chair, intending to go out and help Frankie, when a standard ship's avatar appeared on the monitor screen. The image chosen by the ship's designers was that of a competent-looking, middle-aged human male sporting a military-style haircut. "This is the exploration vessel Vanguard. Welcome to the Medusa system. As soon as power's restored to the shuttle, I will initiate recovery procedures."

Cameron peered through the windscreen, spotted Frankie, and made an urgent beckoning gesture.

Minutes later, the cargo queen machete still clutched in her fist appeared behind him. "What the hell, Chet? I've only cleared part of the starboard panel, the light's failing, and it looks like a storm's blowing in."

313

Cameron jabbed a finger at the screen. "We've found Vanguard."

Frankie gave Cameron a congratulatory punch on the shoulder, leaned forward, and demanded of the avatar, "Where the hell you been, Vanguard?"

The avatar responded, "On arrival in system, I took up station orbiting New Brazil as per program and launched my shuttles. Shortly thereafter, Medusa flared, damaging my systems. I've since been able to maintain an orbit that keeps the planet between me and any further flares."

"And your shuttles?"

"One crashed and burned, but I was able to glide this one into the Sagan tops and effect emergency repairs. Unfortunately, the fast-growing Sagan foliage prevented the solar cells from building up sufficient power for a return flight."

The Kid groaned in her sleep. Cameron reached over, touched her forehead, and said, "She's burning up." He swung back to the avatar. "We have a medical emergency. Are you equipped to treat radiation poisoning?"

The avatar gave its head a human-like shake. "No, but I can fabricate the necessary facilities and medicines."

A flash of lightning, a harbinger of the coming storm, lit up the flight deck. Cameron glanced at the power gauge. While it remained green, it showed no significant increase in power reserves. They wouldn't be going anywhere soon. Rain spattered the windscreen, and the Kid groaned in her sleep.

#

Cameron woke to the sound of Frankie climbing up to the flight deck. The cargo queen dropped a full water bag in his lap, saying, "Make sure the kid gets some of this when she wakes up."

Cameron gave his head an admiring shake. "How the hell'd you manage that?"

"Found some plastic sheeting in the cargo hold and rigged it to catch last night's rain. Tastes funky, but we got enough to keep us going for a couple of days." She handed him a foil-wrapped food tube saying, "Found lots of this crap boxed up in the hold."

Cameron unwrapped the tube, bit off a chunk of its stale-tasting contents and gestured out the side window. "We've got another storm coming in. And we're still getting only minimum power gain from the cells."

Frankie grimaced. "Looks like clearing the foliage was a double-edged weapon. Wind can get under the hull now. Last night it only rocked us around a bit. This time it might blow us right out the trees."

Cameron turned to Vanguard's avatar, "We've cleared away a lot of the foliage from the solar cells. Can you beam power down to us?"

A gust of wind buffed the shuttle.

The avatar looked reflective for the briefest of moments. "Yes, but I no longer have fine control over my lasers. You will have to get the shuttle out from under the remaining foliage and present a flat surface to me before I can risk a power transfer."

At the sound of the avatar's voice, the Kid stirred and woke eyes fever bright. "I move ship."

Frankie shook her head. "No, you won't. Chet, give her some water and try to get some food down her."

The girl gulped down the water but refused the food tube, saying, "Now, I move ship."

Frankie's face purpled. "No, you won't dammit—"

Outside, the sky darkened, and a second gust of wind, far stronger than the first, hit the weather side of the shuttle, pitching the craft sideways and sending Frankie sprawling. Rain thundered against the hull, drowning out her curses.

The Kid, pinched face lined with effort, sat up, and extended a trembling hand. The shuttle began to rise. The wind hit them again. Cameron grabbed for the control stick as the ship slipped off the supporting lattice of branches. He risked a glance out the side window. They were falling leaf-like toward the jungle below. Beside him, the Kid sagged back in her chair, exhausted.

The cargo queen pulled herself up to stand behind him. "If you can't fly this beast, try and bring it down on the other side of the river."

Cameron shook his head. "Not enough fuel. Best we can hope for now is a controlled crash."

Vanguard's avatar interrupted, saying, "I'm going to initiate power transfer. Keep the shuttle on a straight and level course, or the lasers will burn you to cinders."

As Cameron fought to comply with these directions, the power gauge fluttered and snapped from green back to yellow. The controlled crash option was off the table. They were going down and going down hard.

Then a shimmering white light flashed through the flight deck. The power gauge jumped back to green and read full charge. A moment later, however, a proximity alarm howled. Cameron risked a glance out the side window. The jungle canopy was rushing up at them. He heaved back on the control stick, and just as the topmost branches scraped against the hull, the shuttle shot upwards.

The cargo Queen whooped and pounded Cameron on the back. "Son of a bitch, you cut that close. I damn near peed myself."

Cameron grinned and turned to check on the Kid. Her shriveled, unmoving form was almost lost amid her clothing. He touched her shoulder, giving her a gentle shake. "Kid?"

Frankie leaned forward; her broad face lined with concern. "She okay?"

Cameron shook his head. "No, looks like she's gone."

The monitor screen flashed, and the Kid's face appeared in place of Vanguard's avatar. "No, no, up here. Cameron and Frankie come up to Vanguard."

Vincent Morgan lives in the fishing port of Steveston, British Columbia, is an avid reader of science fiction with a particular fondness for space opera, has completed the Science Fiction Writers Master Course with Gotham Writers Workshop and several courses with LitReactor. His short story, "To Allegiance Recalled," was awarded Silver Honorable Mention by Writers of the Future. And his work appears in several anthologies, including *Explorers Beyond The Horizon*, *First Contact Imminent*, and *Aliens Among Us*.

The Messenger

by Frank Sawielijew

The wizard's ghostly image appeared above the fountain in the town square, accompanied by a hideous noise that summoned all citizens to hear his words. His image struck fear into all who beheld him, and not even the boldest young men dared open their mouths in his presence.

"Your lack of devotion disappoints me," he announced when all the town had gathered around him. "For many years I have been your overlord, yet so rarely do you deign to visit. Not once have I seen a man of this town kneel at the gate of my tower and leave tribute in appreciation of my lordship. Yet still I allow your town to exist."

"But Lord," said the mayor, folding his hands in a supplicant gesture, "whenever your collector arrives, we hand over any tribute he asks for! If you want more, we give it willingly. But to journey to your tower on our own – far too perilous is the path, great master!"

"Cowardice is not a trait I desire in my subjects," replied the wizard. "I shall therefore present you with an ultimatum. Before the passing of five days, one among you must journey to my tower and pour out a libation of fresh, clean water before me, taken from the town's fountain." His projected image pointed down to the fountain it hovered above.

The mayor's eyes widened in shock. "Five days? But…"

The wizard pointed to a young red-haired woman in the crowd. "And I choose this one as the town's messenger. Remind me, my dear, what was it called again?"

Susanna met the stare of the apparition's translucent eyes. Its finger pointed to her chest, right at the spot where her heart was pounding rapidly.

"Brunntal, great master."

"Ah yes. I expect you at my tower within five days, messenger of Brunntal. Should you not arrive within that time, I shall lay waste to this town of cowards. Be swift in your journey, messenger – you would not wish to disappoint a wizard."

With these words, the wizard's image vanished, leaving the townsfolk to curse and wail in despair. None could make the journey to his tower in five days, and certainly not alone. Acts of wanton tyranny were common in the wizard's domain, but this was his cruelest yet.

While the others lamented their fate, Susanna picked a waterskin of sturdy cow hide from a market stall and submerged it in the fountain until it was full.

She silenced the crowd with a shout. All eyes were upon her, and only hushed whispers crawled from ear to ear as none dared to speak aloud. There was an atmosphere of uncertainty among the people. Many feared she would leave and seek a better life elsewhere; but those who noticed the bulging waterskin slung across her belly knew better.

"Bring me a horse and provisions for a week. I need both food and water; *this* is for the wizard." She slapped the waterskin at her waist. Then, she glanced down at her sandaled feet. "I also need a sturdy pair of boots. Comfortable socks to go with them. A cloak for protection. A dagger to defend myself. A staff for walking, in case I lose the horse."

Her announcement was met with dumbfounded silence. People exchanged questioning glances; some left the crowd and vanished into their homes, only to return with the requested items in hand. Soon, more and more of the townfolk followed their example, until Susanna had an entire heap of equipment to choose from.

She ditched her sandals, dressed herself in the most comfortable socks and boots she could find, armed herself with a long dagger and sturdy staff, and wrapped a thick woolen cloak around her shoulders; it had deep pockets sewn into the inside, into which she stuffed well-packed rations of dried meat and fruits, flatbread and nuts. Three filled waterskins joined the dagger at her belt.

A rich merchant's daughter presented her with a long silver hairpin with a sharp, needle-like point. She gratefully accepted it and pinned up her long red hair, glad to have it out of the way – and a backup weapon on her head in case she lost her dagger.

Thus equipped, she took the mayor's own horse and set out toward the wizard's tower. The way there led through the treacherous Sinking Marshes, the jagged crags of the Broken Spine, the wild jungles of Ammura, and the scorching desert of Ilra'ka.

The journey was possible to be made in five days; but the dangers that lurked in these hostile biomes had cut many a traveler's journey short before.

Susanna rode out and left the familiar surroundings of her home for the first time in her life. The people looked after her with newfound hope in their eyes.

Even though nobody truly believed she could do it, at least she had given them a spark of hope to cling to.

#

Susanna's southward journey led through rolling hills and vast grasslands populated by peaceable wildlife that posed no threat. Skittish deer fled into the woodland at her approach and tiny birds sang their farewell songs overhead. She rode at a moderate pace, careful not to put too much strain on the horse. If she wanted to reach the wizard's tower before the passing of five days, she had to keep her steed fresh and healthy.

She paused at a brook to drink and pick berries, saving her provisions for less hospitable lands. But she only stayed for five minutes and no more. Rest was a luxury she could not afford.

Only a few hours after she had left her home, the wet bogland of the Sinking Marshes came into view. The shallow water glittered under the midday sun; a treacherous beauty pocked with sinkholes that could swallow men whole. In darker days, criminals were drowned in the swampy waters of the marsh; nowadays, they were beheaded in a clean and civilized manner.

Susanna's horse bucked as it neared the marsh, reluctant to enter. She calmed it down with gentle strokes along its neck, then urged it onward. Hesitantly, its hooves stepped into the brackish wet, sinking down into the soft ground.

It was treacherous terrain. One wrong step could get her horse stuck, forcing her to leave it behind and continue on foot. She guided it through the swampland at a slow, deliberate pace, careful to avoid the ground that swallowed.

She had been riding for over an hour when suddenly, a corpse rose out of the water to her right. Its skin was black and leathery, but all the features of its face were as clear as they were in life. A grimace of agony was frozen into its ancient lips, and its bony fingers pointed towards the wizard's tower many miles ahead.

The horse whinnied and veered off its path, hooves splashing into the treacherous waters of the swamp.

"Ho, be calm! It's a mere trick of the wizard to unnerve us! Be not afraid," Susanna said to her horse, holding a reassuring hand against its neck.

But then, another corpse rose from the depths, and another. Dozens of the ancient dead emerged from their watery tombs, sending the horse into a panic. It galloped away from the strange dead men, paying no heed to the ground underfoot.

Susanna tried to hold it back, but it was no use. Terror had taken hold of her steed and it charged through the swamp in a mad flight, its hooves kicking up big chunks of muddy soil. Her journey's progress was rapid for a while – until the horse's legs sunk deep into the mud and got stuck. The more it struggled, the deeper it got sucked in.

Susanna cursed and wailed, hugging the horse's neck and letting its mane soak up her tears. Her trusty animal companion was stuck for good, and she had to continue on foot.

She carefully dismounted, making sure to step lightly lest the swamp swallow her too. She ended the horse's suffering with her knife, tears rolling down her cheeks, and took up her quarterstaff. It allowed her to test the ground by prodding before she put her feet on it.

The slow, tedious march through the marshland was taxing on Susanna's limbs. Even where the ground was solid enough to tread, it was wet and sticky and sucked at her boots. Each step was laborious, and her legs soon ached with exhaustion.

For hours she walked, pressing on with all her strength. Even when the sun touched the horizon and drenched the sky in red, she kept walking. No matter how tired her legs grew, there was no rest for her in this swamp. The ground was difficult enough to walk on – it could offer her no sleeping place for the night.

But as her exhaustion grew, so did her vigilance shrink, and a careless step found her stuck in the mud like her horse had been. The wet, soupy ground held her boots in a tight embrace, unwilling to let go. No amount of pushing could loosen its grip, no matter how hard she tried.

She yelled and screamed and shouted curses at the sky, damning the wizard and his cruel games. With the premature end of her journey, Brunntal was doomed. In five days, death and destruction would rain upon the place of her birth, and it was all her fault.

As her shouts disturbed the deathlike silence of the swamp, a giant bird of prey became aware of her presence. She saw its shadow passing over her head and looked up. It was a massive creature, twice as large as her horse had been. The giant predator swooped down at her and she raised her staff to defend herself.

The bird's claws closed around the wooden staff and it rose back into the air, pulling Susanna up with it. The ground struggled to hold her, but in the end, it only kept her boots as she slid out of them and rose into the air, borne on the mightiest wings she had ever seen.

She was glad for her thick cloak, for the air was cold at this height and the speed of flight blasted a strong wind into her face. The bird's path led ever southward, towards the dreadful tower that awaited at her journey's end. Even though it was still many miles away, she could feel it getting closer. When the wizard had chosen her as Brunntal's messenger, he must have placed a sort of compass in her heart – an inner sense that showed her the way to his tower.

The swampland below passed rapidly before her eyes, such was the speed at which the bird rode the winds. A faster transport she could not have hoped for. It was a welcome rest for her tired legs, but now her arms had to prove their strength. If her fingers slipped from her staff, she would plummet to her death.

And so, she held on, straining the muscles in her arms and shoulders to fight against the gravity that tried to pull her back to ground, until the bird finally reached its lair.

#

This was the Broken Spine, a tall range of jagged grey mountains that separated the cold northern swampland from the lush and warm jungles to the south. The bird had built its nest on a large protruding slab of stone that jutted out of the mountainside. Like the birds in her homeland weaved nests of straw and twigs, this one was made from thick branches and roots. The bird dropped her into the nest, and she found herself face to face with three man-sized fledglings whose feathers had not yet grown and whose eyes were still blind.

They pecked at her with sharp beaks, and Susanna shielded herself with her thick cloak. The birds tore large holes into the garment with their pecking, and one of them chanced upon a pocket stuffed with beef jerky and dried fruit. The discovery of this little treasure chamber sent them into a frenzy, and they savaged her cloak to get at its precious fillings.

She dropped her cloak, relinquishing the many provisions she had packed for her journey, and climbed out of the nest. The young birds were so busy picking through her rations that they did not notice her escape.

The mother bird had gone out again, gliding across the swamps on its majestic wings. She watched it shrink against the horizon, going on its final hunting trip of the day before the sun passed entirely below the earth.

Susanna turned towards the mountain and climbed down its angled face. She had to find a place to rest before the break of night, for the terrain was too treacherous to brave at dark. The jagged rock was sharp and cut into her palms as she climbed, and a single wrongly placed step could cause her to slip and fall into the yawning depth below.

The loss of her cloak and boots only made the climb more arduous. The biting winds cut effortlessly through her thin tunic, and the grip of her socked feet was slippery.

When she finally reached a cave to take shelter in, the sun had long vanished behind the horizon and only the dim light of moon and stars remained to illumine her surroundings.

She retreated into the cave and laid down, trying to make herself comfortable on the hard-stone floor. Tomorrow, the most dangerous part of her journey would begin – the climb across the Broken Spine.

#

She woke with the first rays of sunlight against her face. Her hands reached for the rations stashed in her cloak but found only nothingness. With a groan, she remembered the fledgling birds of prey and their bountiful prize.

The day would have to start without breakfast.

She left the cave that had sheltered her for the night and followed the narrow pathway leading down from it. The sharp rocks underfoot poked many little holes into her socks, yet she did not want to take them off and go entirely barefoot. Even though it was just a thin layer of cloth, they offered at least some protection to her sensitive soles.

The Broken Spine turned out to be a labyrinth of winding paths leading past jagged rock faces and mighty peaks. Sometimes, they led her to a dead end and forced her to turn back; other times, they led her into caves that carved their way through the rock for miles, offering a shortcut to the other side of an insurmountable peak.

Yet her progress was deceptively slow. While her heart knew the way to the wizard's tower, the tall cliffs and jagged peaks blocked the direct path toward her goal. Only when the face of a mountain was not too steep could she dare to climb across; when she could not climb, she had to find a way around.

And not every path she took brought her closer to her goal. Even though she marched on without rest, the mountains did not want to end. Wherever she looked, only grey stone loomed before her eyes. No feature of the landscape was prominent enough to serve as a point of reference. She walked until the jagged rocks had turned her socks into shredded rags, yet she had no idea whether her wanderings led her any closer to the edge of the mountain range. She might as well be walking in circles, forever trapped in the heart of the mountains.

At the end of the day, she sought shelter in a cave again. In the darkness of night, her progress would be even more uncertain. She went to sleep with a growling stomach, awaiting another morning without breakfast.

#

When Susanna woke, she realized that the cave she had spent the night in was much larger than she had initially thought. She had slept right in the middle of a subterranean crossroads. Three different paths led deeper into the rock, all slanted downward.

As she stared into the darkness below, it seemed to call out to her, beckon her. Even though she had no source of light to illuminate her path, she decided to descend. Outside awaited only insurmountable peaks; in the depths, a possible path out of this labyrinth of stone.

Touching her hand against the wall, she proceeded down the middle path, choosing it by pure instinct. Her steps were slow and cautious. The ripped socks on her feet offered little protection and she did not want to step into something dangerous. Each time she took a step, she carefully probed the ground with her toes, feeling for irregularities, before putting her foot down. In the darkness, her sense of touch was her only guidance.

She walked for a long time, and still the cave went on. It did not lead to a dead end, nor did it expand into a larger space. Her fingers never left the wall, and she never felt it curve. The passage was straight as a spear's shaft, leading only forward and down, all the way down to the foot of the mountain.

After a while, the rays of a distant source of light returned the sight to her. It was a warm, orange light, gently flickering. She lowered her hand from the wall and moved it to the dagger at her belt as she walked into its embrace. The warm glow of fire hinted towards the presence of people, and she had no idea whether they were friendly or not.

As she went further, the light's source revealed itself to be a fire around which a group of people was gathered. The carcass of an animal was suspended over the fire, skewered on a wooden spit. The delicious smell of searing meat crawled into Susanna's nostrils and made her stomach growl.

She couldn't pass up the opportunity to provide her tired body with much-needed nourishment. Raising her hands in a non-threatening gesture, she shouted a greeting to announce her presence.

The people around the fire turned to face her. Only now did she notice their curious appearance: the men only had a right arm, the women only a left. Their torsos were bare, and Susanna couldn't see any scars on their shoulders that implied a wound. It was like they were born one-armed, a strange race of man entirely distinct from her own.

"Hail, dwellers of the cave! I wish to ask for a piece of meat to fill my stomach, for I have not eaten in a day," she said, earning strange looks from the one-armed people. She pointed a finger at the fire while her other hand rubbed her belly, hoping that her gestures would get the point across if they failed to understand her words.

But the strange one-armed people spoke among themselves in a rough and guttural language. They pointed at Susanna, grumbled and shook their heads. Some touched their empty shoulders and muttered under their breaths. The women seemed particularly perturbed, staring at her with apprehension in their eyes.

When the men picked up wooden clubs studded with the teeth of predators, Susanna knew they were not friendly. Angrily, one of them shouted a word: "Dumadan!"

The others took up the shout, turning it into a chant. *Dumadan! Dumadan!*

Their shouts echoed through the subterranean chamber, reflecting off the hard-stone walls. They approached Susanna with raised clubs, and she broke into a run. Along the cave wall she ran, heading towards the exit at the other end of the chamber. Unlike the passage she had emerged from, this one did not lead into darkness – instead, it held the promise of sunlight, of fresh air and a way out of the mountains.

But when her eyes fell upon its guardian, she froze in her tracks.

A one-armed man held the leash of a giant spider wrapped around his fingers. It was larger than the sheep-herding dogs they kept in Brunntal. Its myriad eyes regarded her with a predator's curiosity.

The spider's master looked towards Susanna with a questioning look, but when he noticed that she had two arms his eyes widened in shock. He let go of the leash and released his pet upon her with a barked command.

The giant spider leapt at Susanna with its eight legs stretched to the sides. The impact pushed her to the ground, and she found herself staring into the creature's many eyes, venomous fangs hovering above her face.

She pulled out her dagger and rammed it into the spider's soft underbelly. The creature shrieked and jabbed its fangs downward. Susanna rolled away, barely escaping the spider's venomous bite. One fang caught the sleeve of her tunic, pinning it to the ground. She yanked her arm free, tearing the sleeve off at the shoulder.

The spider struggled to pull its fangs out of the stone, so hard had it stabbed them into the ground. Just as Susanna reached for her dagger to pull it out again, the spider managed to free its fangs. She left her dagger and quickly crawled out from under the monstrous creature, grasping two of its hairy legs and pulling herself through the gap between them.

She charged at the spider's master and shoved him aside, rushing for the exit. Her legs carried her through the small passage into the sunlight. The ground underneath her feet changed from hard rock to soft soil as she ran onward, and soon she was surrounded by vibrant green in every direction.

As welcoming as the jungle's lush vegetation appeared after two days spent among barren rock, she didn't dare slow down her steps. The fight against the terrifying spider still fresh in her mind, she kept running, pushing onward until her lungs burned with exhaustion.

Finally, she allowed herself to collapse to the ground, resting her weary body on a soft patch of moss. Her pursuers had long given up; the only voices she heard were the sweet songs of birds echoing through the canopy.

She lay with her eyes closed for a long while, breathing deeply of the refreshing jungle air. It was thick with the fragrances of leaves and blossoms, so different from the thin air of the mountains.

When the ache in her legs subsided, she sat up and assessed the damage. Her body was miraculously unharmed despite the harrowing encounter with the giant spider, but she had left her dagger in the monstrous creature's belly. Now she was not only without supplies, but without weapon, too.

Her hands went up to her head, touching her hair. It was still fixed in place, held firm by the silver hairpin.

A smile wandered across her lips. She was not entirely disarmed yet.

Her clothes had suffered the worst damage. Her socks were shredded rags that barely covered her soles anymore, and her tunic had lost its left sleeve. But at least her belt was still intact, as were the three small waterskins hanging down from it. One was empty, drained during her arduous trek through the mountains; the other two were full, hopefully enough to last her for the rest of her journey.

The large waterskin slung across her belly was off limits, after all. It contained the wizard's libation. She looked up, trying to find the sun behind the dense canopy overhead. It had reached its zenith – it was noon already.

She only had two and a half days left to reach the wizard's tower.

With a sigh, she got to her feet and marched onward. Rest was a luxury she could not afford. Her tired legs led her southward, each step bringing her closer to her goal. But her legs were not the only part of her body that complained: her stomach was growling, hungry after two days without food. The jungle's berry-bearing bushes looked deceptively inviting, yet she resisted the temptation. She was not familiar with the plants of this region, and a carelessly ingested poison could quickly put an end to her journey.

Hunting did not promise much success, either. There were little furry things that vanished into the underbrush faster than she could catch them, colorful birds high up in the branches far beyond her reach, and thick-bodied snakes who could easily crush her throat if she provoked them.

When the sunlight assumed the red color of evening, she reached a broad river whose waters rushed southward. A smile of relief appeared on her lips and she offered a grateful prayer to her gods. With the last of her strength, she collected thick branches from the jungle floor and tied them together with sturdy vines. She pushed the resulting raft into the water and climbed onto it. It was an unstable construct, but it held her weight – and floated. The river's rapid currents took hold of her rickety raft and carried it downstream. She sat down on the uneven logs and allowed herself to relax. Her raft followed the river's path without any action of her own, and she could finally rest her tired limbs.

She dangled an arm into the cool, refreshing water – and pulled it out again when she felt something bite her finger. A glance into the depths revealed a school of fish swimming downstream, right below the logs of her makeshift raft.

"Oh, you little fishies are a godsend," she said, breathing out with relief. "Finally, something to eat!"

She pulled the long silver hairpin out of her hair and her long red hair broke loose of its tight updo, tumbling down to her waist. The hairpin's tip was sharp as a dagger's, and she stabbed down into the water to catch a couple of fish with it.

The little creatures were quick and agile, but after many tries, she finally caught one. She held her catch before her lips for a long moment before deciding against taking a bite. Her father had always warned her that raw fish could make you sick, so she tore off the right sleeve of her tunic and turned it into a makeshift sack, wrapping the fish into it. Once she got back to land, she could roast it over a fire and eat safely.

As long as some daylight still remained in the sky, she kept hunting for fish in the waters below her raft. The makeshift sack of her torn-off sleeve filled with more and more fish, promising a satisfying breakfast in the morning.

Just as the darkness of night was about to chase away the last remnants of light, a particularly large fish caught her eye. It was half the length of her raft and its massive shape was clearly visible even in the low light of dusk. If she managed to catch it, it could feed her for the entire rest of her journey.

She stabbed at the large fish and hit it right below its dorsal fin. The hairpin got stuck in its flesh and she pulled at it with all her might, but the fish trashed its body around to rid itself of this land-dwelling predator. The smooth handle of the silver hairpin slipped out of her fingers and the fish escaped her grasp, carrying her last remaining weapon with it.

"Damn!" She punched her fists against the thick logs of her raft. "I shouldn't have been so greedy."

She tied the ends of her torn sleeve together to secure her catch and stuffed it into her pants. She couldn't afford to lose that, too.

Lying belly-down on the raft, she tried to catch some sleep. The uneven logs provided uncomfortable bedding, and the sway of her craft upon the river's turbulent current made it hard to relax. But with tomorrow's food resting beneath her womb and the rapid progress towards her goal, her mind rested easy, and after a while she drifted off to sleep.

#

She woke with the first light of morning. Her raft had been swept ashore by an errant wave. A furry little creature had climbed upon the logs and prodded her face with three-fingered hands. She made a grab for it, but it scurried off at her first sign of movement.

So, it was only fish for breakfast, after all.

She got to her feet and pulled her stranded raft completely out of the water to make sure it wasn't swept away. Then, she gathered dry branches from the ground and piled them up to form a

333

fireplace. It took her much effort to light it aflame, but after a long while of rubbing a stick against a dry piece of bark, the fire finally took hold. It spread through the thin sticks and dry leaves she used as kindling and slowly ate its way into the larger logs.

She pulled the wrapped-up fish out of her pants and placed them around the fire. There were six of them, enough to satisfy her growling stomach and have some left for later.

While the fish cooked, she ran a hand through her tangled hair. As much as she loved her waist-long red hair, out here in the wilderness it only got in the way. She paced to and fro, searching the jungle floor for smooth, straight sticks that could serve as a replacement for her hairpin.

When she bent down to pick one up, a black panther emerged from between the trees and lashed out at her with its sharp claws. They tore through the fabric of her tunic and cut bleeding wounds into her flesh.

She stabbed at the great cat with the wooden stick, but the blunt wood couldn't penetrate its thick skin. The panther struck at her again, claws raking across her thigh. She went to her knee and the panther leapt at her, pinning her down with its weight.

Its sharp-toothed mouth descended towards her throat, but she shoved her fist between its jaws before it could go for the kill. She pushed her left arm further down the creature's throat, its teeth cutting deep wounds into her flesh.

But without a weapon, she saw no other way to prevail.

With her arm deep down its throat, she strangled the panther from within. It tried to break free, but she wrapped her right arm around its neck and wrestled it down. The struggle lasted minutes, but the great predator finally passed out from the lack of air, leaving Susanna triumphant.

She winced in pain as she pulled her arm out of the panther's mighty jaw. Her arm was a mess, blood flowing freely from deep wounds, pooling at her fingertips and dripping down to nourish the earth. The panther's claws had torn several shallower cuts into her chest and thighs, less severe but bleeding nonetheless.

She ripped up the remains of her tunic and bandaged her wounds. The fabric was dirty and wet, but at least it stemmed the flow of blood. Even if her wounds got infected – stopping the blood loss would allow her enough time to complete her journey to the wizard's tower. If she died soon after, so be it.

She dragged the panther's carcass to the fire and got to work. Today, she would feast on meat, after all.

#

Using a sharp stone she had found at the riverbank, it had taken her over an hour to carve up the carcass and roast the meat. She had cut it into thin strips, easy for transport, and put it over the fire until it was thoroughly grilled. After a filling breakfast of fish and meat, she cut a hole into her empty waterskin and stuffed cuts of well-done panther into it until it was filled to bursting.

With enough provisions to last for the rest of her journey, she pushed her raft back into the water and resumed her southward path. Her progress was quick, and she felt the tower coming nearer and nearer. One more day until the wizard expected her arrival – she was confident to make it in time.

Riding the river's rapid currents, the hours went by quickly. She passed the time chewing on tough strips of panther meat and rearranging her hair until she was satisfied with the updo, fixing it in place with a smooth wooden stick.

It was long past noon when the river bent east and she had to abandon her raft, continuing the journey on foot. No predators attacked her this time – it had been the scent of roasting fish that attracted the panther, she assumed. As a lone wanderer quick on her feet, she was not the most attractive piece of prey.

Her way through the jungle was uneventful, and she was glad for it. The cuts from the panther's teeth sent waves of pain coursing through her arm, and her legs still ached from exertion despite the half day of rest the raft had afforded her.

Her body was reaching its limit, but she pushed onward.

The desert appeared abruptly and suddenly. Where just a moment ago lush grass and soft moss had covered the ground beneath her feet, now coarse sand crawled into the spaces between her toes and hot winds blew into her face, unobstructed by foliage. It was like an invisible line drawn across the ground, neatly separating the two biomes.

She paused for a moment, closing her eyes and taking a deep breath. One last breath of the fresh, clean jungle air before she ventured into the harsh wasteland of the desert.

"His tower is out there," she whispered. "I can make it by tomorrow morning. I merely have to keep walking."

And so she walked, climbing from shifting dune to shifting dune as her feet sunk into the sand. At least there were no predators here – but neither was there prey. No plants nor animals to give her nourishment once her supplies ran out. No rivers or lakes to slake her thirst.

She still had two full waterskins. They would have to be enough.

Her hands touched the larger one slung across her belly. This one was the wizard's – even if her throat was as dry as the desert itself, she could not drink of it.

She hoped that thirst would never tempt her to.

#

Among the peaks of the Broken Spine, she had thought the labyrinthine paths of the mountains to be the hardest part of her journey. But out here in the desert, with the unrelenting sun bearing down on her without mercy, she knew she had been wrong.

The heat was almost unbearable. There was barely anything left of her clothes, leaving her skin exposed to the burning sunlight. She had undone her hair and wrapped it around herself like a cloak, just to protect her sensitive skin from the sun's relentless glare. Every step she took was exhausting, for the sand gave way underneath her feet, offering no solid ground to walk upon. Her legs had never felt so tired before.

And yet she pushed on. Each labored step brought her closer to the wizard's tower. Out here, so far from home, her life in Brunntal almost seemed like a dream – but the fate of the idyllic little town was in her hands now.

She took a waterskin from her belt and drank. The water was warm and stale, yet it still felt intensely refreshing on her parched tongue. At least thirst wouldn't become much of a problem on her trek through the desert. There were still a few sips left in her waterskin, and once it was empty, she had another, filled to the brim.

Her hand touched the second waterskin at her hip and she froze. Instead of the firm bulge she expected, she felt only flaccid leather. She looked down and spotted a large hole, torn into the leather by the panther's ravaging claws.

After her victory against the giant cat, she had only checked for damage on the skin intended for the wizard. Like a fool, she cut open her third waterskin to store the meat, failing to check if the other two were still hale. Had she filled it with water from the river instead…

"Don't think about could haves, Susie," she muttered, steadying herself with slow, steady breaths. "You still have a few sips of water left. It will soon be night. You'll make it."

She marched on, placing one foot in front of the other, her progress slow but steady. The sun wasn't far from the horizon and she wouldn't have to bear the heat for much longer.

But when night fell, the last sips of water were already gone from her waterskin. She only hoped she could resist the urge to drink from the wizard's tribute and doom her town to destruction.

#

Susanna marched through the night, taking advantage of the cruel sun's absence. While the pain in her wounded arm had subsided to a dull ache, her legs burned with the pain of exhaustion. But she forced herself onward, knowing that it would be hard to get going again if she allowed herself even a minute of rest. And she couldn't afford wasting those precious hours of darkness, for she knew that the lack of water would turn her journey into pure agony once the sun reached its zenith.

The hours of morning were still bearable. But as the sun rose further and further into the sky, the air turned into a sweltering oven. Hot winds whipped up the sand, and every breath was agony as little grains entered her nostrils. She tried breathing through her mouth, but that only made it worse. Her throat was so dry that she couldn't even spit out the sand that got into her mouth.

At high noon, her legs gave out from under her and she collapsed, falling face-first into the sand. She lay unmoving for a while, hugging the thick, full waterskin slung around her belly. The temptation to take a sip was great. For a long time she lay unmoving in the hot, blistering sand, her thoughts focused entirely on the delicious wet within the leather skin.

She closed her eyes and took slow, steady breaths.

"Dear compass in my heart," she whispered, "how far do I have left to go?"

It was hard to concentrate, but when she managed to tear her thoughts away from the water for just a moment, the wizard's gift answered.

The tower was close. One more hour of marching and she would stand at its gates.

One more hour.

She pushed herself up to her knees, then back onto her feet. Fighting against thirst and exhaustion, she summoned her last reserves of strength and pushed on. Every fiber of her body ached with exhaustion and every breath made her lungs burn as if they were on fire. Had the tower been any farther, she would have allowed herself to succumb to thirst and pain.

But with her goal almost within sight, she kept driving her tired body onward with naught but sheer force of will.

It was the longest hour of her entire life.

#

The wizard's tower stretched far up into the sky, a mighty sandstone pillar reminding all who beheld it of the power of its master. It stood in the middle of a fertile oasis, surrounded by the greenest vegetation Susanna had ever laid eyes on. A sparkling stream of water emerged from between two rocks, a source of life within the desert's dry death.

She crawled towards it on her knees, for her legs had long given up their stride. Cupping her hands into the shape of a bowl, she moved the water to her lips and drank.

After a few sips, she got back to her feet and walked towards the tower. Her gait was stumbling and awkward, and she fell down twice before she reached the tower's gates. But she didn't want to meet the wizard on her knees, so she forced herself to walk, no matter how much her legs protested.

She knocked at the door and shouted in a hoarse voice: "Great wizard, the messenger of Brunntal has arrived! You have given me five days, and on the fifth I stand before you, a full skin of water from Brunntal's fountain as my tribute."

The door opened inward, propelled by a magical force, and the wizard's voice replied: "Come on up into my chambers, messenger of Brunntal, so you may pour out your tribute before me."

She walked through the door and ascended the spiral staircase leading to the top of the tower. Grasping the handrail, she pushed herself up the stairs with her arms, as her legs could not do it on their own.

When she entered the wizard's chambers, he beheld his visitor with an amused expression on his bearded face. Her chest was bare and stained with dried blood, the remains of her tunic wrapped around her wounded arm; her long red hair was tangled and matted with sweat and sand; her feet, dirty and clad in shredded rags that once were socks, barely managed to hold her up.

Yet there she stood, a full waterskin cradled in her arms, carried all the way from distant Brunntal to his tower in the desert.

"How quaint," he said with a chuckle, "I did not expect you to make it, messenger. You are stronger than you look."

Susanna uncorked the waterskin and poured its contents into a clay bowl at the wizard's feet. "Your tribute, great wizard. Water from Brunntal's fountain, as you requested."

The wizard looked at the fresh, clear water pouring into the bowl and shrugged. "An unexpected surprise, but not unwelcome. To tell you the truth, I thought you had perished days ago. So, I have already sent my creatures to feast…"

He walked to a pedestal upon which sat a large sphere of translucent crystal. His palms hovered over the crystal ball and images of savage beasts appeared within, winged lizards that spat fire and lion-taloned eagles with massive beaks.

Susanna stared at the crystal dumbfounded. "What?"

"Huh? Oh." The wizard looked up from his crystal ball and met her stare. "As I said, I did not expect you to make it – and as today is the fifth day, I have sent my creatures ahead so they may reach your town at the sixth. Tell me, have you ever seen a dragon rend flesh? It is a delightful display."

"But you promised," said Susanna, walking towards him with slow, wavering steps. "If I delivered your tribute before the passing of five days, you would spare my town."

The wizard shrugged. "And I promised my creatures they would feed. I cannot call them back now – I wouldn't wish to disappoint them." He showed her a broad, mischievous grin, yellowed teeth peeking out beneath his mustache. "But don't be sad, messenger. I'll let you watch as they tear through your town, devouring its unfaithful citizens in their hunger for human flesh. It is so enjoyable to behold."

She stared at the wizard and his crystal ball with mouth agape. All this hardship, all her efforts had been in vain; the wizard cared not for the tribute. To him, idyllic Brunntal and all its citizens were mere playthings to be toyed with at his leisure.

"Oh, and as for you," he said with a dismissive wave of the hand, "I shall allow you to serve me as slave. There is much work that needs to be done in the gardens... and once you clean yourself up, I might even allow you to join me in my bedchamber."

Susanna took a deep breath and steadied herself. Her legs were still shaky, but she found a new source of strength filling her body.

"Great wizard," she said, "I come to you as the messenger of Brunntal. The tribute you asked for has been delivered. Yet there is one more message I must tell."

341

The wizard looked at her with curious eyes. "Oh? And what would that be?"

She jumped at him and slung her hands around his throat, squeezing until he choked. He stared at her with bulging eyes as he tried to push her away, but her grip was too tight, her feet too solid on the ground. Where mere moments ago her legs had struggled to keep her upright, she now stood unyielding as a rock.

She squeezed the life out of the wizard tyrant and tossed his body to the floor, an expression of utter surprise frozen permanently into his face.

She stepped over his corpse and put her hands onto the crystal ball. It still showed the image of the wizard's creatures flying towards Brunntal, driven by man-eating hunger and a tyrant's command.

"Away with you, foul creatures! Away!" she shouted at the ball, and the flying lizards and lion-birds hissed in confusion. Her voice was unfamiliar to their ears, but the magic of the crystalline orb compelled them nonetheless. "Leave your northbound path! Do not enter the lands of men but return from whence you came!"

The creatures scattered at her command, flying off into all directions.

She picked up the crystal ball and sat down on the ground, allowing herself to finally rest. Brunntal was saved, and the wizard tyrant was gone.

She threw the crystal ball against the wall and watched it shatter into a thousand pieces. The wizard's tyranny was over, and no-one else should take up his dark arts, either.

She sat for a while on the cold stone floor, savoring her moment of rest, but then the tower began to rumble. Plaster rained down from the ceiling and fell upon her head, and the walls were shaking as if by an earthquake.

Susanna got to her feet and made for the exit, driven purely by instinct. As her feet slapped against the steps of the spiral staircase, cracks appeared in the walls around her, spreading through the stone until the tower collapsed under its own weight.

She barely managed to reach the exit in time, hurling herself through the door before the tower's heavy sandstone blocks crushed her underneath.

Whether it was the wizard's death or the broken crystal ball that destroyed the tower, she did not know. But she knew that it was for the better.

She crawled towards the stream and filled her undamaged waterskins until they were full to bursting. Then, she laid down in the shallow stream and let the fresh, clean water roll over her until the sand and sweat was washed off her skin. She stayed there until the sun touched the horizon, painting the sky red with the color of dusk.

With her body refreshed, she got to her feet and returned to the ruined tower. Crumbled as it was, some things of use still lay buried underneath the rubble. She managed to find a long knife of a strange material, harder than any metal she had ever seen; a sturdy pair of boots fashioned from soft brown leather; a silken cape of the same red color as her hair; a crooked staff of dark wood, its tip carved into the shape of a face.

She put the knife into her belt, slipped her feet into the leather boots, and draped the cape around her shoulders.

With both hands wrapped around the wooden staff, she turned her back on the tower and marched back into the desert. Night was approaching, allowing her to cross the sands without the sun's scorching rays bearing down on her.

It was time to return home.

Frank Sawielijew, an eccentric Russo-German author with Bulgarian roots, loves to forge fantastic tales set in strange, imaginative fantasy worlds. He writes in both English and German and had a handful of his short stories appear in various anthologies since 2015. He has also written professionally for the video game industry.

Thank you...

Thank you for taking the time to read our collection. We enjoyed all the stories contained within and hope you found at least a few to enjoy yourself. If you did, we'd be honored if you would leave a review on Amazon, Goodreads, and anywhere else reviews are posted.

You can also subscribe to our email list via our website, Https://www.cloakedpress.com

Follow us on Facebook
http://www.facebook.com/Cloakedpress

Tweet to us https://twitter.com/CloakedPress

We are also on Instagram
http://www.instagram.com/Cloakedpress

If you'd like to check out our other publications, you can find them on our website above. Click the "Check Our Catalog" button on the homepage for more great collections and novels from the Cloaked Press Family.

Printed in Great Britain
by Amazon

74091733R00199